rkly

[*Ash*
plot'

rter'

Ash
ded,
your
rless

wish
Zone

bout
igan,

'[A]n addictive na   rom start to
finish. When   er to return'
Renu Shah,

BOOKS BY LAURA SEBASTIAN

Ash Princess

Lady Smoke

LADY SMOKE

LAURA SEBASTIAN

MACMILLAN CHILDREN'S BOOKS

First published 2019 in the US by Delacorte Press, an imprint of Random House
Children's Books, a division of Penguin Random House LLC, New York

This edition published 2019 in the UK by Macmillan Children's Books
an imprint of Pan Macmillan
20 New Wharf Road, London N1 9RR
Associated companies throughout the world
www.panmacmillan.com

ISBN 978-1-5098-5518-6

Text copyright © Laura Sebastian 2019
Map illustrations copyright © Isaac Stewart 2019

The right of Laura Sebastian and Isaac Stewart to be identified as the
author and illustrator of this work has been asserted by them
in accordance with the Copyright, Designs and Patents Act 1988.

1 3 5 7 9 8 6 4 2

A CIP catalogue record for this book is available from
the British Library.

Interior design by Stephanie Moss
Printed and bound by CPI Group (UK) Ltd, Croydon CR0 4YY

FOR GRANDMA CAROLE,
a rebel queen if I ever knew one

AND FOR GRANDPA RICH,
for keeping her stories alive

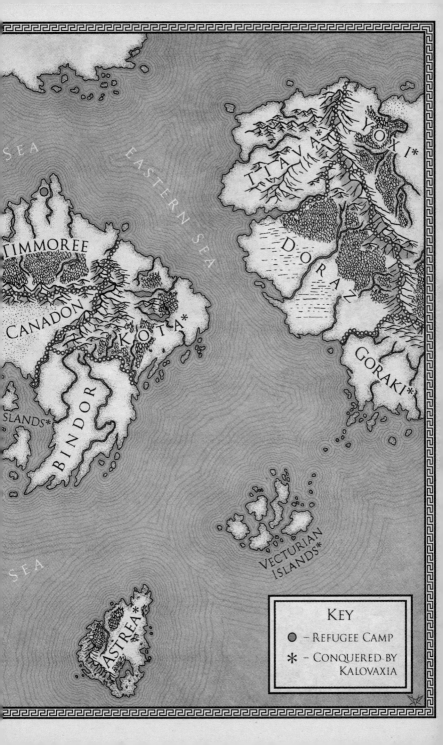

PROLOGUE

M Y MOTHER ONCE TOLD ME that peace was the only way Astrea could survive. We had no need for vast armies, she said, no need to force our children into becoming warriors. We didn't court war like other countries, in an effort to take more than we needed. Astrea was enough, she said.

She never imagined that war would come to us, courted or not. She would live just long enough to see how poorly peace fared against the Kalovaxians' wrought-iron blades and savage greed.

My mother was the Queen of Peace, but I know too well that peace isn't enough.

ALONE

———————•———————

THE SPICED COFFEE IS SWEET on my tongue, made with a generous dollop of honey. The way Crescentia always orders it.

We sit on the pavilion like we have a thousand times before, steaming porcelain mugs cradled in our hands to ward off the chill in the evening air. For a moment, it feels just like every time before, a comfortable silence hanging in the dark air around us. I've missed talking to her, but I've missed this, too – how we could sit together and not feel the need to fill the silence with meaningless small talk.

But that's silly. How can I miss Cress when she's sitting right in front of me?

She laughs like she can read my mind and sets her cup down on its saucer with a clatter that rattles my bones. She leans across the gilded table to take hold of my free hand in both of hers.

'Oh, Thora,' she says, her voice lilting over my false name like a melody. 'I missed you, too. But next time, I won't.'

Before her words can make sense to me, the lighting overhead shifts, the sun growing brighter and brighter until she's fully illuminated, every awful inch of her. Her charred, flaking neck, burned black by the Encatrio I had her served, her hair white and brittle, her lips gray as the ersatz crown I used to wear.

Fear and guilt overwhelm me as the pieces fall into place in my mind. I remember what I did to her; I remember why I did it. I remember her face on the other side of the bars of my cell, full of rage as she told me she would cheer for my death. I remember the bars being scalding hot where she'd touched them.

I try to pull my hand away but she holds it fast, her storybook-princess smile sharpening into fangs tipped with ash and blood. Her skin burns hot against mine, hotter even than Blaise's. It is fire itself against my skin, and I try to scream, but no sound comes out. I stop feeling my hand altogether and I'm relieved for a second before I look down and see that it has turned to ash, crumbled to dust in Cress's grip. The fire works its way up my arm and down the other, spreading across my chest, my torso, my legs, and my feet. My head catches last, and the final thing I see is Cress with her monster's smile.

'There. Isn't that better? Now no one will mistake you for a queen.'

My skin is drenched when I wake up, cotton sheets tangled around my legs and damp with sweat. My stomach churns, threatening to spill, though I'm not sure I've eaten anything to spill, apart from a few crusts of bread last night. I sit up in bed, placing a hand on my stomach to steady it and blinking to help my eyes adjust to the dark.

It takes a moment to realize that I am not in my own bed,

not in my own room, not in the palace at all. The space is smaller, the bed little more than a narrow cot with a thin mattress and threadbare sheets and a quilt. My stomach pitches to the side, rolling in a way that makes me nauseous before I realize it isn't my stomach at all – the room itself is rocking from side to side. My stomach is only echoing the motion.

The events of the last two days filter back to me. The dungeon, the Kaiser's trial, Elpis dying at my feet. I remember Søren rescuing me only to be imprisoned himself. As quickly as that thought comes to me, I push it away. There are a good many things I have to feel guilty about – taking Søren hostage cannot be one of them.

I'm on the *Smoke,* I remember, heading toward the Anglamar ruins to begin to reclaim Astrea. I am in my cabin, safe and alone, while Søren is being kept in chains in the brig.

I close my eyes and drop my head into my hands, but as soon as I do, Cress's face swims through my mind, all rosy cheeks and dimples and wide gray eyes, just as she looked the first time I met her. My heart lurches in my chest at the thought of the girl she was, the girl *I* was, who latched on to her because she was my only salvation in the nightmare of my life. Too quickly, that image of Cress is replaced with her as I last saw her, with hate in her cold gray eyes and the skin of her throat charred and flaking.

She shouldn't have survived the poison. If I hadn't seen her with my own eyes, I wouldn't believe it. Part of me is relieved that she did, though the other part will never forget how she looked at me when she promised to raze Astrea to the ground, how she said she would ask the Kaiser if she could keep my head after he executed me.

I flop down on my back, hitting the thin pillow with a thud. My whole body aches with exhaustion, but my mind is a whirl of activity that shows no sign of quieting. Still, I close my eyes tight and try to banish all thoughts of Cress, though she lingers on the edges, a ghost of a presence.

The room is too quiet – so quiet it takes on a sound all its own. I hear it in the absence of my Shadows' breaths, their infinitesimal movements as they fidget, their whispers to one another. It is a deafening sort of silence. I turn onto one side, then the other. I shiver and pull the quilt tighter around me; I feel the fire of Cress's touch again and kick the quilt off entirely, so that it falls in a heap onto the floor.

Sleep isn't coming anytime soon. I roll out of bed and find the thick wool cloak Dragonsbane left in my cabin. I pull it over my nightgown. It swamps me, hanging down to my ankles, cozy and shapeless. The material is fraying, and it's been patched so many times that I doubt there is anything of the original cloak left, but I still prefer it to the fine silk gowns the Kaiser used to force me to wear.

As always, thinking of the Kaiser makes the flame of fury in my belly burn brighter until it scorches through me, turning my blood to lava. It's a feeling that frightens me, even as I relish it. Blaise promised me once that I would light the fire that would turn the Kaiser's body to ash, and I don't think this feeling will abate until I do.

SAFE

———— ◆ • ◆ ————

THE PASSAGEWAYS OF THE *SMOKE* are deserted and quiet, without a soul in sight. The only sound is the light patter of footsteps overhead and the muted din of waves crashing against the hull. I turn down one hallway, then another, looking for a way up to the deck before realizing how hopelessly lost I am. Though I thought I had a decent idea of the ship's layout during Dragonsbane's tour earlier in the evening, it looks like an entirely different place at this hour. I glance over my shoulder, expecting to see a flash of one of my Shadows before I realize they aren't there. No one is.

For ten years, the presence of others was a constant weight on my shoulders that suffocated me. I hungered for the day I could finally shrug it off and just be alone. Now, though, there is a part of me that misses the constant company. They would, at the very least, keep me from getting lost.

Finally, after another few turns, I find a steep set of stairs going up to the deck. The steps are rickety and loud and I climb slowly, terrified that someone will hear and come after me. I have to remind myself that I'm not sneaking anywhere – I'm free to wander as I please.

I push open the door and sea air whips at my face, blowing my hair in all directions. I smooth it back with one hand to keep it out of my eyes and pull my cloak tighter around me with the other. I didn't realize how stale the air belowdecks was until fresh air is in my lungs.

Up here, there are some crew members working, a skeleton crew to ensure that the *Smoke* doesn't go off course or sink in the middle of the night, but they're all too bleary-eyed and focused on their tasks to spare me more than a glance as I walk by.

The night is cold, especially with the wind as vicious as it is on the water. I cross my arms over my chest as I make my way up to the bow of the ship.

I might still be growing used to being alone, but I don't think I'll ever get enough of this: The sky open all around me. No walls, no restrictions. Just air and sea and stars. The sky above is overflowing with stars, so many that it's difficult to pick out any one in particular. Artemisia told me the navigators use the stars to steer the ship, but I can't imagine how such a thing is possible. There are too many to make any sense of.

The bow of the ship isn't as empty as I hoped it would be. There's a lone figure standing at the railing near the front, shoulders hunched as he stares at the ocean below. Even before I'm close enough to make out any of his features, I know it's Blaise. He's the only person I've met who can slouch with such a frantic energy about him.

Relief surges through me and I quicken my pace toward him.

'Blaise,' I say, touching his arm. The heat of his skin and the fact that he's awake at this hour tug at my mind, pulling it in still more directions, but I refuse to let them. Not now. Now, I just need my oldest friend.

He turns toward me, surprised, before smiling, though a little more tentatively than I'm used to.

We haven't spoken since we came aboard earlier in the afternoon, and truthfully, a part of me has been dreading it. He must know that I switched our cups on the trip here, giving him the tea that he'd laced with a sleeping draught for me. He must know why I did it. That isn't a conversation I want to have right now.

'Couldn't sleep?' he asks me, glancing around before looking back at me. He opens his mouth but closes it again. He clears his throat. 'It can be difficult, getting used to sleeping on a ship. With the rocking and the sound of the waves—'

'It isn't that,' I say. I want to tell him about my nightmare, but I can already imagine his response. *It was just a dream,* he will say. *It wasn't real. Cress isn't here, she can't hurt you.*

True as that might be, I can't make myself believe it. What's more, I don't want Blaise to know how Cress lingers in my thoughts, how guilty I feel about what I did to her. In Blaise's mind, it is clear: Cress is the enemy. He wouldn't understand my guilt, and he certainly wouldn't understand the longing that has taken root in the pit of my stomach. He wouldn't understand how much I miss her, even now.

'I didn't tell you about Dragonsbane,' he says after a moment, unable to look at me. 'I should have warned you. It couldn't have been a pleasant shock, meeting a stranger with your mother's face.'

I lean on the railing next to him, both of us staring down to where the waves lap at the hull of the ship.

'You likely *would* have told me if I hadn't switched our cups of tea,' I point out.

For a moment, he doesn't say anything, and the only sound comes from the sea. 'Why did you?' he asks quietly, like he's not sure he wants to know the answer.

I'm not sure I want to give it to him, for that matter, but there is a part of me holding on to the hope that he will laugh it off and tell me I'm wrong.

I take a deep, steadying breath. 'Before we left Astrea, when Erik was telling me what berserkers were, he mentioned the symptoms,' I say slowly.

Next to me, Blaise stiffens, but he doesn't look at me and he doesn't interrupt, so I push on.

'He said that as their mine madness gets worse, their skin runs hot and they begin to lose control of their gifts. He said they don't sleep.'

Blaise shudders out a breath. 'It's not that simple,' he says quietly.

I shake my head to clear it, then push off the railing, folding my arms over my chest. 'You're blessed,' I tell him. 'It's how you survived the mine, how you've survived in the years since you left. You can't be . . .' I can't force myself to say the words. *Mine-mad.* It's only one word, two syllables, each one innocuous enough on its own. Together, though, they are so much bigger.

I want so badly for him to tell me I'm right, that of course it isn't mine madness, of course it isn't fatal. Instead, he says nothing. He stays frozen, hunched over the railing on his elbows, hands clutched tightly in front of him.

'I don't know, Theo,' he says finally. 'I don't think I am . . .

sick,' he says, unable to utter *mine-mad* either. 'But I've never really felt like I was blessed either.'

The confession comes out in a whisper lost in the night air, never to be spoken of again. I wonder if this is the first time he's said the words out loud.

I touch his shoulder, forcing him to face me before placing my hand on his chest, where I know he bears a mark, right over his heart. 'I've seen what you can do, Blaise,' I tell him. 'Glaidi blessed you, I know it. Maybe your power is different from other Guardians', but it's not . . . it's not that. It's something more. It has to be.'

For a second, he looks like he wants to argue, but then he places his hand over mine and holds it there. I try to ignore how hot his skin is.

'Why couldn't you sleep?' he asks me finally.

I can't tell him about my nightmare, but I can't lie to him either. I settle for something in the middle – a partial truth.

'I can't sleep alone,' I tell him, as if it's as simple as that. We both know it isn't.

I wait for the judgment to come, for him to tell me how ridiculous that is, that I shouldn't *miss* having Shadows to watch my every move. But of course, he doesn't. He knows that's not what I'm saying at all.

'I'll sleep with you,' he says before realizing what he said. It's too dark out to say for sure, but I think his ears turn red. 'I mean . . . well, you know what I mean. I can be there, if that will help.'

I smile slightly. 'I think it will,' I say, and because I can't resist, I don't stop there. 'I would sleep even better if you tried to sleep, too.'

'Theo,' he says with a sigh.

'I know,' I say. 'It isn't that simple. I just wish it were.'

As Blaise and I make our way to my cabin, I feel the eyes of the crew on us. I can imagine how this looks to them, the two of us walking together at this hour. By sunrise, they'll all be whispering that Blaise and I are lovers. I would rather people didn't whisper about me at all, but if that rumor eclipses the ones about Søren and me, I wouldn't mind.

A romance with Blaise is a much better rumor because it's one the crew will support wholeheartedly, if for no other reason than that he's Astrean. And the more support I have from the crew, the better. I can't help but remember how dismissive Dragonsbane was when I came on board, how she spoke to me like I was a lost child instead of a queen. *Her* queen. I worry it's going to get worse.

I force myself to stop that line of thought. How did I become so conniving? I do have feelings for Blaise and I know he has them for me as well, but I didn't even consider that. I went straight to plotting, straight to seeing how he could be used to my political advantage. How did I become that sort of person?

I'm thinking like the Kaiser. The realization sends a shudder through me.

Blaise feels it. 'Are you all right?' he asks as I open the door to my cabin and lead him inside.

I turn to look at him, and push the Kaiser's voice out of my mind. I don't think about who saw us come in or what they'll say or how I can work that to my advantage. I don't think about what we talked about a few moments ago. I just think about us, alone in a room together.

'Thank you for staying with me,' I say instead of answering.

He smiles briefly before glancing away. 'It's you who's doing me a favor. I'm bunking with Heron, and he snores loud enough to shake the whole ship.'

I laugh.

'I'll lie on the floor while you sleep,' he says.

'Don't,' I say, surprising myself.

His eyes widen slightly as he looks at me. It feels like we're going to stand here in frozen, awkward silence for eons, so I break the spell. I step toward him and take him by the hand.

'Theo,' he says, but I press a finger to his lips before he can ruin this with warnings I don't want to hear.

'Just . . . hold me?' I say.

He sighs and I know he's going to say no, that he should keep his distance because I am not his childhood friend anymore. I am his queen, and that makes everything so much more complicated. So I play a cheap card, one I know he won't say no to.

'I'll feel safer, Blaise. Please.'

His eyes soften and I know I have him. Without a word, I let my hand fall away from his lips and I pull him with me to the bed. We fit together perfectly, his body curling around mine, his arms around me. Even here at sea, he smells like hearth fire and spice – like home. His skin is scorching hot, but I try not to think about that. Instead, I feel his heartbeat thrumming through me, falling into a rhythm with my own, and I let it lull me to sleep.

FAMILY

———— ✦ • ✦ ————

WHEN I WAKE UP, BLAISE is gone and the room is too cold without him. There's a note on the pillow next to my head.

> *Had swabbing duty this morning. I'll see you*
> *tonight.*
>
> > Yours,
> > Blaise

Yours. The word sticks with me as I try to smooth my frizzy hair into something presentable and adjust my rumpled clothes. In another life, I would probably flutter over a word like that, but now it rubs me the wrong way. It takes me a moment to work out why that is: it's the same way Søren signed his letters to me.

I try not to let my thoughts linger too long on Søren. He's alive and safe and that's all I can do for him now. It's more than he deserves after what he did in Vecturia, after his hands became too drenched in blood to ever really be clean again.

And what about your hands? a voice whispers in my mind. It sounds like Cress.

I pull on the boots Dragonsbane gave me. They're a size too large and they clunk when I walk, but I can't complain, especially considering that unlike Blaise, I don't have any chores on the ship. Yesterday, during Dragonsbane's tour, she explained that everyone aboard has some assigned daily task to earn their keep. Heron got a daily shift in the kitchens and Artemisia will have to run the sails for a few hours each day. Even the children take on small tasks like pouring water at mealtimes or running errands for Dragonsbane.

I asked Dragonsbane what I could do to help, but she only smiled and gave my hand a condescending pat.

'You're our princess. That's all we need for you to do.'

I'm your queen, I'd wanted to say, but I couldn't make my mouth form the words.

When I step out onto the deck, the sun is surprisingly high in the sky, so bright it's blinding. How long did I sleep? It must be close to noon, and the ship is buzzing with activity. I search the crowded deck for a face I know, but all I find is a sea of strangers.

'Your Majesty,' one man says with a bow as he hurries past, carrying a bucket of water. I open my mouth to reply, but before I can, a woman curtsies and repeats the sentiment.

After a while, I realize it's best to just smile and nod in response.

I make my way across the deck, nodding and smiling and searching for someone I know, but as soon as I find a familiar pair of eyes, I wish I hadn't.

Elpis's mother, Nadine, is standing beneath the mainsail,

mop in hand as she washes the deck, though she stands frozen now, the mop suspended and dripping gray water. Her eyes are heavy on mine, yet her face remains blank. She looks so much like her daughter that it took me aback the first time I met her – the same round face and dark, deep-set eyes.

When I told her about Elpis last night after Dragonsbane's tour, she said all the right things, even through her tears. She thanked me for trying to save her daughter, for being a friend to her, for vowing vengeance against the Kaiser, but the words felt hollow and I would have rather she railed against me and accused me of killing Elpis myself. It would have been a relief, I think, to hear someone give voice to my own guilty thoughts.

She tears her eyes away from me and focuses on her mopping again, scrubbing hard at the deck, as if she wants to wear a hole in it.

'Theo,' a voice says behind me, and I'm so grateful for the distraction that it takes me a moment to realize it's Artemisia calling me.

She stands against the railing of the ship in an outfit like mine – slim brown trousers and a white cotton shirt – though hers somehow looks better, like it's something she's wearing by choice and not because there are no other options. Her body faces the water, with her arms outstretched, though she looks at me. Her hair hangs down around her shoulders in messy white waves that transition to bright cerulean tips. The Water Gem pin I stole from Crescentia is embedded in her hair, and the ink-blue stones glisten in the sunlight. I know she's self-conscious about her hair and I try not to stare at it, but it's difficult not to. At her hip is a sheathed dagger with a gold filigreed hilt. At first, I think it might be mine, but it can't be. I saw mine moments ago in my room, tucked away under my pillow.

It takes me a moment to realize what she's doing. The Water Gem in her hair isn't glistening in the sunlight – it's actually glowing. Because she's using it. When I look closely at her fingers, I can almost see the magic flooding from them, as fine as the ocean's mist.

'What are you doing?' I ask her as I approach somewhat warily. I like to think that I'm not afraid of Artemisia, but I'd be a fool not to be. She is a fearsome creature, even without her magic.

She gives me an impish smile and rolls her eyes. 'My mother thinks we should be going faster in case the Kalovaxians are following,' she says.

'So she asked for your help?'

At that, Artemisia laughs. 'Oh no, my mother would never ask for help from anyone, not even me,' she says. 'No, she ordered this.'

I lean against the rail next to her. 'I didn't think you took orders from anyone,' I say.

She doesn't respond to that, only shrugs.

I look out at the great expanse of blue waves, stretching as far as I can see. I can make out the other ships in Dragonsbane's fleet trailing in the *Smoke*'s wake. 'What are you doing exactly?' I ask her after a moment.

'Twisting the tides in our favor,' she says. 'So that they're going with us, not against us.'

'That's a sizable use of power. Are you sure you can handle it on your own?'

I don't mean offense at the question, but Artemisia

bristles. 'It's not as difficult as it seems. It's pushing a natural body of water to do what it wants to do anyway, just changing direction. Literally turning the tide, as it were. And it isn't as if I'm changing the whole Calodean Sea – just the bit around our fleet.'

'I trust your judgment,' I tell her. Silence falls and I watch her work, her hands twisting gracefully in the air before us, the fine sea mist of magic seeping from her fingers.

She's my cousin, I remember suddenly, though I don't think that thought will ever become less ludicrous. We are as different as any two people could be, but our mothers were sisters. Twins, even.

The first time I saw her, she changed her hair from the blue and white that marks her Water Gift to a deep brown tinged with red, like mine. I thought she'd been mocking me or trying to make me uncomfortable, but that must have been the color her hair was before she was marked, the same as her mother's and my mother's and mine. She must have always known we were cousins, but she never said a word.

The same blood runs through our veins, I think, *and what blood it is.*

'Do you ever think it strange that we're descended from the fire god but you were chosen by the water goddess?' I ask her after a moment.

She glances sideways at me. 'Not particularly,' she says. 'I'm not much of a spiritual person, you know that. Maybe we are descended from Houzzah, or maybe that's only a myth to enforce our family's claim to the throne. Either way, I don't think magic has anything to do with blood. Heron says that Suta saw me in her temple, that of everyone there, she chose me and blessed me with this gift, but I don't know that I like that answer either.'

'What answer do you like?' I ask her.

She doesn't respond, instead focusing on the sea before her, moving her hands through the air with the grace of a dancer. 'Why are you so curious about my gift?' she asks.

It's my turn to shrug. 'No reason in particular. I would imagine most people are.'

'No, not really,' she says, frowning as she jerks her hands suddenly to the left, then back in front of her. 'Mostly, people just tell me how blessed I am. Sometimes they say it while combing their fingers through my hair – I always hate that. Either way, no one ever asks me questions about it. That would dance too closely to talking about the mine, and they don't want to hear about that. Better they think of it as something mystical that exists beyond the realm of their curiosity.'

'I didn't think you would be surprised to find that few things exist beyond the realm of my curiosity,' I say lightly, though her words still have a thorned grip on me.

If Artemisia notices my discomfort, she ignores it. 'You slept in awfully late,' she says instead. There's a barb in there somewhere, but it doesn't land as hard as her barbs usually do. It was the same yesterday, after we came on board the *Smoke* – she mumbled and fidgeted, and I've never known Artemisia to do either. There is none of the bite or sarcasm I'm used to from her. In her mother's shadow, she's become less of herself.

'I didn't mean to oversleep. I was up most of the night—'

'Blaise said you weren't feeling well,' she interrupts, but the smug look she gives me says she thinks that's a euphemism for something else entirely. The rumors must have already begun to spread.

My cheeks burn. 'I'm fine,' I tell her before searching for a way to change the subject. After a moment, I nod toward the dagger sheathed at her hip. 'What's that for?'

She lowers her hands and the flow of magic ceases. She touches the hilt idly, the same way I've seen women at court fiddle with their jewelry. 'I wanted to try to get some practice in after my shift,' she admits. 'There wasn't a lot of opportunity to use it after taking out your Shadows, so I'm rusty.'

'*You* killed them?' I ask.

She snorts. 'Who did you think? Heron says it goes against his gift to cause harm, and Blaise doesn't like to get his hands dirty unless it's necessary. He likely would have if I'd asked it of him, but . . .' She trails off.

'But you like doing it,' I finish.

Her eyes flash and her smile is grim. 'It feels good,' she says. 'To take something back.'

She opens her mouth and I ready myself for a pointed comment about how I couldn't kill Søren when I had the chance, but it doesn't come.

'I can teach you,' she says instead, surprising me. 'How to use a dagger, I mean.'

I look at the weapon at her hip and try to imagine myself wielding it – not like I did in the tunnel with Søren, with shaking hands and paralyzing doubt, but like someone who knows what they're doing. I remember the Kaiser's breath on my neck, his hand gripping my hip, inching up my thigh. I felt helpless in those moments, and I never want to feel helpless again. I push the thought away. I'm not a murderer.

'After Ampelio . . . I don't think I have it in me,' I tell her finally, wishing that it weren't the case.

'I think you'd be surprised at what you have in you,' Artemisia says.

Before I can reply, we're interrupted by the approaching tap of boots against the wood deck, the sound stronger and more clipped than anyone else's step. Art must recognize the gait, because she almost seems to shrink in on herself before turning toward it.

'Mother,' she says, the hand on the hilt of her dagger fidgeting again. A nervous habit, I realize, though yesterday I would have laughed at the idea of anyone making Artemisia nervous.

Steeling myself, I turn to face her as well. 'Dragonsbane,' I say.

She stands tall and poised, taking up more space than it seems like she should, given her size. She wears the same outfit as the rest of the crew, apart from the shoes. Instead of bulky work boots, she wears knee-high boots with a thick block heel. I wondered, at first, how practical they were to wear on a ship, but she never so much as stumbles, and they give her a few extra inches in height that I imagine make her appear more imposing to her crew.

When her eyes meet mine, she smiles, but it isn't the same smile my mother used to wear. Instead, she looks at me the way Cress would look at a poem she was having trouble translating.

'I'm glad to see the two of you are getting along,' she says, but she doesn't sound glad at all. She sounds vaguely cross about something, though I think that might be how she always sounds.

'Of course,' I say, trying on a smile. 'Artemisia was invaluable in getting me out of the palace and in murdering the Theyn. We wouldn't have been able to do anything without her.'

Next to me, Art doesn't speak. She stares down at the planks of wood beneath her mother's boots.

'Yes, she's quite special. Of course, she's the only child I have left, so she's particularly invaluable to me.'

There's an undercurrent in her tone that makes Art flinch. She had a brother. She told me he was with her in the mine, that he'd gone mad and was killed by a guard she later murdered. Before I can think too much about the energy between them, Dragonsbane snaps her attention to me.

'We have plans to make, Theo. Let's discuss them in my cabin.'

I begin to respond, but Art gets there first.

'Your Majesty,' she says quietly, though she still won't look at her mother.

'Hmm?' Dragonsbane says, yet judging by the way her shoulders tensed, she heard perfectly well.

Artemisia finally looks up to meet her mother's gaze. 'You should call her "Your Majesty," especially where others can hear you.'

Dragonsbane's smile is taut as a bowstring ready to snap. 'Of course, you're right,' she says, though the words sound forced. She turns back to me and bows shallowly.

'Your Majesty, your presence is requested in my most humble cabin. Is that better, Artemisia?' she asks.

Artemisia doesn't answer. Her cheeks are bright red and her gaze drops again.

'It'll do,' I tell her, diverting Dragonsbane's attention before she reduces her daughter to a pile of dust.

Dragonsbane frowns at me, then looks back to Artemisia. 'And I'd assigned you to manage the tides until noon. You have another hour, if you think you can manage it.'

The challenge in her voice is clear and Art clenches her jaw. 'Of course, Captain,' she says, lifting her hands toward the sea once more.

Without another word, Dragonsbane turns and motions for me to follow her. I catch Artemisia's eye and try to give her a reassuring smile, but I don't think it registers. For the first time since I met her, she looks lost.

CLASH

As soon as we step into Dragonsbane's cabin, I wish I'd asked Art to come with me. It's a selfish wish – she was clearly anxious to get out of her mother's presence – but I wish it all the same. The two men waiting there are thoroughly devoted to Dragonsbane, and it feels like I've walked into a trap. It isn't the way I felt around the Kaiser and the Theyn – like a lamb in the lion's den, as the Kaiserin said – but it isn't so far off. I will have no allies in this room.

I am the queen, I remind myself, squaring my shoulders. I am my own ally, and that will be enough.

The men clamber to their feet when they see me, though the show of deference might, in fact, be for Dragonsbane.

Eriel, a little older than Dragonsbane, with a full russet beard and no hair at all on top of his head, leads Dragonsbane's fleet – the *Smoke,* the *Fog,* the *Dust,* the *Mist,* and half a dozen smaller ships whose names I can't keep straight. Last night, he told me he lost his left arm in battle a few years back. It's since been replaced with a stub of polished black wood with carved fingers frozen in a fist. The loss would have meant retirement for most soldiers, but

Eriel's strategic prowess makes him invaluable even though he can no longer fight. Dragonsbane's small army has held its own against Kalovaxian battalions three times their size, and it's largely due to his careful planning with the captains of the other ships.

Next to him is Anders, an Elcourtian lordling who ran away from his easy life two decades ago, when he was a teenager in search of adventure. And he certainly found it. He told me yesterday that he barely survived his first few years on his own, as he had no real skills to speak of and little understanding of money. It was not the never-ending resource he'd once believed it to be; it was something to be fought for – to be stolen, if the need arose. So he thieved his way from country to country and later trained others to do the thieving for him. When he grew bored with that, he decided he wanted to be a pirate and bartered his way onto Dragonsbane's ship.

'You may be seated,' Dragonsbane says before I have a chance to speak.

Maybe Artemisia was right to correct her mother for calling me Theo. Maybe Dragonsbane is undermining me on purpose. She won't have a difficult time of it with these two. Though they've all been perfectly civil toward me since I came on board, there is no doubt in my mind that I don't live up to whatever idea they had of Astrea's rebel queen.

But I've been underestimated by far more intimidating people, and for the first time it doesn't behoove me to shrink in on myself and avoid notice. Instead, I draw myself up to my full height, even though Dragonsbane in her block-heeled boots dwarfs me.

'Thank you for meeting with me,' I say, nodding at both men in turn before letting my attention fall on Dragonsbane, daring her to correct my assertion. I sweeten my smile. 'And thank *you*, Aunt, for arranging this. It's time we discussed what comes next. If one of you would be so kind as to find Blaise and Heron, as well?'

Dragonsbane's nostrils flare so slightly that I would miss it altogether if I weren't looking for a reaction. Her jaw tenses before she forces her mouth into an echo of my smile.

'I don't think that's necessary, Theo,' she says. 'I've assembled our best strategic and diplomatic minds.' She motions to the men. 'Blaise and Heron have done much for our cause, but they are boys with little experience in these matters.'

Her dark eyes are unrelenting against mine and it takes all I have not to flinch away. They are my mother's eyes, after all, and looking into them makes me feel like a child again. But I am not a child and I can't afford to feel like one for even a moment. There is too much at stake. So I hold her gaze and I don't let myself waver.

'They are my council,' I tell her, keeping my voice soft but level. 'I trust them.'

Dragonsbane tilts her head to one side. 'You don't trust us, Your Majesty?' she asks, eyes widening. 'We have your best interests at heart.'

The men murmur their agreement a beat behind her.

'I'm sure you do,' I say, flashing them a reassuring smile. 'But we've known one another such a short time, I'm afraid you can't *know* my best interests yet. You will soon, I'm sure, but you'll agree that we have no time to waste.'

'We don't,' Dragonsbane says. 'Which is why it hardly makes sense to be tracking down other people when the group I've already assembled is more than capable—'

I interrupt, sharpening my words to daggers. 'If you'd gone to fetch Blaise and Heron when I first asked you to instead of arguing for argument's sake, they would already be on their way. Now, would you like to waste more time while the Kalovaxians put together a battalion to wipe us out for good?'

For a painfully long moment, she says nothing, but I can feel the resentment rolling off her in waves. I hold her gaze, her fury stoking my own. I'm dimly aware of a dull burn itching at my fingertips, but I don't dare break eye contact to look at them. Something about it feels distantly familiar, the way my skin felt after I woke up from my nightmare about Cress. I cross my arms, pressing my fingertips into the sleeves of my tunic, hoping that if I ignore them they will stop burning.

After what feels like an eternity, Dragonsbane turns toward Anders, though every muscle in her body seems to protest it.

'Go get the boys,' she says, voice tight. 'And hurry back.'

Anders's blue eyes dart between us uncertainly before he inclines in a slight bow toward Dragonsbane, then to me. He hurries out the door without another word, leaving us in an uncomfortable silence.

Triumph sings through me and I forget about my burning fingers.

'You're very unlike your mother,' Dragonsbane says after a moment.

And just like that, the feeling of triumph slips away. The

words land like a hard punch to my gut, but they aren't as painful as the realization that she's right. Antagonizing those who go against me, twisting their words against them, stubbornly clinging to my way of things – those are not tactics my mother ever used as queen. She charmed and mediated and compromised and gave where she could because she had so much to give.

Another realization washes over me, sending a shudder through my whole body that I try to suppress.

I did not handle that like my mother; I handled it like the Kaiser.

A tense few minutes pass before Anders returns, Blaise and Heron in tow. They both look confused as they enter the increasingly cramped space.

'Finally,' Dragonsbane snaps as they come to stand next to me, flanking me on each side without a word.

They must have pieced together what happened, at least somewhat. They must realize that this meeting was called without them, that Dragonsbane tried to shut them out. Or maybe Blaise is glaring daggers at her for an entirely separate reason. Heron, for his part, doesn't glare at anyone. His gaze is heavy and solemn but distant. It's been that way since we came aboard, and I worry Elpis's death is weighing even heavier on his conscience than it is on mine. After all, it was his job to fetch her after she poisoned the Theyn, to bring her to safety here on the *Smoke*.

I smile broadly at Dragonsbane. 'Now that we're all here, let's continue. We're heading toward the Anglamar ruins in order to launch an attack on the Fire Mine and liberate the slaves there.'

Eriel clears his throat, looking at me with a touch of wariness. 'I would recommend against that course of action, Your Majesty,' he says, his voice gruff with an accent I can't place, making the words sound both melodic and dangerous. 'Simply put, coming at the Kalovaxians straight on with as few warriors as we have would be a fool's errand. They would destroy us with ease, no matter what strategies we employ. We're simply outmatched for such a task.'

'This is what we agreed on before I accepted your assistance,' I say, glancing from Eriel to Dragonsbane. Again, I feel my temper rising.

'The key,' Anders interjects, 'is to get more forces.' The posh edges of his words haven't quite been erased by years of thievery and piracy.

Blaise gives a derisive snort. 'More forces? Why didn't *we* think of that? Why didn't Ampelio, for that matter? It certainly would have saved us a lot of trouble. Oh, wait, we *did*. No other country will stand up to the Kalovaxians.'

'Not out of the goodness of their hearts they won't. The rest of the world is too afraid of the Kaiser to help, so we will have to make it worth their while,' Dragonsbane says, her eyes level on me. 'And I would imagine the only thing they want from us is something Ampelio wouldn't have entertained trading for an instant.'

My mouth goes dry. 'And what would that be?'

'You,' she says plainly. 'More to the point, your hand in marriage.'

'Queens don't marry,' Heron says, looking flabbergasted

at the very notion. I'm grateful for him, since I can't seem to form any words myself.

'Let's not pretend this is a normal circumstance, dear,' Dragonsbane says. Heron towers over her by a foot and half at least, but she still makes it sound like she's talking to a child. 'Theo can put her pride aside for the good of her country, I think.'

'It isn't my pride,' I say, fighting to keep my voice calm and hide the panic rising in my chest. 'Those men don't care about me, they just want their own piece of Astrea, and our magic.'

Dragonsbane shrugs as if this is a trivial matter. 'If we let the Kalovaxians keep it much longer, there won't be any magic left. It's a sacrifice, but a necessary one.'

'That's easy for you to say, considering you aren't the one sacrificing anything,' I bite out.

'We don't know that it's necessary,' Blaise says before Dragonsbane can reply. 'There are other options—'

'Such as?' she asks, arching her eyebrows.

'We haven't even leveraged the Prinz yet. If we trade him for one of the mines—'

'Unfortunately, intelligence tells us that he's not exactly the hostage we hoped he would be,' Eriel puts in. 'The Kaiser doesn't *want* him back. He sees him as a threat and an enemy. We did the Kaiser a favor by taking the Prinz off his hands. He's already spreading rumors that the Prinz went with you voluntarily, Your Majesty.'

Not far from the truth, I think.

'So we don't use him as a hostage,' I say, though my voice sounds desperate even to my own ears. 'The plan was always to use him as a wedge between his father and the Kalovaxian people. Killing him and framing one of the Kaiser's guards was meant to cause chaos in the court, but I don't see why we can't spin the story of him running away into a similar outcome.'

'The Kaiser will make sure the rest of the court sees him as a traitor,' Blaise says, though he isn't contradicting me; he's following my train of thought, giving me an opportunity to solve the problem.

'But the court saw the way Søren stood against his father at the banquet,' I say. 'They'd be fools to take the Kaiser at his word. If there was a way to add some whispers to the cacophony, we could change the story. Make them think Søren didn't abandon them, that the Kaiser banished him, maybe. The court heard me accuse the Kaiser of murdering the Kaiserin; they must be whispering about that now as well. It won't be difficult to turn them against him if we have the right voices to whisper in the right ears.'

Blaise nods slowly before turning back toward Dragonsbane. 'Do we?' he asks.

'I have a handful of spies,' she admits cautiously. 'But they pass information to me, they don't interfere at court. It's the only reason I've managed to keep them undiscovered and alive this long.'

I can't help but think of Elpis, who was safe until I asked her to interfere. I see her charred body being dragged out of the throne room, unrecognizable. I hear her screams of pain in her last moments. I swallow, hating myself even as I say the words I need to.

'The time for staying safe has passed. If we don't take the chances we can, all we'll do is survive by the skin of our teeth.

I want more than that for Astrea, and you should as well.'

Dragonsbane's jaw clenches.

'Fine,' she says. 'I'll start spreading your *whispers,* as you call them, but it still leaves us unevenly matched for a battle at the Fire Mine. Eriel tells me it will take four days to reach Sta'Crivero.'

Eriel, who has been listening intently to the conversation while rolling back and forth on the balls of his feet like an impatient child, looks surprised to hear his name, though he quickly nods.

'In Sta'Crivero, we will meet with King Etristo,' Dragonsbane continues.

It takes a second for me to understand where this is heading. 'I'm not marrying this King Etristo,' I say, hardening each word, as if the issue were simply a matter of her hearing me.

She only laughs. 'Oh, my darling, no. Etristo is far too old to make a good match for you, not to mention the fact that he already has a wife. No, he's been kind enough to host an . . . event of sorts. The heads of countries from all over the world will come to meet you and offer their troops in exchange for your hand.'

'I am not some jewel to be auctioned off to the highest bidder,' I say, unable to keep my voice from rising. My body begins to feel too warm, the same way it did when I woke up from my nightmare. Sweat beads on my forehead but I wipe it away. I don't know why Dragonsbane keeps her cabin so hot. I don't know why I seem to be the only one to notice it. 'I am a queen and I will make my own decisions.'

Dragonsbane purses her lips, eyeing me for a moment in thoughtful silence.

'Of course, the decision is yours,' she says finally, with a strained smile and calculating gaze. 'But I urge you to consider it seriously. In the meantime, we will continue on to Sta'Crivero. At the very least, we can take refuge in the chaos of their port while we formulate another plan.'

I agree to consider it, though even that much makes me nauseous.

CONFESSION

———◆•◆———

WHEN I EMERGE BACK ONTO the deck after my meeting with Dragonsbane, the fresh air hits me and my skin begins to cool. I wipe more of the sweat from my brow and upper lip, glancing at Heron and Blaise on either side of me. They both look perfectly fine, not at all affected by the temperature in Dragonsbane's cabin. Maybe I'm getting ill – it wouldn't be surprising, after everything. Or maybe it was only my imagination, a reaction to the stress and anger.

'There has to be a better plan than marriage,' Blaise says, jerking me out of my thoughts.

I swallow. 'There has to be,' I agree without looking at him, or at Heron on my left. Instead, I stare out at the busy ship, full of people rushing to and fro, keeping the *Smoke* moving at full power toward a future that has once more been taken out of my hands. Dragonsbane might have given me the illusion of a choice, but I'm not foolish enough to believe it will be as easy as that.

'I can't believe she tried to corner you alone for that meeting,' Heron says.

I snort. 'I can. Gods, I'm tired of games,' I tell them,

shaking my head. 'I played the Kaiser's games for ten years and I didn't escape just to be forced to play hers.'

I turn to face them.

'I told Dragonsbane that the two of you are my council. I didn't think it best to have Art there today, given the effect her mother seems to have on her, but I include her in that as well. You're the people I trust here.'

Blaise nods, but Heron looks uncertain, his eyes lingering on me a moment too long. Whatever he wants to say won't leave his mouth.

'Blaise, I know you need to get back to work, but will you accompany me for lunch, Heron?'

Blaise inclines his head toward me before walking back to the bow of the ship, where he had been swabbing decks.

Heron nods, but he seems reluctant, so I loop my arm through his and steer him toward the dining hall.

'Is everything all right?' I ask.

'Of course,' he says in a way that makes me more certain than ever that it's not.

It's late for lunch and the dining hall is mostly empty. The handful of people gathered watch me as I take my ration of hardtack and dried meat. I'm used to people watching me – the Kalovaxians stared as well – but now there is no malice behind it. Only expectation, which somehow feels worse. A knot hardens in my stomach as I wait for Heron to fill his plate.

We have no trouble finding an empty table in the corner, away from listening ears. I give him a moment to eat in silence, staring at his food to avoid looking at me. The Heron I know would never ignore me; he would find it disrespectful. There's nothing disrespectful about it now, I realize. He's afraid of me. Could he think I blame him for Elpis's death?

I clear my throat. Maybe telling him my secret will make him feel better about his own. 'I had a chance to kill Søren,' I say. He pauses, a strip of dried meat halfway to his open mouth. 'I had the knife to his back before he knew what was happening. There was no way out for him. I knew it, he knew it. He even told me to do it. *Urged* me to do it. I think he wanted me to kill him. I think he thought it would somehow make us even. But I couldn't.'

He finally meets my gaze, expression inscrutable.

I continue. 'I haven't told anyone else, not even Blaise. I'm sure he and Art assume I didn't get the chance, but I did. I just wasn't strong enough to take it. And it feels good to tell someone else. It feels good to tell you.'

Heron chews the meat slowly, looking down at his plate. He breaks off a corner of a piece of hardtack, then breaks that piece in half.

'I told you about Leonidas,' he says quietly. 'We met in the Air Mine when we were first brought there, became friends right away. He was one of the only things that made surviving there bearable. He was there when they killed my mother in front of me; he was there when my sister missed too many quotas and they took her down to the submine. He was there when they brought her body back. And I was there when they took his brother, then his oldest friend. We held each other and sobbed and somehow, in that ugly nightmare of an existence, we found love. It wasn't a story like the ones parents tell their children about romance and happily-ever-afters, but it was love. It was all that kept me getting up in the mornings.'

He crushes one corner of the hardtack into crumbs beneath his thumb, eyes unfocused and narrow.

'The symptoms started slowly, but we both knew what they meant. His skin was hot to the touch, like he was always running a fever, and he slept less and less until he finally stopped altogether. We never talked about it, not in so many words, but we hid it as best we could from the guards. We managed for a while, but there's no hiding mine madness forever.'

So the weight on his shoulders isn't about Elpis, then. I lean toward him.

'Did they kill him on the spot?' I ask, hoping they did. At least then it would have been a quick death, a less painful one. A mercy killing, though I know the Kalovaxians aren't capable of mercy.

But Heron shakes his head, swallowing. 'They took him away. For his execution, they said. But now we know that might not have been true.'

My stomach sours. It's possible they sent him into battle as a berserker, but there are even worse fates than that. There were experiments – I'd seen them myself, performed on the last three of my mother's Guardians, kept in the palace dungeons for a decade. Blood had been drawn, fingers amputated, skin sliced open. It's possible that happened to Leonidas, but I will never tell Heron that.

He continues. 'I fought the guards when they took him away. I knocked one unconscious, even. So they threw me in the submine,' he says, shuddering. 'I hope you never see such a place, but it haunts my nightmares. There was crusted blood on the walls, and I knew some of it must have belonged to my sister, Imogen. And the smell – sulfur and rot so pungent you never get used to it. When they brought others down there, their screams would pierce the walls of the cave, but I never screamed. I curled up and waited to die.

'I had nothing left,' he tells me, leaning across the table to take my hands in his much larger ones. His expression is strange, not horrified or sad, the way I'd expect him to look. Instead, he is alight with hope for the first time since I met him. 'That was when the gods blessed me, when Ozam gave me his gift. I'd thought it was a gift so that I could get revenge, but what if it's so I can save him?'

'You think Leonidas might be alive,' I realize.

'It's possible.' His grip on my hands tightens. 'I never *felt* like he was really dead. It never felt real. I know I would have felt it if he were dead.'

Part of me wants to tell him that isn't necessarily true. Part of me wants to tell him that sometimes I still don't feel like my mother's really dead, even though I saw her die with my own eyes. A feeling isn't proof. But I can't bear to kill the scrap of hope he's found, though I don't want that scrap of hope to destroy him when it leads to nothing either.

'Most people with mine madness don't live longer than a few weeks,' I point out carefully.

'I know,' he says quickly before giving me a heavy look. 'But we both know it's possible to survive much longer.'

I shake my head. It isn't that I'm surprised Heron has seen Blaise's symptoms – he's suspected mine madness, I'd assume – but it still has the weight of a secret, and one I'm not keen on talking about with anyone. Not even Heron.

'It's *possible*, that's all I'm saying,' Heron says. His grip on my hands has gotten so tight I can't feel my fingers anymore.

'It's possible,' I agree gently. 'But I'm not sure what we can do about it, Heron.'

He's quiet for a moment, and I can tell he's trying to figure out the right words. 'Søren might know something. About mine madness and bersekers. About what might have happened.'

I shake my head. 'He used berserkers, but I don't think he knew much about them. He was following orders.'

'It's possible, though,' he says, his voice turning more desperate.

I shake my head. 'It isn't a good idea for me to talk to him, Heron,' I say. 'But if you ask—'

'I tried. He won't talk to me,' he says. It feels like someone dropped cold water down my back. Heron has visited Søren? Ignoring my surprise, he continues. 'One of his guards told me that he hasn't said a word since we brought him aboard.'

'He's being held hostage,' I say. 'That doesn't usually make people like Søren very chatty. I doubt he'll talk to me either.'

Heron looks at me like he can see through straight to my deepest thoughts.

'He'll talk to you,' he says. 'Please. I know it might be a dead end, I know that chances are Leo is already in the After, calling me a fool right now, but if he isn't – if there's even the slightest chance that he's still out there – I need to know. If anyone can understand that, you can.'

My mother is never far from my thoughts, but now she overwhelms them and I can't help thinking about what might have happened if I hadn't seen her killed with my own eyes, if I hadn't felt her hand around mine go limp as the life left her.

If there was a sliver of a chance that she was still alive, what would I do to find her?

The answer is simple: there is nothing I *wouldn't* do.

'We'll visit him tonight,' I tell Heron.

Blaise has a late-night shift but agrees to stay with me until I fall asleep. Though I'm grateful for the company, my conversation with Heron weighs heavily on my shoulders. I don't mean to lie, but I also can't bring myself to tell Blaise about going to see Søren tonight. I don't want to know what he'll say about that.

'If we get to Sta'Crivero and Dragonsbane still tries to push this marriage business,' he says, keeping his back to me as I change into a nightgown, 'we can leave. There are plenty of other ships in Sta'Crivero. You, me, Heron, and Art in the kitchens.'

He doesn't mention Søren, which only affirms my decision not to tell him about my plan. In his mind, Søren is Dragonsbane's problem now and nothing more. He wouldn't understand. He would only wonder if there was any truth to the rumors that are swirling about our involvement.

'We need Dragonsbane for more than her ships,' I remind him with a sigh, pulling the cotton nightgown over my head. 'And she knows that. You can turn around, I'm decent.'

He does, and his eyes dance down my body before working their way back up to meet mine. He smiles slightly.

'You're never decent,' he tells me, making me smile back. It's another fleeting glimpse of a simpler, more playful life we could have had. His smile fades too quickly, though, and we fall back into the life that's actually ours. 'And you can't really be considering her proposal.'

'Of course not,' I scoff. 'But it isn't as easy as leaving, you know that. Anyone else we accept help from will want something. Everyone wants something from me.'

I don't realize how true the words are until I say them out loud, but once they are said, they are undeniable.

I stretch out under the covers and turn to face the wall my bed is pressed up against, hearing him shuck his own boots off before the mattress gives as he crawls in next to me.

I still feel the lie hanging uncomfortably between us even as he fits his body to mine, his chest pressing against my back, his bent knees curling behind mine, his forehead touching the back of my head. Tentatively, his arm comes around my waist, his skin hot.

He smells like Astrea, like spices and hearth fire and home.

'I just want you,' he whispers, the words tentative.

I trace the tips of my fingers over his arms, words that I want to say back lodged in my throat.

CHAINS

I PRETEND TO SLEEP UNTIL BLAISE leaves for his shift, trying to ignore the pool of anxiety that has taken up residence in my gut. I'm going to see Søren tonight, and though I'd like to pretend my biggest worry about that is being caught, that's not the whole truth of it. The last time I saw him, I had betrayed him and he had told me he loved me anyway. He doesn't. He *can't* love me. But something tells me this meeting won't be any more comfortable.

I did what I had to do, I tell myself again, and though that might be the truth, it doesn't ease the guilt that's worked its way under my skin.

Luckily, I don't have long to think about it before Heron arrives with a knock so soft I almost miss it. I push Blaise's words out of my mind and throw off the blankets, climbing out of bed.

'Come in,' I call out, slipping my boots back on.

The door opens wide and then closes again, and I'd think it was only the wind if I didn't know better.

'Did you tell Blaise what we were doing tonight?' Heron asks, shimmering into view. The Air Gem chandelier earring I stole from Crescentia is now hooked through the material of his shirt, just above his heart like a badge. In the aftermath of its use, the tiny, clear gems glow in the darkness for a moment, giving enough light to see Heron's face, creased with worry and a grim kind of hope.

'Would *you* have?' I reply, tying the laces of one boot, then the other before pulling on my cloak over my nightgown. 'We both know he would have tried to talk me out of it. No one can see me go down there.'

Heron holds a hand out to me to help me stand up, and when I take it, our joined fingers begin to fade from sight, leaving behind a tingling feeling, like they have fallen asleep. The feeling travels up my arm, erasing it as it goes, along with Heron's. Our shoulders, torsos, heads, and legs all disappear, until the room looks empty and my whole body is buzzing.

'I won't be able to hold it over both of us for long, so we'd better get moving now,' he says, shifting his grip so that our fingers are linked before pulling me out the door and letting it slam behind us.

I stay close to him as he hurries down the hallway, nimbly sidestepping the handful of skeleton crew members bustling about.

A couple of them must feel us as we pass: they look around uncertainly, a shiver of fear dancing down their spines as they imagine ghosts and tell themselves it's only the wind.

I have only a vague idea of where Søren is being kept, but Heron knows the way well enough, twisting and turning down passageways and rickety spiral staircases. I only have to follow along and try to keep my thoughts from lingering too long on Søren.

I am only going to ask him questions, I remind myself. We aren't going to talk about his suggestion that Blaise was mine-mad or how he insinuated I might have real feelings for him.

I don't. Maybe I did once, but that was before he'd led his men to butcher thousands in Vecturia. That was before I saw him for who he really was. But even as I think that, I know it isn't the full truth. No, I don't love him, but I do care for him. I don't want to see him in chains. I don't want to know that I was the one who put him there.

Two men stand guard outside a door at the end of the final passageway, both holding crudely made spears at their sides and looking sleep-drawn. Seeing them makes my whole body tense, though I should have expected them – there's no way Dragonsbane would have left Søren unguarded.

Heron feels my panic and he squeezes my hand before uncurling his fingers from mine and moving my hand to his forearm instead. He keeps walking toward them, so I imagine he must have a plan. Stepping out of the shadows, he lets his invisibility fade so that he comes into focus before the guards, startling them.

I wait for visibility to come over me, too, a bevy of poor excuses flying to my lips, but my invisibility holds. I cling to his arm tightly, my heart pounding in my chest.

'Evening,' Heron says, nodding to each of them in turn.

'Looking for a shot at him?' one of them asks.

I'm not sure what he means, but Heron only nods. 'I'll be ten minutes,' he says.

The two guards step aside and let Heron pass, me half a step behind him, trying to puzzle out his words.

A shot at him. It doesn't mean what it sounds like. It can't mean that. Dragonsbane would never allow – but as soon as I start to think it, I know she would. Heron would have told me if he knew, though. He would have tried to stop it. That much I am sure of.

But when the door closes behind us and my eyes adjust to the dimly lit room, my stomach sinks.

Søren is slumped against the far wall, an open porthole the size of my hand above his head the only source of fresh air. Heavy, rusted iron manacles are clasped around his wrists, old and new blood on the skin around them. He's wearing the same clothes he wore the last time I saw him, though now they're tattered and bloody. He doesn't look anything like he did only two days ago; his close-cropped hair looks more crimson than blond and his face is covered in bruises and open cuts.

He doesn't lift his head when he hears us enter, though he does flinch away from the sound.

There is a plank of wood on the ground near him, the edge of which is covered with blood.

Bile rises in my throat and I recoil from Heron, breaking our connection when I do. I turn and retch in the corner, emptying my stomach.

I feel Heron behind me and he reaches a tentative hand out to touch my shoulder, but I shove him away.

'You knew about this,' I hiss. Even with this rage and nausea racking my body, I'm aware of the guards on the other side of the door.

Heron's eyes don't leave mine; he doesn't cower from my anger. He lets it wash over him.

'Yes.' He doesn't sound quite like the Heron I know. It's

like he's been broken into two jagged halves, sharp enough to draw blood.

I swallow the fresh waves of sickness that come over me, placing a hand on my stomach.

'Did you take part?' I ask, though I'm not sure I want to know the answer.

'No,' he says, and I let out a breath of relief. 'Though it was tempting.'

'You didn't tell me—'

'It's the same thing they did to you, Theo,' he says.

But not Søren, I think, even though I know that's a poor defense. I understand how this happened, how so many people on this ship would want to come here and take their fury and grief out on the only person they can reach who is responsible. I understand the desire to take something back from the Kalovaxians, I do, but it isn't right.

'Thor . . . Theodosia?' Søren's voice is hoarse and cracked, barely stronger than a whisper. He tries to lift his head but winces in pain and lets it drop again.

I shoulder past Heron and hurry to Søren, dropping to my knees beside him. There have been times when I've hated him so much I've wanted to kill him – I almost did – but this is something more. I know all about the blood on his hands, the lives he's taken, the wars he's waged on innocent people. I haven't forgiven or forgotten that, and I can't imagine I ever will. Maybe he deserves this. Maybe it's his due. Maybe it's justice.

But it is not a world I want to live in.

I reach out to touch his face, and he flinches.

'Theo,' Heron says behind me, though I'm not sure if it's

a warning or an attempt at an apology.

'You're going to fix him,' I say, without looking at Heron, my voice shaking. 'Use your gift. Heal him.'

'No,' he replies.

'That wasn't a question,' I snap over my shoulder. 'It's an order. From your queen.'

Heron is quiet for a moment.

'No,' he says finally, though he doesn't sound as sure.

'Then consider it leverage,' I say through gritted teeth. 'You need me to get you answers, and I'm not getting them for you until he's healed.'

'You know what he's done, Theo,' Heron says. 'You know what he is.'

'I do,' I say. 'But I also know that we're better than them. We have to be, or what is the point of the war we're fighting?'

He hesitates again. 'If I heal him, they'll only do it again.'

'I'll stop them,' I say, though I'm not sure how.

'Elpis's mother seems to find some comfort here. Is that something you want to take away from her?'

Tears sting at my eyes and I hasten to wipe them away.

'Heal him,' I say again. 'Or I won't get you your answers.'

With a loud exhale, Heron drops to a crouch on Søren's other side, taking his limp, broken hand in both of his.

As Heron's healing power starts to leak into his body, Søren forces his eyes open and they find mine. There is so much pain there that it takes my breath away.

'I'll fix this, Søren. I promise.'

I shouldn't make promises I have no idea how to keep, but the words spill out before I can stop them.

''S'not so bad,' he says with an attempt at a smile. 'Could be worse.'

With Heron's touch, the torn skin of Søren's wrists closes and smooths beneath the heavy manacles; the bruises that cover more of his skin than not turn yellow before fading completely. The broken bones of his face, the cut lip, the black eyes, all of them fade before my eyes as if weeks have passed. When Heron is done, Søren almost looks like himself again. But there is no way to magically heal the weariness in the set of his mouth, or the way his eyes are sunken deep into his sallow skin, underlined with harsh purple half-moons.

'You want something,' he says quietly, trying to sit up straighter. Heron didn't do a thorough job of healing him, and he still winces in pain. Bruised ribs, maybe.

'I didn't realize it was like this,' I tell him. 'I had no idea.'

Søren looks at me incredulously before his gaze softens. 'It's war,' he says. 'This is how it goes. Your friend is right. We both know I've done worse things.'

I can't deny that. I think of him using berserkers in the Vecturian battle. I think of how, when he lost that battle, he ordered the Vecturians' food sources destroyed as they retreated. How many of them are dying now, starving as winter takes hold of the area and their crops stop growing? Maybe this *is* a kind of justice, the only sort people like Elpis's mother have at their fingertips.

In my mind, it almost makes sense, but I've been in his place. I remember the Kaiser having me beaten whenever other Astreans caused him trouble. Only last week I paid for the Kalovaxian deaths in the Vecturian battle. It feels like the same thing, even though I know it's not.

'What is it you want?' Søren asks. 'You didn't come here to pity me.'

I don't pity you, I want to tell him. *I have been where you are, and I know that no one deserves this, not even you with your blood-soaked hands.* But I can't say any of that, not with Heron here listening. I press my lips into a thin line and straighten up, putting a little distance between us.

'What do you know about berserkers?' I ask him. 'What happens between the mines and the battlefield?'

Søren's bloodshot eyes glance between Heron and me. 'The guards at the mines sequester those with symptoms of madness. Sometimes they would be too far gone to use in battle or their bodies would be too weak. Those were executed on the spot. Sometimes, one would turn up with signs of a gift instead of the madness. They would be kept somewhere separate.'

'For experiments,' I say.

Søren nods, looking away and swallowing. 'I didn't like to think about it,' he says, but the words come out weakly.

'Leonidas didn't have a gift,' Heron says quietly. 'And when the guards finally discovered him, he was delirious – he couldn't even stand on his own anymore. We managed to keep it hidden for so long.'

Søren doesn't say anything, he only shakes his head.

'You killed him, then,' Heron says, wiping the back of his hand over his cheeks to catch tears that I hadn't realized had fallen.

'*I* didn't,' Søren says. 'But the guards would have, yes.'

It happens so quickly I don't have time to decide to react. One moment, Heron is frozen in shock; the next he's lunging toward Søren and then I'm standing between them, shielding Søren even though I'm not entirely sure he deserves protection.

I put my hands on Heron's shoulders, and though I know he could bowl past me easily, he doesn't. His gaze is murderous and hateful, feelings I didn't think him capable of.

'Theo, move,' he says through clenched teeth.

'No,' I tell him, enunciating the word carefully so that I sound stronger than I feel. 'It isn't going to help anyone.'

'You don't know that and I'd like to find out for sure,' he says.

'You're right,' Søren says before swallowing. 'It doesn't matter if I didn't do it myself; I stood by while it happened – not just to him but to thousands of others. I'm going to end it.'

Heron sneers at him. 'You can't end anything, *Prinkiti*. You're in chains, on a ship full of people who hate you.'

Søren doesn't have a response to that, so he says nothing. After a moment, Heron's fists slowly unclench.

'After you people came and destroyed everything, I wanted nothing to do with the rest of the world. I just wanted my home back,' he says, each word a dagger. 'Leonidas was different. He still wanted to travel, after the siege. He told me that there had to be more of us out there than you. He thought the world was mostly made up of good people. I wonder if he'd say the same thing now.'

He breaks off with a laugh empty of any kind of mirth.

'He probably would,' he admits, shaking his head. 'He might even have forgiven you. He was a better person than me.'

Søren doesn't say anything, but Heron doesn't expect him to. Heron turns away and starts for the door. 'You can come with me, Theo, or you can stay, but if you stay you're going to have a lot of explaining to do when you're found.'

Søren's eyes dart toward me and away again, settling on the stones in front of him. He looks so lost that for a moment I waver.

I know better than most what a person who has given up looks like. Scanning the room, I see a few ways he could end his own life – slamming his head against the stone floor, wrapping his chains around his neck, cutting his wrists on the nail sticking out of the wooden wall. I'm sure Søren could find half a dozen more if he put his mind to it. Letting him do it might even be a kind of mercy.

But the world isn't done with him yet, and neither am I.

'I'll come back,' I tell him. 'I promise.'

He nods, though his eyes are far away and his jaw is set.

TOGETHER

———◆•◆———

'YOU DID WHAT?' BLAISE ASKS, barely remembering to keep his voice quiet.

With him, Heron, and Artemisia here, my cabin feels smaller than ever. There isn't even room to move around. Artemisia and I sit side by side on my bed while Heron slouches against the wall next to the door and Blaise sits on top of my dresser. I can tell that he'd like to get up, to pace the room to clear his mind, but he can't stand without stepping on Heron's feet and there's nowhere to pace.

'I didn't know what was being done to him, though I'm assuming all of you did,' I say, keeping my voice calm and level as I glance between Artemisia and Blaise. Heron won't look at me – he hasn't since we left Søren in the brig – and I don't particularly want to look at him either. Blaise glances down, guilt written all over his face, but Artemisia holds my gaze, unabashed.

'We knew that if you found out, you would do something stupid. And alas, here you are, wanting to do something stupid,' she intones.

Outside of Dragonsbane's presence, she's prickly as ever,

and as much as her words bristle, I'm glad to have her back.

'Who are we if we let him stay there?' I ask them. 'How are we any different from the Kalovaxians if we act just like them? I've been in his position, only treated *better*. At least I was given a room. I wasn't kept in chains. I was given clean clothes and good food.'

'You did nothing to deserve that,' Blaise says. 'You didn't lead any battalions, you didn't end any lives. You were a child.'

He has a point, and it's one I can't argue with.

'Søren can be a stronger asset if he's on our side,' I say instead.

'*If* he's on our side,' Artemisia echoes.

'He thought he was, before I betrayed him,' I point out. 'He was ready to stand against his father and go to war.'

'He was ready for Astrea to join forces with Kalovaxians,' Artemisia corrects. 'That won't happen.'

'And I don't want it to,' I say.

'You do, though,' Heron says, speaking for the first time. His voice is still raw at the edges, but most of the anger has dissipated. All that's left is grief, which is even harder to bear. 'You want us to join with *him*.'

'He *wants* to be different,' I say. 'You saw that yourself, Heron.'

Heron doesn't reply, but his jaw sets into a hard line.

'We have all the power here,' I continue. 'He can help us and we don't even have to offer him anything in return, no truce or mercy. He just wants his soul. He just wants to prove to himself that he isn't his father. And we can use that to our advantage.'

'Theo . . .' Blaise starts with a sigh.

'It isn't an ideal situation,' I interrupt. 'But right now, we're heading to a foreign country where my hand in marriage is being sold to the highest bidder. Nothing about this is ideal.'

None of them answers, and a thrill of power rushes through me. *We're on the same side,* I remind myself, though I've spent so long on my own side that it's an easy thing to forget sometimes.

'My mother won't let him go,' Artemisia says. 'She'll fight you every step of the way, and she'll have a lot of support behind her. I'm not saying you're wrong – I'm not saying you're right either, mind you – but you can't afford to turn her into an enemy.'

'Dragonsbane isn't the best ally, I know,' Blaise adds. 'But right now she's the strongest one we have. We have to pick our battles.'

I remember thinking the same thing about the Kaiser, that I had to pick what I would fight him on and what I wouldn't, and how I learned quickly that I didn't stand a chance of winning any battles, so I didn't even try to fight. I'm not under his thumb, I'm not powerless anymore, but I feel that way now. Thinking of Søren in that dungeon, beaten and alone, makes me feel sick. I did that to him, I put him there, and now I can't get him out.

'All right,' I say. The words taste bitter. 'But as long as he's down there, I want him as safe as he can be. Heron—' I break off. I have no right to ask it of him, not after what he's lost, but I'm asking it anyway, even if I don't say the words.

Heron swallows and holds my gaze. 'I'll heal him every other day,' he says. 'And only the worst of it. Any more than that and it'll be suspicious.'

After Blaise and Heron file out of the room to get back to their respective duties, Artemisia lingers next to me on my bed, picking at a puckered thread in the quilt and watching me with wariness heavy in her dark eyes. She seems afraid of *me*, which is strange since it's often the other way around.

'You didn't bring me into the meeting with my mother,' she says after a moment, each consonant sharp enough to cut.

'I thought it would be cruel, asking you to take my side over hers like that,' I say, but it's a half-truth that she sees through immediately.

Her eyes narrow and she gets to her feet abruptly. 'I don't need pity, least of all from you.' Her voice is low and dangerous.

The words hurt. 'I don't pity you,' I say, though I'm not sure whether or not that's true. But Artemisia doesn't want nice words, softened and easy to hear. She wants hard, uncomfortable truth, and I understand that.

'You're useless in your mother's presence.' I meet her gaze as I say it. 'I need people who can tell her she's wrong, who will fight her and not cower.'

For a moment, she stares at me in shock. 'You don't know what you're talking about,' she says finally.

'You think I didn't want you in that room?' I ask. 'Of course I did. I needed it. Blaise and Heron have their strengths, but Heron is a broken-hearted dreamer and Blaise has trouble seeing the bigger picture – his focus is always me, not Astrea as a whole. I needed someone to say what needed to be said, and neither of them can do that. But neither can you when your mother is around. You become a mumbly, doe-eyed shadow and I had no use for that.'

She stands stock-still, expression hard and inscrutable. I expect her to argue, I expect her to fight back. I *want* her to. But instead, she lets out a breath and the fierceness in her deflates like a sail without wind.

'What happened in the meeting?' she asks.

I tell her about her mother's plans to have me marry a foreign ruler, about how she's already sailing us to Sta'Crivero. I tell her about the event the King there is hosting. I tell her I haven't agreed to anything.

'That was smart of you.'

'Queens don't marry,' I tell her.

Artemisia snorts. 'Oh, that's the only choice we have if we're going to secure a large enough army,' she tells me. 'But I know my mother and I'm sure she's getting something else out of this arrangement. By not agreeing to betrothal yet, you have something my mother wants and so you have some measure of control.'

It isn't what I want to hear, but it rarely is with Artemisia. It's exactly why I need her, like this, by my side.

'Not enough power to free Søren, though,' I say.

'Not by half,' she says before pausing. 'But it may be a start.'

I consider that for a moment. Then I tell her, 'Whatever it is between you and your mother, get it under control.'

Artemisia hesitates, then nods. She looks away, biting her bottom lip. 'She underestimates you and that's something you can use to your advantage, but don't be foolish enough to make the same mistake. Don't underestimate what she's capable of.'

BURN

———◆·◆———

CRESS STANDS ON THE OTHER side of rusted cell bars, gripping them with her tiny, bone-white fingers. She only comes up to my waist now, though some part of me knows that she has always been just a bit taller, just a bit older, just a bit wiser. She isn't anymore – she's a round-faced child with yellow hair in two plaits that hang down past her shoulders. Her eyes are wide and full of concern.

'Are you all right?' she asks, speaking the Kalovaxian words slowly and clearly so that I can understand them. The way she says the words echoes somewhere deep in my mind, just out of reach. There is a distant, familiar ache in the pit of my stomach, but it's drowned out by relief at the sight of her.

She could be Evavia, goddess of safety, I think, but that, too, doesn't feel like my own thought. Not really. But it doesn't matter. All I know is that I need help, that I have been drowning and here she is, a desperate, gasping breath of air.

Cress reaches through the bars, her small fingers wrapping around my wrist. I struggle not to sob with relief.

Her smile widens, revealing teeth that have been sharpened

to points. Surprised, I pull back, stepping just out of her reach.

A spot of gray at her throat grows and spreads until her entire neck is charred black skin. I try to take another step away, but my back hits cold, damp stone.

Cress takes hold of the bars again, but this time they melt beneath her touch. She walks toward me with her tiny hands outstretched, palms a vivid red with flames licking at her fingertips. I drop to a crouch and press farther back into the wall, desperate to get away from her, but there is nowhere to go. She must realize this as well, because she stops right in front of me, leaning in close to my ear.

'Our hearts are sisters, Thora,' she whispers, hovering her burning hand just above my chest. 'Shall we see if they match?'

My own screams wake me up and I turn, burying my face in my pillow to muffle them. I'm aware of the empty space next to me, the fact that the pillow is still warm. Blaise must have left only moments ago. I take a few breaths to calm myself, closing my eyes before immediately opening them again when I see Cress's grotesque smile behind my eyelids. The sheets tangled around my legs are drenched in sweat, and it takes me a moment to extract myself from them. The braid I put my hair into last night has come unraveled; bits of hair are now plastered to my forehead and cheeks.

Shakily, I get to my feet and cross to the basin in the corner, pouring a bit of water into it from the pitcher beside it and splashing my face and neck. It feels like ice, but it does little to soothe the ghost of the fire I still feel crawling over my skin.

After drying my face with a threadbare towel, I turn back to my bed and barely manage to stifle a scream. There, stark against the white sheets, are two black handprints the size of mine.

Just shadows of my dream, clinging to me, I tell myself. I try to blink them away, but there is no erasing them, no matter how I try.

It's a figment of my imagination, it has to be, but when I reach out to touch one of them, the charred cotton flakes beneath my fingers and falls apart, turning to ash.

I stumble back, my mind a whirl of panic and denials that don't make sense. And what *does* make sense? That I did that? That I scorched my sheets? I turn my hands over to look at the palms, only to find them bright red, though they don't hurt. There is only a faint, hot tingle dancing over the skin. It feels like magic, the way I felt at court when I got too close to a Fire Stone.

I swallow the panic working through me. My thoughts are too jumbled to make sense of. I press my hands against my nightgown, as if that can solve anything.

What is happening to me? I thought I'd imagined the heat that came over me in Dragonsbane's office, but I can't pretend I'm imagining this, not when there is proof right before my eyes.

I've always felt an affinity with Houzzah, the fire god; I've always felt drawn to Fire Gems. I thought it was because I am descended from him, but that can't be true. I share his blood as much as Artemisia and Dragonsbane do, but neither of them seems to feel drawn to Houzzah. Dragonsbane doesn't believe in any of the gods, and Artemisia was blessed by Suta, the water goddess. It can't just be my blood. This is something else, something dangerous.

I think of Cress as I last saw her in the dungeon, surviving a dose of poison that would have killed a man twice her size but looking like death had left its fingerprints on her nonetheless. *How had she survived?* And not just that – her touch hot enough to scald. That, too, should have been impossible, but I saw her with my own eyes and felt those bars with my own hands. Hot as my own touch was just moments ago.

I don't know how any of that is possible, but I can't bring myself to believe that my god would see fit to save a Kalovaxian – to *bless* her with his gift – as thousands of his own people went mad in the mines.

I have to force myself to breathe.

I still feel Cress's hand on my chest just over my heart, feel the fire of her touch as she turned me to ash. I can't be sure, but I could swear my own hands begin to grow warmer again.

Without thinking about it, I pull the sheets off the bed, bundling them in my arms so that the scorch marks don't show. I try to still my shaking hands as I walk into the hall. It doesn't take long before I find a skeleton crew member scrubbing the floors – a boy only slightly older than I am.

'Y-Your Majesty,' he stutters.

'Good evening,' I tell him, managing an embarrassed smile as a plan falls into place. 'I'm afraid there was an . . . incident with my monthly bleeding.'

For an instant, he stares at me bewildered before his face turns scarlet and he looks away. 'Oh, er . . .'

'Can you please ask someone to bring me new sheets?

There's no hurry, but by tomorrow evening would be wonderful.'

'Oh . . . of course,' he says warily. 'Should I . . . er . . . take those?' he asks, nodding toward the sheets I'm carrying. He looks terrified of them, as if they're some kind of dangerous animal instead of ruined linens.

'No need, I can take them to the washer,' I tell him, and he visibly sags with relief.

He nods and mercifully doesn't ask any more questions. But I don't go to the washer. Instead, I take the ruined sheets to the empty kitchen and feed them into the furnace, watching as the flames take hold and burn through them until there is nothing left but ash. Watching the proof disappear, I can almost let myself believe that I imagined all of it, but I know I didn't. I can still feel my palms tingling and warm. I'm not imagining it; I'm not mad. I don't know what I am. I don't know what to do. I don't know anything.

The idea of going back to my empty room and being alone with my thoughts is unbearable. Childish as it makes me feel, I want someone to hold me and tell me everything is going to be all right, even if I can't imagine talking about any of it out loud. Blaise is my first thought, but he must have left for his work shift and I don't want to bother him. Artemisia is not someone familiar with sympathy, and I don't want to go to Heron either, after everything that has passed between us.

There is another option, though I don't need Artemisia to tell me it's a foolish one. But already my mind is churning out lies and excuses for my presence in the dungeon, and foolish as it may be, that is where my feet lead me.

SØREN

———◆•◆———

IT'S DIFFICULT TO NAVIGATE THE ship's passageways on my own, but after a few wrong turns, I find myself in the familiar narrow hallway, walking toward a door flanked by the same two guards from last night. Though they didn't hesitate to let Heron past, when they see me, their eyes narrow and I know it won't be so easy.

'Your Majesty,' they both mutter.

'I'm here to see the prisoner,' I say, trying to make my voice sound cold and detached, though I don't think I quite manage it.

'The prisoner isn't allowed visitors,' one guard says with such certainty that I almost believe him even though I've seen the truth with my own eyes.

I swallow and stand up a little straighter. 'I'm not any visitor,' I say. 'As your queen, I'm telling you to let me past.'

The guards exchange a look.

'For your own safety, Your Majesty, you mustn't—' the other guard begins.

But as soon as he says *mustn't* instead of *can't,* I know he's lost his ground.

'He's chained to the wall,' I say before hastily adding, 'I assume.'

'Yes, but he's a dangerous man,' the guard insists.

'And luckily, I have the two of you right outside in case I need you. That is your job, isn't it?'

Again, the guards exchange a look before hesitantly stepping aside and opening the door for me. I slip past them into the brig, immediately hit by a cloud of stale air and the tang of fresh blood. Like yesterday, Søren is slumped against the far wall, chains around his ankles and wrists. The healing Heron did yesterday has already been undone, with fresh cuts and bruises covering much of his skin. Unlike yesterday, though, he looks up when I approach. Though his mouth is too bloody to say for sure, I think he attempts a smile.

'You came back,' he says, the words more breath than voice.

'I told you I would,' I say, trying to inject some pep, though the sentiment comes out flat. I almost ask how he is, but it's such a ridiculous question that I can't bring myself to voice it. Instead, I glance around the room, my eyes landing on the bloodied plank of wood, the chains biting into his skin, a tray of food next to him. It must be his dinner ration, a few pieces of hardtack and dried meat. It hasn't been touched.

'You haven't eaten?' I ask, looking back to him.

He shakes his head slowly, eyes still guarded and wary. His right eye is bruised and swollen and there's a cut along his cheekbone.

I take a step closer to him, close enough that if he were to lunge for me, he might be able to just grab at the hem of my nightgown. I'm not afraid of him, but I hesitate to get any closer. 'When was the last time you ate?' I ask.

He thinks about it for a moment. 'That gods-forsaken banquet when I returned from Vecturia,' he says, his voice raw. 'I couldn't stomach much, with everything.'

Everything. I don't think I'll ever forget the revealing dress the Kaiser made me wear that night, the way he treated me like I was his to display however he liked. His hands on me, searing like a brand. Søren had looked ill, though I'd imagine it was a good deal easier to witness than it was to withstand.

'You're supposed to be getting rations like everyone else,' I say. 'Dragonsbane promised me you would be fed.'

He glances away. 'Rations have been delivered thrice a day without fail. They force water down my throat but they haven't yet forced me to eat.'

He still won't look at me, so I let myself look at him. In just a few days, his skin has stretched tightly over his bones, making him look more specter than person. Unbidden, I wonder what his mother would think if she could see him now, but I push that thought away before the Kaiserin can shame me from beyond the grave.

'Why aren't you eating?' I ask him.

He pulls his knees up, curling in on himself. I take a step closer.

'Many years ago, my father had the Theyn train me how to be a hostage,' he says. Talking seems to pain him, but he continues. 'My father said we had a lot of enemies and that we had to be prepared. The first thing the Theyn taught me was not to eat their food.'

I can't help but snort. 'You think we poisoned it?'

He shakes his head. 'It's about control. As long as I refuse to eat, you are on my terms. You don't want me dead or you would have killed me already, which means you need me. But the second I accept your food, I become dependent on you and lose that control. It's a mind game, little better than a staring contest.' He pauses for a second. 'Back then I made it three days without food. It's easier this time – mostly I'm in too much pain to remember to be hungry.'

He doesn't say it like he's looking for pity or an apology, just stating a simple fact. I close the distance between us and pick up the tray, setting it down in front of him.

'I need you to eat, Søren,' I say, but he doesn't move. 'I'm not your enemy.'

At that, he laughs, but the sound is weak.

'Friends, enemies, I don't think it matters anymore. The chains are just as heavy, no matter who holds the key,' he says.

'I know a thing about chains, even if my own were usually metaphorical,' I tell him.

He has the grace to look shamed by that, his eyes finally finding mine. 'Is it everything you thought it would be? Freedom?'

It should be a simple question, but it lodges in my gut, a dagger slipping between my ribs. I used to dream about the day I would finally leave the palace, how I would stand under an open sky without enemies on all sides, how I would breathe without that weight on my chest.

'I'll let you know when I get it,' I tell him.

Something sparks in his eyes. 'The woman who had me brought down here. I've seen her a couple of times. The others respect her. The captain, I would assume – the notorious Dragonsbane?'

I hesitate before nodding. 'My aunt,' I admit. 'My mother's twin.'

The shock plays over his face, clear as words on a page.

'You're working with her?' he asks.

'That was the plan, but . . . it's more complicated than I thought,' I tell him. 'I want to get you out of here, but she won't let you go easily. When you do get out, though, I'm going to need you strong. I need you to eat.' I nudge the tray toward him again.

His eyes linger on mine for a moment before he unfolds his legs and looks down at the tray. 'Start at the beginning,' he says, picking up a piece of hardtack and trying to break it in two. It takes more of an effort than it should, but he gets it eventually. 'And tell the truth this time.'

I expect there to be a barb in that, but it isn't there. Once more, he says it like a simple fact.

So I tell him everything. I tell him about killing Ampelio, who I always thought would be the one to rescue me. I tell him how I decided to save myself. I tell him about Blaise showing up and how much worse things were in Astrea than I realized, how many thousands of people the Kaiser had killed. I tell him how I realized that saving myself wasn't enough.

Though the words stick in my throat, I force myself to tell him about the plan Blaise and I hatched, how I was supposed to seduce him for information and turn him against the Kaiser. I force myself to admit that I was the one who decided to kill him in order to turn the Kalovaxians against one another and start a civil war.

I expect him to balk at that, to look at me like he doesn't know me at all, but his mind is already plotting. I can see it in the faraway look in his eyes, the way his mouth is pursed and twisted to one side.

'If you had done it, it might have worked,' he admits.

'I know.'

Neither of us talks about the moment in the tunnels beneath the palace, when I held my dagger to his back and he was so ridden with guilt about the lives he had taken in Vecturia that he told me to do it. Neither of us talks about why I didn't.

'What happened to Erik?' he asks.

Erik. I haven't thought about him since the last time I saw him.

'I told him to get Hoa and get out of the palace. I imagine he must have or the Kaiser would have brought her out with Elpis. I hope they're somewhere nice, wherever it is,' I say.

He nods slowly, eyebrows drawn tightly together. 'He's my brother,' he says slowly, and I wonder if it's the first time he's ever said it out loud.

'Half,' I say.

'And what a half it is,' he agrees, voice dripping with derision. 'Tell me about Dragonsbane.'

I tell him how she tries to undermine me every chance she gets, how she paints me as a well-meaning but incompetent child who cannot possibly rule, and how she acts like my loving aunt who only wants what's best for me and Astrea.

'What do you think she *does* want?' he asks.

'I don't know,' I admit. 'I think she wants to help Astrea – it's her country, after all – but she also wants to profit from it. Blaise said she charged Astrean families for safe passage to other countries. Helping them, but profiting. And she's trying to marry me off to someone royal. She said they would have the troops needed to take Astrea back, but I'm sure there's something else in it for her for managing me.'

At that, Søren gives a wry smile. 'She doesn't know, though, how difficult you are to manage.'

'I think she's starting to get an idea.'

He eats the last bit of dried meat and his stomach grumbles, already demanding more.

'So we start there,' he says. 'If we left for Sta'Crivero four days ago, we should be there in three days. We can use that time to strategize. I know a little bit about the other rulers and I have a decent idea of who will send their heirs to woo you.'

'I have no desire to be wooed,' I say before hesitating. 'But hypothetically, would there be any decent choices in the lot?'

He considers it for a moment. 'It would depend on what you're looking for.'

'Ideally? A way to get my country back without giving full sovereignty over to a stranger with the highest bid,' I tell him.

He shakes his head. 'No one will go up against my father if they have nothing to personally gain from it.'

'I was worried you might say that,' I say, taking the tray from him. I glance at the small porthole above his head, where dawn light filters through. 'I'm going to go get breakfast, but I'll come back right after. I'll bring you some more food as well, and you can tell me more about the potential suitors.'

For an instant I think he might protest, but instead he nods.

I start to stand up, but before I can, he reaches out and

grabs my wrist. His bloody fingers encircle it completely and hold firm in a way that makes my breath catch, despite the atmosphere of the brig and the chains and the blood. I'd forgotten the effect his touch has on me. I want to pull away but I also don't.

'*Yana Crebesti,* Theodosia,' he says.

The words catch in my throat. *I trust you.* After everything I've done to him – everything we've done to each other – trust shouldn't exist between us. But here he is, putting his faith in me.

I look down at his hand around my wrist and then back at him. 'Theo,' I tell him. 'You can call me Theo.'

'Theo,' he repeats before letting go of my wrist.

I leave the brig quickly, hearing his voice echo in my mind even as I bid farewell to the guards and try to wipe the blood from my wrist before they can see.

I hear him say my name over and over and over again, and I wish Artemisia were here to tell me to snap out of it. I always thought that my feelings for Søren were not really mine but Thora's, the broken, twisted girl that the Kaiser had created out of the ruins of me. I thought that they were kept separate enough that they didn't overlap. I thought that when I left the palace, I left her as well.

But here I am, hundreds of miles away, and my feelings for Søren are as complicated and knotted as they were the night I left.

LESSON

——— ◆ • ◆ ———

I DON'T GO STRAIGHT BACK to Søren. I know he's still hungry and needs some more company from someone who doesn't want to beat him, but the thought of being alone with him again paralyzes me. It isn't that I don't trust myself around him. It's that the way he looks at me highlights my vulnerabilities and brings back little pieces of who I was in the palace. Being around him makes me forget that I'm a queen and that there are tens of thousands of other people depending on me. It takes all I have not to order the guards to give me their keys and break him out of there regardless of the consequences.

Changing course, I walk toward the aft of the boat, tray balanced in my arms as I look for a shock of blue hair.

Artemisia is easy to find in the chaos, her hair bright amid the various shades of brown and black hair that most Astreans have. She's standing in the middle of an open space on the aft deck of the ship with a sword in each hand. They're smaller than the swords the Kalovaxians favor, though they aren't quite small enough to be called daggers. They're about the length from her elbow to her outstretched middle finger, with filigreed gold hilts that gleam in the sunlight.

I don't recognize her opponent, but he looks a couple of years older than she is and is much taller, with broad shoulders and a face with angles sharper than broken glass. His dark eyes are intent on Artemisia as they circle one another, his mouth set in a firm line. For her part, Artemisia dances instead of walks, each move graceful as a cat's. She even smiles at the boy, if it can truly be called a smile.

All at once they lunge at each other, metal clanging against metal as their swords clash.

It's immediately clear that they are unevenly matched, though not in the way they first appear to be. Though the boy is twice Artemisia's size and strong, his movements are slow and clumsy, and Artemisia is quick enough that he misses more often than not, wasting energy he needs to keep up with her.

She is showing off, throwing in a twirl here, an unnecessary but dramatic arc to her swing there. It's more performance than fight for her, until it's not. She sees the moment his breathing becomes too labored, his steps dragging, and in that moment she doubles her own efforts. Her strikes rain down one after another, though he blocks them all. She seems to want him to and uses his distraction to back him up farther and farther until he stumbles over an uneven plank in the deck and falls backward. Before he can register what is happening, Artemisia is on top of him, her swords crossed over his neck and her grin triumphant.

I'm not the only one watching. Dozens of others have stopped their work to gape at the spectacle, and now they cheer for her.

'I'd say I missed sparring with you,' the boy says, more

amused than annoyed at his loss. 'But I'd be half lying. I'll be sore tomorrow, you know.'

Artemisia clicks her tongue. 'You let yourself slip while I've been gone,' she volleys back, sheathing her swords at her hips and extending a hand to help him up.

He's prideful enough to ignore it, pushing himself back up to his feet with a groan. He retrieves his swords and sheaths them. 'I didn't expect you to come back this good,' he says. 'When did you have time to practice in the mines?'

She shrugs her shoulders, though a dark cloud passes over her face. 'I didn't, but I managed to stow a lot of anger, and that makes up for rusty muscles, at least somewhat.'

The boy looks like he wants to say something, but then his eyes find me and widen.

'Y-Your Majesty,' he stammers, dipping into a hasty bow before I can tell him not to.

Artemisia whirls around to face me, cheeks pink with exertion.

'That was impressive,' I tell her.

'It would be more fun with an opponent who'd lifted a sword in the last year,' she says, shooting a halfhearted glare at her partner.

He rolls his eyes. 'I'll practice more,' he says. 'And you'll wish I hadn't when I beat you.'

She snorts. 'As if you ever could,' she says. 'Theo, this is Spiros.'

'Nice to meet you,' I tell him. 'Trust me, you did far better than I could have.'

'I did offer to fix that,' Artemisia reminds me before she notices my tray. 'Taking breakfast in your room?'

'Not quite,' I say. 'Do you have a few moments free?'

She nods before turning back to Spiros. 'I'll see you at supper.'

'If I can walk by then,' he says.

Artemisia and I don't speak until we are out of earshot. When I confess about my visit to Søren, she wastes no time telling me how foolish I was.

'As soon as the guards' shift is over, they'll be tattling to my mother about your visit and she'll find some way to use it against you,' she says.

'I know,' I reply. 'But I have an idea about that.'

Artemisia arches a dark eyebrow and purses her lips, waiting for me to continue.

'Your gift can change your appearance. Can it change mine?'

She looks surprised for a half second before her mouth bows into a smile. 'It can. But in return, I'm going to put a sword in your hand and teach you how to use it. Deal?'

I start to protest again, but then I think about the way she fought a few minutes ago, unafraid and powerful and ready to take on any enemy. I still don't know if I have that in me, but I would like to find out.

'Deal,' I say.

Artemisia gives a curt nod. 'Well then, whose face would you like to try on?'

It is a strange thing, to be wearing my mother's face. *Dragonsbane's face,* I remind myself, though it doesn't feel like Dragonsbane's. I try to mimic her posture as Artemisia and I walk toward the guards. Art managed to change the appearance of my clothes, but she couldn't do anything about my boots – I hope my straight-backed stance will help to disguise the fact that I'm a couple of inches shorter than Dragonsbane.

When the guards see us approach, they stand up a little straighter.

'Captain,' they say in sync.

'I'm here to see the prisoner,' I reply, clipping my words the same way Dragonsbane does.

'Of course,' one of the guards says, fumbling to open the door as quickly as possible.

'Is there anything you would like to report?' I ask, knowing that there is.

The guards don't disappoint. They trip over each other to tell me about my own visit, how long I stayed, what they overheard through the door. I make a note to myself to speak softer, even if they didn't hear anything particularly damning this time. Only my concern, only me convincing him to eat.

'You'll speak of this to no one, am I understood?' I say, looking between the two of them with what I hope is the same intensity that Dragonsbane always has.

They both nod frantically and step aside, letting Artemisia and me pass.

I should have brought paper and a quill with me. I hadn't expected much from Søren – the names of a handful of other countries similar to Astrea willing to join with us against the Kaiser – but he lists close to a dozen, and Artemisia has plenty more to add. It turns out that growing up on a ship crewed by people from all over the world has given her a unique insight into the elements of their cultures that Søren never picked up during his visits to their courts.

Each country seems to have a different structure. None of them is a matriarchy, the way Astrea is, though plenty follow the same patriarchal structure as Kalovaxia, even if the names of the rulers change. There are kings and emperors and potentates, yet as far as I can tell they all mean the same thing, more or less.

'I never understood the concept of the bloodline tracing through male heirs,' I admit after Søren tells me about Prince Talin of Etralia, whose legitimacy as an heir is questionable at best.

'It's how most of the world operates,' Søren says. Though Artemisia doesn't have Heron's healing powers, she's managed to use her Water Gift to clean him up and rinse out his wounds to keep them from getting infected. Again, it's only temporary. After we leave, it will only be a matter of hours before he's roughed up again. The thought weighs heavily on my conscience, but I know Art is right: there's nothing I can do about it. Not now, at least.

'Patriarchies are awfully fallible, though,' I say. 'It's easy to cast doubt on the paternity of an heir, but almost impossible if you follow the maternal line. No one can say for certain who my father was, but my mother's identity has never been called into question. No one would ever doubt my legitimacy as an heir to her throne.'

Artemisia makes a noise in the back of her throat. 'Unless there are twins, of course,' she says.

When Søren and I both turn to look at her, she sighs and sits up from her spot slouched against the wall diagonally across from Søren. 'There's a story about when our mothers were born,' she says to me. 'They say they tied a ribbon around the firstborn's ankle. Flimsy a system as it was, there was no precedent, so they did their best. Of course, babies are squirmy things and the ribbon fell off after less than an hour. So the queen – our grandmother – picked one of them. It was a random choice, based on her intuition, she said. That was how the fate of our country was decided.'

She says it plainly, a story she's heard so many times it's become its own kind of mythology, but it prickles at the back of my neck like a gnat. Søren catches my gaze and I see the pieces coming together for him as well. It's almost a relief, for Dragonsbane to have some kind of goal aside from creating chaos and hoarding control, but if she wants my crown she's going to have to pry it from my corpse's fingers.

'Tell me about the Bindorians again,' I say to Søren, changing the subject, though I stow that bit of knowledge in the back of my mind. 'You said they were a . . . religious . . . ?'

'Oligarchy,' he finishes. 'Ruled by five high priests, who are in turn elected by smaller delegations of regular priests, one for each sub-country. Though the common belief is that each high priest is chosen by God himself.'

'God?' Artemisia asks.

'They're monotheistic, yes,' he says.

She rolls her eyes. 'Just say there's only one. You aren't in court, your fancy words don't impress anyone.'

His cheeks turn pink. 'There's only one,' he amends. 'There are a few countries that are mono . . . that have only one god. In some religions he's benevolent and kind, protecting his people. In others he's vengeful, ready to reach down and punish them for any kind of indiscretion.'

'So how would this work?' Artemisia asks. 'If a religious oli . . . whatever it is shows up to try for Theo's hand. Would one of them marry her?'

A bonus of this briefing is that it's an immersion lesson in keeping my expression placid while they throw around words like *marriage* and *husband* and *wedding*. It's all hypothetical, I remind myself. I haven't agreed to anything and I won't, but it would be foolish to walk into the Sta'Criveran court blind.

'I don't imagine so,' he says. 'They are all celibate. They would be interested solely in Astrea and ruling there.'

'Partially ruling. *Hypothetically*,' I correct him, though even that is a horrifying thought. 'Something tells me that they wouldn't be too keen on respecting our beliefs.'

Søren hesitates before shaking his head. 'I visited Bindor once a few years ago and I didn't have a single conversation with any of them that didn't get forced back into them trying to convert me.'

'Lovely,' I say with an exhale. 'They're out, then.'

It's the same thing I've said about most of the heirs Søren has mentioned, and even the ones I haven't outright rejected haven't sounded like valid options. But I could tell Søren and Art were getting frustrated with me, so I said I would at least consider them. The problem isn't any of the prospective matches. I know that and they must as well. The problem is that I can't stomach the thought of marrying anyone, let alone some stranger with ulterior motives. If there was another choice – any other choice – I wouldn't even entertain the idea. But as awful as all these prospects seem, I can't deny that we need more troops, and that won't come without a high cost.

'Let's go back to King Etristo again,' I say, but Artemisia and Søren exchange a tired look. Even to them, King Etristo of Sta'Crivero is something of an enigma. Søren's actually met the man before, but still couldn't say much. I can count the things I know about him on only three fingers.

First, he is either in his sixties or seventies – Søren and Artemisia disagree here.

Second, he has several daughters but only one legitimate son, who himself has his own heir. The Sta'Criveran royal lineage is secure for at least another two generations.

And third, since the Kalovaxians began their conquering nearly a century ago, Sta'Crivero has accepted refugees from the countries that were ravaged. They are one of the few countries too strong for the Kalovaxians to target.

'There's nothing else?' I press, but Søren and Artemisia both shake their heads.

'What about him personally?' I ask. 'Is he kind or cruel, wise or dim?'

Søren shrugs but Artemisia purses her lips.

'I don't know any more about the King, but I do know that Sta'Crivero is a wealthy country. They haven't fought a war in centuries. They don't need to value useful things, so they value pretty things.'

The implication is clear. 'I'm not a thing,' I say.

'I know that and you know that,' Artemisia says, rolling her eyes. 'But they don't. And they won't care enough to make the distinction.'

ATTACK

———— ✦ ————

A RINGING SOUND PIERCES THROUGH THE haze of sleep surrounding my mind and drags me back to the world after what feels like only a few minutes, though the early dawn light filtering through the porthole window means it must have been hours. I blink the sleep from my eyes and sit up before realizing that something is wrong.

It isn't the sound that signals a crew change or meals or an announcement from Dragonsbane. Those are all a single gong, struck only once. Now it's three different bells, clanging in tandem with no sign of stopping.

It's an alarm.

I throw the blanket off and clamber to my feet, pulling my cloak over my nightgown and quickly shoving my feet in my too-big boots. My heart pounds against my rib cage as a thousand thoughts stream through my mind, heightened by the bells' constant ringing.

The Kaiser's men have found me.
They'll drag me back in chains.
It's over.
I've failed.

I push those worries aside and head for the door, determined to find out what all the fuss is about, but when I open it I find Spiros on the other side, swords sheathed at his hips and his fist raised to knock.

'Y-Your Majesty,' he stutters, eyes darting around and looking anywhere but at me as his hand falls to his side.

'What's happening?' I ask him. I have to shout to be heard over the bells.

'We've caught wind of a Kalovaxian trade ship a few miles east, and the captain has decided to give chase. It's all hands on deck now as we prepare for an attack.'

My body sags with relief and I have to grip the doorframe to stay upright. *We're* attacking *them,* not the other way around.

'Captain says you're to stay put in your cabin until it's safe.'

The order wraps around me like a too-tight corset, though I know it's for the best. I'm of no use in an attack. The best thing I can do for anyone is stay out of the way.

'And are you tasked with being my nanny?' I ask instead of arguing.

He frowns. 'I'm your guard, Your Majesty.'

'Yes, I've had guards like you before,' I say, though I immediately regret it. This is hardly Spiros's fault. 'This happens often enough, doesn't it?' I ask.

He nods. 'Every couple of weeks.'

'Will there be casualties? Of ours?' I ask.

Again he hesitates. 'There is usually a cost,' he says carefully.

Ampelio thought the cost was too high, I remember Blaise saying once, about Dragonsbane and her methods.

I open the door wider. 'You might as well come in. It'll be a long morning.'

Spiros nods, the dark cloud not leaving his face as he enters my cabin.

'How long does it usually last?' I ask him.

'A few hours. She's pretty efficient about it by now – we could probably take the ship with blindfolds on. Approach their broadside and get as close as we can before turning our cannon side to them – you want to avoid turning too quickly, because then you give them a larger target,' he explains. 'It's much harder to do damage to the bow of a ship.'

I nod and wait for him to continue.

'Sometimes they'll surrender before we even shoot. They know Dragonsbane's reputation by now and there's a rumor that she's merciful to those who surrender, that she lets them sail off to Esstena or Timmoree or some small country and live so long as they swear to never return to Astrea. But the captain's never shown mercy to any Kalovaxian.'

'And if they don't surrender?'

Spiros shrugs. 'We fire on them until they do, or until the ship sinks. If they do surrender, we loot them and then sink the ship and all the Spiritgems on board.'

He pauses, but I can tell he isn't done, so I don't interrupt.

'I used to think it was an insult to the gods, to let all of those gems litter the ocean floor, but I think it's the kindest thing we can do. It isn't as if we can put them back in the mines. At least this way, no one can abuse them.'

For a beat, I don't say anything, but I can hold my tongue only so long. 'I'm more concerned about the slaves who go down with the ships that refuse to surrender.'

He isn't surprised by my retort. Instead, he only seems tired. It's not a new argument.

'It's a high cost to pay,' he allows, though he sounds distant, lost in his own thoughts. 'Sometimes it seems worth it, sometimes it doesn't.'

When the *Smoke* fires her first cannon, shaking the ship so strongly that my unlit candle falls off my desk, Spiros doesn't jump in surprise like I do. He barely even seems to hear it, though it leaves my ears ringing. He leans against my door like he half expects me to bolt through it at any moment.

'How many years have you been with Dragonsbane?' I ask him from my perch on the edge of my bed. I feel like I have to shout to hear myself. Once the cannon fire begins, it's constant, though at least it all seems to be coming from our ship.

He shrugs and slides down the door until he's sitting, arms braced on either side of him to prepare for the next cannon blast.

'Since before the siege,' he says. 'I don't really remember life before, honestly, but I know my father joined her crew after my mother died. Before that, we were in Naphia,' he says, naming an Astrean town at the base of the Grulain mountain range.

'Naphia is beautiful,' I say. 'I only went there once with my mother before the siege, but the lavender fields had just bloomed and it was so lovely.'

Spiros only shrugs again. 'I suppose. We went back a few years ago – Dragonsbane had been hired by refugees hiding out in the mountains and we passed through Naphia on our way. It was . . .' He pauses. 'There was nothing. The village had been leveled and burned. The lavender fields, too. It was just barren land, like no one had ever set foot there before us. Dozens of generations, obliterated.'

My chest tightens. 'I'm sorry,' I tell him. 'I know what it is to lose your home.'

He shakes his head. 'The *Smoke* is my home.'

Another cannon fires, making the ship shudder. I wince, clenching my hands at my sides until it stills. 'I can't imagine growing up like this. Always under attack.'

He gives me a funny look and I realize what I said.

'Well, not like *this,* at any rate,' I amend. 'Those attacks were—' I break off for another cannon blast. 'Quieter.'

'They aren't firing back,' he says after a few beats. 'It's only our fire. We must have taken them by surprise and now they'll be scrambling. It'll be an easy haul.'

It's difficult to imagine the Kalovaxians scrambling. In my experience, they have always been stoic and steely warriors always two steps ahead of their enemies, but there's a reason Dragonsbane has managed to evade them for so long. In spite of everything, I respect her.

'What'll happen now?' I ask.

He considers it for a moment, dark eyes growing thoughtful. 'They'll wave the white flag soon – that means surrender.'

'I know what a white flag is,' I say. 'The Kalovaxians use it as a metaphor, though I always heard that their ships aren't equipped with them – death before surrender and all that.'

He laughs. 'Those are strong words, but they're only words. Kalovaxians have a survival instinct, just like anyone.

They'll fly their undershirts if they need to.'

Gods know I saw enough Kalovaxian courtiers trample over one another in order to save their reputations and pride – I can only imagine how they would act if their lives were at stake. But even as I think that, I remember being in that tunnel with Søren and holding my dagger to his back. I remember him telling me to do it.

'I assume Søren is secure in the brig?' I ask Spiros.

Spiros frowns. 'He has his guards to keep him there.'

'Just like I have you?'

He gives a snort. 'His aren't nearly as friendly as I am.'

'And after the Kalovaxians surrender?' I ask. 'What's next?'

Spiros leans back against the door opposite me, crossing his arms over his chest. 'We'll pull up alongside them and secure our ship to theirs. I don't have to tell you that Kalovaxians are crafty – they'll have men lying in wait, hoping to surprise us when we board. I suppose they think it's a clever ploy, but they all do it. We send our strongest on first, ready for a fight, and what resistance they have is taken out quickly. Usually that's my job.'

'Sounds like a dangerous one,' I say. 'Especially since Artemisia beat you so handily when you dueled.'

Spiros smiles sheepishly and rubs the back of his neck. 'Dueling is different from battle – Art knows that, too. There's no grace to battle, no need for style. You only need to move faster and hit harder than your opponents. Dueling is more like a dance – you respect your partner, you understand them. It's as much a chess match as a physical sport. That's the part I've gotten rusty with.'

'And then?' I prompt.

He shrugs. 'Then the rest of the crew boards. We take what we need – money, clothes, valuables. The captain tries to pry some information from them, but even with her knife at their throats, they still fear the Kaiser more. They rarely say a useful word, and when they do, it usually proves false.'

'So she kills them,' I finish. It's hardly sportsmanlike, but neither is conquering defenseless countries.

'It'll all be over before much longer,' Spiros says.

I nod, but I'm hardly listening to him. A wisp of an idea is taking shape in my mind, slowly becoming corporeal. It will mean acting quickly, and it will mean going against Dragonsbane's orders, but I only let myself hesitate for a few seconds before giving Spiros my most charming smile.

'I'd imagine it's difficult for you, Spiros, being stuck down here with me while all the action is happening.'

Spiros frowns, lifting a shoulder in a shrug. 'I don't mind,' he says, but his eyes give away the lie.

'At least you're much safer down here,' I say.

Instead of placating him, my words only agitate him further, and he pushes off from the door, beginning to pace.

'It'll be over soon,' he says again.

I pretend to consider it for a moment. 'Wouldn't it be something,' I say slowly, 'if the last thing those Kalovaxian men saw before they died was me?'

Spiros is quiet for a moment. 'Dragonsbane gave specific orders that you were to stay in your cabin,' he says.

'Of course,' I say. 'My aunt wants to keep me safe, I understand that. But I won't be in any danger after we've boarded them. You said so yourself.'

He hesitates, and I can see my words getting to him – not to mention his own desire to be a part of the action – but it isn't enough. His loyalty to Dragonsbane is unwavering. I try another tactic, making my voice small.

'Art told me that when she kills Kalovaxians, she takes back a little of what they took from her,' I tell him. His wince is slight, but it's there. I continue. 'I would like to take something back from them as well, Spiros. Please.'

'If I did let you,' he says slowly, 'you wouldn't do anything foolish? Art says you're prone to foolishness.'

I can't help but laugh, knowing that Artemisia would call what I'm about to do the height of foolishness. 'I promise I won't,' I tell him. 'But we'll also need to bring Prinz Søren with us.'

He's alarmed at the idea. 'The Prinz is a prisoner, a *Kalovaxian* prisoner,' he says. 'Why would we bring him to interrogate other Kalovaxians?'

I smile. 'Because those men respect Søren as much as you respect Dragonsbane. And he will be on our side.'

'You can't guarantee that,' Spiros says, shaking his head. 'He's an enemy. Dragonsbane will get information from the Kalovaxians, just as she always does.'

'Good information?' I ask, and he hesitates. 'You said very little of it ever actually checks out. Because they're talking to an enemy, not someone they believe to be an ally. Like Søren. He's weakened and unarmed, easy for his guards to handle even without chains.'

'I won't go against my captain's orders,' Spiros says quietly, but that isn't a no.

'You aren't,' I tell him. 'You're following your queen's. You're going to go fetch Heron. He isn't one for violence, so you'll find him in his cabin. Once you have him, you're going to meet me in the brig.'

HOSTAGES

———◆·◆———

B Y THE TIME THE CHEERS erupt from the deck – which Spiros says means we've officially taken control of the other ship – I have Heron on one side and Søren and his guards on my other. We didn't have time for Heron to heal all of Søren's injuries, but the cosmetic ones have been taken care of, at least. The only outward sign that he is anything other than a guest on board is a limp he hides so well I wouldn't notice if I weren't looking for it. My dagger is sheathed at my hip, though it looks a bit silly strapped over my gray nightgown. It took some convincing for the guards to let Søren out without chains, but my weight as queen helped push them. It isn't a card I'll be able to play forever, the Kaiser taught me that. A title is all well and good, but it doesn't guarantee respect. Actions do.

'Would you like to fill me in on whatever you're planning?' Søren whispers to me as we walk up the stairs, Spiros, Heron, and the guards trailing a few steps behind.

I hesitate for only a second. 'When Dragonsbane orders the Kalovaxians killed, you can't say a word about it.'

Though the lighting belowdecks is dim, I can see Søren go

a shade paler. 'Theo . . . ,' he says. 'I understand that this is war, but don't ask me to *watch* it.'

'You need to prove that you're on our side unequivocally if we're going to get you out of the brig.' I glance behind us at the guards before turning back to Søren and lowering my voice. 'Please. *Yana Crebesti.*'

His eyes meet mine for just an instant before he drops his gaze and nods.

I take a deep, steadying breath before pushing open the door and stepping out onto the deck of the *Smoke*. It's surprising the ship hasn't tipped over, given how many people are gathered against the port side railing, peering over to where I can just make out the mast and collapsed red sails of the Kalovaxian ship.

Søren struggles to see past the crowd – easier for him than me. After a moment, he lets out a curse under his breath.

'What is it?' I ask.

'The ship. It's the *Dragon's Pride.*'

The name means nothing to me, but Søren is rattled.

'I trained on the *Pride,*' he explains. 'So I could understand trade routes.'

'You'll know some of the men,' I realize.

He nods, but doesn't say more, his expression tense.

'That means that they'll know you,' I point out. 'It'll be easier for you to get them to talk.'

And harder for you to watch them die.

Spiros and the other guards move in front of us, clearing a path to the gangway – a thick wooden plank leading from our ship to theirs. The sight of it makes my stomach clench and I imagine all the ways I could topple off it. Spiros crosses first, the plank rattling beneath his feet with each step he takes, though he hardly seems to notice it. He's done this before, of course. So has Søren – I'm the only one new at this.

'If it helps,' Søren murmurs to me, 'I've never seen anyone fall off a gangway unless someone pushed them.'

'Thank you,' I reply dryly, before taking my first step onto the rickety plank.

I've done harder things than this, I remind myself as I place one foot in front of the other. I remember escaping the palace, swimming against that icy current and climbing those jagged rocks, my palms and soles bleeding by the time I was through. I try not to think about the board shaking beneath me or how far of a drop it is if I fall, straight into churning dark water. I keep my mind empty until my feet find the solid ground of the Kalovaxian ship. My shaking hand finds Spiros's and he helps me step down.

But as soon as my mind clears, I almost yearn for the quivering plank again, because suddenly I'm faced with dozens of Astreans and Kalovaxians, staring at me and Søren, bewildered, alarmed, and expectant. None of them speaks, though. Instead, they glance between us and Dragonsbane, waiting to follow her lead. I find Blaise and Artemisia in the crowd, both staring at me with their mouths gaping open. Most of the crew are armed, their knives aimed at the pale throats of the Kalovaxians kneeling before them. I don't have time to count them all, but I'd guess fifty Kalovaxians, many wounded, and a handful more Astreans. For once, we outnumber them.

'Theodosia.' Dragonsbane's voice cuts through my thoughts. Her voice is a warning with an undercurrent of confusion, but it does not match the fury in her eyes. But that is a good thing – it means that angry as she might be to see Søren out of the brig, she is trying to hide it. To show her emotions would be to lose face in front of her crew and the Kalovaxians, and she can't have that. I can almost see her mind working: Søren is out of the brig, yes, but there are enough armed crew members around him that he's still effectively powerless. She has more to gain by letting this play out than by confronting me and setting us in opposition to each other. She knows that if it came to it, some of her crew would follow a queen over a captain – not many, not enough to put up a real rebellion, but still too many by her standards.

So she plays along. She stands on the raised bow of the ship, Eriel behind her. On his knees in front of her is an older, broad-shouldered Kalovaxian man who I assume to be the captain. If the length of his hair is any indication, it has been many years since he lost a battle. Now that he has, he'll be losing more than just his hair. He knows this. While most of the men in his crew are looking around fearfully, his eyes are lowered and empty – a man who has already given up.

At least until Søren crosses the gangway and comes to stand beside me.

'*Min Prinz,*' the man says, his gruff voice sharply accenting the Kalovaxian words. *My Prinz.*

'Captain Rutgard,' Søren says, impassive. I sneak a sideways glance, only to find that his eyes are as emotionless as his voice. He might as well be speaking to a stranger, but he isn't.

Dragonsbane clears her throat. Her eyes are daggers piercing Søren. 'You were meant to stay on the ship, darling,' she says in Astrean, and I realize she's speaking to me and not Søren, on account of how syrupy her voice has become. It's the way a person speaks to a child or an invalid.

I curse my decision not to change out of my nightgown. What a sight I must be in this too-big gray shift, with my too-big boots and my hair loose and wild. I must look like some sort of specter, not like a queen at all. I fight the urge to cower and instead stand up straighter, lifting my chin and forcing my voice to stay level.

'Spiros assured me all was safe, and he was right,' I say, sticking to Astrean as well, since the Kalovaxians won't understand. I pan my gaze slowly around the ship at the dozens of Kalovaxian men cowering on their knees before Astreans with blades held to their throats. It is not a sight I'm used to and I savor it. I begin to wind around the deck, with Søren and his guards following a step behind, and I examine each Kalovaxian I pass. A boy of maybe fifteen looks up at me with fear plain in his eyes. I hold his gaze until he drops his.

'What news do they bring us from Astrea?' I ask, looking back up at Dragonsbane.

'None,' she admits, through clenched teeth. '*Yet*.'

'I thought they might be a bit more forthcoming to their Prinz,' I say, gesturing to Søren beside me.

Søren doesn't understand what I'm saying either, but he recognizes his title, his forehead creasing.

'They'll tell us what we want to know, eventually,' Dragonsbane says, waving a dismissive hand.

'Will they really?' I ask her. 'I was under the impression that was not usually the case.'

Dragonsbane's eyes find Spiros behind me, but before she

can reprimand him, I continue. 'Søren is their Prinz; they'll tell him the truth if he can convince them to turn against the Kaiser. Many of these men know him – or at least they know of his legendary skills in battle. They may be more loyal to him than to his father.'

I turn my attention to Søren, keeping my Kalovaxian to a whisper. 'We need news from Astrea and they won't tell us anything, so she's going to kill them.'

His expression flickers briefly before settling back into placidity. 'It's wise,' he manages. 'It's why no one has been able to describe her or the ship. It's why no one knows who she is.'

'No one will be able to spread rumors of you rebelling against your father to a court where you still have allies either,' I add.

Understanding sparks in his expression.

'Get the information and we can spare a couple of them. Turn them into our own spies.'

He nods before facing Dragonsbane.

'Captain,' he says, stumbling over the Astrean word. It's an admirable attempt, but it's as far as he can go, so he switches to Kalovaxian. 'If you would let me be of assistance, I can prove my loyalty.'

Dragonsbane hesitates, eyes darting around to the watching crowd. 'Make it quick,' she says in Kalovaxian before switching to Astrean. 'It'll all end the same anyway.'

The Astrean crew members laugh. Though Søren can't decipher what exactly she said, he understands enough. He takes a deep breath before looking around at the Kalovaxian men on their knees. It takes me a few seconds to realize that he's searching for a familiar face. It takes a few more before he finds one.

Søren crouches in front of a man in his early twenties with blond hair long enough to brush his collarbones. The man looks up at him with angry, bright green eyes. His arms are twisted behind him, bound by fraying rope, and an Astrean man I don't recognize stands over him, a knife at the man's neck.

'Mattin,' Søren says, his voice low and soft. I suppose he's trying to sound soothing, but the man is far from soothed. 'Help me help you, Mattin.'

Mattin stays quiet, his eyes fixed on the deck at Søren's feet.

'Do you want to see your wife again?' Søren asks, his voice sharpening. 'Your daughter – how old is she now? Four?'

That gets Mattin's attention and he finally looks up at Søren, expression wavering, but still he says nothing.

Søren pushes himself to his feet. 'Fine. There are others,' he says, starting to turn away from Mattin, though he does so slowly.

'Wait,' Mattin says feebly after a few seconds. 'I'll talk to you. If you'll let me live, I'll talk to you.'

Søren's eyes dart to me for a brief second, a flash of uncertainty there, before he turns back to Mattin and nods.

The other Kalovaxians erupt in jeers, calling Mattin a traitor and far less savory words I only half understand. But not all of them, I notice. There are some who are staring quietly at the ground, thoughtful.

MATTIN

———— • ————

MATTIN IS MORE DIFFICULT TO get information from than Søren anticipated, and with each moment that passes, I can feel his frustration grow. My own patience is wearing thin, and Dragonsbane doesn't even bother trying to mask her irritation as she paces the deck in front of him. A few of the crew members who were willing to talk were taken belowdecks, so that the information they provided could be corroborated, but many Kalovaxian men are still here, kneeling before their Astrean captors with the blades of knives pressing against their necks.

'Has the Kaiser's search party already returned to Astrea?' Søren asks for what must be the fifth time.

Again, Mattin shrugs as much as he can with his wrists bound tight behind his back. Though he volunteered, the jeers of his shipmates are giving him second thoughts.

The Astrean man who was guarding Mattin – whose name I've learned is Pavlos – digs the edge of his blade a little harder into Mattin's neck, making him flinch.

'I'm saying that I wasn't privy to the Kaiser's plans regarding the heathen Ash Princess and the kidnapped Prinz,'

Mattin says, his tone flat. Though it isn't any kind of answer, some of the Kalovaxians still shout insults at him, ignoring their Astrean captors who try to quiet them.

Dragonsbane's lips curl and for an instant I expect her to pounce on him, but instead she looks at the man through narrow eyes like he's an equation she can't figure out how to solve. She motions to one of her crew members, who drags his dagger across a jeering Kalovaxian's neck without hesitation. Blood flows from the wound and the body falls to the ground with a thunk. There isn't even time for him to scream, and I have to bite my tongue to keep from crying out in surprise. For his part, Søren doesn't even blink. He doesn't take his eyes off Mattin.

After a moment, Dragonsbane's gaze shifts to Søren.

'You're proving quite a useless interrogator, *Prinz* Søren,' she says in Kalovaxian, drawing out each word so that everyone gathered can hear it.

Søren shakes his head and opens his mouth to speak before quickly closing it again.

'Not useless,' I say, stepping forward. 'He's not answering the question you asked, but he's said an awful lot.'

Dragonsbane tilts her head. 'I'm not sure what you're hearing—'

'*The heathen Ash Princess and the kidnapped Prinz*,' I repeat. 'That's the story that's being told. But you aren't a prisoner, are you, Søren? You wear no chains, you're free to roam. You're on our side willingly.'

Søren meets my gaze, his eyes sparking with understanding.

'I wasn't kidnapped, Mattin,' he lies, resting a hand on the man's shoulder. Mattin shrugs him off.

'Then the whore must have tricked you – used her heathen magic to put a spell on you,' he bites out, loud enough that everyone watching can hear. 'The Prinz I served with would never betray his brothers otherwise.'

Whispers break out across the deck, but it takes a moment for me to realize that he's talking about me. Søren winces at the word *whore*, but I don't know whether to laugh or retort. Neither would help. Nothing I say will sway Mattin into believing Søren is trustworthy enough to talk to. There's nothing Dragonsbane can do either, short of torture – though I'm not sure he would fold even then. No, Søren is the only one who can break him, so I keep quiet and let him do it.

'There was no magic,' Søren says. 'Only truth that I was too frightened to see before. Truth that I think you know as well: my father is a coward and a tyrant.'

For a long moment, Mattin is silent. 'The Kaiser has expanded our reach during his reign and opened more trade,' he says finally.

'No, Mattin,' Søren says, glancing at the crowd gathered and amplifying his words so all can hear. 'My father has sat on a throne and grown lazy. He is content with feasting and being worshipped like a god. But what sort of god sends his men off to fight a battle he's too frightened to fight himself? He hasn't gone to war in more than two decades because he thinks his own life is more precious than yours, but I don't think that's true. Your wife and daughter would disagree as well.'

Mattin straightens up before turning his head to glower at Søren. 'Do you think you would be any better? How, when you put an Astrean whore above your own people?'

Before I can feel the sting of that word again, Søren's fist collides with the side of Mattin's face and he doubles over, blood dripping from his mouth. Søren grabs his bound wrists and yanks him upright again, turning him to face me.

'You'll apologize,' he says, pulling Mattin's arms until they are nearly yanked out of their sockets. Mattin winces. When he meets my eyes, there is little more than hate there.

'No,' Mattin spits out.

Søren clenches his jaw and yanks the man's arms until he cries out. 'Her name is Queen Theodosia, and if you won't apologize for disrespecting her, I'll let her men have you and I'll describe your last moments to your wife so that she knows how pathetically you died.'

Mattin grunts, eyes dropping away. 'I apologize,' he says through gritted teeth.

Søren looks tempted to extract something more sincere out of him, but that would hardly be productive. I clear my throat.

'I accept your apology,' I say coldly. 'I hope you come to see that a woman can wield power beyond what's between her legs – for your daughter's sake if nothing else.'

He flinches before Søren forcefully turns him back to face him.

'I'm trying to help you, Mattin,' Søren says. 'When I was on board the *Pride,* you had more grievances with the Kaiser than anyone. He raised taxes and your parents had to scramble to work harder on the farm to pay them. Your father worked himself to death, you said, because his five sons were all called to fight the Kaiser's wars. When you received word that your daughter was born, you told me you were glad it wasn't a boy so that he wouldn't . . . what were your words? "Die for an old man's selfishness"?'

Mattin doesn't reply at first but I can see him waver. 'You wouldn't be any better,' he says finally.

Søren glances at me before looking back at him. 'I never had any desire to be Kaiser – I was always open about that, even back when we crewed together. I wanted a ship and the sea around me and nothing else – I still do want that. If I had my way, I would never go back to court, but I've led men who died for my father's selfishness – just like your brothers have, just like your father did. The Kaiser will never be satisfied until the entire world is scorched earth. Or until someone stops him.'

'So you're joining *them*?' Mattin asks, looking at Dragonsbane, Pavlos, and me. 'They would see every Kalovaxian put to death.'

At that, Søren hesitates, his eyes meeting mine. He can't lie, I realize. So I do.

'We want Astrea back,' I say. 'That's all. We are joining our forces to remove the Kaiser, and in exchange for our help, Søren has promised to take his people away from our home.'

I half expect Dragonsbane – or any of the other Astreans gathered – to laugh or contradict me, but everyone remains mercifully silent. Søren nods.

'Times are desperate,' he adds. 'We might not be ideal partners, but we're far more formidable together than we are on our own.'

Mattin looks at all of us before he sighs, slumping forward. 'I told you: I don't know anything about the Kaiser's plans. I'm too far from court.'

Søren's face falls but he nods.

'You can go back home, though,' I say. 'And ensure the Kaiser's lies aren't the only story the people are hearing. Let them know that Søren is alive and well and fighting his father.'

'If I do, you'll let me go?' he asks, looking at Dragonsbane skeptically.

'Yes,' I say before she can answer. I know even as I say it that it's a promise I'm in no position to make.

Dragonsbane narrows her eyes. 'Pavlos, take him down to our brig,' she says, sounding bored. 'We'll compare his story to the rest and figure out who is the most useful to spare.'

Pavlos lowers his knife and steps forward to take hold of Mattin's shoulder and haul him away just as Søren comes toward me, eyes intent with a look I recognize only an instant before Pavlos's scream pierces the air. With Søren blocking my view, I can only make out a flash of silver and Pavlos crumpling to the ground with a thud before Mattin lunges toward Dragonsbane.

Panicked shouts from the crew pierce the air, but Dragonsbane is quicker than I thought and dodges out of the way an instant before Mattin buries a dagger in the mast she had been leaning against. A second earlier and the blade would have found her throat.

Before I can process what's happening or where Mattin got the dagger from, Søren is grabbing my dagger from its hilt at my hip, and without hesitating, he sends it flying through the air. It embeds itself in the back of Mattin's neck just as he's closing in once again on Dragonsbane.

He dies quickly, with barely a gurgle as he slumps to the ground at Dragonsbane's feet.

For a few beats, no one moves – not Søren or me or the Astrean crew or even the Kalovaxians still on their knees. The only sound is our labored breathing and the waves crashing against the ship's hull. It all happened so quickly, but as far as I can tell, when Pavlos took hold of Mattin again, it gave him the opportunity to somehow grab Pavlos's dagger, cut his own bindings, and stab Pavlos before turning to Dragonsbane, even though Søren and I were closer. Søren saved Dragonsbane's life when he had a lot of reasons not to.

And one good reason to do just that.

HONOR

———— • ◆ • ————

T HERE IS NO SAVING THE other Kalovaxians after that, and their deaths are quick and bloody, staining the deck of the *Pride*. Dragonsbane instructs a handful of her crew to take care of the bodies. Her voice doesn't waver. She might as well be asking them to clean up spilled ale.

The men and women do as she asks without hesitation before she dismisses the remaining crowd. Anders comes up from belowdecks, eyes scanning the body-strewn deck with a cold detachment. When he sees Pavlos, though, he freezes. He pushes his way through the crowd toward us as everyone leaves, coming to stand closer to Dragonsbane than I think is entirely appropriate, with his brow creased in concern. She must feel uncomfortable with his proximity as well, because she takes a step away.

'What happened? Are you all right?' he asks her.

She waves his concern away. 'I'm fine,' she says before pausing, her eyes narrowing at Søren. 'One of the hostages attacked me, but the *Prinkiti* stopped him.' The effort it takes for her to admit her own weakness in the same breath as she commends Søren is clear.

Though Søren doesn't understand the words, he seems to guess the sentiment. He nods at Dragonsbane, but wisely says nothing.

'He saved you,' Anders says slowly, disbelief evident in every word.

Dragonsbane bristles at the phrase. She looks at Søren, her curiosity winning out. 'Why?' she asks him in Kalovaxian.

Søren shrugs. 'I meant what I said – I am on your side.'

Dragonsbane frowns, and I can tell she still doesn't believe him.

'We can use him,' I say again in Astrean. 'His guilt is real and it's driving him. He's of much more use to us as an ally than as a prisoner.'

Dragonsbane's nostrils flare. 'He's one of them. He can never be an ally,' she says before turning to Anders. 'I'll need to speak with Pavlos's family as soon as possible. Did you get information from any of the hostages we took below-decks?'

For a moment, I think Anders is going to ignore her question and press for more about Dragonsbane's near assassination, but he finally nods. 'They each talked easily enough, but in the end, most of it couldn't be verified with the other prisoners, as usual.'

'What could be verified?' she asks.

Anders's eyes flicker to me, then Søren, then back to Dragonsbane.

'I'm not sure it's wise to discuss in front of mixed company, Captain,' he says carefully.

'The *Prinkiti* wants to be of assistance,' she says in Astrean. 'Perhaps we should let him try to suss out what information is true. He and Theo know the Kalovaxians better than anyone, after all.'

'"*Prinkiti*" is me, isn't it?' Søren whispers to me in Kalovaxian. 'I really don't like that nickname.'

'I think you're stuck with it,' I whisper back.

'Hush,' Dragonsbane snaps at us. 'What information, Anders?'

He still hesitates, glancing uncertainly at Søren. 'The story traveling the country is that the *Prinkiti* was kidnapped by the Queen after she murdered the Theyn and ran away. The Kaiser is offering a million gold pieces for her head, but five million if she's brought back alive.'

The implication slithers across my skin. I vow to myself that I'll end my own life before I let anyone take me to the Kaiser alive.

'We heard the same, more or less. Are there any rewards for the *Prinkiti*?' Dragonsbane asks.

Søren lets out an annoyed huff.

'Ten million for the *Prinkiti*,' Anders says. 'On the condition that he is handed over alive and unharmed. If he has so much as a stubbed toe, the reward is forfeit.'

'The Kaiser doesn't really want his son back, but the people love their Prinz, so he's creating that illusion to keep their goodwill, all the while ensuring that there's too much risk to tempt most bounty hunters,' I say. Dragonsbane and Anders turn to look at me, surprised that I spoke. I continue. 'Everyone knows Søren is a warrior. If he was kidnapped, he wouldn't have gone without a fight. Injuries are a given, so as far as they're concerned, Søren is a lost cause. They'll be focusing their efforts on me, just as the Kaiser wants them to.'

Dragonsbane's eyebrows rise but she nods, turning back to Anders. 'Any rumors about where they're searching hardest?'

'There was a rumor that she escaped to a refugee camp in Timmoree,' he says.

'Good,' Dragonsbane says. 'That's three days north of Sta'Crivero, and I've been assured that once we're in the city, King Etristo will protect Theo with his own life.'

'Words are easy,' I point out. 'Do you trust him?'

She shrugs. 'I trust that he's motivated by money,' she says. 'And I trust that his cut of your dowry will bring him far more than five million gold pieces.'

I can't argue with the logic of that, though my stomach sours at the word *dowry*. It was a custom in the Kalovaxian court as well, girls being sold off with a pile of gold to show their worth. It bothered me then, when it was girls I didn't really know and whom I disliked on principle. Now, though, I am the one being sold off, earning a profit not just for Astrea, but for King Etristo and presumably Dragonsbane as well. I feel like a thing instead of a person, the way I always felt around the Kaiser.

'What of the hostages?' I ask Anders, trying to push the feeling away and focus on the present. 'Are they willing to turn spy for us?'

'They're willing to not be executed,' Anders says, words clipped, but Dragonsbane is already shaking her head.

'No,' she says. 'It was a ridiculous plan before and this business with Pavlos only confirmed that. They can't be trusted. Anders, give the order.'

The order to kill them. I glance at Søren, who doesn't understand any of this but would protest if he could.

'That wasn't the agreement,' I say, looking back at Dragonsbane. 'They made a deal for their lives.'

'A deal is only as honorable as the people who make it,' Dragonsbane says. 'And we all know that the Kalovaxians have no honor.'

'I'm going to need to pick up Astrean very quickly,' Søren mutters to himself.

I ignore him. 'Do you have honor?' I ask Dragonsbane.

She bares her teeth in what might pass as a smile but isn't. 'No,' she tells me. 'That's why I've stayed alive as long as I have. The men aren't worth the risk and so they'll die. That's why the *Prinkiti* is going to be returned to the brig, no matter how useful you think he might be.'

I glance at Søren. I did not drag him out here and make him watch his own people be slaughtered just so he can be put back into chains. Artemisia's words echo in my mind.

By not agreeing to an arranged marriage yet, you have something my mother wants and so you have some measure of control. I feel sick, but I know what I have to do.

'Søren isn't going back to the brig,' I tell Dragonsbane, swallowing down my doubts and meeting her surprised gaze. 'I don't know much about the world outside of Astrea, and I will need Søren's assistance in selecting the most suitable husband when we reach Sta'Crivero.'

Dragonsbane stares at me in shock. 'You have me for that, Theo, and Anders. There is no need to trust a traitor Prinz.'

'I trust Søren,' I insist. 'If you want me to go through with this plot of yours, I want him out of the brig and treated as my advisor.'

She considers my words, her lips pursing. 'Very well,' she

says after a moment, her voice dangerously low. 'I suppose he has proven some measure of loyalty today, though I've always found the loyalty of men to be a fickle thing. He is your responsibility, Theo, and at the first sign of treason, his life is forfeit, am I understood?'

'At the first sign of treason, I will kill him myself,' I say.

Dragonsbane's expression is sour, but she nods.

'Was there any other information?' I ask Anders.

He clears his throat, looking like he would rather step on rusted nails than intrude on our conversation. 'There was only one other thing we could verify,' he admits. 'About the Kaiser.'

Even the thought of the Kaiser makes my whole body seize up, though I try to keep my expression level and distant. *I'm an ocean away,* I remind myself. He can't touch me, not even for five million gold pieces.

It's another rare word that Søren recognizes and he stiffens beside me, glancing back and forth between Anders and me with a guarded expression.

'He took a wife after you fled – a rushed marriage that's been plagued by some unkind rumors.'

For a second, my breath leaves me.

'Who?' I finally manage to ask.

'The Theyn's daughter,' Anders says. 'Lady Crescentia.'

TRUST

---·---

S øREN IS SILENT AT MY side as we walk down the hallway that leads to my cabin. I barely notice him. My mind is a whirlpool, spiraling my thoughts until they're jumbled and senseless.

'He said *Crescentia*,' Søren says finally, when we're close to my room. 'And the color drained from your face. Is she . . .' He trails off.

'She's not dead,' I tell him, and his face relaxes. I don't tell him that I think death would be a preferable fate.

'I'm glad,' he says. 'When I got back to court, my father had laid my whole life out for me, including Crescentia. I resented her for that, but it was never about her. You truly care about her, don't you?'

I think of Cress as I last saw her on the other side of my cell bars, wild-eyed and brittle, with singed skin and white hair and a touch that turned the cell bars scalding hot. My friend, once, my heart's sister. But not anymore.

'One day, when I am Kaiserin, I will have your country and all the people in it burned to the ground,' she said to me in her raw, pained voice. Now she is Kaiserin, and there is

nothing to stop her from fulfilling that vow.

'I don't know her,' I tell Søren. 'And she doesn't know me.'

I open the door to my cabin only to find Blaise, Heron, and Artemisia already waiting for me. As soon as they see me, Blaise jumps up from where he's sitting on my bed.

'Are you all right?' he asks in Astrean. 'We were below-decks handling other interviews, but we heard that a hostage attacked—'

'We're fine,' I assure him, switching to Kalovaxian so that Søren can understand as well. 'He killed Pavlos and tried to kill Dragonsbane, but Søren stopped him.'

All three sets of eyes go to Søren, who is standing just behind my shoulder. None of them speaks, but I can hear a dozen unspoken questions.

'He saved Dragonsbane's life and proved his loyalty to us,' I say.

Artemisia isn't fooled. Her eyes narrow, making her look frighteningly like her mother. 'And?' she prompts.

I glance away. 'And I pointed out that Søren's diplomatic experience would make him a necessary asset to me if I were to agree to marry one of these suitors in Sta'Crivero,' I say, though the words come out pinched.

Blaise's expression is a rolling thundercloud. 'You're a queen, you can't marry a stranger.'

'It would have happened anyway,' I point out, sitting down on the edge of my bed. 'Dragonsbane would have goaded me into it, pushed me and pushed me until I was backed into a corner without another choice. It would look like she controlled me.' I draw my blanket around my shivering shoulders. 'But by offering it up like that, I did it on my terms.'

Blaise makes a disapproving noise in the back of his throat but doesn't say anything. I look at Søren, still lingering in the doorway. The healing Heron did on him, though only superficial, was enough to make it look like he was a guest among us and not a prisoner, but away from the audience it's clear he's still in pain. He favors his right leg and grimaces whenever he moves either arm.

'This hostage, he didn't try to go after you?' Artemisia asks me, drawing my attention away from Søren.

I can't help but snort. 'Thank you for that, Art, but no.'

She rolls her eyes. 'I just mean that it's surprising, considering the Kalovaxian I interrogated said there's a bounty on your head.'

'I can't imagine what thoughts were going through his mind. I suppose he must have known that he wasn't going to survive, but if he could kill Dragonsbane, he would at least die a hero. I don't think the reward even crossed his mind,' I say, though something about that explanation nags at me.

'Mattin always had fantasies of heroics, but never the brains to see them through,' Søren says, shaking his head. It's a plausible explanation, but Søren's an easy liar to read, and sure enough, there's the tell – his nostrils flare.

'So there are bounties on both of our heads,' I say, turning away from Søren. 'And there are Kalovaxian forces searching for us in Timmoree. And the Kaiser married Crescentia. Is that everything we learned?'

'He *what*?' Søren asks, face twisting in disgust.

'They were married two days after we left Astrea, and she was crowned the day after that,' Blaise confirms. 'Each of the prisoners we interrogated said the same thing.'

'But . . . he was trying to betroth her to me,' Søren says, looking nauseous.

'You're a lost cause,' I tell him. Even though my own stomach is twisting, I push my feelings down and try to stay logical. 'The Theyn was growing more popular with the people than the Kaiser was. Being murdered would have added to that, turned him into a folk hero. That popularity would have even touched his daughter – Cress will be seen as sympathetic at court and that sympathy will now also spread to the Kaiser, who could sorely use some of it.'

'Not to mention she's beautiful,' Søren adds. 'There were dozens of men trying for her hand. My father likes to take what everyone else wants.'

She isn't beautiful anymore, though, I want to say. Not in a way the Kaiser would appreciate, at least. Though maybe he finds her power frightening. Maybe that horror is its own kind of beauty, a kind the Kaiser would want to take ownership of. I don't let myself say any of that out loud. Even thinking it makes me feel sick.

'Why would she do it, though?' Søren asks, horror still clear in his voice.

Because of me, I think, though again, I keep that to myself.

'Cress was raised to be Kaiserin,' I say instead. 'I'm sure she would have rather married you, but that wasn't an option anymore. She did what she had to, to get what she wanted.'

'You can't pity her,' Art says, though I can't tell if she's saying it in disbelief or as a command.

'She was my friend,' I say. It's the first time I've admitted that to them, though they must have known it to be true. 'And as someone who came perilously close to being married to the

Kaiser myself, of course I pity her.'

'You came close to *what*?' Blaise asks, eyes widening until they nearly bug out of his head.

I wince. I forgot that I hadn't shared that bit of information with my Shadows.

'If you knew, you would have insisted on pulling me out of the palace too soon,' I say, keeping my voice level. 'I didn't tell you and we still got out before anything happened.'

It's true enough, though I can't help but think of that last banquet and the Kaiser's hand on my thigh, his breath on me. I suppress a shudder and look to Søren. I think he's remembering that night, too. If we'd left even a day later . . . no, I won't think about that. The Kaiser will never touch me again.

But he's touching Cress, I remind myself. She's his wife now, and though I'm sure she married him willingly, I can't imagine that she was too willing about what followed.

I push the thought from my mind and focus on the present, on what I do have control over.

'Søren, you need sleep,' I tell him before turning to Heron. Though I hate to ask more of him, I do. 'Can you finish healing him? Please?'

Heron's brow furrows and he opens his mouth to answer, but Søren beats him to it.

'I'm fine,' he says, though he realizes how false it sounds. 'I will be fine,' he amends. 'Nothing fatal, nothing time and care won't fix.'

Heron exhales slowly, shaking his head. 'I can fix them.'

'I won't take anything more from you,' Søren says. 'It's some cracked ribs, a sprained ankle. I've had worse. The rest of the world heals from injuries like these just fine without magic.'

For a moment Heron says nothing, only stares at Søren like he isn't quite sure what game he's playing. Finally he shrugs.

'You'll need some help with the bandages,' he says. 'Not to mention clean clothes. Mine will be too big, but Blaise's will be too small, so you'll have to make do.'

Søren nods. 'Thank you.'

Art looks at Søren for a few seconds, as if she's trying to decide something. 'I know where my mother keeps the spare clothing. I can steal a couple sets for you tomorrow, and some boots.'

'Thank you,' Søren says again.

Blaise doesn't look at Søren, even when he speaks to him. 'You can take my bunk. I'm spending my nights here with Theo anyway.'

I want to pummel Blaise for the way he says that, like he's staking some kind of claim on me. Like a dog urinating on a favorite tree. I open my mouth to say as much, but Søren interrupts.

'Is that wise?' he asks, concerned. His eyes dart to the others, brow furrowing. 'I just mean . . . with everything we talked about,' he adds to me.

I bite my lip, glancing at Blaise, who is slowly putting the pieces together, then to Artemisia and Heron. I remember my talk with Søren when we were on our way to the *Smoke*, how he told me he thought Blaise was a berserker and I told him he was wrong, that it wasn't possible, even when I believed it might be. Heron puzzled it out on his own and I would be surprised if Artemisia hasn't done the same, but it isn't something the lot of us have ever acknowledged.

'You're wrong. Blaise isn't dangerous,' I say after a moment, looking at Blaise as I say it. I half expect Søren to protest but he doesn't. Artemisia doesn't ask what we're talking about and a quick glance her way confirms that she's not having trouble deciphering what isn't being said.

'It's been a long day for all of us,' I say after a moment of uncomfortable silence. 'Heron, please get Søren something to sleep in for tonight. Blaise, show him the way to your room. Art, see if you can charm whoever's working in the kitchen into giving you a few extra pieces of hardtack and a canteen of water. We'll discuss more tomorrow.'

I have just enough time to change into my nightgown and swipe a damp towel over my face before Blaise returns, expression drawn tight. It should be unreadable, but I know him well enough to see the anger hiding in the corners of his mouth. It's easy to guess what put it there.

'I didn't tell him,' I say before he can accuse me. 'He's seen berserkers up close before; he knows the symptoms better than any of us.'

His mouth tightens even more but he nods. 'And Heron and Artemisia know as well?'

I shrug. 'Heron mentioned it. Artemisia hasn't said anything to me, but she seemed to understand what Søren was alluding to and she didn't look surprised by it.'

'Everyone knows, then.' He laughs, but there's no joy to the sound. The walls and floor of the cabin suddenly thrum to life, beating like an erratic heart – like Blaise's heart now, I'd imagine. At first, I think I'm imagining it, but when I place a hand on the wall, the thrumming grows stronger and my own heartbeat quickens. Blaise's Earth Gift, I realize with a twisting stomach. It's connecting with the wood of the ship, affecting it, though he doesn't mean to. He doesn't even notice, his eyes fixed only on me.

It's a subtle enough tremor now, but he started an earthquake once. How easily could he turn the ship into splinters?

I swallow my panic and try to keep my voice calm and soothing. 'Blaise,' I say, locking my eyes onto his. 'They understand that it isn't like that. They know better than to be afraid of you.'

Even as I say the words, though, I know they aren't true. I might know Blaise better than anyone, but in this moment I am afraid of him. Not Blaise – not necessarily – but what he's capable of. What he can do without even meaning to. I force myself to breathe, to speak softly. I don't want to be afraid of him, but fear races through me all the same.

He would never hurt me, I remind myself, but fear is not a thing to be controlled by logic.

Blaise catches himself, closing his eyes and taking deep breaths until the room stills once more. Even when it does, I can't bring myself to relax. I hear Søren's voice again in my mind, telling me that Blaise is dangerous. *He's not,* I argue to myself. Even if he loses his temper from time to time, he's always been in control enough to stop it before it becomes serious. Blaise said it himself: his gift might not feel like a blessing, but it doesn't feel like mine madness either.

He catches his bottom lip between his teeth and hesitates for a moment before some of the tension leaves his body. 'If Dragonsbane finds out,' he says after a moment, his voice so quiet I can barely hear him, 'she won't let me stay on the ship. Assuming she doesn't have me killed on the spot, she'll exile me.'

'I won't let her do either,' I say.

Blaise shakes his head. 'You just used the only piece of leverage you had to free the *Prinkiti*,' he points out. 'The whole ship will be saying you're in love with him by morning,' he says.

I turn away from him so I'm facing the bed, though I know he's right. Agreeing to meet with suitors was the only card I had to use with Dragonsbane, and now I am fully at her mercy. I peel back the covers and slip beneath them before letting myself face him, careful to keep my face impassive. 'I can't control what people say.'

I hope he'll leave it there, but I know Blaise too well for that. I'm not even surprised when he asks, 'Are you?'

'No,' I say without missing a beat. 'But I also don't appreciate you treating me like a toy you're carving your name into to keep it away from someone else.'

'I didn't—'

'You did,' I interrupt. 'You told him we were spending our nights together.'

'We are.'

'That's not the way you said it, and you know it,' I say.

He doesn't say anything for a moment, standing in the middle of my cabin looking wounded and angry. 'You're agreeing to *marry* a stranger to save him. Him. A Kalovaxian.'

My stomach churns again, though I keep my voice placid. 'I'm agreeing to marry a stranger for *Astrea* – because it's the best chance we have of matching the Kalovaxians in battle,' I say. 'But I didn't see why I shouldn't get as much out of the arrangement as possible.'

Blaise shakes his head. 'You just put your own wants above the wants of your people, and they'll remember that.'

The words are a stab to my gut.

'It was the right thing to do,' I say, my voice barely louder than a whisper. 'For Søren, yes, but also for Astrea. It was the only way.'

He looks at me for a long moment, eyes bright and unflinching. 'You keep telling yourself that, Your Majesty.'

Without another word, he turns and walks out my door, leaving me alone.

'You untied Mattin,' I say to Søren the next morning when we eat breakfast in the cabin he's sharing with Heron. The others are all on duty, but Søren and I don't have assignments, so instead I'm trying to teach him some Astrean before we arrive in Sta'Crivero tomorrow.

He looks up from the piece of parchment I'd given him, where I'd written down the sounds that make up our language, translated into Kalovaxian phonetics.

'I don't know what you're talking about,' he says, but his nostrils flare again and he glances away, focusing again on the parchment.

'It was smart,' I say. 'And it worked – you're free, in a sense. Unchained, at least. Pavlos is dead, though, and so are all the other hostages we tried to turn into spies.'

He doesn't respond at first, though his face pales at the mention of the other hostages. He shakes his head.

'If I *had* untied Mattin, it would have been a calculated risk,' he says finally, his eyes not leaving the parchment. 'I would have chosen the worst swordsman out of the *Pride*'s crew, but one with a history of doing foolish things in the name of bravery. I would know that in untying him, I would be telling him I was on his side, and in shielding you, I ensured that protection would apply to you as well. I would have known he would take Pavlos's weapon and attack him first, but poor a swordsman as Mattin is, I would have hoped it wouldn't have been a fatal injury. I would have been certain that I could get your dagger and stop him before he killed Dragonsbane.'

Even though he clings to his hypotheticals, he knows I know that's the truth of it.

'You killed one of Dragonsbane's crew in order to prove that she could trust you,' I say slowly. 'Do you realize how convoluted that is? Why am I supposed to care about what you *hoped* would happen? You were wrong and a man died because of a risk he never consented to take.'

He says nothing, only staring at the ground, shame turning his cheeks red.

'Sacrificing someone else to improve your own lot – it sounds like something your father would do,' I say.

'I know,' he admits, though each word costs him. 'When I was standing on that deck, going over all of it in my mind, it was his voice I heard.'

The confession hangs in the air between us, neither of us knowing what to say.

'I hear it sometimes, too,' I say after what feels like an eternity. 'Any time I confront Dragonsbane or use the word *queen* as a weapon to get what I want. I heard it when I convinced Spiros to let you out of the brig.'

Søren lets out a mirthless chuckle. 'The difference is, my father would have let me die in that brig without a second thought.'

I shake my head. 'Not if getting you out gave him a tactical advantage, even as it hurt the people who were depending on him to help them,' I say. 'Getting you out was the right thing to do, I know that, but it isn't why I did it. *That's* what scares me.'

Søren hesitates. 'A lot of awful things can be said about my father – we've said most of them. The idea of sharing anything with him is enough to make me want to tear my skin from my bones. But it can't be denied that he wins his battles. He's a monster, but maybe understanding him is the only way we can hope to beat him.'

His words reassure me more than they probably should. I still hate the idea of being like the Kaiser in any way, and I'm not sure that will ever change, no matter how Søren tries to justify it. Still, there is something to be said for someone seeing your darkest parts and accepting you anyway.

ETRISTO

———— • ————

THE *SMOKE* GETS AS CLOSE to the Sta'Criveran shore as it can without the risk of running aground. Most of the crew will remain on the ship for the duration of our visit, but Dragonsbane and I are supposed to stay in the palace as King Etristo's guests. I can't deny that I'm looking forward to sleeping on solid ground again – no violent rocking, no moldy sea smell, no worry that a storm might come along.

As my council, Søren, Blaise, Artemisia, and Heron are allowed to join me in the palace, just as Dragonsbane's council are joining her. Though she won't be Dragonsbane here. She will be Princess Kallistrade, my beloved aunt, who came out of hiding when I escaped and has been aiding me ever since. That is the story Dragonsbane spun for King Etristo in their correspondence to keep her pirate identity secret. We all must remember to only call her *Aunt* or *Princess* but never *Captain*.

Though this was a directive, I didn't miss the fact that it gives me an amount of power over her. With one word, I could reveal her identity as a wanted pirate and change her fate forever.

I cram into a small rowboat with my council, glancing

after Dragonsbane, Anders, and Eriel in a second boat ahead.

'Any sign of trouble and we'll get you out immediately,' Blaise says while Heron and Søren row us toward the shore. Blaise offered to row, but Heron and Søren are visibly stronger and Blaise begrudgingly agreed to let them do it.

'We're at war,' I tell him. 'Trouble is inevitable, and I'm ready to handle my share.'

'Running is the last option,' Artemisia adds. 'It's all well and good to act like Theo's made of glass – by all means, keep that illusion up once we get to Etristo's court – but she isn't. And as much as we might not want to admit it, we need Etristo. We need his help far more than he needs anything from us, and you ought to believe he's keenly aware of that fact.' She turns to me. 'You are sweet and docile and dumb.'

I recoil. 'Excuse me?'

She smirks. 'Another role to play. You're very good at playing roles.'

I'm tempted to look at Søren, who's too busy rowing to talk but can certainly hear every word.

'Let them believe you are dim,' Artemisia continues. 'The King, his court, your suitors. If they believe you to be an idiot, they will underestimate you. Let them.'

I swallow before nodding. The idea of going back to pretending to be someone I'm not rankles, but I know she's right.

Sta'Crivero is a country of sand. As we approach the shore, I scan the horizon but there is little to see. Rolling dunes crest like waves all the way to the horizon, unbroken by trees or any kind of foliage. It doesn't look like the sort of place where anything could survive.

As the boat beaches, I see a hint of movement on the horizon. A line of white carriages approaches, though the sun's rays make the shape of them hazy and unclear.

The first thing I notice once Blaise helps me out of the boat and onto the Sta'Criveran shore is the heat. It was hot enough on the boat, but the water surrounding us cooled the air somewhat. On the shore, there is no solace. The sun is so bright I have to squint and shield my eyes to see anything.

The carriages stop a good distance away, fanning out into a semicircle. Now that they're closer, I can see the open tops, covered only by white cloth awnings. Each carriage is filled with a handful of men and women dressed head to toe in loose white clothing.

'The King and his entourage,' Søren says, coming to stand at my side.

'Is the white of cultural significance?' I ask, dragging the back of my hand across my forehead to wipe away beads of sweat.

'No,' Artemisia says, appearing at my other side. 'It deflects the sun's rays to keep them cool while they're out of the palace. Once they're inside, they'll wear more color.'

I can see the appeal of the lighter garments. My dark purple gown is sleeveless and made of airy silk, but I am already sweating under the heat of the high sun. Even though Heron mended its tears and Artemisia used her Water Gift to clean it, it still reminds me of the last time I wore it, back in the dungeon. Art and Heron did a good job of fixing it – it looks the same as the day Cress gave it to me, which seems unfair somehow, given how much I've changed since then.

'They aren't moving,' I point out, watching the Sta'Criverans watching me.

'They expect us to go to them,' Dragonsbane says, approaching from her boat with Anders and Eriel. She looks uncomfortable in her own gown, black silk and so high-necked that it looks like it's choking her. 'Etristo wants us to remember who is in control here.'

She doesn't sound happy about that, but she's resigned. Artemisia moves back as her mother approaches, giving Dragonsbane room to loop her arm through mine and pull me into step with her.

'You'll let me do the talking,' she says, not bothering to soften the command into a request. 'Smile and nod and keep your answers short and charming. You can do that, can't you?'

I resist the urge to pull my arm from hers, but I'm acutely aware of everyone watching. What she's saying isn't so different from what Artemisia said just moments ago, but it feels a world apart. Artemisia told me to act stupid; Dragonsbane is treating me like I *am* stupid.

'Of course, Aunt,' I say with a saccharine smile. After all, there's no reason playing stupid shouldn't extend to Dragons-bane as well. I can't imagine that her underestimating me won't end up coming in handy.

As we draw closer, I get a better look at the Sta'Criverans. Though their clothing is similar, the people are all strikingly different from each other. Unlike Kalovaxians, who are uniformly fair-haired and pale-skinned, or Astreans, who are tawny-skinned with dark brown and black shades of hair, Sta'Criverans have a variety of different skin tones, from a near jet-black to the color of the sand around us. And the hair! Though hats cover most of it to block out the sun's rays, what bits stick out are every color imaginable. Deep bluish black, white blond, fire red, and everything in between.

As we get closer, I realize that the horses hitched to the carriages have jewels woven into their manes and tails that glitter in the sunlight. My first thought is that they are Spirit-gems to help them go faster, but no. There are too many different colors, none of them the telltale clear of Air Gems. They are just for show.

I remember what Artemisia said about the Sta'Criverans – they have no need for useful things, so they value pretty things instead.

When we're halfway between the shore and the carriages, Dragonsbane stops short and I follow suit. The others fall in behind us.

'We can't seem *too* eager, can we?' she asks me. 'They'll come the rest of the way.'

I nod, though I'm not sure she's right. For an uncomfortable few moments, the Sta'Criverans stay put in their carriages, watching us like we're a group of strange new beasts brought in for them to ogle. A handful of them bring gilded telescopes to their eyes for a better look. Under their expectant gaze and the hot sun overhead, I start to sweat more through my dress, and I will myself not to. That is hardly the first impression I want to make on King Etristo.

I open my mouth to suggest to Dragonsbane that we

surrender what little pride we still have and walk the rest of the way to them, when the Sta'Criverans' attention is diverted to something happening on their side, out of my view.

'Finally,' Dragonsbane mutters under her breath.

Four white-clad men are now making their way toward us, carrying a large cloth-draped box between them. They move quickly, the box balanced between them on metal rods, marching with such ease across the sand dunes that I'd imagine they do this regularly.

The rest of the Sta'Criverans hurry in their wake.

When they're ten feet from us, the men all stop perfectly in sync before lowering their cargo as one. It's impressive – I don't think one of their corners touches the sand a half second before another.

For a long moment, nothing happens. Dragonsbane and the Sta'Criverans gathered behind the box all watch it expectantly, so I do the same. Finally, the white covering parts down the center on one side and a weathered copper hand emerges, pulling the cloth back. Then comes a cane of carved lapis lazuli. With a pained grunt, a figure emerges, hunched over and dressed in the same white as everyone else. The only difference is the crown that circles his bald, spotted head, an ornate thing of gold curlicues and jewels of so many different colors that I can't name them all.

The man himself is unassuming, and if it weren't for the crown, I don't think I would look twice at him in a crowd. Swathed in white and hunched over his gleaming cane, he almost reminds me of a priest from one of the mines, before the siege. Søren and Artemisia were both wrong in their estimates – he is eighty at least, maybe even ninety – and judging by his labored breathing and how painful every step seems to be, I wouldn't be entirely surprised if he expired somewhere along the ten-foot walk to us. The Sta'Criverans who carried him seem to think the same thing, hovering just behind him as if he might fall at any moment. They must be his personal guards as well as his transportation.

With a wheeze, he waves them off and takes the last few steps alone, until he's standing directly in front of Dragonsbane and me. Hunched over as he is, he barely comes up to my shoulder, and Dragonsbane towers over him even more in her heeled boots.

'Your Highness,' Dragonsbane says in Astrean, bowing her head. 'It is a pleasure to meet you in person. You look very well.'

The King wheezes again, though I think beneath it is a snort of disbelief. He turns his eyes to Dragonsbane for barely a second.

'I never had the honor of meeting your sister, though they tell me you were twins,' he says.

Dragonsbane hesitates for only a beat but it's long enough to glimpse her discomfort. 'Yes, Your Highness. I'm Princess Kallistrade. As Dragonsbane told you in his letters, I've recently decided to come out of hiding to protect my niece, Queen Theodosia Eirene Houzzara of Astrea.'

She gestures to me. My full name sounds strange coming from her, like she's draping a cloak around my shoulders that she doubts I'll ever grow into.

'Shame he couldn't make it to shore himself,' King Etristo says to Dragonsbane. 'I would have liked to meet this elusive pirate.'

'But then he wouldn't be elusive, Your Highness,' Dragonsbane says with a smile.

King Etristo makes an annoyed noise in his throat before finally turning to me. His watery eyes rake from the top of my head to my feet. I force myself to stand tall and proud.

'Queen Theodosia,' he says after a moment, his voice raspy and quiet enough that it nearly disappears into the air. Though the action costs him, he attempts a bow.

'King Etristo,' I reply, dipping into a curtsy. I decide to speak Astrean as well, since he seems to understand it. 'I'm so grateful for your generous hospitality and your interest in my situation.'

'You've been through quite an ordeal, I've been told,' he replies. His Astrean is passable, but clumsy, too heavy to pass for a native speaker. 'We are happy to come to your assistance against these Kalovaxian beasts, though I see you are bringing one into our midst. How peculiar.'

His eyes dart over my shoulder to where Søren is standing beside Heron, Blaise, and Artemisia. King Etristo regards him in much the same way he looked at me, as if trying to decide exactly what he might be worth to him. He doesn't spare so much as a glance at my other advisors – I imagine he doesn't think them to be worth anything at all without a pedigree to back them up.

'The best sort of ally is one who understands the enemy, don't you agree?' I say, looking back at the King with the kind of smile I haven't worn since Astrea – the kind that's been thoroughly coated in honey. 'Who understands the Kaiser better than his own son?'

'Mmm,' King Etristo says, though his eyes linger on Søren and his mouth purses.

'He's proven his loyalty,' Dragonsbane says, drawing King Etristo's eyes to her. 'And if that loyalty ever falters, he will be quickly disposed of. Isn't that right, Theodosia?'

I would be a fool to miss the tone of her voice, the condescending smile, the way she looks at King Etristo as if to say *Children will be children, what can one do?* I want to retort, but I hold my tongue. Let him think me a silly child – let *her* think me a silly child.

'Of course, Aunt,' I say.

King Etristo grunts before looking back at Søren and switching to Kalovaxian. 'Last time I saw you, Prinz Søren, you were answering to another sovereign. Of course, you're hardly the first man to be swayed by a pretty face.'

I worry that Søren will say something we'll all regret, but King Etristo doesn't give him a chance to reply before continuing in Astrean.

'And what a pretty face it is, my dear,' he says, lifting my hand to his dry lips. 'A shame for a girl like you to be alone in this world, but that is what we are here for, no?' he asks, glancing behind him. It seems to be a rhetorical question but the crowd murmurs in agreement. 'Our other honored guests will arrive tomorrow, and you will all stay in the palace with me.'

Without another word, he drops my hand and turns away from us, hobbling toward his carrier and climbing inside. As soon as the white cloth settles behind him, he's lifted into the air and we are ushered into an empty carriage led by a duo of bejewled horses. After we're settled, the driver snaps the reins, and with a jolt, we begin our journey across the sand.

STA'CRIVERO

———— • ————

THE WALL THAT SURROUNDS STA'CRIVERO'S capital city is so tall that I can't quite tell where it ends and the sky begins. During the hour-long journey, there was little more to see than sand. It stretched out in every direction, rippling over the land in wavelike patterns. Only twice, I spotted signs of a village in the distance, not large enough for more than fifty people.

'Eight in ten Sta'Criverans make their homes in the capital,' Søren had said during our lesson. 'The conditions outside it are brutal – scalding summers with little opportunity to find food and water, and the winters aren't much better.'

'Why do even the two in ten remain outside?' I had asked.

Artemisia had shrugged. 'It's home,' she'd said.

Now, looking up at the wall from the outside, I wonder if it's more than that. The city hardly looks inviting and I know that walls are generally built for one main reason – to keep people out.

Not us, though. We pause in front of ornate, heavy gates and they creak open, guided by an elaborate set of ropes and pulleys. It's a slow process, but as the capital gradually comes into view, I gasp.

Though Astrea's capital as it exists in my childhood memories is the most beautiful place in the world, even I have to admit that the Sta'Criveran capital might be her equal.

On the journey here, my eyes grew accustomed to the bright sunlight, but the splendor of the capital makes them ache all over again. No matter where I look, everything is either polished gold or richly colored, a blinding beauty that is almost gaudy in its overwhelmingness.

Dozens of spindly towers rise over the streets like golden blades of saw grass, so delicate that I worry a light wind will send them toppling. No two are the same exact color, and atop each one a flag hangs limply in the still air. Closer to the ground are rows of houses and shops with flat roofs and large windows, each wall painted with its own work of art. One shows two human figures dancing in bright clothing, while another shows the night sky, littered with stars that seem to actually sparkle. Some are painted more simply, with colors swirling over the surface.

Even the roads look like they should be on display somewhere – each brick is glistening white and without so much as a scuff mark that I can see, despite the mass of carriages and crowds of people trampling over them.

'They have magic,' I say, because there is no other explanation. 'I thought Astrea was the only country that did.'

Dragonsbane's laugh is mocking. 'No magic,' she says, shaking her head.

'But the streets are so clean,' I argue, 'and the air is cooler, and those towers can't possibly be staying up there on their own.'

'You were right, no other countries besides Astrea have magic the way you do, apart from the gems they buy from the Kaiser,' Anders says. 'But because they lack magic, they strive to replicate its effects with advancements in science and . . .' He pauses, searching for an Astrean word. After a moment he gives up. '*Technology*,' he finishes. I'm not sure what language that is, but it's certainly not Astrean. He continues, 'The streets stay clean because they are coated with a compound that repels marks and stains. The air is cooler because the capital was built on an underground spring. The towers are held aloft because they were built to exact specifications that a team of mathematicians devised.'

'Science and *technology*,' I repeat slowly, sounding out the strange word. *Science* is at least a familiar concept, the study of organic materials and chemistry and medicines and plants and animals, though I have a feeling *this* kind of science is something entirely different from what I'm familiar with. I can't begin to guess what he means by *technology*, though, and I'm too embarrassed to ask. This seems like something I should know. It's one thing to act like a fool, but I'm painfully aware of how little I know about the world outside of Astrea. Artemisia and Søren might have prepared me for the suitors, but they didn't prepare me for this.

I can't imagine how the palace can be any more exquisite than the rest of the city, but it is. Instead of the single towers spread throughout the city, here there is a cluster of at least two dozen spindly towers of various heights and colors, each with a conical roof topped with its own flag. The tallest tower is at the very center, painted a rich red, and it has a flag that is crisp white with an orange sun.

I don't have to ask anyone to understand that the flags are the sigils of different families who live in those towers and that the largest therefore must belong to the royal family.

'It really is something,' I murmur to Blaise. Our earlier fight lingers distantly in my mind, though neither of us has acknowledged it since. I don't think either of us *wants* to acknowledge it. Try as I might, though, I can't forget the thrum of the wood around us when Blaise lost his temper, as if the whole ship was about to shatter into nothing but splinters.

'It's very . . . pointy,' he says, shrugging his shoulders. 'I prefer home.'

Home. What was it I told Blaise when we left? *'It's only walls and roofs and floors.'* And maybe that's the truth, but now that he's said it, I can't help but feel the ache in my gut for my palace – not as it was the last time I was there, with its burnt garden and cracked, dirty stained-glass windows and the Kaiser sitting on my mother's throne, but how it was before the siege. The Sta'Criveran palace would have dwarfed it, but Blaise is right; I prefer it, with its round rooms and domed ceilings and the gold and mosaics and stained glass everywhere you looked. Sta'Crivero is beautiful, but it will never compare to the memory of home that I cling to.

After the seven of us pile out of the carriage, we're escorted through the arching palace entrance by a quartet of guards dressed in pressed cerulean uniforms with gold epaulets. The entryway is dominated by a large spiral staircase with tiled stairs in a rainbow of colors and a gold railing. When I look up, the stairs spiral high enough that I can't see where they end.

'You must be our Astrean guests,' a female voice calls out, echoing in the large space. I glance around, but it's impossible to tell where the voice is coming from. Finally, my eyes fall on a woman stepping around the edge of the stairway, dressed in a draping gown of peach cotton cinched at the waist with a thick yellow ribbon. She's maybe five years older than I am, with bronze skin and dark brown hair that falls to her shoulders in loose curls. She has a kind face, but I've learned not to trust appearances.

She smiles, showing two rows of gleaming white teeth. 'My name is Nesrina. King Etristo has asked that I show you to your rooms so that you can settle in before dinner. We realize that the palace can be quite confusing to newcomers.'

Nesrina gives a light chuckle that sounds rehearsed, and I wonder how many times she's given this tour.

Dragonsbane clears her throat. 'I'm Princess Kallistrade,' she says, though she can't manage to say *princess* without wincing. 'This is Anders and Eriel,' she says, motioning to them; each man gives a nod of acknowledgment. 'Artemisia. Blaise, Heron, Prinz Søren . . . and, of course, my niece, Queen Theodosia.'

Nesrina nods to each of us as Dragonsbane points us out, but when it's my turn, she dips into a graceful curtsy with a few extra flourishes worked in.

'Your Majesty,' she says. 'If you will all come with me, we're going to head upstairs.'

Again I look up at the seemingly endless spiral staircase.

My legs already ache at the thought of climbing them. The prospect of sleeping on the rocking ship is suddenly not as disagreeable as it was this morning.

'How far up is it?' I ask, hoping I don't sound rude. The last thing I want to do is insult my host.

Nesrina laughs and shakes her head. 'Not to worry, Your Majesty. We have a riser – we aren't savages.' She turns and motions for us to follow.

I seem to be the only one who doesn't know what a riser is, and I don't want to show my naïveté by asking. Warily, I trail behind her until she stops before a large brass cage at the base of the stairway, nestled in the center of its spiral. Inside is plush red carpet and a shirtless man, skin the same color as the bars behind him, standing at attention. His shoulders are broad and his arms are the biggest I've ever seen – I think each one might be bigger around than my waist.

Nesrina steps into the cage and gestures for us to follow, but I hang back, my mind circling over every way this can go wrong. It's a trap. King Etristo thinks I'm foolish enough to step into a cage so that he can deliver me to the Kaiser and collect his five million gold pieces. I know I'm supposed to play the fool, but not that much a fool, surely.

Søren lingers by my side. 'The risers are the easiest way to get to the tops of the towers,' he murmurs. 'The man uses that crank to lift the box up, bit by bit.'

I glance sideways at him, unable to keep the disbelief off my face. 'We'll fall to our deaths,' I say.

He shrugs. 'The Sta'Criverans have been using them for decades, and they've sold the design to other countries around the world. We even adapted the design to use in the mines in

Astrea. No deaths have been reported. They say you're more likely to fall by taking the stairs.'

Though my stomach is still churning, I follow the others into the cage. When the door closes behind me with a clang, my whole body goes tense. I force myself to take deep breaths, but I know it'll be difficult until I'm out of this contraption. With the rest of our eight packed in, giving the riser attendant plenty of space, there's barely room for me to move my arms.

'To the twenty-fifth floor, please, Argos,' Nesrina says. She's perfectly relaxed, as if she does this all the time. She likely does.

The riser attendant – Argos – nods and takes hold of the large crank, beginning to turn it. His muscles bulge with the effort.

'There's a jolt to start,' Søren whispers to me an instant before the jolt comes. Søren's warning aside, it still scares me and I jump, reaching out to grab whatever I can, which turns out to be Søren's arm and Artemisia's shoulder. Art shrugs me off and at first I think Søren does as well, but after a second, he takes my hand, lacing his fingers with mine. The riser is so crowded that no one can see him do it, but I feel the urge to pull away. Though I know I should, I can't bring myself to.

We rise slowly at first, but gradually get momentum and pick up speed until we're ascending at a decent clip – much faster than we would if we took the stairs. The stairs pass in a blur of colors, but even though it's easier than I expected, I can't bring myself to relax. I feel my shoulders bunched all the way up to my ears, and I squeeze Søren's hand like I'm trying to break it.

To his credit, he doesn't pull away and I can't help but think of the last time we did this, in the dark dungeons beneath the Astrean palace, racing through the corridors with the Kalovaxian guards and their dogs getting closer with each passing second. I don't want to think about that, but I suppose it's somewhat preferable to imagining what would happen if the crank broke and the cage plummeted to the ground.

'Last time I was here,' Søren says quietly, though I'd imagine everyone in the riser can hear him, 'was when my father sent me on a diplomatic expedition to try to make the Sta'Criverans allies. It was the first time I was ever in a riser and I think I nearly fainted, which was not exactly the image of strength my father wanted to project. Of course, the Sta'Criverans had no interest in an alliance, as I came to find out. But they wanted to make sure I – and my father – understood how strong they were and how, even if we weren't allies, it would be a mistake to consider them enemies.'

'It's true,' Nesrina says, glancing at us over her shoulder. 'The Kalovaxians would never dare invade Sta'Crivero. Which is precisely why it's the safest place for you, Your Majesty.'

'I'm so grateful,' I say with my sweetest smile, as if she's given me a gift by extending to me what should be a basic human courtesy.. 'Your kindness to me will never be forgotten.'

Yet, as the elevator finally lurches to a stop so sharp it makes my stomach tumble, I can't help but wonder what Sta'Crivero's kindness will cost me.

PALACE

———◆•◆———

Nesrina escorts us down a long hallway, passing half a dozen doors before stopping at the one at the very end. She twists the gold and crystal knob and pushes the door open.

'For the Queen,' she says, inclining her head toward me. 'We hope that it is to your liking.'

I step inside and the room swallows me. It's an expansive space, with high, vaulted ceilings painted with clouds and cherubs and so big I think merely walking from one side to the other would take some effort. In the center is the biggest bed I've ever seen – a family of six could sleep in it comfortably – draped in fire-coral satin with a jewel-box array of pillows covering most of it. Yards of matching silk canopy over it, dancing in the breeze coming through the open windows that line three of the walls. Midafternoon sunlight pours in, making the lapis lazuli tile floors glow beneath my feet.

In one corner is a cluster of plush chairs around a mosaic table set with a glass water pitcher and four cups. On the other side of the room is a lacquered armoire with bone-inlay doors and ivory handles. There is also a writing desk and chair, a table with a water basin, and a basket of sponges and soap that's been carved into birds that look so real I half expect them to fly out the windows. Next to the basin is a large vanity with more birds carved into the mahogany edge of the mirror.

Even the Kaiser would find the decadence of this room to be too much. I certainly feel out of place, like an alley cat that's been dropped into the middle of a ball. Though Astrea's palace was opulent, it was nothing like this. I try not to let my discomfort show.

'Will cots be brought in for my advisors?' I ask Nesrina.

Her forehead furrows and she shakes her head. 'You misunderstand me: this is *your* room. They will be close enough – just down the hall – but the Sta'Criveran palace is certainly grand enough to afford you your own space, Your Majesty.'

The words grate. In a strange palace in a strange country, the last thing I want is to be alone and in a room this size – I feel like I could get lost in it and no one would ever be able to find me.

'There are no guards outside,' Blaise says, sounding as alarmed as I feel. 'King Etristo guaranteed the Queen's safety, but without guards—'

'Crime of any kind is not tolerated in Sta'Crivero,' Nesrina interrupts with a patient smile. 'Even petty theft has been punishable by death for many decades now. As a result, we have wiped out crime completely. I can assure you, there is no safer place than this palace.'

'I don't think the Kaiser would care about your laws or the lives of the assassins he would send after her,' Blaise counters.

Nesrina's smile falters only for an instant. 'I can, of course, bring up this concern with King Etristo,' she says.

'There's no need to concern the King with a boy's unfounded fears,' Dragonsbane tells her, giving Blaise a severe look. 'In order for an assassin to get into Theo's room, they would have to get past the guards at the gate, past the guards at the palace doors, and past the riser operator. As I understand it, this is the same level of security given to the King himself.'

Nesrina nods in agreement. 'The King would wish Queen Theodosia no less security than he requires,' she says. 'She is in very good hands here with us.'

Blaise looks ready to argue but I stop him with a hand on his arm. Though it may be my imagination, his skin feels even hotter than normal.

I only realize I've done something wrong when Nesrina's smile slips from her face altogether. Her eyes are locked on my hand where it rests on Blaise's arm. I can practically see her thoughts turning.

I drop my hand, but the damage has already been done. Though on the *Smoke* it was nothing to touch Blaise – or Heron or anyone else for that matter – we are not on the *Smoke* anymore. My actions will be monitored more closely here and I need to remember that. It's difficult not to feel like I'm back in the Astrean palace, where I had to constantly be aware of how I was being viewed.

'This room will do just fine,' I tell Nesrina. 'Please pass along my gratitude to King Etristo.'

Blaise simmers next to me, but he says nothing.

Nesrina nods, her smile back in place but stiffer at

the corners. 'We'll leave you to freshen up, then, and I'll show the others to their rooms.'

As they file out, Blaise catches my gaze, his expression loaded with worry. I give him a reassuring smile, but it doesn't seem to do much to lift his mood.

I watch them walk back down the narrow hall toward the other guest rooms before I close the door, letting out a sigh of relief. At least there are no holes in these walls, no spies watching me in my own room. That is something of an improvement.

Pacing the room, I examine all the fine decor and furniture, running my fingers over the lacquered armoire and the plush silk canopy over the bed. I feel a bit like a marble rolling around the too-big space, but I can't deny the overwhelming beauty of it.

Sta'Criverans value pretty things, Artemisia told me, so I shouldn't be so surprised, but still. The Kalovaxian courtiers rarely met a surface they didn't want to gild or embellish, but this is a different sort of beauty – a more ephemeral one without any strength or purpose behind it. It's pretty for the sake of prettiness, a silk flower with no life and no perfume.

Before I know what I'm doing, I'm tumbling into the mountain of pillows and satin face-first with my dress and shoes still on.

After a week in a narrow bed with a thin mattress, this bed feels like a cloud. I never want to get up. Surely there's a way to save Astrea from right here?

Before I can relax too much, a sharp knock sounds at the door. I bolt back up and smooth out my dress, trying to look somewhat presentable. I can't bring myself to get off the bed completely, but I scoot to the edge and cross my ankles primly, setting my hands in my lap the way I remember Kaiserin Anke used to sit.

'Come in,' I say, trying to ignore the pang brought on by the memory of the Kaiserin.

I expect a single woman to come in to help me dress, but instead the door opens and a small army pours in. There must be more than ten people but they all flitter around so quickly that it's difficult to get a proper count. Two women cross to the wardrobe while another three settle in near the vanity, unloading various pots and powders and brushes from the baskets they carry. The rest flutter back and forth, a couple of them surrounding me and combing their fingers through my tangled hair, circling my waist, chest, and arms with a measuring tape, tilting my face toward the sunlight and eyeing me critically without ever saying so much as a word.

'Queen Theodosia,' one woman finally says, pausing in front of me to dip into a curtsy. Her silver hair is pulled back from her face in a severe bun that does little to soften the wrinkles around her forehead, eyes, and mouth. She has sharp, dark brown eyes that flitter from the top of my head to my boots, her nostrils narrowing more the more she looks at me. 'My name is Marial and I'll be the head of your staff while you're with us.'

'It's a pleasure to meet you, Marial,' I say.

Her pinched mouth and narrowed eyes don't move and she doesn't bother with a reply. 'You're to attend a dinner with the King and his family tonight. A bath first, then we'll try to do something with your hair. I understand you've brought no suitable clothing of your own?'

I don't let my smile waver. 'I had to leave Astrea in something of a hurry to avoid my own execution,' I tell her. 'Unfortunately, I didn't have time to take anything more than the dress I was wearing. This one.'

Her smile is so tight-lipped that it's hardly a smile at all. 'Yes, well, we had the foresight to prepare for such an occurrence.' She gestures to the wardrobe, where the women who just took my measurements are now pulling out various draped gowns and attacking them with threaded needles, their nimble fingers moving quicker than I thought possible. 'We'll have some options ready by the time you're out of the bath. Come.' She snaps her fingers and two women appear, one on either side of me, pulling me to my feet and helping to remove my dress, while another woman twists a knob on the bathtub. After a moment, there's a gurgle and water begins to spew from the curved pipe into the tub.

It's difficult not to stare at it in wonder, especially once steam begins to rise from the water. Where is the water coming from? In Astrea, boiling water was brought up a pail at a time, so that by the time it was full, the water had gone cold. The Kalovaxians used Fire Stones to keep the water warm, but the Kaiser never trusted me enough to get that close to them, not that I would have used them anyway. The thought brings back the memory of the scorch marks on my bedsheets, and I quickly push it away. It's surprisingly easy to pretend that it never happened. Most of the time, it lingers on the outskirts of my mind like a bizarre dream that only appeared to bleed into reality. It's impossible that it truly happened. But I know what I saw and touched with my own hands.

I want to ask what kind of magic the Sta'Criverans have

to summon water out of nowhere, but I remember what Anders said earlier – what they lack in magic they make up for with science and technology. Something tells me that asking Marial questions will only earn me more pinched, impatient looks, so I swallow my curiosity and resolve to ask someone else later.

The women strip me naked, and a distant part of me knows that I should feel uncomfortable being nude in front of strangers, but I suppose my sense of modesty was broken a long time ago.

When I finally slip into the bath, the hot water envelops me and I want to just sink to the bottom and stay there forever, wrapped in warmth. The feeling doesn't last long, though. As soon as my hair is wet, three women begin to attack it, combing through the tangles and nests that have grown during my week on the *Smoke*. By the time they're finished, my scalp feels raw, but my wet hair hangs down in a heavy sheet, finally smooth. But they aren't done with me yet. They move on to my body, scrubbing every inch of my skin with rough, wiry sponges and soap, until the water turns grimy and dark. They help me out of the bath and towel me off before rubbing on oils to soothe the skin they just abraded until I'm as smooth and shiny as a pearl and I smell like jasmine and grapefruit.

Marial flitters over from where she's been inspecting the seamstresses' handiwork, her hands clasped tightly in front of her and her forehead even more creased. She purses her lips and eyes me critically. My sense of modesty might be broken, but I still feel the need to pull the towel tighter around my torso under her gaze.

'Better,' she proclaims. 'But there's still much to do. Come.'

I follow her back to the wardrobe area, hurrying to keep up with her brisk pace.

'Who else will be joining me at this dinner?' I ask, trying to make my voice commanding even though Marial terrifies me.

'I already told you,' she says slowly with a belabored sigh, though she doesn't spare me a glance. All of her attention is focused on examining one of the seamstresses' stitches on a sapphire-blue gown with an intricately beaded bodice. After the seamstress knots and cuts the thread, Marial takes the gown and brings it to me. 'The King and his family.'

'And what about my advisors?'

She gives a derisive sniff, helping me step into the heavy gown, pulling its thin straps over my shoulders. The scars on the top half of my back are on full display, spilling out from the silk of the gown like red and white snakes. No one gapes openly, but I feel their gazes on me all the same and it is somehow even worse.

'Their presence is unnecessary for such an event,' she says, each word crisp. 'But an invitation has now been extended to the Kalovaxian Prinz,' she adds after a moment.

I'd feel better if Blaise, Artemisia, and Heron were there as well, but at least I'll have Søren.

'And my aunt?' I ask, though even as I pose the question I'm not sure which answer I prefer.

'She has made it clear that her presence is required wherever yours is,' Marial says, though she makes no effort to hide her disdain. She laces up the back of my gown tightly, and after that I can scarcely breathe, let alone keep up a conversation.

CHASTE

———◆•◆———

THE ROYAL DINING ROOM IS somehow even more elaborately decorated than my room. Three out of four walls are covered in frescoed murals of cherubs lounging on pillowy pastel clouds, dining on grapes and drinking from gold wine goblets. The fourth wall isn't much of a wall at all – the top half of it is open, with violet drapes pulled aside to show the sun setting in the distance. A chandelier hangs from the ceiling, but instead of crystals, it's hung with bits of blue and green sea glass that cast a cool glow on the room. The long, carved-oak dining table is edged with gold leaf and set with seven matching chairs.

Six of those chairs are already occupied. King Etristo sits at one end, hunched over, his ornate crown slipping down awkwardly on his forehead, but the others stand when I walk in. Etristo is flanked on one side by a man in his thirties who I assume is his son, Avaric, and on the other side by a woman only a few years older than me who is fair and blond as a Kalovaxian but with a rounder, kinder face. She's also heavily pregnant. On Avaric's right is a woman with skin the color of rich honey and black hair in elaborately coiled braids.

Dragonsbane is next to the blond woman; Søren stands between the dark-haired one and an empty seat at the other end of the table, which I assume is for me. I'm gratified to see that both Dragonsbane and Søren have also been dressed in the uncomfortable but ornate styles that the Sta'Criverans seem to favor. They even managed to get Dragonsbane into a gown of black satin without any straps at all.

I walk toward the empty seat, though it's difficult to cross even that small a space in the heeled slippers Marial gave me. Perhaps it would be easier if I weren't so worried about tripping on the hem of my heavy, gem-laden gown, but as it is I have to take small, careful steps, and an eternity stretches out before I make it to my seat, between Søren and Dragonsbane.

'I hope I haven't kept you waiting,' I say when I sit down. It's as difficult to talk as it is to walk in this gown, but I find that I can manage if I take shallow breaths.

The others retake their own seats as soon as I'm settled into mine.

'Not at all, my dear,' King Etristo says in Astrean. 'To wait on such beauty is an honor.'

To the Sta'Criverans I am a pretty thing in a glittering dress, an investment they expect a good return on if Artemisia's theory about my bridal price is to be believed. I am a tool they think they can use, and Art was right when she said that it's easier to let them think that. For now.

So I plaster a smile on my face. It doesn't feel at all real, but I doubt anyone is looking close enough to notice that. It's *pretty* and that will be enough.

'I'm so grateful for your hospitality, King Etristo,' I say. 'It's more kindness than I ever expected to find from strangers.'

'*Yesterday* we were strangers, my dear,' he replies, lifting his gold wine goblet in a toast that I hasten to meet with my own glass, though we're too far apart for our glasses to come close to touching. 'Today we are friends.' He takes a sip before replacing it and I do the same, since not doing so would be construed as an insult. The wine is darker than what we drank in Astrea, more spice than fruit. It burns my throat when I swallow.

King Etristo coughs before speaking. 'All Sta'Criverans speak Astrean, of course, in addition to a few other tongues, though I suggest we keep to Astrean since that seems to be the most common tongue here.'

I glance at Søren, who doesn't understand a word of what's being said. He keeps his eyes forward and his expression blank.

'I'd like to introduce you to my son,' Etristo continues, gesturing first to his right. 'Avaric and his wife, Amiza,' he says, motioning to his son and the woman with the braided hair. Etristo gestures to his left. 'And my wife, Lilia.'

I struggle to hide my surprise. I'd assumed the blond woman was one of his daughters, though they look nothing alike. King Etristo is in his eighties at the very least, and Lilia is practically my age. She must be his second wife, or even his third or fourth. The baby she's carrying can't possibly be his.

'It's a pleasure to meet you,' I say, smiling at the three of them. 'You have other children as well, don't you?' I ask the King.

He waves a dismissive hand. 'My daughters all left home when they were younger than you,' he says. 'They've done wonderfully for themselves, securing alliances and trade contracts with other countries all over the world. We write from time to time, but visiting one another is . . . difficult.'

I nod and make what I hope is a sympathetic noise, though I find I have little pity for a man who sells his daughters to foreign lands to make his own life easier. I've been a stranger in a strange court, and though I know that was a different sort of experience, I still remember how it feels to be surrounded by unfamiliar faces, not being able to communicate, missing my family.

'Well, let's not stand on ceremony here,' King Etristo says before clapping his hands twice. 'I'm ravenous.'

At the sound of his summons, servants pour in through the side door, each carrying a large gold plate. The smells that waft from the dishes are unlike anything I've ever experienced, and I'm not quite sure how to describe them. Spicy, yes, but there's a sweetness as well and something else I can't quite put my finger on. When one of the servants sets a full plate down in front of me, my mouth waters at the sight of the food – an array of beautifully arranged vegetables, seasoned rice the color of the night sky, and seared meat of some kind.

'Small bites,' Søren whispers to me. 'Sta'Criveran cuisine takes some getting used to.'

I smile my thanks but after weeks of hardtack and dried meat, it's difficult to heed his advice. I want to devour it as quickly as possible, but I force myself to eat slowly, savoring each spice and texture. I must not eat slowly enough, though, because Avaric watches me intently, leaning forward with bright, curious eyes.

'Did they starve you in Astrea?' he asks me.

I swallow the bite of fish I'd just taken. 'No, never,' I say.

'At the palace, I ate the same as any Kalovaxian courtier, though most of my advisors spent years in the mines, doing grueling physical labor on meager rations. And they've gotten worse in the last few months, I've heard.'

'Of course,' Avaric says, trying and failing to look sympathetic. 'But . . . well . . . your aunt told us so many stories of your suffering at the hands of the Kaiser.'

I buy myself a moment by dabbing at my mouth with a napkin, fighting the urge to glare at Dragonsbane.

'It was a very difficult decade,' I say slowly, hoping it will be left at that.

But Avaric doesn't take the hint.

'Were you beaten?' he asks. 'That must have been awful. How often did it happen?'

'Yes,' I say, anger seeping into my chest. I'm more aware than ever of my scars, on full display, how harsh and barbaric they are amid all the Sta'Criveran beauty. I wish the dress had sleeves of some sort – some way to hide them, to hide the story they spell out on my skin. My arms begin to grow warm and I fight the urge to scratch at them. It feels the way it did when I woke up from my nightmare to find my sheets burned. It feels like fire is pressing against my skin from the inside, desperate to seep out. *It's not real,* I tell myself, as if I can will myself to believe that. I force myself to breathe through the anger; I imagine ice in my veins.

These people don't care about me. They only care about what happened to me, like it's some kind of sick story written to shock and horrify and entertain them. I grip the arms of my chair so tightly that my knuckles turn white, though at least it distracts from my tingling arms and hands. I keep my face soft, ducking my head and looking up at the Prince through lowered eyelashes.

'I'm sorry,' I say, letting a hint of tears work its way into my voice. 'It's still so difficult to talk about. But it happened often enough that I fear I will always bear the scars of it, both physically and mentally,' I admit with a mournful sigh. 'I survived, thanks in large part to my advisors and my aunt.' I give my aunt a sad smile that she isn't remotely moved by. She sees right through it, but the Sta'Criverans don't.

'That's so awful,' Lilia says, clutching the string of pearls wrapped around her pale throat. Her Astrean isn't as fluent as the others', still a little sharp around the consonants. 'I cannot imagine how horrid that was.' She pauses briefly. 'What was used?' she asks, lowering her voice. 'A whip? A cane?'

My jaw clenches and I hold her gaze for a few seconds before answering. 'Whatever was handy,' I say. 'Though I suppose the whip was the Kaiser's favorite.'

I feel a glimmer of satisfaction when she drops her eyes away from me and goes back to her food without another word.

'And, of course,' Avaric continues, 'your aunt also told us what the monster made you do to . . . what was the man's name who died?'

'Ampelio,' Dragonsbane answers without hesitation, her voice level. 'Guardian Ampelio.'

My grip on my chair tightens more until I fear I'll break the arms off altogether, and I can't seem to relax my hands. I can't talk about Ampelio; I can't give them that piece of my heart, no matter what they are giving me. What happened is between him and me; I haven't even told Blaise much more than the basics. I can't exploit what I did for these people's entertainment.

Something warm rests on top of my left hand and I look down to see Søren's pale, rough fingers covering mine, though his eyes stay firmly stuck on his food. He doesn't understand most of what's being said, but he heard Ampelio's name and I suppose he can guess the rest. He was there, after all, when I drove the sword into Ampelio's back, and maybe he didn't understand then what kind of torture it was, and maybe he still doesn't know that Ampelio was my father, but he still saw firsthand how awful it was for me.

'The Kaiser made it clear that it was his life or mine,' I say slowly, struggling to keep my voice soft. 'Necessary as it might have been, I don't think I will ever forgive myself for it.'

The table is quiet for a moment, though it's a pregnant kind of silence that hints at worse things to come. I busy myself with my dinner, hoping that I'm wrong and that the subject will be dropped.

'The Kaiser is a demon incarnate,' King Etristo says finally. 'For what he's done to you, he will surely spend an eternity suffering in the underworld.' He pauses, but there's a weight in the silence that implies he's not quite finished. He looks at me like he's measuring my every inch with his gaze. 'Are you still a . . .' He hesitates, searching for the word. He must not find it in Astrean, because he switches over to Kalovaxian. 'A virgin?'

I freeze mid-bite, forcing myself to swallow even though I'm fairly certain it will come back up again any moment. Beside me, Søren stiffens; he understands that word and must have cobbled together the context.

'Are you asking if he raped me?' I ask slowly in Astrean, holding King Etristo's gaze. Avaric, Amiza, and Lilia flinch from the word and drop their gazes to their plates, but Etristo is unabashed.

'Yes,' King Etristo says after a moment. 'I suppose I am, though there have also been rumors of your involvement with Prinz Søren that I am curious about as well.'

At the sound of his name, Søren looks even more confused. I hold King Etristo's gaze for another moment before tearing my eyes away and looking at Søren instead.

'King Etristo is wondering if your father raped me or you deflowered me,' I explain to him in Kalovaxian, not bothering to lower my voice.

Søren's face reddens, more in anger than embarrassment, I think.

'No,' he says to King Etristo in biting Astrean. It must be one of the few words he's picked up.

King Etristo throws his hands in the air as if he's being attacked. 'I apologize if you take offense to my question,' he says, which doesn't sound like much of an apology at all. 'But you understand that I must ask it before we continue on our road to finding you a husband. Most men of high birth would never take a sullied woman for a wife.'

I frown, unsure where to begin with that sort of logic. I decide to call out the worst of it. 'I would be considered sullied even if it had been rape?'

King Etristo smiles tightly and shrugs his shoulders. 'It is how it is,' he says. 'Men marry women who are chaste, and take women who *aren't* as mistresses. Surely this is not surprising to you – they have the same customs at the

Kalovaxian court, as I understand it.'

'Yes,' I admit. 'But surely you didn't take anything I've said to be a commendation of their behavior?'

At that, King Etristo's face reddens. 'There's no need to take offense, my dear,' he says. 'If what you say is true, you have nothing to fear. After all, my own wives – both departed and still with us – underwent an examination before we were married to ensure their virtue. My daughters did it before their weddings. Amiza did as well, isn't that right?' he asks.

'It is tradition,' Amiza says, but she doesn't look at me. Instead, she keeps her eyes on her plate.

'The examination is a simple thing, easy to endure,' King Etristo says, waving a dismissive hand.

I force a saccharine smile. 'You've undergone it yourself, Your Highness?' I ask. 'That makes sense. If highborn men should only marry chaste women, then surely highborn women should only marry chaste men.'

'Theodosia,' Dragonsbane hisses at me, her face sharp and drawn tight.

I'm tempted to point out her own hypocrisy in taking his side. After all, she can hardly claim to be a virgin, having had two children. But I hold my tongue and smile innocently at King Etristo.

'I'm sorry, Your Highness,' I tell him, fluttering my eyelashes. 'It's just such a strange custom for such a civilized world. There's a reason you can't find the word *virginity* in Astrean. The concept doesn't exist.'

The table is quiet for a moment. 'Well, this is not Astrea,' King Etristo says. 'The suitors will begin to arrive tomorrow, so it would be our hope that you will have the examination before meeting them.'

I don't know what that *examination* entails, but I don't need to. Even though whatever it is will prove that I haven't been touched in that way, I shouldn't have to prove it. It shouldn't matter. I know that I'm supposed to be sweet and pliable and unassuming in order to keep the Sta'Criverans' favor, but this is a line I will not cross, not even for Astrea.

'Unless the men will be going through similar examinations before they meet me, I will not,' I say. 'Marrying me will bring these men untold riches when we take back Astrea. If they want to forfeit that wealth because they're too preoccupied with tradition, they are welcome to. I'm sure there will be plenty who would rather have the money.'

GAME

———◆·◆———

DRAGONSBANE MANAGES TO HOLD HER tongue for the rest of the quiet, tense dinner and even during the riser ride back to our floor. Her mouth stays tightly pursed the entire time, eyes hard and staring straight ahead. Once we're in the hallway, though, and it's only her, Søren, and me, she grabs hold of my arm and spins me to face her, fingernails digging into the soft skin of the underside of my arm.

'Tomorrow, you will apologize to King Etristo and consent to whatever examinations they feel necessary.'

Søren steps between us.

'If you don't remove your hand,' he tells her in Kalovaxian, his voice low, 'I'll do it for you, and it'll be an unpleasant experience for both of us, but certainly more painful for you.'

Dragonsbane clenches her jaw and stares at him for a moment, as if debating whether or not his honor will actually let him hurt a woman. Wisely, she decides not to take the risk and releases my arm.

'You will apologize for your outburst,' she says again, not taking her eyes off me.

'Of course, Aunt,' I say finally, pitching my voice higher

and softer. 'I'm sure King Etristo will understand how alarmed I was at the thought of having my person prodded at again after all the abuse I suffered at the hands of the Kaiser. And I'm sure he will agree that it would be best to wait at least until I've recovered more. If the husband I choose insists upon an examination, I will comply before my wedding.'

She looks at me with narrowed eyes. 'You're playing a dangerous game,' she says.

It takes effort to hold back a laugh. 'I've played worse.'

Blaise, Heron, and Artemisia are already waiting in my room. I suppose I should have expected that – of course they'll want to know about the dinner. Of course I'll have to tell them, mortified as the thought makes me.

But first I need to get out of this torture device of a dress.

'A little help, please, Art,' I say, grabbing a nightgown from the armoire and stepping behind the painted trifold screen. 'And you might want to bring your dagger.'

Artemisia cuts me out of the gown that the seamstress sewed me into, though she does it with less grace, sending glass beads spilling across the floor, the sound like a hollow rainstorm.

I pull the nightgown over my head, savoring a few deep breaths. Though I was only wearing the gown a few hours, I forgot how nice it feels to take air fully into my lungs instead of little gasps here and there. Maybe that's why Amiza and Lilia were so quiet at dinner – they couldn't breathe, let alone speak.

'All right,' I say, stepping back around the screen. I'm

aware of how ridiculous I must look now, with my loose cotton nightgown and my face fully painted and lacquered, but there are more pressing matters. I join the others in the seating area, taking the open chair next to Blaise. 'We're going to have to speak in Kalovaxian for Søren's sake. Is everyone all right with that?'

The others groan but ultimately agree. I can't blame them – speaking Kalovaxian makes me feel like I'm back in the Kaiser's court.

'We need to keep teaching you Astrean, though. It'll save us a lot of time, to say the least,' I tell Søren.

He nods. 'I feel like an ass, but I'm picking up bits and pieces, I think. Slowly.'

'What happened tonight?' Blaise asks me in Kalovaxian. 'We tried to go with you but we weren't allowed.'

'The Sta'Criverans value their exclusivity,' Søren says. 'I was surprised they invited me, though I suppose they found it amusing since I didn't understand a word they said.'

I tell them about the royal family and their interest in the Kaiser's treatment of me, how they seemed not just fascinated but enthralled with the details of my captivity and punishments.

'It's as if they don't see me as a person, just a rare collectible with a story attached to it,' I grumble.

'Sta'Criverans in the capital tend to lead charmed, soft lives,' Søren says. 'Especially the royal family. I imagine they draw some excitement over your misery because they can't quite fathom it to be real. It's like you're a character in a play.'

I frown, but before I can respond, he continues.

'What was the argument at the end?' he asks, though he looks uneasy. 'I understood bits and pieces but . . . well, it seemed important.'

Part of me doesn't want to answer – especially since I'll have to explain to Blaise, Heron, and Artemisia what virginity even means – but Søren's right. It is important. The argument isn't over yet and I can't keep secrets from them again.

So I explain the conflict as simply as I can, though I feel my cheeks redden as I do. It takes all I have in me not to shudder when I tell them about the King's proposed examination. Though he didn't detail the specifics, they're easy enough to surmise.

'It is common practice,' Søren says when I finish, looking a bit green. 'You were right to refuse, though.'

Artemisia nods, but there's a crease between her eyebrows. 'It will make it all the more meaningful when you finally consent.'

I stare at her, my mouth gaping open. 'I'm not consenting to that,' I say. 'I thought you of all people would understand—' I break off. Artemisia told me about her assault in the mines in confidence, though Heron was there, too. I doubt she wants that to be common knowledge. 'You're a woman as well,' I say instead. 'Would you let them examine you like some sort of experiment?'

'No,' she says, shrugging her shoulders. 'But then, I don't want to get married.'

'Neither do I!' I exclaim, louder than I mean to.

Artemisia remains unfazed by my outburst, merely arching her eyebrows.

'Fine. I don't *need* to get married in order to use another country's army to reclaim my throne. Is that better?' she asks.

I roll my eyes but can't bring myself to answer. 'It's another problem for another day,' I say instead.

'There are getting to be a few of those building up,' Heron says, his voice quiet and unsteady around the Kalovaxian words he's probably heard more often than spoken.

'I know,' I say, rubbing my temples. 'And King Etristo said the suitors will arrive tomorrow, so I'm sure there will only be more problems to come.'

A heavy silence falls over us, pushing in at all sides. Tomorrow, suitors will arrive to bid on me, and my country and I will be put on display like one of the Theyn's war souvenirs. The conversation at dinner tonight will be repeated tenfold with every one of them, I'd imagine, each king and emperor prodding for details of my suffering, each examining me like the hog they're about to slaughter for their feast.

'Soon,' Artemisia says with a sigh, pushing herself up to stand. 'But not tonight.'

She traipses across the room to a small cabinet I hadn't paid much attention to. When she flings open the doors with a flick of her wrists, I see three shelves of wine bottles. She plucks one out at random and brings it back over, using her dagger to pry the cork from its mouth.

'We're out of Astrea,' she says, pouring the wine into the water cups on the table. 'We're safe, in a beautiful palace in Sta'Crivero, and the rebellion is *alive* because of us. That's cause for celebration, don't you think?'

Artemisia's optimism is unexpected but welcome and I smile when she passes me a cup. One by one, she passes them out to everyone else, even Søren, who looks surprised by the gesture.

'To Astrea,' Artemisia says, lifting the bottle. 'What it was once. What it will be again. And all that we sacrifice for it.'

And just like that, the pointed tip of Artemisia's words digs into my skin. *I've sacrificed enough for Astrea*, I want to say, *I can't give any more*. But that isn't true and we both know it. If it comes down to it, there is nothing I won't give up to save my country.

Not my will.

Not my body.

Not my life.

It won't come to that, I tell myself, but deep down I know it very well could. A fair world wouldn't ask anything more of me, but this is not a fair world.

We clink our cups together with Art's bottle and we drink.

'Are we not going to talk about how absurd this place is?' Heron asks, surprising me. He's been quiet more often than not since we brought Søren out of the brig, but he seems to be trying. 'Everything is drenched in gold and jewels and color. That dress you were wearing must have cost enough to feed a family for a year in Astrea, Theo.'

I can't help but laugh, sinking deeper into my chair and taking another sip of the wine. Like the dinner wine, it's dark and spicy and not what I'm used to, but it's slowly growing on me. 'You're lucky you didn't have to wear it. It was suffocating and it weighed more than a bushel of bricks. And that contraption!' I add. 'The . . . what was it? The lifter?'

'The riser,' Søren says with a snort of laughter. 'The men who operate them – that's their entire job. And most men don't have the strength to do it, so the ones who do are paid handsomely for it.'

'Do they ever wear shirts?' Heron asks him. 'I'm not complaining, but it is a very . . . strange uniform.'

'Shirts get in the way, apparently,' Søren says.

'A likely excuse,' Artemisia says with a snort. 'I've heard of a few affairs between the operators and the noblewomen here. It's fairly commonplace. One of the perks of the job, as it were.'

'At least until the husbands find out,' Søren adds, laughing. 'It happened when I was visiting a couple of years back. This lord was furious and called for the riser operator's execution, but the King had to deny his request because it turns out a riser operator is more valuable than a nobleman.'

'Just wait a few years until the towers are overrun with barrel-chested children who refuse to wear shirts,' I say with a smirk.

The others burst out laughing at the image and it goes on for far too long. As soon as we get a hold of ourselves, a couple of us will make eye contact and then the laughter begins anew.

It feels good to laugh this freely, the five of us together. To let everything outside the room be forgotten for just a few moments – and even some things inside the room. Heron and Søren aren't speaking directly to one another, but I'm no longer worried that Heron is going to try to hit him again, and I suppose that's the best I can hope for, all things considered.

When we finish the first bottle, I consider calling it a night and sending the others back to their rooms, but I can't bring myself to do it. I don't want to be alone. I don't want to stop laughing. As soon as I do, the reality of what tomorrow will bring will set in, and I don't want to think about that just yet.

I drag myself up from my chair to grab another bottle, a lighter wine this time, passing it to Artemisia to uncork.

We toast to riser operators.

We toast to the gods.

We toast to those we've lost.

We toast to ourselves.

We toast to the past.

We toast to the future.

By the time the early dawn light is streaming through the windows, I'm only barely conscious. I'm sprawled out on my bed with Artemisia on one side and Heron on the other, both of them snoring quite loudly. Blaise is stretched across the foot of the bed, doing battle with Heron's long legs to make room. He isn't sleeping, just staring at the ceiling with glassy, faraway eyes, but it's the closest I've seen him come to it since I drugged his tea. Søren sleeps on the sofa instead, one of the decorative throw pillows over his face to block out light and sound.

The last thing I think before letting my mind fade into darkness is to wonder if we will ever get to a point where he truly is one of us.

SUITORS

———————◆•◆———————

EVERYTHING FEELS NUMB BUT MY head, which is pounding, intensified tenfold by the bright sunlight beating down on the palace steps. My mouth is dry as sand, and even though I've been brushed and buffed and painted by Marial and her team again, I feel like last night is written plainly on my face. My mind is a fog, but in a way, I suppose that's a good thing – I'm too exhausted to remember to be anxious.

The suitors are arriving in a long procession of canopied carriages that weaves through the white stone streets.

'Not to worry, my dear,' King Etristo says from his seat next to mine, misreading my expression. 'There are a lot of them, but this will only be a brief introduction. The whole event should take an hour – two at most.'

An hour or two. I stifle a groan. I can't imagine sitting out here more than a few minutes, even if the chairs brought out for the royal family and me are comfortably padded and somewhat shaded with palm fronds. Between the hot sun and my aching head and the dress pinching my ribs, I feel like I'm going to pass out.

But I smile at King Etristo in a way I hope looks natural.

His manner toward me has cooled since my outburst last night, though outwardly he's been nothing but polite. When I apologized for my words, he accepted it with a strained smile.

'Wonderful,' I tell him. 'I'm so excited to meet everyone. Thank you so very much for putting all of this together for me.'

It sounds like too much to my ears, but King Etristo only returns my smile and pats my hand with his, the skin of his palm wrinkled and clammy. 'It's a pleasure to help, my dear, after everything that has befallen you.'

I lean back against my chair and glance at Søren, who is standing behind me and slightly to the side. The others are pressed farther back in the crowd of Sta'Criverans gathered behind us – even Dragonsbane, much to her displeasure. But Søren is on full display, though whether he is being shown off as an ally or just as a trophy is unclear. Since King Etristo is still speaking Astrean and not bothering to translate, it's difficult to imagine he sees him as anything more than decoration.

I translate what the King said and Søren nods, but his face is paler than usual and there are dark shadows under his eyes. I had those this morning as well, before they were painted and powdered into oblivion.

'Last night, it felt like I was fluent in Astrean,' he says. 'But I can't remember a word of it today.'

I laugh, though it makes my head ache even worse. 'Whatever it was you started speaking last night, it was *not* Astrean,' I tell him. 'You kept talking about *amineti,* but apart from that I didn't hear a single Astrean word.'

His cheeks redden. 'I suppose that's one of the only ones I remember,' he admits.

My own face grows warm as I remember the night I taught him the word, demonstrating with more *amineti* – kisses – than I could keep count of.

'Well, you're sober now,' I point out. 'Can you tell me about the suitors when they arrive?' I lower my voice, casting a glance toward King Etristo, who is deep in conversation with his son. 'I have a feeling my official introductions will be much rosier than the truth on their side and mine.'

He nods, though a crease appears between his brows.

I turn back to King Etristo, drawing his attention away from his son and to me.

'After the introductions are made, I would like to visit the refugee camp,' I tell him.

King Etristo looks at me like I've just suggested we jump into lava. 'Why on earth would you want to do that?'

It's a struggle to hold on to my smile. 'You've been so kind to take in my people over the years, and those from other fallen countries. I would enjoy seeing people from Astrea, and I think it would help them to see me, to know that I'm trying to get us home.'

Again, King Etristo pats my hand and smiles at me like I'm a charmingly misbehaved puppy.

'You are kindness incarnate, my dear, but the camp is no place for a girl like you.'

I open my mouth to argue and quickly close it again. After last night, I need to watch my step more carefully, even if the temptation to slap his hand off mine is almost too much to bear.

What does that mean, a girl like me? And can he truly consider me a girl while at the same time planning my marriage to men who, if Søren's intel is to be believed, are mostly much, much older than I am? The Kalovaxians believed children became adults at fifteen, though at least they were consistent. In Sta'Crivero I am both infantilized and sexualized, and I'm not sure what to do with that.

The line of carriages snakes forward until the first one pulls to a stop in front of the palace. I straighten up in my chair, catching myself in a very un-regal slouch. Finally, we seem to be starting.

Two men dart from their place at King Etristo's side and go to meet the arrival. One rolls out a thin red carpet that leads right from the steps of our dais to the steps protruding from the carriage. The other opens the carriage door with a sweeping bow that has a few more flourishes than seems practical.

Several tense seconds pass before a man emerges from the carriage door, forgoing the steps and simply hopping down onto the carpet. He's tall – taller than Søren even – and broad-shouldered, with umber skin and close-cropped black hair that is already receding in the front, though he can't be more than twenty-five. He has a severe face with sharp bones and a mouth that looks like it's permanently down-turned. His eyes are dark brown and intent below thick eyebrows.

He makes his way down the red carpet and up the stairs of the dais, one hand idly reaching to his hip, where I'd imagine a sword would usually rest in its scabbard. He must have been told to leave that behind today – it is against Sta'Criveran law to approach the King with a weapon.

Beside me, Søren makes a noise of recognition as the man approaches. 'Archduke Etmond of Haptania,' he whispers to me, his voice tinged with awe. 'Brother of the King there, but everyone knows the King is sterile. Etmond is next in line. One of the best military minds I've ever met – he's turned the tables in battles where he was outnumbered ten to one.'

Søren sounds half in love with Etmond already, but there's something about the man that I can't quite place. He seems to have trouble looking anyone in the eye, even when he approaches me with a stiff bow.

'Archduke Etmond, may I present Astrea's famed beauty, Queen Theodosia,' King Etristo says.

The Archduke's eyes dart toward Søren and narrow before turning back to me. 'Queen Theodosia,' he says, reaching out for my hand, which I offer. He bows to me again, kissing my knuckles. His thick mustache scratches my skin. 'Your beauty is indeed legendary. It's an honor to make your acquaintance.'

He speaks like he's memorized what he's meant to say, rambling it off in a flat tone, his eyes not quite meeting mine.

'It's an honor to meet you as well, Archduke Etmond,' I say. 'I'm so pleased you came all this way.'

His bushy brows knit together. 'Haptania is only a day's journey, Your Majesty,' he says. 'I didn't have to come very far at all.' He seems to hear the implication in his words as he says them, because he straightens up and clears his throat. 'What I mean to say is that any journey to have the chance to meet you would be considered short, and I would have gladly traveled much longer if I'd had to.'

The Archduke is ushered into the palace, his entourage of

Haptanian courtiers trailing behind him like baby ducks.

'I don't think he cared much for me,' I whisper to Søren.

He laughs. 'I wouldn't take it personally. His mind doesn't work the way yours or mine does. He understands charts and figures and diagrams – he's an ace at chess – but he has more difficulty with people.'

I smirk. 'It seems like perhaps *you* should marry him,' I tell Søren. 'You seem enamored enough already.'

Søren shrugs. 'He's brilliant, though from a personal standpoint I don't think he'd be a good husband for just about anyone, you and me included.'

I sigh. 'Well, we aren't looking at this from a personal standpoint, are we?'

'Just wait,' Søren tells me, nodding toward the next carriage pulling up. 'I'm sure worse is yet to come.'

It's difficult for my eyes not to glaze over as the introductions drag on, especially since many of them seem identical and I can't imagine agreeing to marry any of these men.

King Wendell of Grania, for example, is fifty and has already accumulated three wives and what Søren tells me is the largest harem in the world. He is short in stature, with thinning hair that has already gone gray and skin like old milk. When he bows and kisses my hand with soggy lips, his lecherous gaze makes me want to take a bath immediately, though I make do with subtly wiping the back of my hand on my dress. Grania has a large army, Søren tells me with some regret.

There are so many kings! Ten pour out of the next carriage, all of them bickering among one another, taking only a small break to introduce themselves to me. Their names are all a blur, though, and I can't remember a single one. All of them are rough-faced and in need of a good shave. When they disappear into the castle, the Sta'Criveran courtiers give them a wide berth.

'Esstena is a nation of clans,' Søren explains when they're gone. 'Each of those men is a minor king trying to take control of the entire country. They've all been at war for centuries. No doubt they think if one of them marries you, they'll be able to call themselves high king.'

'Difficult to imagine they'll be anxious to take Astrea back with so much on their plates,' I murmur. Another lost cause. The Archduke is starting to seem very appealing.

Prince Talin of Etralia is next, accompanied by his father, Czar Reymer – or, as Søren says he's known, Reymer the Handsome. He must have been once – even now, in his forties, he's quite dashing. His son is remarkably less so. He's the one Søren said was rumored to be illegitimate. I can under-stand why, looking at them side by side: where the Czar is dark-haired and broad-shouldered, with a strong square jaw and high cheekbones, Prince Talin is scrawny and small, with wheat-colored hair and a round, unstructured face. He also hangs back, staring at the ground while his father makes introductions and kisses my hand.

'He's a child,' I tell Søren when they're gone. 'What is he, ten?'

'Eleven, I think,' Søren says, but he's fighting laughter. 'Don't worry, I doubt there would be pressure to consummate the marriage for a few years.'

I fight the urge to gag. 'No,' I say firmly.

Next is another prince, this one from Brakka. Prince

Tyrannius looks far too old to still be a prince – fifty or so, with weather-beaten tan skin and hair that's gone silver. According to Søren, that's exactly the problem.

'His father won't give up his throne. He's in his nineties and rarely leaves his bed anymore, but he's holding on to his crown tightly. Rumor has it Tyrannius is planning a coup. I'd imagine you're a part of that plan.'

I give a dramatic huff and watch Tyrannius exchange pleasantries with King Etristo. 'It's awfully rude of everyone to try to use me to their own ends when I'm trying to do precisely that to them.'

When the next carriage pulls up and its door opens, I have to bite back a gasp. After the parade of men, the woman who steps out is a welcome shock to me before I remember that she's also competing for my hand. Other women have never appealed to me in that way, though I realize she's beautiful – strong and golden-skinned with long chestnut hair looped into elaborate braids. Even Søren looks a bit enchanted by her.

'Empress Giosetta of Doraz,' he whispers to me as she approaches, sounding as surprised as I feel. 'I didn't think she would be coming.'

I have so many questions, but before I can ask them, she approaches me and kisses my hand, offering the usual introductions and flattery – did King Etristo send lines to be recited with his invitations? – before moving on to say hello to our host.

'Is an empress like a queen?' I whisper to Søren.

'Doraz is not a matriarchy, though it isn't a patriarchy either. Giosetta's parents weren't rulers – the last emperor chose her when she was a small child and adopted her. He raised her to be empress, just as she'll choose and raise her own successor.'

I purse my lips. 'That's actually quite sensible, isn't it?' I say. 'Choosing a ruler instead of leaving it up to bloodlines. What will she want from me?'

Søren shrugs. 'Marriage in Doraz isn't limited to being between men and women. . . .'

'It wasn't in Astrea either,' I tell him.

'In this specific case, I'm not sure what the protocol would be. It would likely be open to discussion; you may be able to get her to agree to the two of you being partner rulers.'

'That's certainly preferable to the others,' I tell him.

He shrugs. 'I'm sure she'd still want a cut of Astrea. Famed as they all say your beauty is, they wouldn't have come all this way for that alone.'

Next up is Bindor and one of the high priests Søren mentioned. He's younger than I expected, with limbs he hasn't quite grown into and a shaved bronze head that gleams in the afternoon sunlight. He looks at me with his nervousness clearly written on his face.

'His Holiness the High Priest Batistius has been raised in a monastery,' Søren whispers to me. 'And in the Bindor capital, women are strictly forbidden. It's quite likely he doesn't remember seeing one before.'

I have to stifle a giggle as he approaches me uncertainly. Unlike the others, he doesn't kiss my hand, only bowing.

'May God smile upon you, Queen Theodosia,' he tells me, his voice shaking.

'And you as well,' I say, which seems to be the right answer. He gives a quick nod before turning to King Etristo.

'Still a no,' I whisper to Søren. 'And let's try to get him home as soon as we can – something tells me Sta'Crivero might well be enough to kill him.'

I almost sag with relief when I realize we've reached the last carriage.

A man steps out in a tailored jacket-and-trouser set that matches the violet of his carriage perfectly. He must be around thirty, with milk-pale skin and dark hair that has been styled with so much pomade that it looks like it would be hard to the touch. He holds himself with a kind of practiced air that seems strange, though it takes me a moment to pinpoint exactly why – he holds himself like a man who had to learn to seem powerful, not one to whom power was a natural birthright. During our lessons on the ship, Søren and Artemisia mentioned that there were some countries whose leaders were chosen by the citizens themselves, and I would wager this is one of them.

'Chancellor Marzen of Oriana,' Søren whispers to me, confirming my guess. Chancellors are voted into power and so they can rise from anywhere. 'And that will be his sister, *Salla* Coltania.'

Coltania follows her brother closely in a matching violet gown that hugs her figure. She's younger than him, but older than me – twenty, perhaps. Her gaze is sharp and serious, her full, painted lips in a permanently straight line.

I open my mouth to ask Søren what *Salla* means, but before I can, the Chancellor turns his gaze on me. He has the sort of contagious smile that elicits one in return. Even before he opens his mouth, there is something intrinsically compelling about him. I suppose it's a handy trait to have if you're going to convince people to vote you into power.

'Our neighbors to the west, my dear,' King Etristo explains. 'In fact, they used to be under our domain before they demanded to run things themselves several centuries back.' He turns to the Chancellor. 'From what I've been hearing, Marzen, many of your countrymen might be missing our unified country after the stress of the election.'

Though his tone is jovial enough, there's no disguising the bite to King Etristo's words. The Chancellor's smile freezes but never falters.

'I can't imagine that would be the case unless I quadrupled their taxes and put a toll on all imports and exports, as your grandfather did,' he says.

Both men fall silent and I half expect King Etristo to leap out of his chair – frail bones and all – and attack the Chancellor, but after a moment he laughs instead, a loud, wheezing sound. The Chancellor joins in and I force a laugh as well, even though I'm not quite sure what's funny.

'This one has such a sense of humor,' King Etristo says to me. 'And charm, that's why *almost* half the people in his country voted to elect him.'

The dagger is unmistakable, but again, the Chancellor continues to smile as though everyone in the country were watching him.

'Make sure to make my home your home, Marzen,' King Etristo says, reaching out to shake the Chancellor's hand. 'I'll have someone explain how the bath works. I know it's a foreign concept in Oriana.'

'Ah, but *I'm* simply excited to try some of this Sta'Criveran wine I've heard about,' Marzen says, matching the King's tone. 'Is it true it can be used to clean carpets as well? How magnificent to have so many uses for a single product!'

Again, both men laugh and shake hands, though their grips are white-knuckled.

When Marzen disappears into the palace, I lean toward Søren.

'Did I fall asleep at some point and miss the part where they compared the size of their—'

'You see, my dear,' the King interrupts, drawing me back to him, 'I've found you some fine prospects. What are your thoughts so far?'

I consider my words carefully before answering. 'They were all wonderful, to be sure,' I say with a smile. 'And I'm so pleased that they all left their homes to come and meet me.'

'You'll get to know some of them better at dinner tonight,' he says.

Without waiting for my response, he waves his hand and a group of attendants rushes over to lift him out of his chair and into a transport similar to the one he used when we first met in the desert. They carry him inside and the gathered Sta'Criverans follow.

'Thoughts?' Søren asks me as we stand as well.

I think my expression manages to say it all better than words ever could, because Søren stifles a laugh. He eyes me for a long moment. 'As badly as I'd like to go back to my room and sleep off this infernal headache, you look like you have other plans.'

'I was hoping to visit the refugee camp,' I admit. 'But

King Etristo refused. He said it was no place for a girl like me.'

'Something tells me that isn't enough to dissuade you,' Søren says.

I smile. 'Tell the others. We'll leave in an hour's time.'

SNEAK

———◆·◆———

MARIAL DOESN'T LOOK AT ALL surprised when I say I'm not feeling well and would like to rest, which makes me think that I must look as awful as I feel after last night. Which means the suitors were awful liars for telling me how lovely I was all morning.

After Marial and the rest of my attendants help me out of my suffocating dress and unpin my hair from its elaborate style, they leave me tucked into bed in another gauzy nightgown. When the door closes behind them, I wait a moment to make sure no one comes back before throwing the satin quilt off and climbing out of bed again. Comfortable as my bed is, I'm worried that if I stay in it for another moment I actually will fall back asleep, and I can't do that.

My wardrobe is so full I can't move the hangers more than a hair's breadth, and almost all the dresses are embellished and heavy with layer upon layer of material, with so many hooks and buttons and ribbons that I could never put one on myself. After searching for a few minutes, I finally manage to find one that might perhaps be described as plain, if only by Sta'Criveran standards. Bottle-green silk with cap sleeves and a bodice that is somewhat looser than the other dresses I've worn. The skirt bells out in a cascade of chiffon, trimmed with small jewels along the waist and hem. Even with the embellishments, it's far lighter and simpler than anything else in the wardrobe. It will have to do.

It's a struggle to fasten the hook-and-eye closures that run up the back of the dress without assistance, and for an instant, I nearly call for help from one of my Shadows before remembering that this is a different palace entirely and one without holes in the walls.

I've just managed to hook the last closure when there's a soft knock at the door, and without waiting for a response, Artemisia slips in. She's wearing her tunic and leggings from the *Smoke* again, and her cerulean hair is gathered into a messy pile on top of her head. Her dark eyebrows arch almost into her hairline as she looks me over from the top of my head to my toes.

'We're going to the refugee camp,' she says slowly. 'Not a ball.'

My cheeks warm. 'If you can find something less flashy in there, I'll gladly change,' I say, gesturing to the wardrobe.

'Hmmm,' she says with what might be a scoff or a laugh – it's difficult to tell. 'It's almost as if the King doesn't *want* you sneaking out of the palace to go visit the camp. You didn't bring your clothes from the *Smoke*?'

'It didn't occur to me to,' I admit. 'And even the purple gown I wore to shore would have been better, but I think they sent it to the launderer when I got here. Or the furnace, maybe,' I add, thinking about the disdain with which Marial's attendants handled the patched and fraying dress that had been through far more than it was made to withstand.

'I'll see about getting you something for the future, but this time—'

She breaks off when the door opens again and Blaise, Søren, and Heron slip in, all dressed in plain clothes from the *Smoke* and long cloaks.

'Ah, perfect,' Artemisia says before they can so much as say hello. She traipses over to Heron and tugs his cloak off. His bewilderment is clear but he lets her take it.

'It'll swamp me,' I say when she hands it to me. It came down to Heron's knees and he's at least a foot and a half taller than I am, with shoulders that are twice as broad.

'Which means that dress will be well and truly covered,' she replies.

I shrug it on, laughing when the hem pools on the ground around me.

'You'll have to walk carefully,' she says with a smirk. 'Though I doubt it will be harder than trying to balance in those heeled slippers they've been forcing you into.'

She has a point there. I gather the material of the cloak in front of me and take a few tentative steps. It isn't too bad, I suppose. Certainly manageable.

'All right, what's the plan then?' I ask them.

As it turns out, the plan – if it can even be called that – involves walking out of the palace and taking horses from the stable near the front gates. It's far less subterfuge than I'm used to, and as we walk through the brightly painted city bursting with afternoon life, I can't help but feel naked, even as I sweat under Heron's overlarge cloak.

'This isn't Astrea. You aren't a prisoner,' Blaise tells me, seeing my discomfort.

'King Etristo doesn't want me going to the camp,' I remind him.

'And he won't know,' Blaise replies, jangling a velvet bag of coins, the same one he used to bribe the riser attendant to take us to ground level. 'Money solves most problems, I've found.'

'And I suppose you aren't going to tell me where you happened upon so much of it so quickly after we arrived here?'

Blaise shrugs and flashes me a grin that reminds me of how he used to smile in the years before the siege. He's lighter here, happier than I've seen him in a long time. Not that I can blame him for that – it's easier to feel happier when there isn't an ax hanging above your neck at all times. Sta'Crivero might not be ideal, I'm the first to admit that, but it's infinitely preferable to the Kaiser's court.

Blaise seems to be thinking along the same lines. He looks at the city around us with a peculiar expression on his face, half awe and half fear.

'It is something, isn't it?' he says, his voice low. 'All the color and the art and the happy people . . . I see the appeal.'

I nod, looking around as well. 'You were right, though. It's not home,' I say.

Blaise is quiet for a moment. '*You're* my home,' he says finally, his voice barely louder than a whisper. 'The place we happen to be is inconsequential.'

A smile tugs at my lips and I'm tempted to reach for his hand, but with the others here I stop myself. It's not just about Søren – in the three days he's been out of the brig he hasn't said anything that can be construed as romantic – it's about the others as well. We're a team. We have to be if we're going to save Astrea. If Blaise and I form our own team, that would tarnish us somehow.

Still, I let the back of my hand brush the back of his hand as we walk, and the warmth of his skin sends a tremor through me.

Blaise was right – as soon as a few coins change hands, the stable boys bring out four horses for us. Each one tall and intimidating and graceful, ranging in color from a pale reddish brown to black as the night sky. I'm struck again by how even Sta'Criveran *horses* are embellished with jewels and ribbons braided into their manes and tails, like they're getting ready to go to some kind of party.

In another life, I would have learned to ride a horse – I might have even been good at it like my mother was – but in this life I wouldn't know where to begin. I have vague memories of Ampelio leading me around the palace grounds on his horse, but that wasn't the same thing.

Blaise, Artemisia, and Søren mount their horses while Heron lifts me into the saddle of the one we're going to share. I was relieved when he offered to ride with me, because at least with him I won't have to fret about where to put my hands or how close we're sitting or the warmth of his skin. And I feel a lot safer with him than I would with Artemisia, who I'm sure will take every opportunity to gallop and jump and show off.

Heron swings up in front of me and I knot my hands

around his waist, struggling not to look down at the ground. Though the horses seemed large enough when I was standing next to them, sitting on the back of one is a whole other matter. It feels like I'm so much farther up, and the chances of falling off . . . well, I won't think of that. Instead, I keep my eyes firmly fixed on Heron's back and pretend that I'm on solid ground.

But as soon as we take off, it's impossible to pretend. Each step the horse takes jostles me to my bones, and I tighten my grip on Heron, sure that I'm going to fly off at any moment. The hot, dry wind whips through my hair as we cross into the desert that surrounds the capital, grains of sand stinging my skin. I manage to get my cloak over my face to cover it without falling off. I can't imagine how the others are doing, since they can't cover their faces without blocking their much-needed sight.

Somehow, time passes and I don't fall off. I don't think I could ever grow used to the jostling pace and the wind, but it eventually does become almost calming in its predictability. The journey yawns out in front of us, but before I know it, Heron is pulling the horse to a halt.

He hops down onto the ground before holding out his arms to help me. 'The *Prinkiti* says it'll be easier to get into the camp if we go on foot.'

I take hold of his arms and let him help me down, squinting into the distance where I can just make out another wall – this one much different from the one around the capital. That wall was tall and gilded and regal, a promise of what awaited inside, but while the wall around the camp is nearly as tall, it's a grisly-looking thing of craggy, uneven stones that don't appear to have ever been cleaned. There is no grand, ornate gateway, instead a small wooden door in one corner that's easy to overlook.

The capital wall was made to keep people out, I realize. This wall was made to keep people in.

CAMP

❖━━━◆・◆━━━❖

THE TWO GUARDS STATIONED ON either side of the single door wave us through without question, which strikes me as odd until I realize that those swords sheathed at their hips aren't meant for those trying to enter the camp.

'Visitors happen often enough,' Heron tells me, answering my unasked question. 'I was walking around the palace invisibly last night and I heard some people talking about it. The refugees are cheap labor, so people will hire them when they have some kind of task they need done. Jobs no one else wants to do – construction work, sewing cheap clothing, stable mucking. And they pay them next to nothing to do it, because they can.'

Dread coils around my heart and squeezes.

As we come out through the other side of the door, though, I nearly lose my stomach altogether. After the ornate shine of the capital, with its bright colors and elegant spires, the decrepit state of the refugee camp seems all the more ghastly. The streets are cramped and dirty, with clusters of shacks on either side, none of which could be larger than a single room. Thatched roofs look ready to collapse and the wooden doors are moldy and hanging off their hinges. The smell of dirt and rot hangs heavy in the air. I'm tempted to wrap the edge of Heron's cloak around my mouth and nose again, but I resist, worried about how that might come across to the people who live here.

And the people! Men and women and a handful of children crowd the streets and peer out from cracked open doors, all dressed in dirty scraps of clothes that don't cover much more than absolutely necessary. A couple of children who can't be more than five are completely naked and caked in grime. Their hair is matted and cut short or shaved completely, even the women's. *Cheap labor,* Heron said, and it shows. They are all callused fingers and rough, sunburnt skin stretched too tight over muscle and bone.

The way they look at us hollows me out until I can't feel anything, not even the ground beneath my feet. Their eyes are hungry and wary and fearful, like they aren't sure if I'm here to feed them or spit at them.

'We should have brought food,' I say, more to myself than to anyone else.

The others don't respond and I realize that they're as shocked as I am. I didn't expect to find the opulence of the palace here, but I didn't expect it to be like this. As soon as I think it, though, I realize how naive that was of me. There is a reason they are kept in a camp still, ten or more years after they arrived. There is a reason they haven't been brought into the capital or the villages around it. They are seen as less than.

I let go of Heron's arm and take a tentative step forward, casting my eyes around in search of someone Astrean, though it's surprisingly difficult to tell what anyone looks like under all the grime. I clear my throat and hope my voice doesn't waver.

'We're looking to talk with someone in charge,' I say in Astrean, trying to channel my mother. She had a way of speaking that felt like it could travel a mile even though she didn't so much as raise her voice.

There's whispering at that, low murmurs that I can't understand, though bits and pieces of it sound Astrean. Finally, a man steps forward. He must be in his late forties with a shaved head and gaunt face. Under the dirt, his skin looks similar to mine, but a few shades darker.

'You speak Astrean well,' he says, in the same tongue, but rougher around the edges, similar to the way Heron speaks it. 'What do you want with us?' Though he's speaking to me, his hard gaze keeps flickering behind me. The rest of them aren't so subtle about it; they stare just over my shoulder with an intensity that could be described as hate. With a sinking stomach, I turn to see what they're looking at.

Immediately I realize my mistake in bringing Søren. How can they believe that I'm here as a friend when I bring their enemy with me? But it's too late now.

I turn back to the man and draw myself up to my full height. 'My name is Theodosia Eirene Houzzara,' I tell him. 'Queen of Astrea. I want . . .' I trail off, suddenly at a loss. What *do* I want? I thought I wanted to see the camp, to talk to other Astreans who weren't enslaved by the Kaiser. I wanted to talk to those who had been lucky enough to escape, but *lucky* doesn't seem like the right word now.

'I want to help,' I say finally, though my voice shakes around the last word.

The man stares at me for an uncomfortably long moment before he throws his head back and laughs, showing a mouth with more gaps than teeth. The sound is hoarse and after a few seconds it turns into a hacking cough.

'*Queen of Astrea,*' he repeats, shaking his head. 'You're hardly more than a child.'

I try to think of a retort but can't. He's right, after all. In Astrea, sixteen was still considered a child, though I hardly feel like one anymore myself. In another life, I would be, but I stopped feeling like a child the moment the Theyn slit my mother's throat.

Instead of saying so, I shrug. 'Maybe,' I allow. 'But my mother's dead and so it falls to me. Who are you?'

He doesn't answer right away; instead he gives me a long look that I've come to recognize. He's sizing me up. 'I remember you, Theodosia Eirene Houzzara,' he says. 'You were a babe on your mother's hip when she came to visit my village some fourteen years ago now, thumb in your mouth and stubborn, defiant eyes that dared anyone to tell you to remove it.'

'I don't suck my thumb anymore,' I tell him. 'But I think you'll still find me stubborn and defiant.'

At that, he laughs again, but this time I know he isn't laughing at me. 'I suppose you must be, to have come so far,' he allows. 'Last I heard, you were being kept as the Kaiser's toy. I'd ask how you managed to escape but I fear that would be a very long story.'

'Maybe in time I'll tell it to you in full,' I say. 'But for now, suffice to say that I ran away after killing the Theyn, and I managed to take the crown Prinz hostage with me.' I gesture behind me, toward Søren.

It doesn't feel right to take so much credit. Elpis killed the Theyn; I only told her to do it. And Søren didn't realize he was my hostage until we were already gone; it isn't as though I managed to capture him myself. And I couldn't have done any of it without Blaise and Artemisia and Heron. But that isn't what this man wants to hear, or what he *needs* to hear. He needs to see me as someone formidable and intimidating, so that is who I'll be.

He nods toward Søren. 'You call him a hostage?' the man asks.

I lift a shoulder in a shrug. 'The Kaiser is an evil man – I doubt anyone here would argue that point, his son included. It turned out the Prinz was more valuable on our side than in chains.'

The man makes a noise in the back of his throat that I'm not sure how to interpret, though his eyes are still wary.

'It hardly seems fair that you know me but I don't know you,' I tell him.

He eyes me for another few seconds before spitting at the ground between us, not close enough to me to be taken as an insult, but the lack of respect is clear. I'm not his queen, I'm just a girl with a long name.

'Sandrin,' he says finally. 'Of Astrea. Nevarin in particular.'

Heron clears his throat. 'I grew up not five miles away from Nevarin,' he says. 'In Vestra.'

A gap-toothed smile stretches over Sandrin's face. 'I knew a girl in Vestra,' he says. 'I think I might have married her if the Kalovaxians hadn't come.'

'I think I might have done a lot of things if the Kalovaxians hadn't come,' Heron replies.

Sandrin nods, along with most of the people in the crowd around him. 'Who are you?' he asks.

'Heron,' he answers, before gesturing to Blaise and Artemisia and giving their names as well. 'We were in the mines for years,' he says, eliciting gasps and murmurs from the crowd. 'Until a man named Ampelio rescued us. He taught us how to use our gifts, and he told us that if anything should happen to him, we were to find the Queen, save her, and follow her.'

'We've done as Ampelio asked,' Artemisia says, her voice unusually thin. I don't think I've ever heard her say his name. 'And she's brought us here.'

'You're Guardians,' Sandrin says, eyes alight with sudden understanding.

I half expect Blaise to deny it, but instead he inclines his head. 'We are Guardians,' he agrees. 'And she's our Queen.'

Sandrin looks between us for another moment, appraising. After what feels like an eon, he nods. 'Come on, then,' he says, voice weary. 'I'll introduce you to the others.'

ELDERS

———— ◆ · ◆ ————

S ANDRIN LEADS US THROUGH THE crooked, dirt-caked
streets, and I spy skittish, spectral figures peering out
from doorways as we pass, until we reach a house at the end
of one of the lanes. It looks very much like all the others:
the thatched roof is collapsing in places, and the walls are a
hodgepodge of scrap stones that I'd imagine are left over from
other building projects. The wooden door is too small for the
frame, leaving gaps of space. Hardly a door at all, really, since
I can't imagine it keeps much out.

The door swings open and a woman appears in a ragged
dress that has been torn and patched over so many times it's
difficult to imagine what it looked like originally. Her skin is a
deep, russet brown and her hair has been plaited close to her
scalp so that I can see rows of skin between the dozen or so
braids. It's difficult to tell her age, though if I had to hazard
a guess I would say she's in her fifties. Her face is made up
of sharp angles, and she has the narrow, suspicious eyes of a
person who has seen far too much bad to expect anything else
out of life.

'Tallah,' Sandrin says before approaching her alone

and launching into a long spiel of words that I can barely understand, though I do manage to pick up some pieces that sound Astrean. *Visitor. Help. Queen. Child.* Others sound half-familiar – there's a word that sounds like it might be *traitor,* but it's been twisted and embellished too much for me to be sure. Most of what he says, though, I can't make any sense of whatsoever.

'That's five languages,' Søren says next to me. 'I heard Astrean and Gorakian and Kotan. I think that was Tiavan and Lyrian as well.'

'Six,' Artemisia says, a bit smug. 'You missed the Yoxian. I think I heard Manadolian as well, but it's so close to Kotan that it's difficult to tell them apart when everything's being mixed together like that.'

'Those are all countries that have been conquered by Kalovaxia,' I say. 'All countries who would have refugees here.'

I can't help but think of how much Cress would love hearing about this. She's always had an ear for languages and could teach herself a new one in a matter of months. Dissecting and analyzing a language made up of an array of different ones would be a party for her.

I push the thought of Cress aside and focus on Sandrin and the woman – Tallah? Was that her name or something in another language I didn't understand? – who are now deep in a hushed conversation punctuated every few seconds with a glance in our direction.

'I only understand the Astrean,' I admit. 'Does anyone know what they're saying?'

Artemisia makes a humming noise under her breath. 'I only have a passing understanding of most of the languages, but I *believe* they're arguing over whether they should trust us or steal whatever food or valuables we have and send us on our way.'

'That's encouraging,' I mutter under my breath. 'Did we bring food?'

'Just lunch,' Heron says. 'But I can wait another couple of hours to eat.'

My stomach grumbles in protest, but I ignore it and nod. 'I can, too.'

The others agree, though we all know it won't be enough. Lunch for five won't do much to feed the thousands here.

I step toward Sandrin and the woman.

'We only have a little food, but you're welcome to it,' I say in Astrean, making them both stop their arguing and look at me. 'As for valuables, we have some coins and my dress, though I hope you won't take that from me, since it would be difficult to explain its absence to King Etristo. If he learns I came here, he'll prevent me from returning. I'd like to return and bring more food.'

They both stare at me for an uncomfortably long time before the woman lets out a loud, irritated sigh and says something to Sandrin again. Most of it is lost on me but I hear the Astrean word for *child* again. I open my mouth to protest, but before I can she starts back inside her house, beckoning us to follow.

The woman's house is only a single room a quarter of the size of mine in the palace. There is a small stove in one corner, four threadbare mattresses on the floor, and next to nothing else. Somehow, though, there are six other people crammed into the space, three men and three women, all with shorn or braided hair and ragged clothes. Not one of them is wearing shoes, even though the ground is barely cleaner than it was outside.

The woman who led us in motions to me.

'Queen Theodosia of Astrea, come to be our savior,' she says, her Astrean passable but heavily accented.

There are some chuckles from the others, but I try not to let them bother me. I can't blame them for seeing me as a naive, overambitious child, can I? It might not even be that far from the truth.

'King Etristo has invited me to stay in the palace as a guest,' I explain. 'He hopes to find me a husband with armies to help us defeat the Kalovaxians and reclaim our home.'

There's more laughter at that, though the loudest comes from Sandrin.

'Queens don't marry,' he says. 'Have you been among the barbarians so long that you've forgotten that?'

My face grows hot.

'Some traditions are difficult to keep in times of war,' I say, choosing my words carefully.

No matter how true the words might be, Sandrin still scoffs. 'One might argue that it's most important to keep traditions in the midst of difficulty.'

Annoyance prickles at my skin. I don't want to marry either, but I'm certainly not doing so because it's easy.

'If you have an army you're hiding somewhere, I'd be happy to take it, but I doubt that's the case. If you have another suggestion, by all means, I would love to hear it.'

That, at least, seems to silence them. Even Sandrin looks somewhat cowed. Unfortunately, no one actually offers a suggestion.

'I'd heard of the refugee camp here and I suppose I'd gotten it into my mind that I would find happy Astreans here, ones lucky enough to have escaped the Kaiser's tyranny.'

'Tyranny is everywhere, Your Majesty,' Sandrin says quietly. 'The Kalovaxians don't own the concept.'

'That's very philosophical.'

He shrugs. 'So was I, before,' he admits, voice becoming thin and wistful. 'People used to travel hundreds of miles to hear me lecture on philosophy.'

'You're Sandrin the Wise,' Heron says suddenly. 'My mother heard you speak once. She said your mind had been gilded by the gods.'

Sandrin gives a harrumph. 'She wasn't the only one,' he says. 'Now I'm Sandrin the Elder of Astrea.' He gestures to the people gathered behind him. 'These are my fellow Elders, one from every country here. We keep the peace and we do what we can to make things easier.'

'I can't imagine that's a simple job,' I admit.

'It isn't,' says another man, pale-skinned with close-cropped hair the color of copper.

I glance back at my friends, who all look the same way I feel. Shaken, like the world has shifted beneath their feet. And so full of guilt that it just might drown us. *It isn't our fault,* I remind myself, *it's the Kaiser's.* But still, I should have known about this. I should have done something. Blaise catches my eye and nods, a thousand words passing between us without us voicing a single one out loud.

I turn back to the Elders.

'What can we do to help?' I ask.

The help the camp needs is simple enough. They need food, first and foremost, and our meager lunch is a drop in that pot. The Sta'Criverans deliver rations every week, leftovers from the capital, but more often than not the food has gone bad by the time it arrives. We can come back with more, take some from the palace kitchens that would still be fresh, but it will only ever be drops. Never enough to put meat on their bones or keep their stomachs from constantly growling. It will be a start, though, until we can think of another solution.

They need fresh clothes and soap and clean water – more things that we can bring only in small amounts, though there's a lake nearby and Blaise, Heron, and Søren make half a dozen trips back and forth on the horses, filling up whatever makeshift containers the Elders can find so that the refugees will have enough water to last them at least a few days.

While they're gone, Artemisia and I thatch one of the sagging roofs – a process that is foreign to me but that Art seems somewhat practiced at. She climbs up onto the corner of a house, nimble as a cat, and instructs me to pass her handfuls of straw from the ground below. Art gains no small pleasure in bossing me around, but I know better than to take it personally by now, and it isn't long before we fall into a comfortable conversation that lures out the neighbors, who have all been hiding from us since we arrived.

The children are the bravest, as children often are. Small and wraithlike, they have a surprising amount of fire burning in their bellies. A small cluster keeps daring one another closer, as if Artemisia and I are dangerous. The younger ones don't even need dares; they wobble up on dirty, bare feet and stare at Art and me with eyes that take up most of their faces.

Artemisia is too preoccupied with the thatching to notice them at first, but I do.

'Hello,' I say to one of the children, who can't be a day older than four, with bony arms and legs but a round belly. His golden skin and black hair make me think of Erik, and I wonder if he's from Goraki as well – or if his parents are, at least.

He says nothing in reply, just continues to stare at me with solemn eyes, hands fisted at his sides. I set down the bushel of straw I'm holding and feel around Heron's cloak, hoping to find something tucked away in the pockets – a bit of hardtack, a piece of candy, a coin – but there's nothing except a snippet of string and balls of dust. When I pull my hands from my pockets, though, I hear a clinking sound and remember the dress I'm wearing underneath. The one embellished with jewels.

I hike up the cloak and reach for the dress's diamond-trimmed hem. Each stone is the size of my thumbnail. With a sharp tug, I pull one of them free and hold it out to him.

He looks at it like it's a weapon, which breaks my heart. For someone so young, he's known far too much cruelty. But after staring at it for a few seconds, he seems to realize that it won't hurt him. He takes it, grubby, rough fingers brushing mine. It sparkles in the sunlight when he holds it up, sending rainbows dancing on the ground below. Before I can stop him, he sticks it into his mouth.

'No!' I say.

He seems to realize it isn't edible without testing the theory and spits it back into his hand, drying the saliva off on his rough-spun tunic. He looks up at me and grins broadly, teeth yellow and chipped, before scampering back to a woman I assume is his mother. I smile at her, and after a second of clutching her child in her arms, she smiles back tightly, nodding her head once.

After that, what timidity the other children possess disappears entirely. The whole flock of them presses in around me, with eager faces and dirty hands and words I only understand bits and pieces of.

'Whoa, slow down,' I say, though I can't help but laugh. I manage to clear a bit of space between them and me before pulling a few more jewels from my dress's hem, passing one out to each child there.

'You're going to have some explaining to do when your maid finds that dress,' Artemisia says, peering down at me from the roof with an amused expression that seems wholly out of place on her. As she looks at the children, though, her amusement fades. 'The Sta'Criverans believe the refugees are cursed,' she says, disgust punctuating her words. 'As if misfortune is somehow contagious.'

'That's the most foolish thing I've ever heard,' I say.

'It is,' she agrees. 'But people will believe anything if it makes them think they have more control than they do in this world. Pass me a bit more straw and then we're done and you can go back to your legion of devotees.'

I pass her another handful of straw before turning back to the children. I have nothing more to give them but they don't seem to care. Their fingers reach out to tug at the material of Heron's cloak or my hands, anything they can reach to get my attention. I laugh, turning from one to another and another and another. I can't understand most of what they say, but it doesn't matter. They just want to be heard and I'm happy to listen.

'It's a shame they're too young to wield weapons,' Artemisia says before leaping down from the roof, landing lightly next to me. 'A few more years and they'd make for the start of a fierce and devoted army.'

I know she means well, but the words still gnaw at me. The idea that these children would grow up to fight battles, to feel the blood of others on their skin, to know the bite of a sword – I don't want that for them. Not in service of me or anyone else.

MARIAL

———◆•◆———

THE RIDE BACK TO THE city is quiet, but it isn't the uncomfortable kind of silence. I think we're all too fatigued and hungry to talk much, but aside from that, I know my thoughts are still back in the refugee camp and I'm sure the others feel the same. Even Søren's face is drawn and pale, though part of me wants to slap him. He can't be horrified by the way the Sta'Criverans have been treating those people when it's the Kalovaxians' fault that they had to seek refuge in the first place.

It isn't Søren's fault, I know that, but it's an easy distinction to overlook sometimes.

When we get back to the city, we return the horses to the stables and slip through the busy streets as quietly as we can. The sun is starting to sink in the sky now – we stayed out longer than we meant to – and I pray to all the gods that might have followed us across the Calodean Sea that our absence has gone unnoticed.

And if it hasn't?

I would like nothing better than to tell King Etristo exactly where I have been and how vile I think he is for the way he treats the refugees who came to his land seeking safety. I want to tell him that I think he's a monster and that if he doesn't send them food and clean water immediately I will leave, marriage be damned. But even as I think it, I know that's something I cannot do. Loath as I am to admit it, I need his help to save Astrea, to give those people a place to go home to.

But the second I am on Astrea's throne again, I will make sure he knows exactly what I think of him.

It isn't until we're in the riser on the way up to our floor that Heron breaks the silence.

'I can steal food over the next few days if I use my gift,' he whispers, casting a wary glance at the riser operator, who doesn't seem to be listening to us. 'Gather up more bit by bit than I could all at once. Then we'll go back. Or, I will. You don't have to—'

'I'm going,' I say. 'If anyone wants to stay behind, you're welcome to, but after what we saw today I can't imagine that will be the case.'

The others say nothing and I take that for assent.

When I slip inside my room, I think for one blissful second that my absence went unnoticed. Everything looks exactly as I left it – the bed rumpled, my nightgown pooled on the floor, the wardrobe door open. But Marial is so still perched in the chair by the fireplace that I don't notice her until she stands.

'You foolish girl,' she says, her voice low and her expression furious.

I take a step back toward the door but there isn't anywhere to go. This isn't something I can run from.

'I felt better,' I tell her instead. 'I thought a walk would do me good.'

She levels a look of disbelief at me, one perfectly arched eyebrow rising. 'A walk?' she says dryly. 'I suppose that's why you smell like a gutter and are covered head to toe in dirt?'

I can't think of an answer for that quickly enough.

'After how well we've treated you, all the fine things we've given you, you decide to repay it by lying and going behind the King's back?' she asks, her voice low and dangerous.

Something in me snaps, and before I can stop them, words force their way past my lips.

'I don't care about your fine things. I'm grateful for the kindness the King has shown me in allowing me to stay, but I am here for my people – the ones in chains in Astrea and the ones being starved and caged in what you have the nerve to call a refugee camp. *Refuge* means safety, and what I saw today can hardly be called that.'

It isn't until Marial recoils from my words that I realize I've said too much. 'You went to the camp?' she asks quietly, her voice wavering. Though she's always seemed so fearsome, for the first time she looks afraid.

I want to deny it, but there's no way I can now. I kick myself for letting that slip. 'I asked the King to bring me there,' I tell her, deciding that if I can't take the words back, I might as well commit to them. 'He refused. He said it was no place for a girl like me and he was right. It's no place for anyone.'

Marial shakes her head. 'They're cursed,' she says. 'We've taken pity enough on them, but we won't put ourselves at risk for strangers. Now you bring their filth and bad luck with you.'

She says it like a line she's heard spoken so many times she's memorized it.

'If you believe that, you're the fool,' I say. 'You can tell the King if you like, but I would imagine that would get you into more trouble than it would me. After all, I left on your watch. And I'm sure he can get another lady's maid far more easily than he could find a new displaced queen to marry off for his own profit.'

The words don't feel like mine, and when Marial stumbles back a step, looking like I physically struck her, guilt pools in my stomach. I remind myself of what she said about the refugees, and that she would find a way to keep me from going back to the camp if I didn't stop her, but that logic does nothing to make me feel better. Again, I can't help but hear the Kaiser in my mind, guiding my actions. I want to apologize, but I can't bring myself to say the words.

Instead, we merely stare at one another for a painfully long moment. Marial's expression is inscrutable. Just as the silence starts to become unbearable, she finally speaks.

'You need a bath,' she says finally. 'No use having the girls see you this way. I'll just have to draw it myself.'

CHARM

——— ◆ ◆ ———

IN THE RISER WITH DRAGONSBANE on the way to dinner with some of the suitors, I make the mistake of yawning. I can't help it: after last night and the hours spent working in the sun at the camp, I'm surprised I'm still standing up straight. Dragonsbane, however, can't know about any of that, and when she sees me yawn, her eyes narrow.

'Tonight is important.' She says each word slowly, as if talking to a small child. She's clad in another black dress, this one fitted like a sheath and embroidered with black pearls. It's a perfect contrast to my own dress of flounced white chiffon. In Astrea, white is the color of mourning, but Marial told me quite bluntly that in Sta'Crivero it symbolizes virginity. Which is hardly subtle, but nothing about the Sta'Criverans seems to be subtle.

'I know it's important,' I say. 'But you'll excuse me if I pace myself. There will be a lot more of these over the coming days if I'm to get to know all of the suitors.'

'These first three will be our best options,' she says.

I frown. 'What do you mean?'

Dragonsbane shrugs. 'Every country in the world was

invited to try for your hand, apart from Elcourt, which is too closely aligned with Kalovaxia. Etristo is collecting a sum from each suitor, so he wasn't particularly motivated to keep the list to those who actually have the force to take on the Kalovaxians. Many of the countries are too weak to actually be of assistance, though I suppose their presence only makes you look more desirable.' She pauses, letting that sink in, though it doesn't exactly surprise me.

'Haptania, Oriana, and Etralia are arguably the strongest countries in the world, after Sta'Crivero,' she continues. 'Any of those three has the power to take Astrea back. The others *may* have the power, but more than likely would only prolong our inevitable defeat.'

'If Sta'Crivero is the strongest country in the world, why don't they help us directly?'

Dragonsbane smiles at me like I'm a pet who just did an amusing trick. 'Because helping you directly doesn't get them anything. They don't want Astrea's magic – you've seen how they live, what use would they have of it? They want money, and that is easier to get elsewhere, with far less bloodshed.'

I swallow down my frustration. No one seems to understand that there are Astreans *dying* in the mines. All they're concerned about is money and gems and their own safety. If everyone put aside their selfishness, the Kalovaxians could be stamped out as easily as an ant under a boot heel, with minimal effort or risk. But there's no money in that, so no one bothers.

* * *

I expect dinner to be held in the same dining room as last night, but instead we're brought to a large open-air pavilion with no dining table – just plush sofas and chairs and low tables that are laden with golden plates of finger food and glasses of deep red wine.

We are the last to arrive. King Etristo is already seated in a high-backed chair, frail shoulders hunched over in what seems to be his usual posture, an attendant holding a glass of wine at his side. The three suitors are spread out around the room, each speaking with his own entourage. I recognize Chancellor Marzen's sister – *Salla* Coltania, Søren called her – and Prince Talin's father, Czar Reymer.

When they notice me, they all get to their feet – apart from King Etristo, who remains seated, though I don't take it as a sign of disrespect. I don't think he could stand on his own if he wanted to.

'I told you she would be worth the wait, didn't I?' King Etristo calls out to the suitors with a laugh, grabbing the wineglass and taking a swig before pushing it back at the attendant without sparing him so much as a look.

'I hope I haven't kept you long,' I say, noticing that Søren isn't here. His presence has been requested at all other official events, but I understand why he's been left out of this one. King Etristo already mentioned the rumors about Søren and me; the last thing he wants is that shadow cast over tonight, especially when I've refused the purity examination. Suddenly, the white dress seems like even more of an obvious ploy.

'Not at all, not at all. I just thought it would be best for you to all get to know one another in a more comfortable setting. No stuffy dinner here, just an easy night of conversation. How does that sound?'

It sounds like it will be anything but easy or comfortable.
'It sounds wonderful, Your Highness,' I say with what I hope
is a gracious smile. 'Thank you.'

He inclines his head before reaching for his wine again.

I glance around the pavilion, feeling the gazes of the
suitors and their guests dragging down on my shoulders.
Chancellor Marzen and his sister are sitting closest to me, so
I make my way to him first, Dragonsbane trailing behind me
like a shadow.

'Hello, Chancellor,' I say, holding out a hand to him. He
stands and bends to kiss it with a graceful flourish before
letting it drop and gesturing to his sister. Tonight her glossy
black hair is piled in a braided bun on top of her head. Her
mouth is painted vermilion red and her eyes are rimmed with
kohl. She looks like the kind of woman who would bite you
as easily as she would smile at you.

'Queen Theodosia, may I present my sister, Coltania,' he
says in Astrean that is proficient but stilted.

Her red mouth bows into a cold approximation of a smile.
'Pleasure,' she says. 'I've heard so many things.' Her Astrean
is a bit rougher than her brother's, but I don't have trouble
understanding her.

'You have me at a disadvantage, then,' I say lightly. 'But
it's lovely to meet you as well. This is my aunt, Princess
Kallistrade,' I add, gesturing to Dragonsbane. Petty as it
might be, it gives me some measure of delight to see her flinch
at her formal title.

Dragonsbane and I both take our seats as the Chancellor
pours us each a glass of wine.

'How are you finding Sta'Crivero?' he asks me, passing me my glass.

The thought of drinking after last night makes me want to retch, but I force myself to take a small sip. 'It's beautiful,' I say, without really thinking about it. It hardly matters, though – a shallow answer for a shallow question is all that's expected.

'It is very bright,' Coltania says, though in her mouth that doesn't sound like a compliment.

Chancellor Marzen scoffs. 'The Sta'Criverans are excessive and . . .' He trails off, saying something to his sister in what I imagine must be Orianic.

'Tacky,' she finishes, flashing a full smile.

'Tacky,' Chancellor Marzen replies with a chuckle. 'That is the word.'

'Sorry to interrupt,' a deep voice says as a shadow falls over me, and I look up to see Czar Reymer with Prince Talin cowering at his side like he's trying to disappear into the air. 'Your Majesty, might we steal your attention for a moment?'

I glance at the Chancellor and his sister, but even though they look like they want to protest, they both nod.

'We'll speak again soon, Your Majesty,' the Chancellor says with a smile that I can only describe as oily.

'I look forward to it,' I tell him before taking hold of Czar Reymer's proffered hand and letting him help me to my feet and lead me – and Dragonsbane – to another corner of the room.

The rest of the night yawns on, a daze of being handed off between the three suitors and trying my best to make pleasant conversation so that they find me charming, which seems to be easier than I thought it would be.

It quickly becomes clear that Marzen sees a union between our countries as inevitable – as I speak to him and his sister throughout the night, they make it sound like his proposal has already been made and accepted, which I find I don't care for. So much of my life has happened without my consent. Feeling like I have no control even here and now makes my chest feel like it's caving in around my heart and lungs. I suppose he thinks his arrogance charming, especially when paired with his oily smile and charisma, but instead I find myself recoiling from him so much that Dragonsbane finally pinches my arm.

'Smile,' she whispers, leaning toward me like she's fixing my hair. 'You look like you've swallowed a frog.'

Repulsive as Marzen might be, I prefer the company of him and his sister to that of Czar Reymer and Prince Talin. I have a feeling that the Prince and I might actually get along decently without his father present, but there seems little chance of that. The Czar lingers over every conversation like the sun, blinding and disorienting the both of us with his handsome smiles and overconfident air. I begin to pity Prince Talin – though he must be used to his father's presence, he still wilts beneath it, a sapling doomed to grow weak in the shadow of a great oak.

And if he is intimidated by his father, he is absolutely *terrified* of me. Throughout our conversation, his eyes flicker around the room as if he's looking for some kind of escape, and he goes to great lengths to avoid having them ever meet mine.

If we were alone, I would put his mind at ease and tell him

that I have no desire to marry him either, but if King Etristo got word of that, I fear his patience with me would finally reach its end.

I suppose Archduke Etmond is the most pleasant of the lot, though that title largely falls to him by default. Most of our time is spent in an uncomfortable silence that I'm actually grateful for – it gives me a moment of peace in what has been a very chaotic day – but there are a few moments when he surprises me, like when he very shyly asks how I escaped the Astrean palace and seems to actually care about the answer.

So I tell him the story, surprised when I realize it occurred not two weeks ago now, though it feels like another lifetime. I leave out the bits about Søren, too aware now of what others might think of our relationship, but I tell him the rest.

His eyes are wide and awed, so I take the opportunity to peel back the white satin gloves Marial made me wear and show him the light scars on my palms from clawing my way up the boulders. Heron tried but hadn't been able to heal me completely. I thought them ugly, but the way Archduke Etmond looks at them makes me think that there is something lovely about them. I certainly prefer them to the scars on my back, though I suppose they mean the same thing now – I went through hell and I survived to tell the tale.

Unfortunately, my time with the Archduke is too short. The Czar and the Chancellor seem to realize that he's an easy one to take advantage of – in social situations if not on the battlefield – and every time I make my way over to speak with him, it's only a few minutes before one of them appears and asks to speak with me alone. By the third time it happens, I almost refuse, but Dragonsbane at my side is a clear reminder that doing so would be frowned upon.

Make them like you, she said to me in the riser, but there doesn't seem to be any trouble in that area. They like me perfectly well with little effort on my part. They like me because when they look at me they see magic and money and that is enough for them to swoon over. The Archduke is the only one who looks at me like he actually sees *me,* though there's nothing romantic in it. I'd imagine it's similar to the way he looks at the soldiers he commands – with respect.

The realization hits me like a slap – he's the only person I've met in Sta'Crivero who looks at me that way. Everyone else treats me like a fragile doll, to be kept high on a shelf, played with on occasion, and protected at all costs but never respected as an equal.

GORAKI

———— ◆·◆ ————

As THE NIGHT DRAGS ON, my limbs grow heavy and it becomes a struggle to keep my eyes open, though I've been careful to take only the smallest sips of wine. I feel like a ball of yarn being pulled between a group of cats, unspooling more and more with each passing moment. What charm I may have been able to muster earlier in the night is wearing thin now, and I'm not the only one who notices.

'Get yourself together,' Dragonsbane hisses at me as she leads me back to Czar Reymer and Prince Talin.

'If the Czar tells me about his prize-bred horses again, I will fall asleep altogether,' I warn.

'You will not,' she snaps. 'You will smile and nod and tell him how fascinating he is and then you will do your damnedest to make that son of his say more than two words. Need I remind you that Astrea is at stake?'

Her words sow shame beneath my skin. Though I'd like nothing better than to jerk my arm out of hers and run out of the room as quickly as my tired legs will carry me, I know she's right. I don't know if I can truly call Dragonsbane my ally, but she is not my enemy either. We are on the same side – Astrea's side.

'Fine,' I tell her, fixing my smile so that it's broader and toothier, even though it makes my cheeks ache.

Before we can make it to the Czar and Prince, though, the brass door swings open with a clang that makes everyone jump in surprise. The entrance is across the pavilion, with a dozen potted plants between, so I can't see who's arrived now. Another suitor, most likely, though the idea of someone else to charm and impress forces a quiet groan past my lips. Luckily, Dragonsbane is the only one who notices, and she fixes me with a stern look.

King Etristo, who had dozed off in his chair, jerks awake, looking toward the entrance with tired but narrow eyes.

'What is this?' he demands, craning his neck to see what the interruption is. 'This is a private dinner! Who are you?'

'My apologies,' a voice says. Something about it nudges at my memory, but I can't place it. I frown, taking a step closer and pulling Dragonsbane with me, though I still can't see who it is. A scrap of violet and gold brocade, a patch of black hair, but I can't manage a good look at his face. 'I know we're late but I was told that you were entertaining some suitors here.'

It *is* another suitor after all, but I'm sure that I know that voice. That bravado so loud that it distracts from insecurity, the charm painted on so thick that you don't notice the doubt layered beneath it. I know that voice.

I let go of Dragonsbane's arm and step toward the entrance, weaving between potted plants until I can finally get a proper look at the intruder.

'Erik,' I say, the name little louder than an exhale. For a moment, all I can do is stare at him and blink, waiting for him to disappear before my eyes. It must only be an illusion after all, crafted by my exhausted, bored mind, because Erik can't be here, parading as one of my suitors. But he doesn't disappear. Instead, he stands tall and straight by the entrance, dressed in clothing so strange it nearly renders him unrecognizable. I've only ever seen him in Kalovaxian garb – fitted trousers and tunics and stifling velvet jackets – but now he wears an ankle-length brocade tunic with wide, sweeping sleeves. It's patterned with intricate designs of animals and trees that look like they've been painted by hand. A thick sash is tied around his waist. His hair – always long and unruly – has been slicked back, secured in a bun at the nape of his neck.

But when his eyes land on me, he smiles and suddenly he looks just like the Erik I remember.

He drops into a sweeping bow. 'Queen Theodosia.'

It isn't the first time he's called me by my name. He said it in the garden, too, after I told him to take his mother – Hoa – and leave the capital. Clearly, he listened.

'What are you doing here?' I ask, walking to his side. I want to hug him, but I know I shouldn't, considering our present company.

'I thought that was obvious,' he says. 'I'm here to compete for your fair hand.' Though he says it lightly, I can see the doubt behind his eyes, the discomfort lingering just beneath this polished and confident surface. Glimpse him from just the right angle and his illusions slip away, leaving a boy playing dress-up, reciting lines that have been given to him.

'Sir,' King Etristo growls from his chair, 'who, *exactly,* are you?'

'Oh, where are my manners?' Erik says, turning toward the King and bowing again and producing an envelope from the pocket of his robe. 'I've just arrived from Goraki.'

King Etristo scoffs, but takes the envelope. 'Goraki is a ruin,' he says, tearing it open, his eyes scanning the piece of parchment. 'We sent an invitation there merely as a formality, but everyone knows there has been no ruling family there since the Kalovaxians slaughtered the last emperor and his children.'

'That is what everyone *thought*,' Erik says, idly taking a glass of red wine from one of the servers. I wonder if anyone else is looking close enough to see how the glass quivers in his hand, the dark liquid rippling like the surface of a pond when a school of fish swims beneath. 'Imagine their surprise when the last emperor's youngest daughter returned to them after being held by the Kalovaxians for two decades. And imagine her son's surprise when she passed her claim to the throne on to him.'

He pauses, but no one else speaks. 'The son was me,' he adds. 'In case that wasn't clear.'

'You have my congratulations,' King Etristo says dryly. 'But the fact remains that Goraki is a wasteland with no money and no troops. You are trifling with our time.'

Erik shrugs, though his eyes dance across the room. 'Your requested sum has been brought, Your Highness,' he says, looking back to King Etristo. 'I left it with your son when he greeted me with the same questions you're asking now. He counted it himself before allowing me into the palace. I've as much right to be here as any suitor.'

King Etristo lifts a thick gray eyebrow. 'And how much is

left in your coffers after that expense, Emperor?'

Erik's mouth twitches. 'Enough,' he says, but he doesn't elaborate. Instead, he turns to me and offers me his free arm. 'If I might have a moment of your time, Queen Theodosia?'

It takes all I have not to seem too eager when I agree, though that excitement is quickly dampened when Dragonsbane follows us to a secluded corner of the pavilion. The eyes of the other suitors trail after us, but none of their gazes are darker than King Etristo's.

'It's good to see you again, Erik,' I say to him, casting a look at Dragonsbane a step behind us. She makes no effort to hide her disapproval. I turn back to Erik. 'Or should I call you *Emperor* now?'

'You can call me Erik if I can call you Theodosia,' he says with a small, grim smile. 'All of this title business is tiring, isn't it?'

'Only when it comes to friends,' I say. 'You can call me Theo.'

'Alas, I can't shorten *Erik* any more without it sounding ridiculous,' he says with a dramatic sigh.

When we reach the sofas clustered in the corner, I let go of Erik's arm and sink down into one. 'If we're done being clever,' I say, 'would you like to tell me what you're really doing here?'

Erik's bravado slips as he sits down across from me, leaning forward with his elbows on his knees. He glances warily at Dragonsbane when she sits down next to me.

'Can she be trusted?' he asks.

It's a tricky question but I can't imagine Erik would have anything to say that Dragonsbane shouldn't hear. Besides, if she thinks I'm trusting her, it will be easier to keep other things secret.

I nod.

'How's Søren faring?' he asks, lowering his voice. 'I'd imagine he's not used to being a prisoner.' Though he keeps his words indifferent, there's a flicker of real concern behind them. They are brothers, after all, and friends besides.

'He made an exceptional prisoner, actually,' I tell him, leaning back against the plush cushions.

'Made?' Erik asks, eyes widening. The careless facade slips another inch. 'He's not—'

'He's not a prisoner any longer,' I clarify. Relief streaks across his face. 'He has his own room here, no chains. I wouldn't recommend he try to leave, but I don't think he wants to.'

If news of Søren's pivot surprises Erik, he doesn't show it. 'Vecturia changed him,' he says. 'It changed many of us, but Søren more so, I think. Most of the Kalovaxians didn't see the Astreans as people – they saw weapons. When Søren gave the order—' He breaks off when he sees me flinch. I can't help it. I don't want to know about what happened next. I don't want to hear details of how horrifically my people were murdered. I don't want to hear about how bad Søren felt when he gave the order to kill hundreds of my people and thousands of innocent Vecturians who were only protecting their home.

'How did you feel, Erik, when you watched Astrean men and women forced to destroy themselves to protect you?' I ask instead, my voice coming out like tinder just waiting for a spark.

He doesn't answer right away.

'I'm glad that we can finally speak frankly, Theo,' he says finally, his voice quiet. 'Honesty doesn't come easily for me, after so many years with the Kalovaxians, but I'll try.' He takes a breath. 'By the time Vecturia happened, I think I was numb to the suffering of others. I was nine when we left Goraki, when I watched my home burn to the ground. Even before that, I watched the Kalovaxians treat my people the same way they treat their Astrean slaves now. The Kaiser beat my mother in front of me, and when she tried to rebel against him, he made me watch while a man sewed her mouth shut. It's not a good answer, that I was too numb, but it's the truth. I am sorry for what happened, truly I am, and I will do everything in my power to keep it from happening again.'

I'm stunned to silence, but Dragonsbane isn't.

'And what power is that?' she asks him. 'King Etristo is right – Goraki has nothing to its name anymore. There are no more expensive silks to sell, no more goods at all as far as I've heard. You can't have much of an army either. It's estimated that less than two thousand Gorakians survived the Kalovaxian invasion. Is that number false?'

Erik, to his credit, does not wither under Dragonsbane's stare.

'I haven't counted them myself,' he says. 'But that estimate sounds accurate.'

'Then how?' she presses.

But Erik doesn't have an answer. 'We're stronger together,' he says instead, speaking to me. 'Our countries united against the Kalovaxians are stronger than we would be alone.'

'Yes,' I say with a sad smile. 'But still not strong enough.'

PHIREN

———— •◦• ————

BACK IN MY ROOM, I ring the bell that summons Marial and she arrives a few moments later. As she changes me into my nightgown, she gives me a warning look, as if she suspects that I'm breaking rules once more. I smile innocently in return, but I don't think it fools her. After what feels like an eternity, she finally takes her leave with a stiff curtsy. I wait a few minutes before stepping out into the hallway myself, finding Erik waiting for me. He leans against the wall opposite my door, arms folded over his chest, still dressed in his brocade robe from dinner, though it looks a bit more disheveled now. His hair is down from its bun, hanging loose to his shoulders.

'Awfully forward of you, Theo,' he says with a smirk. 'Asking your suitor to meet you in your bedroom.'

'*Outside* my bedroom,' I correct. 'I thought you'd like to see Søren.'

The cocky smile slips from his face. 'Thank you,' he says, but there's a note of fear in his voice.

'What is it?' I ask, leading him down the hall toward Søren's room.

'It feels like a lifetime has passed since I saw him last, even though it's only been a couple of weeks. I might as well be an entirely different person,' he admits.

'You still seem like yourself to me,' I say. 'Besides, Søren's done some changing as well.'

'That worries me even more,' Erik admits. 'I've known Søren since the day he was born. I don't like the idea of us being strangers.'

I remember Blaise appearing out of nowhere at that banquet months ago, the first time I had seen him in a decade. He was a stranger to me then, even though once we had been close.

'Being strangers is an easy enough thing to fix,' I say, squeezing his arm. 'But you have to start at some point.'

There's a guard outside Søren's door who doesn't even try to hide his disapproval at my late-night visit.

'The Emperor is here to see Prinz Søren,' I tell the guard with a sweet smile. 'They were raised together, you see.'

The guard gives a skeptical grunt but steps aside for us to pass. I lift my hand and knock.

'Come in,' Søren says, his voice muffled through the door.

I push the door open and step inside first. Søren is lounging on top of his bed with a leather-bound book in his hands. When he sees me, he puts it aside and sits up, frowning in confusion.

'Theo? What are you . . .' He trails off when Erik appears behind me, going from merely confused to bewildered. He scrambles to stand. '*Erik?*' His voice is tentative, as though he might be imagining him.

Erik smiles shyly, rubbing the back of his neck. 'Hello, Søren.'

'What are you doing here?' Søren asks, stepping toward him. He doesn't wait for an answer. Instead he folds Erik into a hug that looks tight enough to break bones. After a moment, Søren pulls back, holding Erik at arm's length. 'And what are you *wearing*?'

Erik laughs. 'That is a long story,' he says, but he tells him anyway.

When I make my move to leave them alone to catch up, Erik follows me to the door.

'My mother wants a word with you,' he tells me.

'Hoa's here?' I ask, surprised. 'Why didn't you say so before?'

He shrugs, though he looks uncomfortable. 'I thought King Etristo might want to meet her, the Kaiser's escaped concubine. I didn't want to subject her to that kind of attention any sooner than necessary.'

I think about the way King Etristo and his family treated me at dinner my first night here.

'Some people enjoy reveling in the misery of others,' I agree.

'*Most* people, I've found. It seems to be a human trait.' He hesitates for a moment. 'We've removed the stitches, so she can speak again,' he says. 'But it's been so long since she has that it can be difficult to understand her at times. And she's still a little—' He breaks off, shaking his head.

'Ten years under the Kaiser's thumb was a nightmare I

can't fully describe to anyone,' I say. 'I can't imagine how she managed twenty.'

Hoa is waiting in my room when I open the door. She's perched delicately on the edge of a chair by the empty mosaic fireplace that I imagine is purely ornamental, her back ramrod straight and her hands folded primly in her lap. Like Erik, she's dressed in a long brocade robe, but hers is a pale peach, tied around her waist with a red silk sash. The wide sleeves swallow her thin arms so that only her bone-pale hands are visible. Her black hair is threaded with silver, though she wears it loose around her shoulders now instead of in the tight bun I've always seen it in. The stitches across her mouth are gone, but the holes remain, three on the top and three on the bottom. I doubt they'll ever close completely.

She must hear me come in but she doesn't look up, her eyes fixed on the empty fireplace as if she expects a fire to spark to life at any moment.

'Hoa,' I say carefully. Though I know she's actually here before me, she feels ephemeral and I half expect her to disappear if I spook her.

She doesn't. Instead, she turns to look at me. Though she's not yet forty, she looks so much older, as if a dozen lives have been sucked out of her. The Kaiserin had the same look about her before she died. I suppose the Kaiser has a way of doing that to women, draining them.

It's Hoa's smile that breaks me, because I've never seen it. I don't think she was capable of it when her mouth was stitched shut, and even if she had been, there wasn't much for her to smile about. It's a shame, because her smile is bright enough to clear the sky during a storm.

'My *Phiren*,' she murmurs, getting to her feet.

The word is strange, but I barely hear it. My body is frozen, even when she crosses to me and puts her hands on either side of my face. She kisses one of my cheeks, then the other.

It occurs to me that I never expected to see her again. In my mind, she is a ghost, already dead and buried. Only she isn't – she's here, flesh and bone, and I don't know what to say to her.

'I hate this language,' she tells me in Kalovaxian. 'It tastes like funeral dirt in my mouth, but it is the only one we share, isn't it?'

'You shouldn't have come here,' I say. 'You should have gone far away, somewhere the Kaiser won't find you.'

She raises her thread-thin eyebrows. 'If it is safe enough for you, it is safe enough for me.'

'And if it isn't safe for me?' I ask. 'The Kaiser has offered an enticing reward for my death or return to him. King Etristo has promised me safety, but I'm not foolish enough to believe that such a promise is a guarantee. You can go somewhere else, somewhere the Kaiser will never look.'

Hoa is quiet for a moment. 'Fear gives monsters power,' she says finally. 'I am not afraid of him; he does not get that power over me. Not anymore, my *Phiren*.'

I frown. It's the second time she's used this word that I do not know. Erik said that she was difficult to understand at times. Maybe I'm not hearing her correctly.

'*Phiren*,' I repeat, trying to make sense of it.

She laughs, a full throaty sound that is somehow prettier for its roughness.

'It is what I've always called you in my mind,' she explains. 'I forget that you never heard me. I had so many conversations with you over those years, but you never heard any of them.'

She leads me back to the seating area and sits down on the sofa, pulling me down next to her.

'In Goraki, there is a legend of a bird made of fire,' she says. 'It never dies, the *Phiren*. First, it is made of embers, glowing bright and new before they burst into flames. The *Phiren* burns brightly for many years, but no fire burns forever – it is smothered into a bird of smoke, wispy and dark. It stays like that for a stretch of time – sometimes centuries even – but the day always comes when an ember within it sparks and its life begins anew.'

'Is it a real bird?' I ask.

She laughs. 'That I cannot say,' she admits. 'It's a story we tell children to keep them occupied. "*Look for the* Phiren *while the adults talk about adult things – if you spy it you get a wish!*" Or a way to explain away bad weather or a poor showing of crops. We would say that the *Phiren* had molted into smoke but it would turn to flame again soon and Goraki's luck would turn with it. Sometimes people would claim they'd seen it, but I think most don't believe it to be more than a myth.'

She pauses, regarding me thoughtfully. 'Still, you reminded me of the legend. With your bright eyes and crown of ashes and Fire Queen mother. *Lady Thora,* everyone called you, but I thought of you as *Lady Smoke*. I knew it would only be a matter of time before your ember sparked again, until you once more burned bright enough to escape him.'

The lump in my throat swells and tears sting at my eyes.

'Sometimes I felt like I hated you,' I admit. 'I wanted you to do something, to help me, to save me. I don't think I realized just how much of a prisoner you were as well. Until Erik told me, I didn't realize the Kaiser had . . .' I trail off, unable to say it. She understands what I mean, though.

'That I'd shared his bed,' she says before shaking her head. 'No, that isn't right. That sounds like I had a choice in it, though I suppose you understand what I mean better than most.'

'He didn't touch me,' I tell her. 'Not like that.'

She lets out a slow breath. 'I will always be grateful for that,' she says. 'I dreaded the day that would happen. I like to think I would have stopped it somehow, that I would have found a way to get you out before then, but I'm not sure that's true. There was no way out for us, not until you cut the path yourself.'

She rests a hand on top of mine and squeezes. Her fingers are all bone, like the Kaiserin's were, but Hoa's are warm to the touch. She is alive and I am alive, and sometimes the Kaiserin is right and that is enough.

'I'm proud of you, my *Phiren*. You may be just brave – and just foolish – enough to triumph.'

PICNIC

———— ◆ · ◆ ————

THE WORD *PICNIC* MEANS SOMETHING different in Sta'Crivero than it did in Astrea. In Astrea, a picnic meant a blanket outside in the shade of a tree; it meant a basket of finger foods and a pitcher of fruit juice; it meant an easy day lying languid in the sun.

In Sta'Crivero, however, it is as elaborate as everything else. That it is outdoors is the only difference between it and a regular banquet. There's a heavy gilt table with plush chairs set up on top of a sand dune just outside the capital's walls. A large cloth awning shields the diners from the unforgiving sun, and two servants stand near us waving large cloth fans to keep the air a tolerable temperature. The plates and utensils are gold and laden with jewels. The food is a full five-course meal complete with an entire turkey – which seems excessive considering there are only four of us and three of us are women with waists corseted so tightly in Sta'Criveran dresses that we can scarcely breathe, let alone eat.

Chancellor Marzen arranged for this private outing with me, though I wonder how much he paid King Etristo for my company. If it weren't for Dragonsbane and *Salla* Coltania's presence as chaperones, I would feel like a courtesan whose company can be bought by the hour.

'You look very sharp in that color, Queen Theodosia,' the Chancellor says to me, refreshing my glass of lemon water, even though I'd only taken a few sips.

I glance down at the dress Marial selected for me today, pale blue chiffon. Pale blue has never been my color. Cress used to say that I was made of fire and she was made of ice the way we dressed – I in warm colors, she in cool ones.

'Thank you' is all I can think to say.

Dragonsbane elbows me, harder than seems strictly necessary, and nods meaningfully toward the Chancellor, who is waiting expectantly.

'Oh,' I say, realization dawning. 'You look very dashing as well, Chancellor Marzen.'

But, of course, it's too late and too halfhearted to sound genuine. I don't think it matters, though; the Chancellor is charmed enough by his own company. He hardly needs me here at all.

He clears his throat, glancing at my aunt and his sister before turning his attention back to me and lowering his voice. 'I look forward to getting to know you better,' he says in a way that slides over my skin like grease.

'And you as well,' I echo, keeping my voice level. 'Isn't that the point of these outings, Chancellor? To get to know one another better?'

'Of course,' Coltania cuts in with a blinding smile, all white teeth and red lips. She idly runs her manicured fingers over the rim of the gold plate in front of her. 'You know, Marzen and I didn't have things like these when we were growing up.'

'Coltania,' the Chancellor says, his voice heavy with warning.

She only laughs, giving her brother a teasing nudge. 'Oh, come now, the fact that you are so relatable is what led our people to elect you,' she says to him before turning back to me. 'We grew up on a farm, if it can truly be called that. There were animals, I suppose, though most of them were too old or ill to be of much use.'

'I'm sorry,' I say, because it seems like the only thing *to* say.

She shrugs her sharp shoulders. 'It was the only life we knew,' she says. 'It was normal. My mother died giving birth to a third bastard, which turned out to be the best thing to happen to us.'

'Coltania,' the Chancellor says again, his voice sharpening.

She ignores him. 'That isn't the way he tells it in his heartfelt speeches, but it's true nonetheless,' she says. 'After she died, Marzen and I – we must have been nine and ten at the time – left our shack behind and went to the city to try our luck there. Marzen always had more charm than he knew what to do with. He managed to talk himself into apprenticeships above more qualified boys. First it was a blacksmith, wasn't it?' she asks. 'You used to come home covered in sweat and coal.'

The Chancellor nods, though his eyes have grown distant. 'Then a silversmith,' he adds.

'You weren't very good at either,' she says with a laugh. 'But you made friends. He's always been very good at making friends,' she says to Dragonsbane and me. 'Not me. People tend to dislike me.'

'You put them off,' Marzen says, not unkindly. 'You say what you mean and it makes people uncomfortable.'

Coltania considers this before shrugging her shoulders. 'Well,' she says, 'I don't like most other people because they don't say what they mean. But that isn't the point.'

'What *is* the point?' Dragonsbane asks, sounding bored.

Coltania smiles again, but this time there is something hard and feral to it. She doesn't so much as glance at Dragonsbane – all her attention is focused on me. 'The other rulers here have had everything handed to them,' she says. 'Their crowns are their birthright, they haven't been *earned*. None of them have suffered like we have and so no one can understand you like we do.'

I don't flinch away from the intensity of her stare, though I very much want to. There's a hunger in her eyes, as though she'd swallow me whole if it meant she never had to know hunger again. It should frighten me, but it doesn't. I recognize that look – I'm sure I've worn it myself too many times to count.

'We're like sisters, don't you think?' she asks.

Considering that we haven't spoken for more than five minutes total, the word *sisters* seems a bit much, but I respect the tactic. She can't know that the word chafes against my skin, that it reminds me of the last girl who called me her sister.

I force myself not to think about Cress, not here and not now. I can't miss her, I can't feel guilty. Wherever she is, she certainly doesn't miss me.

'What does your title mean, *Salla* Coltania?' I ask her to change the subject. 'I've heard others use it but I'm afraid I don't know its origin.'

Coltania smiles. 'It's simply a term of address, like *Lady* or *Miss*,' she explains.

'A bit more than that,' Dragonsbane laughs. 'It's an Orianic honorific. It means she's an expert in her field.'

'Oh,' I say, surprised. 'I didn't realize, *Salla* Coltania.'

She shakes her head, cheeks reddening. 'It's a silly formality.'

'What field are you an expert in?' I ask.

'Science,' Chancellor Marzen says. 'She's studied with the best minds around the world to learn all about biology and chemistry and things I can't begin to pronounce.' His self-deprecating smile is as charming and practiced as everything else about him.

'I admit, I don't know much about science,' I say, leaning forward.

'It's all quite boring,' Chancellor Marzen laughs. 'She's driven off all her suitors with talk of chemical compounds. It's a talent, really.'

'One I employ intentionally,' she replies, but her smile is warmer this time. 'As women, we must have our weapons in this world, whether they're our minds or our fists or our wiles or our tears.'

My own smile feels more real as I lift my wineglass. 'I couldn't agree more,' I say.

'I don't like him,' I tell Søren later that afternoon, while we walk together through the palace's roof garden, which Søren says is renowned across the world. I can see why – there are more flowers here than I can name, in a prism of colors that I didn't know could exist in nature. Gold-paved trails wind through a veritable maze of foliage while fingers of sunlight filter down through the branches of trees overhead. A complex web of piping stretches over the garden like a canopy, letting down a constant stream of light mist to negate Sta'Crivero's dry air. There's no one else in sight.

'The Chancellor?' Søren asks, his brow creasing. 'He doesn't seem too terrible. He's certainly ambitious, but that isn't a negative trait.'

'Not in and of itself,' I admit, stopping to examine a cluster of white flowers shaped like stars. Pretty as they are, they smell of nothing. I straighten up and take Søren's arm again. 'Something about him and his sister troubles me. They're a team – he's smooth and well-spoken, but she's the attack dog when his charm isn't enough. I don't think one knows how to function without the other.'

'Do you think there's something untoward between them?'

It takes me a moment to realize what he's insinuating. I wrinkle my nose. 'Gods no, I didn't mean *that*. Just that they're like two halves of one person, each distilled.'

He's quiet for a moment. 'There were rumors surrounding the election he won, though I'm sure they were twisted and convoluted by the time they made their way to me,' he says carefully.

'What sort of rumors?'

Søren shrugs. 'Bribes. Threats. Hired assassins, in some of the more outlandish tales. They say she carved his way to the chancellorship and the path is lined with blood and greed. I doubt the veracity of most of the claims – they have many enemies in Oriana. Many wealthy, old families still bristle at the thought of a young upstart taking their highest seat. Rumors usually have only a grain of truth to them, if that.'

'I think we know that better than most, given what people are saying about us,' I point out with a laugh.

For an instant, Søren looks like he wants to say something, but he only shakes his head, as if he's clearing the thought away. 'Do you have any favorites yet?' he asks instead. I let out a groan and he quickly rephrases it. 'Are there any who aren't as awful as you expected?'

I consider it. 'I know Erik, I trust him more than the others, and he would accept an alliance without marriage, but that alliance would get us nothing. Goraki is too weak after the Kalovaxian invasion. They can't protect themselves, let alone declare war on another country.'

Though I know it's the truth, my heart sinks when Søren doesn't contradict me.

'Of the suitors with enough power to help me take Astrea back, I prefer the Archduke,' I tell him, though saying the words aloud makes me want to vomit. 'Haptania has a large enough army to be of assistance, and he treats me with more respect than any of the others. I think we could be friends, in the long run.'

I can't bring myself to even think about what it would mean to join our countries, to give him and his country some slice of control over mine.

Søren considers it for a moment, his brow creased deeply in concentration. *This is what he looks like on a battlefield,* I think, *surveying the terrain and coming up with strategies.*

When he turns his head to look at me with that same intensity, my stomach flutters. For a moment, it feels like we're back in Astrea, before we betrayed each other and salted the earth between us.

This is how he looked in Vecturia, before he gave the order to use my people as weapons. I tear my gaze away.

'Is there an option that doesn't include marriage?' I ask him, though I know that if there were, he would have said so already. Still, I hope.

He considers it, reaching up to touch the low-hanging leaves of a tree as we pass beneath its shade.

'Hypothetically,' he says, 'if you were to take the few warriors Erik could offer, plus the maybe sixty percent of Dragonsbane's crew who may be convinced to follow you – and that's being optimistic . . . No, it's not enough. Not by half. Not by a quarter.'

I rub my temples and close my eyes tightly, as if I can shut out the reality of the situation. 'Then I suppose it's the Archduke, unless another option comes along.'

He hesitates. 'What if . . . what if I came along?' he asks.

I laugh. 'Søren, be serious,' I say.

He stops short, reaching for me, callused fingers taking hold of my arm so that I have no choice but to look at him. 'I am being serious. That was your original plan when we were in Astrea, wasn't it? Divide the Kalovaxians so that some are following me and some are following my father?'

'It was more complicated than that,' I say. 'And the rest of the plan was to kill you in order to start a civil war, in case you've forgotten.'

He winces. 'I'm not terribly keen on *that* part.'

I shake my head. 'Half the Kalovaxians think you're a traitor. The other half think you weak enough to get captured by a girl. Do you remember what Mattin said on the ship? He thought I'd cast a spell on you. I'm sure he isn't the only one to hold that belief.'

He considers it, that same quiet intensity etched into his features. 'There are men I've fought beside for years who might still be more loyal to me than to my father,' he says. 'It can't hurt to write a letter.'

'It can if it shows our enemies where we are and what we're doing here,' I point out. 'There is a price on my head, Søren, and if the Kaiser finds out I'm here, I don't think even Etristo will be able to protect me, especially if he learns we're planning on robbing him of his cut of my dowry.'

'We can work through other channels,' he says. 'Send the letters through several messengers so that they're untraceable.'

'And what would all of that effort get us? A few dozen warriors? It still won't be enough.'

He's quiet for a moment, but the intensity doesn't fade from his gaze.

'I just don't want you to have to do it,' he says finally. 'I don't want you to marry any of them.'

'And here I thought you liked the Archduke,' I say, keeping my voice light and teasing. 'You idolize him.'

'He's a brilliant warrior,' Søren agrees before lowering his voice. 'But that doesn't mean he deserves you.'

His words knock the air out of my lungs, flustering and angering me at once. The anger wins out, because it's so much simpler.

'I'm not a prize to be deserved,' I tell him sharply. 'King

Etristo might treat me that way but I expected better from you.'

'I didn't mean it like that,' he says before sighing. 'But it's been . . . difficult, watching them squabble over you even though I know they're only fighting for a faraway country, for gems, for money. I've held my tongue, Theo, and I won't say another word about it after this, I promise, but you have to know it's driving me mad.'

For a long moment, I can't think of a single thing to say. I'd thought we were on the same side of this, that whatever was between us was buried so deep now that we could just ignore it. I don't like being reminded of how recently I thought I was falling in love with him, how even now he has the power to quicken my heartbeat, to turn my thoughts upside down.

When I don't reply right away, Søren steps closer to me, his grip on my arm tightening. The scent of driftwood still clings to his skin, and despite all the reasons I know I shouldn't, I lean into him. His mouth is so close that I can smell the coffee lingering on his breath, so close that if I just tilt my head up, his lips would find mine. The desire to do just that is overwhelming, but instead I bring my free hand up to his shoulder and push him back.

'It was an act, Søren,' I say quietly, though I can't meet his gaze. 'All of it. I saw you, I knew what you wanted, and I *became* what you wanted. But it was never me. That girl was only smoke and mirrors.'

Søren winces before his own mask falls into place. He takes another step back from me, his fingers releasing my arm. The skin he was touching suddenly feels too cold, even in the Sta'Criveran heat.

'As I said before,' he says, the words crisp-edged, 'I'll go back to holding my tongue.'

He leaves me standing alone in the garden. What anger I felt toward him slips away quickly, but I'm not sure how to describe the feeling left behind. It's like walking down stairs and thinking there's one more step than there is. My whole world seems suddenly off-kilter. Nothing I said was a lie – it might even be the most honest thing I've ever said to Søren – but the words still tasted wrong.

PRACTICE

———◆•◆———

THE SWORD SWINGING TOWARD MY face is blunted, but it'll still hurt plenty if it actually hits me. I duck my head, throwing my arm up to protect myself. The blade hits with a dull thwack that I'm sure will leave a bruise.

'*Ow,*' I say to Artemisia, shoving her sword away.

We're in my room after lunch, finally having one of those lessons we discussed on the *Smoke*. It's difficult in my room, with all its heavy, oversized furniture, but we've managed to clear a space big enough for us both to move around. I bore no illusions about my skills with a sword, but I expected Artemisia would at least go easy on me at first.

No such luck. She hadn't even wanted to use practice swords, though I'm glad I insisted – if our swords were sharp she would have killed me by now. As it is, I'm on the floor by the fireplace and she's standing over me, one hand on her hip, the other still holding her weapon like it's an extension of her arm.

'Your arm is gone now,' she says, bored. 'Not your dominant one, though, so I suppose you still technically stand a chance.'

A chance. I could have four arms and still not stand a chance.

'I surrender,' I tell her. 'Can we start at the beginning? How to stand? The proper way to grip a hilt?'

Artemisia raises one contemptuous eyebrow. 'I suppose,' she says, disdain dripping from every word. 'Get up.'

It's not as easy as it sounds. She's already left her mark on both of my legs and my left arm, and every one of my muscles screams as I make my way to stand. At least she brought a set of clothes from the *Smoke* for me; I'm not sure I'd be able to so much as lift a sword in one of my stiff, embellished Sta'Criveran gowns. It's easier to move in leggings and a tunic, though it's difficult to imagine I could fight worse than I already am.

'Legs shoulder width apart,' Artemisia says, kicking the inside of my calves until my feet are sufficiently separate. 'One slightly in front of the other for balance.'

I oblige, though I feel somewhat ridiculous. Artemisia examines me with a critical eye before giving me a firm shove with her free hand. I wobble, but manage to hold my ground. She nods.

'Good enough,' she says. 'Now lift the sword.'

I do and she grips my hand, adjusting my fingers. Again, it feels awkward, but steadier than it did before. It's bigger than my dagger and much heavier, but Art says it's a good size to start with.

'When you're defending yourself, you'll want to cross your body with your sword. Let's say the attack comes from above.' She poses my arm so the sword is above my head, parallel to the ground. 'Then they go for your left leg,' she continues, moving the sword across my torso until it's in front of my left leg and slightly to the side. 'Attacking from the outside will only push your opponent's weapon into you – hardly the desired effect.'

'You couldn't have told me this *before* you covered me in bruises?'

She smirks. 'I thought they would add a little more weight to the lesson. Shall we go again?'

'I suppose we have to,' I say with a sigh. 'You aren't going to teach me how to fight back?'

'Of course I will,' Artemisia says with a shrug. 'As soon as you get the hang of defending yourself. One step at a time.'

This time I manage to fend off a couple of hits before her sword thwacks my elbow hard enough to send a jolt of pain through my whole body. I drop my sword and it clatters to the ground.

'I get the feeling you're enjoying this,' I mutter, holding my sore elbow.

Artemisia doesn't deny it, and her eyes twinkle as she picks up my sword for me, passing it to me hilt first. 'My mother was not exactly a nurturing teacher. It was largely a matter of learning from my own errors.'

'Well, if your skills are any kind of testament, it works,' I say. 'You're one of the best fighters I've ever seen.'

It might be the first time I've made Artemisia smile in a way that seems completely genuine, not mocking or sarcastic or at someone else's misfortune. It's a small, brittle smile, almost shy, though that's never been a word I'd use to describe Art.

'My mother never really knew what to do with me,' she admits. 'I thought that if I could become good enough, strong enough, hard enough, she would be proud of me, though I think that possibility died when my brother did.'

Her brother, the one who died in the mines. The guard who murdered him was the first person Artemisia killed, though certainly not the last.

'I'm sorry,' I say.

She shrugs again, but her shoulders are tight and the movement looks sharp and violent. 'Around that time, I stopped wanting my mother's approval anyway, so we arrived at an impasse.' She frowns at me. 'Talking won't make you better, you know. We're going again.'

I'd rather keep her talking, but I lift my sword and fix my stance, even though my arm is starting to shake under the weight.

This time when she hits, there seems to be an extra dose of power behind it, and even though I block it, the force makes me take a step back. She doesn't give me a chance to recover, instead matching my step and swinging again, to my right hip this time. I block it, stumbling another step back, but my foot tangles up in the edge of the rug and I fall back to the ground, landing hard on my rear.

'Does it help?' I ask, scrambling back up to my feet. 'Hitting someone instead of talking?'

She only glowers at me. 'Would you like to try? If you fought half as well as you talked, we would actually be getting somewhere.'

I feel my face heat up. 'Queens are supposed to speak better than they fight,' I point out. 'One day, Astrea won't be at war and she'll need a leader.'

'Better you than me,' she says. 'Let's go again.'

I groan. 'I need a break and some water,' I say. 'Ten minutes.'

Artemisia purses her lips. 'Five,' she says, though mercifully she sets down her sword and sits on the sofa that has been pushed back against the wall.

I walk toward my basin and pour us each a cup of water. After I pass one to her, I sit next to her.

'Søren's being difficult.' The words force their way forward even though I don't really mean to say them. His confession in the garden is weighing so heavily on me, though, and there is no one else I can talk to about it. Blaise and Heron are out of the question and the idea of confiding in Dragonsbane is laughable. I take another sip of water and continue. 'I thought everything was all right between us, but yesterday he said he didn't want me to marry someone else because he still has feelings for me.'

Artemisia takes a long sip of her water, glaring at me over the rim of her cup.

'And?' she asks me when she's done, wiping away the droplets left on her top lip with her sleeve. 'Do you expect me to ask you how you feel about that? I can't stress how little I care about your feelings, Theo,' she says.

'I was only talking,' I say, trying to hide my hurt. 'It's what friends do.'

She gives a snort of laughter. 'We aren't that kind of friends,' she says before leveling a look at me, like she can see straight through to my heart. 'I'm not her, you know. I'm not your Kalovaxian friend.'

Artemisia knows Cress's name, but she won't say it out loud. I'm almost glad she doesn't, because I don't think

I'd be able to hold on to a neutral expression. Even now, I falter.

'I didn't say you were,' I tell her. 'I only meant—'

'The extent to which I care about Søren is limited to his use to me,' she says. 'If you want to talk about alliances he may have to other countries or intel he might possess about Kalovaxian battle strategy, I'm happy to hear it. But if you want to wax poetic about his muscles or his eyes or whatever nonsense you find handsome, I would recommend finding someone else. Or better yet, keep it to yourself. It makes you look like a weak sixteen-year-old girl, and that's hardly the image you want to be presenting to those who would look to you for leadership.'

Her words sting and burn through me. I set down my water cup and pick up my sword.

'Let's go again,' I tell her.

She smirks and gets to her feet, picking up her own sword.

I still lose, but this time I manage to get in a few sloppy hits of my own before she hits me hard on the shoulder.

'That's more like it,' she says with a satisfied nod. 'I'll have to irritate you more often.'

I snort. 'I'm not sure that's possible,' I say.

We are interrupted by a sharp knock on my door. I freeze, panic coursing through me, but Artemisia only laughs.

'Relax,' she says. 'We aren't in Astrea. We aren't doing anything wrong.'

I smile slightly. 'Still,' I say, 'I doubt sword fighting is King Etristo's idea of ladylike behavior.'

She shakes her head. 'Gods, I'm glad I don't have to be around him as often as you do. I think I'd kill him.'

She says it casually enough, but I can't help but wonder how serious she is.

'He must be in his eighties,' I tell her, crossing the room to answer the door. 'It wouldn't be a fair fight.'

I pull open the door to find an attendant waiting, dressed in a uniform in the King's colors of white and orange, which likely costs more than she makes in a year. Her eyes widen as she takes in my own outfit.

'Queen Theodosia?' she asks, flustered.

'Yes, that's me,' I say with a smile that I hope will put her at ease, but it seems to have the opposite effect.

She holds out a letter with shaking hands, her eyes dropping to stare at the floor.

'From His Highness, King Etristo,' she says.

'Thank you,' I say, taking the letter.

Before I can ask if there's anything else, she scurries back down the hall.

'Frightened little thing,' Artemisia says from behind me. I ignore her, opening the letter with my pinky nail. 'Well?' she presses.

I scan the letter quickly – it's quite short.

'"*Dear Queen Theodosya*" – he spelled my name wrong,' I say.

She shrugs. 'Probably not him; I'd imagine it was dictated.'

I know that it's a small thing and I shouldn't be annoyed, but my name was taken away from me for ten years. Now that it's mine again, seeing it butchered hurts more than I thought it would. I continue.

'"*Another suitor has arrived in hopes of wooing you. You will meet Chief Kapil of the Vecturian Isles at dinner tonight.*"'

'The Chief of Vecturia?' Artemisia asks, frowning. 'But he's got to be over a hundred. Maybe one of his sons?'

'It doesn't say that,' I tell her, wrinkling my nose. 'It sounds like it's the chief himself.'

Artemisia considers it for a moment. 'Well,' she says finally. 'I suppose it's a bit like the boy Prince, isn't it? I doubt the man is capable of consummating, so you might luck out there.' She manages it with a straight face but I can tell she's holding back laughter.

I take a small pillow off one of the sofas and throw it at her, but of course she nimbly ducks out of the way, laughing even harder.

'Not that it would do me much good anyway,' I say. 'Vecturia doesn't have the kind of resources to take on the Kalovaxians. Especially after the battle a few weeks ago, they can barely afford enough food, never mind armies.'

'The Chief must know that as well,' Artemisia points out. 'Why come all this way and pay that much when he doesn't stand a chance?'

'I don't know,' I admit. 'But I suppose I'm going to find out.'

MURDER

———◆·◆———

Marial had a difficult time covering the marks my practice with Artemisia left, but now they are barely visible, buried under so many creams and powders that my skin looks unnatural, like a painted doll's. It also itches terribly.

'Stop fidgeting,' Dragonsbane snaps as we walk down the hall toward the dining pavilion. 'And for gods' sake, try to control yourself around the Emperor.'

My cheeks grow warm. 'Erik is a friend.'

'A useless friend,' she counters. 'You would be better off spending your time making new ones.'

I force myself to swallow down a retort.

'What do you know of the Vecturian Chief?' I ask her, to change the subject.

She scoffs. 'He's a doddering old fool. You don't want to marry him.'

'I don't want to marry *anyone*,' I remind her. 'But I'll do what I must for Astrea.'

Dragonsbane glances sideways at me, a surprised smile tugging at her mouth. 'Good girl,' she says before pushing open the door to the pavilion.

She doesn't see the effect those two words have on me. She can't know that they were the same ones the Kaiser used to say to me when I did something he approved of. It isn't the same thing, I know, but it feels a bit similar.

I push the feeling aside and follow her into the candlelit pavilion, which looks much the same as it did the night before, with the artfully arranged sofas and chairs, the countless small pillows, the paper lanterns hanging from the cloth ceiling.

The suitors are in their usual places as well, but there are more of them now. Empress Giosetta is here tonight, sitting in a corner with a young girl with plaited hair. There are also a few of the red-haired Esstenian kings, bickering over who gets to drink the last bit of wine in the bottle, and going at it with so much ferocity that I worry it will come to blows. Erik and Hoa sit together on the other side of the room, both dressed in their traditional Gorakian robes, and a strange old man with copper skin, a bald head, and a hawklike nose sits alone near them in a loose brown chiton that looks similar to fashions in Astrea, but much simpler, without the ornamentation or color. Chief Kapil, I'd imagine. He's as old as Artemisia led me to believe, but he doesn't wear the years the same way King Etristo does. Though he must be at least a decade older, there's a spryness to his movements that the King doesn't possess.

All the suitors rise when they see me, even Chief Kapil, though he has to lean heavily on his cane to do so. The only one who doesn't stand is King Etristo, who is dozing in his chair. I pray to the gods that he doesn't wake before the end of the night. If I have to hear him call me *my dear* tonight, I just might snap at him.

'Please, be seated,' I say, smiling at each of them. 'Those of you who were here last night know that this is all rather casual – just an opportunity for us to get to know one another a little better to ensure our interests align.' I gesture to Dragonsbane. 'My aunt and I will be spending time with everyone, though there are quite a lot of you and there is only one of me, so it might take a while. Luckily, King Etristo was kind enough to offer what looks like a delicious spread of food and plenty of wine.'

King Etristo stirs for a second at the sound of his name before settling back into sleep. There's a bit of laughter at that, and Erik lifts his wineglass.

'Hear, hear,' he says to me.

'Shall we greet Chief Kapil first?' I ask Dragonsbane. 'He's the only one I haven't met.'

'No, no,' she says, waving a dismissive hand. 'We'll start with the more important ones. Come, let's say hello to the Empress.'

I follow her without complaint. Though I'd rather meet the Chief and find out why he came all this way, I'm also curious to speak more with Empress Giosetta.

When we make our way toward her, the Empress smiles and gets to her feet, the young girl standing a second later. They're wearing matching gowns of teal silk that drape elegantly over one shoulder, leaving the other bare in a style similar to that of Astrean gowns. But while Astrean gowns are loose and light, these are fitted more tightly and embellished so heavily they more closely resemble armor than gowns. The Empress's hair is down and loose in brown waves that have been threaded with jewels.

'Queen Theodosia,' she says to me with a curtsy that the girl tries to mimic. 'May I introduce you to my daughter and heir, Fabienne.'

I smile at the girl, who beams back at me. 'Lovely to meet you,' I tell her before introducing my aunt.

'I've been looking forward to speaking with another female ruler,' I tell the Empress once we're all seated.

She laughs. 'Yes, it is overwhelmingly male here, isn't it?' she asks. 'I think that's what would make us an excellent match. I daresay I respect you far more than anyone else here.'

'I don't doubt that,' I tell her. 'Though I do have questions.'

The Empress smiles. 'You would like to know if our partnership would be romantic in nature?' she guesses. I nod, glancing uncertainly at Fabienne, who doesn't seem fazed. 'Well, I myself am attracted to both men and women equally.'

'Oh,' I say. 'I . . . am not.'

'Pity,' she says. 'But I've never had trouble finding love and I would be more than happy to agree to a platonic partnership if it would suit you.'

I smile and nod, even though the truth of the matter is that even if she could be content with not bedding me, I doubt she would be as understanding if I asked to keep sole reign over Astrea.

Dragonsbane stands, claiming we need to visit with others, and I agree, saying polite goodbyes to Giosetta and Fabienne.

Dragonsbane surprises me. Instead of leading me toward Archduke Etmond or the Esstenian Kings or Czar Reymer, as I expect her to, she veers toward Chief Kapil. He looks as surprised as I feel when he sees us coming toward him. He makes an effort to reach for his cane to stand, but I stop him.

'Really, no need, Chief Kapil,' I say, sitting down across from him. 'I'm not very fond of curtsying, and I can do without another one.'

Relief is evident in his eyes as he takes hold of my hand, kissing the back of it.

'It is a pleasure to meet you, Queen Theodosia. I've heard enough about you that I feel as if we know one another already.'

There's that uncomfortable feeling again. He's heard so much about me yet I know nothing about him apart from his name. But unlike the others, he doesn't look at me with pity.

'You're a brave young woman,' he says, surprising me. 'And I understand that I owe you a debt of gratitude.'

It takes me a moment to understand what he's thanking me for – interfering when the Kalovaxians went to invade Vecturia.

'I'm only sorry I couldn't do more,' I tell him. 'I heard about the burning of your country's food stores. How are your people faring?'

His face darkens but he shakes his head. 'Vecturia has faced worse than a famine; she will survive it.'

Vecturia will survive it, maybe, but not all her people will. And Søren gave that order. I might have forgiven many of his sins, but some sins aren't mine to forgive.

'I wish there were something I could do,' I tell him.

'Pah,' he says, leaning against the back of the sofa. 'I am more concerned about what I can do for you.'

I swallow, wary of where this is going. He's old enough to be my grandfather, and an alliance with Vecturia wouldn't be enough to retake Astrea.

'I can't marry you,' I tell him as gently as I can.

He laughs quietly and pats my hand with his weathered, liver-spotted one. 'I know, Your Majesty,' he says. 'Not all of us old men seek child brides to recapture our lost youth. My youth was well spent but it's long gone now. I have no desire to rob you of yours.'

'Why are you here then?' Dragonsbane interrupts.

He doesn't look at her, all of his attention focused instead on me.

'I needed to meet you,' he says. 'I needed to look you in the eye and tell you how sorry I am that Vecturia didn't help Astrea when the Kalovaxians attacked. I will spend what is left of my life atoning for that mistake. I am grateful that you were braver and kinder than I was.'

'It was the right move, strategically,' I tell him, uncomfortable with the way he's looking at me, like I'm some sort of savior. I'm not.

'Then it was brave and kind and *wise* as well,' he says with a smile. 'I have no desire to marry you, Queen Theodosia, but you have an alliance with Vecturia nonetheless, if you so desire it. You have our armies, however meager they may be.'

I don't have to consult with Søren to know that they're meager indeed. Strong enough to beat a faction of Kalovaxian warriors while having the advantage of Vecturian soil, but not strong enough to stage an attack. Still, the gesture means more to me than I can put into words.

* * *

Chief Kapil takes his leave shortly after – his country can't afford for him to spend more than one night in Sta'Crivero. I'm sorry that he had to spend any amount of money for such a short conversation, but he won't hear any of that. We will be in touch, he promises, lifting my hand to his lips for a brief kiss.

I find that I am sad to see him go. When he does, I make my way toward Archduke Etmond, and Dragonsbane doesn't try to steer me elsewhere. She would approve of the match, I'm sure. Etralia is a wealthy country, with a strong military presence. That his company doesn't suffocate me is merely a bonus, I suppose.

'I was hoping to have a chance to speak with you tonight, Your Majesty,' Archduke Etmond says, his voice low. 'I'm afraid this whole ordeal is . . . well, it's trying for me and I'm sure it's doubly so for you.'

I smile slightly. 'It *is* overwhelming,' I admit.

His smile grows a little easier. 'My brother sent me here,' he admits. 'And I think he meant it as more of a prank than anything. I'm not . . . I've never been very good at talking to people, you know. And women . . .' He trails off, shaking his head. 'I'm sure he believes I will come back embarrassed and rejected.'

He doesn't say it like he's looking for pity. He's only stating a simple fact. Before I can say anything to soothe his mind, he continues.

'But . . . would I be right in surmising that you aren't looking for a romantic partner?' he asks.

Next to me, Dragonsbane goes still. I ignore her. Instead, I move closer to the Archduke.

'Yes,' I tell him. 'You are quite right. Though marriage seems to be the only way to take Astrea back, and so I will do what I must.'

For the first time since I met him, the Archduke holds my gaze, nodding once before he looks away. 'I believe that we can help each other,' he says, lowering his voice. 'You need an army to defeat the Kalovaxians. I have an army.'

'Your *brother* has an army,' Dragonsbane interjects.

The Archduke shakes his head. 'My brother wears the crown, but his army listens to me. He knows this as well as anyone; he is content with the arrangement. After all, we rarely have need for our army. We've fought no wars in years. I can get troops to fight for you.'

'How many?' I ask him.

'Enough,' he says.

I try to keep my expectations in check, but a stupid hope works its way into my chest anyway.

'And what would you need in return?' I ask him. 'Sovereignty over Astrea?'

He shakes his head. 'No, no. Nothing like that. The idea that I might inherit Etralia if my brother fails to produce an heir is horror enough. No. Several years ago, the Theyn came to visit Etralia and my brother gifted him my favorite chess set. Centuries old, carved from onyx and bone.'

I remember the chess set. I saw it often when I visited Crescentia; it was kept on a shelf like a decoration, never actually used.

'My brother gave it to him to spite me,' the Archduke continues. 'But I have always mourned the loss of it. I understand the Theyn is now dead.'

'You want your chess set back,' Dragonsbane says slowly, disbelief punctuating every word.

'A family heirloom,' he says. 'It is more precious to me than anything.' He straightens up, a shy smile tugging at the corner of his mouth. 'And besides, it's been many years since Etralia has fought a war. It sounds like it could pose quite an interesting challenge.'

I exchange a skeptical look with Dragonsbane before nodding. 'I think we can agree to that partnership,' I tell him.

He smiles broadly and motions to a serving girl carrying a bottle of wine. It's the same skittish girl who delivered the King's message earlier. She's even more ill at ease here, her hands shaking as she pours two glasses of rich red liquid. Dragonsbane waves her off before she pours a third, since her own glass is still half full. When the Archduke passes a glass to me, I force a smile. In truth, I know that I can't drink anything more. I haven't eaten all night because the dress is too restricting, and already I can feel the little wine I've had clouding my mind.

'To new friends,' Archduke Etmond says, lifting his glass toward me.

I lift my glass to meet his, but when he takes a sip, I only pretend to. It's all I can do not to get to my feet and shout with joy. I want to throw my wine in King Etristo's face and tell him exactly what I think of him. I want to dance until my feet bleed. For the first time in a long time, the hope in me is not a fragile thing. It is growing firmer, growing bolder.

I open my mouth to thank the Archduke, but before I can get the words out, a bewildered expression settles over his face. His hands rise to clutch at his throat and his eyes grow wide and panicked. He scrambles to his feet, knocking into our table and sending both of our glasses careening to the ground, then collapses beside them.

Everyone is on their feet but my mind is still a bewildered blur. Dragonsbane grabs my wrist, her fingers digging into my skin painfully as she pulls me away.

'Get back!' a voice calls, breaking through the panicked murmur. Coltania rushes toward him, moving surprisingly fast in her heavy dress. She drops gracelessly next to him, rolling him over onto his back and feeling his chest. 'He isn't breathing, I'm going to have to do it for him.'

She leans over the Archduke, fixing her lips to his in what looks at first like a kiss, but it isn't. Her cheeks puff up, then his do before she pulls back and does it again.

I wrench my arm out of Dragonsbane's grip and move toward him, horror coursing through me as the Archduke's skin takes on a purple tint. I feel like I'm walking through a dream, my mind unable to comprehend what is happening right before my eyes.

'Theo,' a voice says, cutting through the fog. Erik steps in front of me, blocking the Archduke from my sight. He grips my shoulders, giving me a gentle shake, but I barely feel it. I barely feel anything at all. 'Theo, you need to leave. It's poison and there may be more. The wine – did you drink it?

I find my voice. 'No,' I say, though I don't sound like myself. 'I didn't have any.'

Erik nods, looking relieved. 'We need to get you out of here until it's safe.'

I finally drag my eyes to his and realize what he is and isn't saying. Poison, but maybe not intended for the Archduke at all. He isn't the one with a million gold pieces on his head. He isn't the one the Kaiser wants dead or alive. Erik swallows, his eyes wide. We both know too well that the Kaiser always gets what he wants, sooner or later, and that no decree from King Etristo can stop him.

Without waiting for a response, Erik leads me out of the room and down the hall, leaving the panicked clamor behind us.

PROTECT

———— ✦ · ✦ ————

THE TRIP BACK TO MY room passes in a blur of shock. I don't even remember the ride in the riser. All I'm aware of is my erratic heartbeat thundering in my ears. By the time we reach my room, my mind is slowly coming back to me, like fingers of sunlight through a dense forest.

'He's dead, isn't he?' I ask Erik, though my voice sounds far away.

He lingers uncertainly in the doorway. 'Maybe the Chancellor's sister saved him,' he says, but I don't think either of us believes that. We both saw the Archduke's face turn purple, and Coltania said he wasn't breathing. When I saw the Kaiserin fall from the window after the Maskentanz, there was a stupid, hopeful part of me that believed she'd survived, up until I saw her face. But like trust, stupid hope is something I can't afford anymore.

It's only then that I realize how shaken Erik is as well. He's good at hiding it – I suppose he's seen death often enough on the battlefield. But this is different; the palace is supposed to be safe. If the Kaiser can get to me here, is there any place that is truly safe as long as he draws breath?

It might not be the Kaiser, though. The room was full of royals, each with their own conflicts and enemies. The poison wasn't necessarily for me. But even as I think that, the Kaiser's face looms large in my mind and I feel his hot, drunken breath on my skin. Five million gold pieces for me alive, but one million dead. One million is still plenty.

'I should stay a while, until we know the threat is contained,' Erik says. I wonder suddenly if he knows about the reward.

For a treacherous instant, I wonder if I can trust him, but I quickly banish the thought. If Erik was loyal to the Kaiser, he wouldn't have brought me back to my room. He would have taken advantage of the chaos and taken me out of Sta'Crivero. He would have taken the five million gold pieces.

I sink down onto the sofa, the stiff material of my gown crunching underneath me. 'I liked him,' I tell Erik. 'At least, I liked him better than the others. He was . . . awkward, but he was kind. He didn't look at me like I was a roast carved up on the table for him. And he just . . . he just offered me his army. No strings attached, no cut of the magic, no marriage, just a chess set of his the Theyn had.'

It's only after I say the words that I realize I am already using the past tense.

Erik shakes his head, dropping his gaze away from me. 'With the power of the Haptanian army, we could have wiped out the Kalovaxians in a month.'

A month. My heart lurches in my chest. In a month, I could have been back in Astrea, sitting on my mother's throne. In a month, my country would have been liberated and I would have made the Kaiser pay for everything he'd done to us.

Everything I've ever wanted was so close to being within my grasp, only to be yanked away.

I close my eyes, but there is no hiding the tears that come. I press the heels of my hands to my eyes and let the sobs rack through me.

You're crying about your own loss while a man lies dead, I chide myself. *You're just as self-centered as the Kaiser.* That only makes me cry harder.

Erik is at a loss – I imagine he hasn't seen many crying women during his training – but after a moment, he reaches out to pat my back awkwardly. Still, I'm grateful for his attempt.

Outside the door, footsteps thunder by, followed by panicked shouts. The entire palace must be in an uproar.

'Do you have a weapon?' Erik asks me, his voice low. He doesn't take his eyes off the door.

I nod, getting up and crossing to my bed. I'd wedged my dagger under the mattress, but now I draw it out, showing it to Erik, who eyes it appraisingly.

'Very pretty,' he says. 'Do you know how to use it?'

I think about my lessons earlier with Artemisia, but suddenly all that feels very far away. That was a different size blade and it wasn't even sharp. What little I did manage to learn in a single lesson suddenly seems useless – Erik is asking if I can defend myself if we're attacked. That's not sparring with dulled long blades, that's life and death.

'You should take it,' I tell him, passing it to him and retaking my seat on the sofa.

He turns the blade over in his hands, his fingers running over the filigreed handle.

'It's so delicate – I think I'm likely to snap it in half if I try to use it.'

My smile wobbles. 'It's stronger than it looks,' I say.

More footsteps echo in the hall outside but this time they don't pass. Erik is on his feet between me and the door, blade poised; the instant the door swings open, though, he steps aside.

Søren leads the charge into the room, with Blaise, Heron, and Artemisia at his heels. When they see me, they all let out a collective breath of relief.

'We heard someone was poisoned at dinner,' Blaise says, panting. 'We thought—'

He doesn't finish, but he doesn't have to.

'It was Archduke Etmond,' I say, recounting everything that happened.

Søren swallows, his eyes finding mine. 'That doesn't make sense,' he says quietly. 'Haptania doesn't have many enemies, and even if they did, murdering Etmond wouldn't do anyone much good. And if anyone did want him dead, they would have had an easier time doing it in Haptania, even during the months he spends in the barracks. Sta'Crivero's security is higher.'

'No one said anything about him being murdered,' Heron says, holding up his hands. 'We shouldn't jump to conclusions. It could have been from natural causes.'

'Or the poison was meant for Theo,' Artemisia says. 'She is the one with a price on her head.'

Erik frowns, looking from them back to me. 'Who are these people?' he asks me.

'Oh, right,' I say, realizing that Erik had never actually met

Heron, Art, or Blaise, though they've seen him from afar. I make quick introductions and explain what Erik is doing in Sta'Crivero.

'Poison is new to me,' Erik tells Heron when I'm done. 'But I know what I saw, and there was nothing natural about that death.'

Heron's eyes widen but he gives a solemn nod.

'And I can't imagine that it was intended for Etmond,' Søren says, looking at me. 'Artemisia is right. Of everyone in that room, you're the most likely target.'

'Everyone in that room is important in their country,' I say, though my voice shakes.

'Important, yes,' Artemisia says. 'But not in anyone's way, not disliked. No one else had serious threats made against them, let alone a bounty on their head.'

'We might not know who delivered the poison, but we know who gave the order,' Blaise says quietly.

Though I didn't eat anything at dinner, my stomach still flips and twists, my mind swimming in thoughts I won't – can't – entertain. I thought I was safe here, I thought I was finally beyond the Kaiser's reach, I thought he would never be able to touch me again. It was a foolish hope and now a man is dead because of it. Because of me.

It isn't until after midnight that a sharp, official knock sounds on the door. All of us have been too tense to talk, though Artemisia has insisted on making the most of this time and practicing some more. It's been especially fun, what with everyone watching and adding their own critiques of my posture and technique, but at least it distracts from my nerves.

At the sound of the knock, everyone goes on alert, their weapons drawn. Artemisia switches out her practice sword for her real one.

'Back corner of the room,' Blaise says to me, and I hurry to oblige, my heart pounding in my chest even though I realize, logically, that an assassin wouldn't bother knocking.

Sure enough, when Heron opens the door, it's only one of the King's guards. Even he looks on edge, though, eyes darting around the room as if expecting an attack to come at any moment.

'Queen Theodosia,' he says, looking at me. If he thinks it strange that I'm cowering in the corner, he doesn't show it. 'The threat has been secured. If you'll join King Etristo in the throne room, you can see the fiend for yourself.'

INTERROGATION

———◆———

THE GUARD LEADS ME INTO the throne room; Søren, Erik, and my Shadows follow at my heels. I must be growing jaded by all the Sta'Criveran opulence, because the room's frescoed walls, marble floors, and ornate gold chandeliers barely register in my mind. All I see is the throne at the center, so large and hulking that at first I don't even notice King Etristo's frail frame. He practically disappears into the plush velvet cushion.

I walk up the aisle between the rows of seats, feeling the suitors' eyes on me as I pass. We must be the last ones here, because every seat in the audience chamber is filled, apart from a few chairs in the front and one with the Gorakian delegation that Erik takes. What are these people looking for? Grief? Fear? Though I feel both of those things, I am mostly just numb. They all look wary and suspicious, as if whoever poisoned the archduke is sitting right beside them. A terrifying thought that I try to dismiss.

The guard escorts us to the front row of chairs and we take them, Søren on one side of me, Artemisia on the other.

'There you are, my dear,' King Etristo says with his usual

condescending smile. He sits up a little straighter in his throne. 'I'm happy to say that we caught the person responsible for the Archduke's murder.'

Murder. So he *is* dead. What scrap of hope I'd been clinging to shrivels and dies. I didn't know him well enough to truly mourn him, not after everyone else who has been taken from me, but I still feel his death like a sharp jab between my ribs. Though I hate myself for it, I mourn the loss of his promise more. I mourn how close I came to reclaiming Astrea, only to have it snatched away once again.

'Who was responsible?' I ask

King Etristo claps his hands twice. A different guard enters through the door behind the throne, escorting a girl in manacles. It takes a moment for me to recognize her as the attendant from earlier, the fearful one who delivered my letter just this afternoon, who poured the wine for the Archduke and me. Her eyes are even more terrified now, rapidly roving across the room, looking for a friendly face. She doesn't find one.

I clear my throat and look back at King Etristo. 'Of course I trust your judgment, Your Highness, but what ill will could this girl bear toward the Archduke?'

The King's smile is grim. 'That, my dear, is precisely what we're here to find out.' He turns to where Chancellor Marzen and his sister are sitting. '*Salla* Coltania,' he says. 'I understand you've brought us truth serum from Oriana.'

Coltania stands up from her place beside her brother in the row behind me. Her face is pale and her expression drawn tight. 'Yes, Your Highness,' she says, voice wavering. 'We always keep it on hand while traveling, in case we need to discover if any strangers mean us harm. Of course, we never expected something like this.'

'None of us did, my dear,' he says with a sigh before gesturing her forward. 'I'll leave it to you to administer, as you are the professional.'

Coltania steps toward the attendant girl with a vial in hand, and the girl immediately begins fighting against the guard holding her bound hands – as if there's any way she can flee. Unbidden, I think of Elpis in a similar situation. Elpis didn't deserve what was in that vial, though, and this girl does. It won't kill her, only bring forth the truth. Why would she fight so hard if she has nothing to hide?

Coltania forces the potion down her throat and the fight leaves the girl's body. She slumps back against the guard holding her, blinking uncertainly.

'It will take a minute to work,' Coltania says to King Etristo.

If it truly is only a minute, it stretches on for what feels like an eternity. Finally, Coltania speaks again, this time to the girl.

'Please state your name,' she says.

The girl swallows, looking like she's coming out of a daze. 'Rania,' she says quietly.

Coltania inspects the girl's pupils and measures the pulse at her wrist before nodding to King Etristo. 'You may proceed,' she says.

King Etristo leans forward, eyes on the girl. 'Did you poison the Archduke's food?' he asks her.

'No,' she says, sounding dreamy and faraway, like she's on the other side of a glass wall. 'I poisoned the wine.'

A murmur goes through everyone gathered, even my Shadows. After all, I drank the wine – everyone did.

'With what?' King Etristo asks.

The girl's eyes dart around the room before landing on the King once again, struggling to remain focused. 'With poison,' she says, sounding confused. 'I don't know what kind, it's what I was given.'

'Given by whom?' King Etristo asks.

She swallows. The truth serum makes her wobbly on her feet and she lurches side to side, steadied by the guard. 'The Kaiser,' she says. 'The Kaiser sent it, with payment.'

More murmurs, but this time I'm numb to them. It's no more than I expected, but hearing her confirmation feels like all of the air has been sucked out of the room. I almost don't hear what she says next.

'He won't stop,' she says, voice beginning to slur. 'He won't stop until she's dead.' She lifts her manacled hands and points to me.

The ground drops out beneath me and I almost fall out of my chair, but Artemisia's hand on my arm anchors me.

The girl sways harder on her feet until the guard is struggling to keep her standing. Her head lolls from side to side.

King Etristo looks to Coltania. 'Is this normal?' he asks her.

Coltania is bewildered. She steps toward the girl and grabs her forcefully by the chin, wrenching her jaw open. The words she mutters under her breath aren't ones I can translate, though I'm sure they're curses.

'Her tongue is black. Spit!' she commands, her voice sharp. The girl blinks in confusion before doing as she's told and spitting on the ground. The spit is tar black but there is something else there as well. Coltania crouches down, touching the spit and rubbing a bit of it between her fingers. She holds it up close to her eye.

'Shards of glass,' Coltania says, wiping the spit on the hem of her dress. She looks up at King Etristo. 'A poison pill she must have had in her mouth since before you arrested her. Given to her to take if she was questioned,' she explains to him.

Then why did she only just take it? Why didn't she take it as soon as the guards arrested her?

Before I can follow that line of thought, King Etristo's voice pierces the air in a panicked shout. 'What are you waiting for? Save her.'

Coltania looks at the girl and shakes her head sadly. 'I can't,' she says. 'She was dead the moment she broke the capsule. There's no cure for deathdrake. She only has a moment left and she won't be lucid for it. There's nothing to do but let it take her.'

Black foam begins pouring out of the girl's mouth and she sags against the guard, tremors rocking through her. I wish I could ask her why she did it, if it was just the money or if there was malice there as well. I wish I could understand what new game the Kaiser is playing from his throne across the ocean. But the life is already leaving her eyes and I can't watch another person die.

I say a silent prayer to the gods and get to my feet, my advisors following a second later. I start to make my way out of the room, but King Etristo's voice stops me.

'Just a moment, my dear,' he says, though there is no

cloying sweetness to his voice now. Instead he sounds angry and panicked, like a cornered animal. Distantly, I know that is what makes him dangerous, but I force myself to turn back toward him.

'Yes, Your Highness?' I say.

Instead of responding, the King leans down toward his guards and murmurs something I can't make out, gesturing toward me before getting to his feet. As he exits the throne room, the guards come toward us. I notice only an instant too late that they draw their weapons.

'Prinz Søren, by the order of King Etristo you are under arrest for the murder of Archduke Etmond.'

Without thinking about their drawn weapons or the suitors still present, I step between the approaching guards and a shell-shocked Søren.

'Prinz Søren was not responsible for the poisoning of the Archduke,' I say, enunciating each word carefully so that the entire throne room can hear me. 'If Søren wanted to kill me, he's had plenty of opportunities to do so,' I say. 'He wouldn't use something as cowardly as poison, and if he *had,* I'm sure he'd have succeeded in properly killing me.'

It hardly feels like a solid defense, even to my own ears.

'I'll go willingly,' Søren says quietly, his hand coming to rest on my shoulder. 'I did nothing wrong and I'm sure King Etristo will see that.'

He moves to step toward the guards, both his hands held up and clearly visible. Before I know what I'm doing, I reach out and grab his hand, forcing him to turn back to face me. It's only then that I remember that we are not alone and that there are a dozen suitors watching who will read far too much into one simple touch. I pull my hand away quickly and let it fall to my side.

'We'll get you out,' I tell him quietly. 'I did it once, I'll do it again.'

Søren's smile is brittle, but he at least pretends to believe me as the guards clap bejeweled manacles onto his wrists and drag him away.

ARREST

———◆•◆———

'HE IS PART OF MY council,' I tell King Etristo, struggling to get the words past my clenched teeth. 'When you promised me protection, I was under the impression that that protection applied to my entire party.'

From his place behind his large marble desk, King Etristo barely spares me a glance. He gives a beleaguered sigh and rolls his eyes skyward. It's hardly respectful, but he doesn't see me as an equal so much as he sees me as female body who speaks far more than strictly necessary. He wouldn't even meet with me until after he'd had breakfast, which means Søren has been stuck in a Sta'Criveran prison for eight hours.

'As I have explained several times already, my dear, I cannot guarantee the safety of those who break Sta'Crivero's laws. Do you not consider murder against the law in Astrea?'

Warmth seeps through my skin until my hands begin to feel hot. I ball them into fists at my sides, though that does little to smother the heat. The warmth coursing through my veins grows hotter every time he says the words *my dear*. I force myself to take deep breaths. Nothing like the singed sheets has happened since we left the ship – only the occasional heat in my hands and arms – and I can almost convince myself I imagined the whole thing, but at times like this I know I didn't. I feel the fire inside me and I know that if it gets out now . . . I can't let it.

'Of course we do,' I say, forcing my voice to stay calm and level. I look to Heron, Blaise, and Artemisia standing behind me before turning back to the King. 'But such a serious accusation requires proof and you have provided none apart from his bloodline. If that is a good enough reason to imprison someone, I'm surprised your prisons aren't overflowing.'

King Etristo steeples his fingers atop his desk and the sheaf of papers that I suspect he was only pretending to read to avoid me. 'As we speak, *Salla* Coltania is instructing my apothecaries in how to make another draught of truth serum. I understand the process can take some time,' he says. 'If that clears his name, I will release him with my humblest apologies, but one can't be too careful with your safety, my dear. Especially since, as I understand it, he was spending quite a few nights in your bedroom.'

The implication in his voice makes me blush and I'm glad my Shadows are the only ones who hear him, though I'm sure that bit of gossip has already taken root, no doubt helped along by my own actions in the throne room. I stepped between Søren and the armed guards, after all.

'Two nights,' I say before gesturing to my three Shadows. 'Along with the rest of my advisors. If he'd truly wanted me dead, there would have been no easier time for him to accomplish it than when I was asleep.'

The corners of the King's mouth pull down into a deep

frown, and he finally looks at me. 'Well, then *Salla* Coltania's potion should clear him of all charges and he will be let go in just a few days,' he says, as if speaking to an irritating child.

I want to scream, but instead I force a smile. 'Very well,' I say tightly. 'But since Prinz Søren was my trusted advisor on matters of international affairs, I can't in good conscience meet with any suitors until he is free to advise me. You understand, of course? I must protect my interests.'

King Etristo looks like he wishes he could strike me, but after a second, a pleasant mask falls into place.

'If you insist, my dear,' he says. 'Though I worry your lack of trust will be seen as a slight.'

The men who would demand proof of my virginity, slighted because I don't trust them. I could laugh at the irony if I weren't so angry.

'No slight intended, of course,' I say sweetly. 'In the meantime, I would like to be able to visit Prinz Søren in the dungeon at my leisure to ensure that he's being treated fairly.'

King Etristo's expression turns icy once more.

'My dear, now *I* am beginning to feel slighted by your lack of trust.'

I keep my smile pasted on. 'Again, not my intention, Your Highness. But I do think it's necessary for my peace of mind.'

King Etristo grits his teeth, but after what feels like an eternity, he nods. 'Very well.'

I dip into a shallow curtsy before turning and walking out of the room, my Shadows at my heels.

* * *

Artemisia, Heron, Blaise, and I barely have time to settle back into my room before Dragonsbane thunders in, her expression a storm cloud. For a moment, I think she's angry about Søren being arrested, but of course that's ridiculous. If she had her way, he'd still be in the brig of the *Smoke*.

'You shouldn't seek an audience with the King without me present,' she snaps. 'Do you have any idea how foolish you've made yourself look?'

I let the venom in her voice roll off my back.

'The King arrested my advisor and I handled it,' I say coolly. 'I daresay I got further than you would have, since you do little more than jump when he tells you to.'

She reels back as though she's been slapped. For a moment she looks like she wants to skin me alive right here, but I hold my ground.

'I have Astrea's best interests at heart,' she tells me. 'And it is in Astrea's best interests not to insult the most powerful ally we have.'

I can't help but snort. 'He isn't an ally,' I say. 'If he was, he would give us troops himself. He merely sides with whoever can get him the most money. If the Kaiser was willing to pay enough, he'd turn on us in an instant. Right now, my marriage dowry is worth more, so I have some power. I'm going to use that as best I can, and if you don't do the same, *you're* the fool.'

'Theo,' Artemisia whispers, a warning I don't heed.

Dragonsbane's eyes are full of ice-cold fury. 'Leave us,' she says to my Shadows, her voice barely louder than a hiss.

'We stay with the Queen,' Heron tells her firmly.

I meet Dragonsbane's stare without flinching. I'd like

nothing better than to keep my Shadows close right now, but I have a feeling what Dragonsbane has to say isn't anything I want anyone else to hear.

'Go on,' I say. 'This won't take long.'

'Theo . . . ,' Blaise cautions.

'Go,' I repeat.

My Shadows exchange wary looks, but they file out, leaving me alone with Dragonsbane. I would be lying if I said I didn't fear her still, but I'm careful not to let it show – she can sense fear and she preys on it.

'The Kaiser made an attempt on my life,' I say, crossing my arms over my chest. 'Here, where King Etristo promised me safety. A man is dead because he underestimated the Kaiser's reach, and instead of looking for the Kaiser's real agent, he's arrested Søren. Meanwhile, whoever actually gave that girl the poison is still out there, and it's only a matter of time before they strike again. I'm not safe here.'

'No,' she says, voice level. 'You aren't safe here. But you don't want to be safe.'

At that, I can't hold back a laugh, but even I am surprised at how biting it comes out. 'Are you saying I *want* to be murdered?'

Her expression remains placid. 'I'm saying,' she says slowly, 'that you want to be a queen, and that is not a safe role to play.'

'I don't *want* to be a queen. I *am* a queen,' I correct her. 'And that is a fact that you seem to forget unless you can use it to your advantage.'

Now it's her turn to laugh. 'Queen of a country that doesn't exist anymore,' she says. 'A queen without a crown, without a throne, without a coronation. What, exactly, do you imagine you're queen of? Three silly subjects who follow you like a mother duck because a man told them you were special and they were silly enough to believe it?'

I stumble back a step, but she isn't done.

'I'm trying to help you, but you're too stubborn and self-important to understand that,' she says, her voice rising. 'Gods, you're just like your mother.'

It isn't the first time someone's said that to me, but it's the first time it's been an insult.

'Don't talk about my mother!' I don't realize I've shouted until I see the look of surprise on her face and her eyes dart warily to the door. 'My mother was fifty times the person you are,' I continue, careful to keep my voice low.

She looks at me for a long moment before letting out a sharp bark of laughter and crossing to the wine cabinet. She spends a quiet moment picking out a bottle and uncorking it and pouring herself a glass, filled nearly to the brim. She takes a long swig, draining nearly a quarter of it, then looks back at me.

'You aren't the first person to say that, you know,' she says. 'Maybe not *fifty times,* exactly, that's a bit dramatic, but the same sort of thing. *"Stand straighter, like Eirene." "Smile like Eirene." "Why can't you be more like Eirene?"* I don't think a day went by when I didn't hear it at least once. It got to be where the sound of her name felt like someone was hammering a nail into the base of my skull.'

She pauses to take another drink, but I've heard enough.

'It wasn't her fault you were jealous,' I say.

But that only makes her laugh again. 'Of course I was

jealous. But no more so than she was of me. *"Kallistrade,"* she'd say, *"you're so lucky you don't have to take decorum lessons."* And *"I wish I didn't have to get up at sunrise to greet the Guardians with mother."* And *"Why can't I spend the afternoon riding horses like you do?"* She asked me to switch places with her often enough, but I never wanted to. I didn't want to be crown princess any more than she did.'

'That's a lie,' I say. 'My mother loved being Queen.'

Dragonsbane shrugs. 'I wouldn't know about that,' she says. 'I left before she was crowned and I never went back, but she certainly didn't care for the training.' She takes another drink, a smaller one this time, before looking at me thoughtfully. 'You're lucky that you didn't really know her.'

Her words feel like cold water down my back. 'Did you just say that I'm lucky my mother died?'

'I didn't say that,' Dragonsbane says, rolling her eyes. 'But it's nice, in a way, to have her preserved so purely in your memory – a perfect mother and a perfect queen, brilliant and kind and valiant. She's practically a goddess in your mind, isn't she? I suppose all girls must feel that way about their mothers at one point. There's always a moment, though, when that illusion of perfection shatters and you realize that your mother is just a person, same as you, flawed, with her own vices and blind spots. You'll never have that epiphany, and yes, I do think you're lucky for that. In a way.'

For an instant, she looks so heartbroken that I'm not sure whether to slap her or apologize, but as quickly as that sliver of vulnerability appears, it's gone once more, sealed away behind her hard, impenetrable eyes.

'Your mother was a fine queen, from what I heard,' she

says. 'She did her duties without complaint and she was well liked, but she will always be the queen who lost Astrea.'

'That wasn't her fault,' I protest. 'She couldn't have known the Kalovaxians were coming.'

For the first time, Dragonsbane falters, hesitating just long enough that I can see a choice weighing behind her eyes, before she steels herself.

'She did,' she says slowly. 'I sent her a letter months before the attack, warning her that they were coming.'

'You're lying,' I say, but my stomach sinks. I don't want to hear this, but I can't bring myself to walk away either.

She ignores me and continues. 'She called me a liar,' she says. 'Said I was an embarrassment, sailing around and calling myself a pirate.'

I have a bevy of insults I want to throw at her, denials that I'm aching to say, but none of them makes it to my lips. I have to remind myself to breathe.

After a moment, her expression softens just a touch. 'Perhaps I should have let you go the rest of your life with that pure, uncorrupted view of her in your mind.'

'I don't believe you,' I say, even though a small part of me does. She has no reason to lie about it, after all.

Dragonsbane takes another drink. 'I loved my sister fiercely, all illusions to the contrary aside. She was my complete opposite, and also the other half of me. But she was a flawed woman.'

She pauses, finishing off her wine before looking at me with clear eyes, frightening in their ferocity. I don't let myself flinch away from her.

'Your mother was a mediocre queen,' Dragonsbane says

quietly. 'You could be a great one. If I didn't believe that, I wouldn't be here. But it isn't something that will come easily. It will not come fairly. It will not come without sacrifices and I'm tired of being treated like your enemy for pointing that out. If you won't give up everything for Astrea – your pride, your independence, your friends – you will never take her back.'

When I say nothing, she sets her empty glass down on the credenza and walks toward the door. Hand on the knob, she pauses.

'All humans make mistakes, and your mother was no exception. She loved you dearly and she loved Astrea, and I believe she thought she was doing the right thing. She was human, no more and no less.'

DREAM

———◆•◆———

FOR THE FIRST TIME SINCE leaving Astrea, my dreams aren't haunted by Cress's ashen face. Instead, I see my mother, but not as I remember her. I see her as she would be now, with the same creases around her eyes and mouth that Dragonsbane has. Her hair isn't the same vibrant auburn that it used to be, though it hasn't turned gray. It's simply faded, pulled over her shoulder in a single long braid. On top of her head is her crown, only it isn't really her crown at all – it's one of the ash crowns the Kaiser used to make me wear. Though she sits still, ash flakes down onto her white chiton.

She looks at me with sad, heavy eyes, but when she speaks it's with Dragonsbane's voice.

'I'm sorry,' she says. I wait for her to say more, to explain to me why she ignored her sister's warning and let the Kalovaxians take us, how – with one decision – she let Astrea fall to ruin. How she so easily handed me over to a man who made my life a terror for a decade.

But it's only a dream and she can't have answers that I don't already know, so all she does is apologize and apologize and apologize until I finally wake up, my mouth tasting of ash.

The sky outside my window is still dark, lit only by stars and a sliver of a moon, but I know I won't be able to sleep again tonight. My mind is still whirring, repeating Dragonsbane's words about my mother over and over again.

Artemisia is fast asleep on the other side of the bed – though it's so big she doesn't even stir when I slip out, carefully tiptoeing around Heron's large form that doesn't quite fit on the sofa. He refused both Art and me when we offered to switch with him. Blaise must have gotten restless and gone back to his own room at some point.

I remember falling asleep with all of them around me. There was never a conversation about whether or not they should stay. Whoever is actually working for the Kaiser is still on the loose and I don't think any of us trust the Sta'Criveran guards.

I should wake one of them up – especially since someone tried to kill me last night – but it doesn't seem right to force them up at this hour just because I can't sleep.

Besides, I don't want any of them with me when I visit Søren.

Quietly as I can, I pull on a dressing gown and take my dagger from its place on my bedside table, wedging it between the gown and the sash around my waist. I step into the slippers next to my bed and tiptoe out the door, closing it behind me with barely more noise than an exhale.

Still, even with my dagger, I shouldn't go alone – especially since I doubt I could do much more with it than wave it around and try to look menacing. Even just walking down the hallway, I find myself on edge, glancing behind me every few minutes as if another assassin is going to spring from the shadows. One very well could.

This was a stupid idea, but even as I acknowledge that fact, I can't bring myself to turn around. I make it to the riser and step inside, relieved to be near another person.

As far as I know, *he* could be an assassin. If he is, though, he's in no hurry. He stares at me blankly, waiting for a destination.

'Fifteen, please,' I say, naming the floor Erik directed me to before, where the Gorakian delegation has been housed.

He nods curtly and begins to crank, sending us gliding down. As smooth as the journey is, I still can't help but grip the bars of the riser wall behind me. No matter how many times I do this, I don't think I'll ever grow used to it. Luckily, it's only a moment before we pull to a sharp stop and he opens the door.

As soon as I'm out, he closes the door again and the riser lowers away, leaving me alone in a dark hallway, lit only by moonlight filtering in through the windows. Ahead of me, the hall is lined with doors on either side, but I have no idea which one is Erik's. Though I visited Hoa here, it was an entirely different place then, bustling with life and people who directed my way. Now I don't even know how to begin to guess which room is which.

I walk slowly down the hall, hoping for some kind of sign, but each oak door is exactly the same. Even the designs carved into them and the cut-crystal doorknobs are identical. Being alone again is beginning to make the hair on the back of my neck stand on end. If an assassin wanted to attack, this would be the perfect moment – they could do the job without any trouble and then blame it on the Gorakians, who don't seem to have many friends in Sta'Crivero to begin with.

Tilting my head, I look at the doorjambs for light bleeding out, a sign that someone inside is awake. It's well past midnight, so most of them are dark, but eventually I find one that isn't and knock softly.

There's a long pause before footsteps thud softly toward me and the door creaks open. A small, wiry Gorakian man appears, with a gleaming bald head and round spectacles perched on the end of his hooked nose. He peers at me irritably, his forehead heavily creased. He might not be happy with me for interrupting whatever he was doing, but at least there is very little chance of him being an assassin.

'I . . . I'm sorry to bother you,' I tell him. 'I'm looking for Eri – I mean, the Emperor. Which room is he staying in?'

He frowns and I realize that he doesn't understand Astrean. I open my mouth to repeat myself in Kalovaxian since he'll probably understand that after living through the Kalovaxians' occupation, but he speaks first.

'Emperor,' he repeats.

Relief courses through me and I nod.

The man leans out the door and points down the hall away from the riser, but there are too many doors for me to make out which one he's pointing to. He must realize this as well, because with a labored sigh he shuffles out of his room and leads me to the door he means, knocking much louder and longer than I would have. I suppose it's a good thing, though, because it's a few moments before Erik finally answers the door, eyes half-hooded with sleep. He blinks blearily at us for a moment, as if trying to make sense of the picture before him.

'Tho – Queen Theodosia?' he asks in Kalovaxian. 'Master Jurou? What's happening?'

The man – Master Jurou – frowns and launches into fast Gorakian that I can't make out a word of. I don't think Erik can either, because all he does is stare at Master Jurou and wait for him to finish. When he does, he looks at Erik, waiting for a response Erik has no idea how to give. Master Jurou realizes this and gives a loud harrumph before stalking back to his room and closing the door with a slam.

Erik winces at the loud noise. 'I see you've met Master Jurou,' he says.

'I didn't know which room was yours,' I admit. 'Who is he?'

He opens his mouth to answer before closing it and frowning, considering the question. 'He's . . . an alchemist,' he says. 'Best in Goraki, even before the siege. If we're being honest, I'm not entirely sure what he does, but everyone seems to think it's very important. As you can see, I don't speak Gorakian, though my mother's doing her best to remedy that. Something to do with gold, I think.' His frown deepens and he shakes his head, eyes refocusing on me.

'What are you doing here, Theo? It's the middle of the night.'

'I couldn't sleep,' I tell him.

'And you decided to share your misery with me? Very thoughtful, but I wish you wouldn't have,' he says, yawning around the last couple of words.

'I want to go visit Søren,' I say. 'And since the Kaiser has a bounty on my head, I don't think it's wise for me to go down to the dungeon alone.'

'Not unarmed, though,' he notes, nodding toward the dagger at my hip.

'More for show than anything,' I admit. 'You saw me yesterday – I'm more likely to hurt myself if I try to wield it.'

'Fair enough,' he says with a sigh. 'Let me grab my sword and we'll go together. I wouldn't mind seeing Søren myself.' He ducks back inside, but before the door closes behind him I hear him mutter, 'Though I'd rather we'd waited until daylight to do it.'

DUNGEON

———— ◆ • ◆ ————

T HE DUNGEON BELOW THE STA'CRIVERAN palace is the kind
of place that doesn't get many visitors – in fact, it has
the feel of a place that one doesn't enter expecting to leave
again. The riser operator balked when Erik and I asked him
to take us down here, but when I told him the King had given
me permission he begrudgingly acquiesced, though as soon as
he dropped us off he couldn't leave fast enough, whirring off
back to the surface before the doors had even closed behind us.

'Hardly inspires confidence,' Erik murmurs, looking
around the dim hall, lit only by rows of small sconces. The air
down here is stuffy and rancid, making me nauseous. I don't
want to put a name to whatever that smell is. It doesn't smell
like it's coming from anything – or anyone – alive.

We follow the hallway until we reach an iron gate that
stretches from ceiling to floor, wall to wall. Leaning against
it on our side is a young Sta'Criveran man who looks half-
asleep. When he hears us approach, though, he bolts upright,
eyes widening in surprise. He looks about twenty, but his skin
is sallow and there are dark circles under his eyes. I wonder
when he was last above ground.

'What are you doing here?' the man asks, flustered, before swallowing and trying again. 'I mean, how can I help you?'

'We're here to visit Prinz Søren. King Etristo has given me permission to visit at my leisure.'

He frowns, looking bewildered. 'But it's the middle of the night,' he says.

I shrug. 'Such is my leisure,' I say. 'My name is Queen Theodosia and I would like the prisoner brought to a secure, separate room away from other prisoners. Has he eaten?'

'I . . . yes, Your Majesty,' he says.

'I'm glad to hear it,' I say. 'He can be a bit stubborn about that sort of thing. Is there a room like the one I described?'

'Prinz Søren is being held in a solitary cell,' he says. 'It's quite comfortable – for a cell, I mean. Certainly better than anything else down here, and far from the other prisoners.'

'That sounds like it will do nicely,' I tell him with a smile. 'What's your name?'

'Tizoli,' the man says before hastening to bow. When he's done, he turns to the gate, fumbling with the ring of keys hooked onto his belt. It takes a couple of tries, but he finally unlocks the door and leads us through.

Søren's cell is a little bigger than the brig on the *Smoke* and at least thrice the size of the cell I had back in Astrea. Unlike on the *Smoke,* he isn't cuffed, so he can stand and walk and do whatever he likes within its walls. Unfortunately, what he wants to do is sleep, which he does quite soundly, curled up in the corner with his face turned away from us.

'Søren!' I shout through the bars of the door for what

feels like the hundredth time, but he still doesn't move. I turn toward Tizoli, who's lingering behind us, unsure whether he should stay or go. 'Is he well?'

'I . . . er . . . I think so, Your Majesty,' he says, looking around nervously.

'He's fine,' Erik says. 'He could sleep through a hurricane – has, in fact.' He cups his hands around his mouth and bellows Søren's name so loudly that I have to cover my ears. Søren, though, only rolls over, burrowing closer to the wall.

'If you could just open the door for a moment, we could nudge him awake and come right back out,' I say to Tizoli, but he shakes his head again, just as he has every time I've asked him since we came down here ten minutes ago – it must be at least five times by now.

Erik takes a deep breath, preparing to yell again, but I cut him off by grabbing hold of the button on the sleeve of his cloak and yanking it off in one sharp tug.

'What did you do that for?' Erik demands, looking at his torn jacket in disbelief. 'That was brand-new – my mother is going to kill me.'

I ignore him and step right up to the bars and reach my arm through, clutching the button tight in my hand. I throw the button as hard as I can at Søren's head, hitting him square in the middle of the forehead. It was a small button, but it was enough. Søren's hand flies up to belatedly swat it away before his eyes crinkle open and he stares at us sleepily.

'Finally,' I say. 'You sleep like the dead.'

Søren pulls himself up to sit, still looking dazed. 'I think I'm still sleeping,' he admits. 'What are you doing here? And what time is it?'

'Nearly dawn, I'd guess,' I say before turning to Tizoli. 'Would you mind giving us some privacy?' I ask him. 'We'll come get you when we're done.'

Tizoli hesitates but after a moment he nods and goes back down the hallway. I listen to his footsteps fade before speaking again.

'Quite the reversal of fortunes,' I say to Søren, smiling even though there's nothing funny about any of this.

Søren smiles back, though it looks halfhearted. 'Are you here to rescue me, Theo?' he asks wryly.

I shake my head. 'They're brewing up a truth serum for you, so as soon as they give you that, you should be in the clear. King Etristo said it could take some time, though.'

Søren nods but he looks unconvinced. 'Any clue who actually *is* working for my father?'

'None,' Erik says, his voice heavy. 'It could quite literally be anyone. Hell, if they knew we shared a bloodline, I would probably be down here with you.'

'Yes, let's keep that secret,' I say before sighing. 'I got a reprieve from the suitors, at least. I said I couldn't meet with anyone unless you were present to advise me.'

Søren snorts. 'I'm sure your aunt is pleased about that,' he says.

He means it as a joke, but the mention of Dragonsbane is like sandpaper against my skin and Søren must see me cringe.

'What is it?' he asks.

I hesitate. 'I have a question about the Astrean siege.' I take a deep breath and consider not asking at all. Maybe I don't want to know the answer. 'If we'd been warned that you were coming, what would have happened? Would it have been like Vecturia? Would you have turned around?'

Søren frowns, thinking it over for so long I start to worry he'll never answer, but finally he shakes his head. 'Maybe it would have lasted longer. Maybe it would have turned into a war instead of a siege, but we still would have outmatched you. Astrea wasn't prepared for an attack like that – they'd never had to face one before. I'm sorry if that's not the answer you were looking for.'

'It is, actually,' I say. 'But it still doesn't make me feel any better.'

What Dragonsbane said pours out of me, and for their part, Erik and Søren listen.

When I finish, my words are barely louder than a whisper. 'I've always imagined my mother as a perfect queen, but that image has been ruined and I don't know how to get it back.'

Erik and Søren exchange a look, but it's Erik who finally speaks.

'Well, our father is the Kaiser,' he says slowly. 'We don't have much experience with shattered illusions of parental figures.'

'But was there ever a time when you admired him?' I ask, looking between them.

They're both quiet.

'No,' Søren says finally. 'Even before I understood what he was doing to other people, I knew what he was doing to my mother. I don't remember a single kind word. I do remember her cowering in fear every time he approached her and wincing whenever he addressed her, like she'd been slapped. I saw my father as a monster from the very start – I just didn't realize how wide his reach was.'

Erik clears his throat. 'I think there was a time I aspired to be like him,' he admits. 'It wasn't for very long, yet it was there. He never acknowledged me as his son or even spoke to me, but it was no secret. I knew. And as a child, I thought that if I were bigger, if I were stronger, if I were better, he would love me. I hated you,' he tells Søren.

Søren frowns. 'You did? I didn't know that.'

Erik shrugs, glancing away. The light is too dim to say for sure, but I think his cheeks redden. 'I didn't know you then – only from a distance. You were just this boy who had everything I wanted so desperately, and you didn't seem to appreciate it at all. Of course I hated you. But when we apprenticed together and became friends, I understood. I think that was when my illusions were shattered, though that's a different sort of thing.'

'No, I think I understand,' I tell him. 'Thank you.'

Søren heaves a heavy sigh. 'So, will you go back to the camp now that you don't have to worry about suitors for a few days?'

'I suppose so,' I say, though the idea fills me with both excitement and dread. I loved helping out there and talking to other Astreans, but the guilt was almost unbearable – how can I sit in King Etristo's palace, eating sumptuous dishes until my stomach feels like it will burst, wearing dresses that cost a fortune each, while all of them are dirty and starving and sick? But, of course, I have to go. If I don't do everything I can to help them, I'll never forgive myself. I certainly couldn't call myself their Queen.

An idea occurs to me and I turn to Erik. 'You should come, too,' I say. 'There are Gorakians there. You should see them, if you're to be their Emperor. I don't think they know Goraki is safe again; they might want to return.'

Erik considers it. 'I'm not counting on that,' he says, shaking his head. '*Safe* is a relative term and they honestly might be better off here.'

The idea makes me queasy. 'Don't say that until you've seen it,' I tell him, then look back at Søren. 'Is there anything you need?'

Søren considers it for a moment. 'Just for time to pass quicker. Do you have anywhere to be before breakfast?'

'No,' I say. 'We can stay awhile.'

Søren stretches out on the dirty floor, leaning against the brick wall. 'Well then,' he says. 'How do you feel about another lesson in Astrean?'

'Now?' I ask, frowning. 'Surely there's a better time and place.'

'I'm quite literally a captive pupil,' he tells me. 'And it'll take my mind off other things, like King Etristo deciding to execute me.'

The idea of that ties my stomach into knots. 'I would never let that happen,' I say.

Søren smiles, though it doesn't make it all the way to his eyes. 'I think you've worked enough miracles for me already, Theo. This one might be beyond even you.' He sits up. 'But see? I'm proving my point – we need a distraction. Erik could stand to learn a few words, too.'

'Actually, I think trying to learn two languages at the same time will only confuse me,' Erik says with a yawn. He leans against the hallway wall, crossing his arms over his chest and closing his eyes. 'Just wake me when you're ready to go, Theo.'

I stare at him in disbelief. 'You can't honestly just fall asleep like that.'

Though his eyes stay closed, his mouth quirks into a smile. 'I'm a sailor,' he says. 'I can sleep anywhere.'

And either he's true to his word or he does a very good imitation of it – snores and all – as I teach Søren some basic Astrean words. *I, you, have, does, water, bread.*

It's difficult to tell how much time passes without any sunlight, but when Erik and I leave the dungeon, Søren seems to be in somewhat better spirits. We promise to visit again soon, but Søren doesn't look like he believes us.

LOVE

———— ◆ • ◆ ————

As soon as I get back to my room, I'm greeted with a barrage of panicked shouts.

'We thought you were dead,' Heron says, his normally tranquil eyes burning a bright amber. 'What were you thinking, leaving in the middle of the night?'

'And you took your dagger?' Artemisia adds. 'Were you trying to save the Kaiser's assassin the trouble?'

'You could have been *killed*,' Blaise says. Anger radiates off him so strongly that I can practically see it simmering in the air. His hands shake, but he doesn't seem to notice it.

I notice, though, and so do Heron and Artemisia. In that instant, their anger and fear disappear, drowned out by Blaise's. The ground beneath my feet trembles so slightly that I could attribute it to the whirring of the riser down the hall – but this isn't that sort of tremor. It's a hum, as if the stones are speaking, as if they are being spoken to in return.

'Blaise,' I say, careful to keep my voice soft. But even when his dark eyes lock on mine, they are strange and faraway, as if he's not seeing me at all.

The tremor in the ground grows stronger, until the glasses

left on the table begin to rattle. I know that I should do something, say something, but I am frozen in place, unable to do anything but stare at him. Dust flakes down from the ceiling, falling over us like the ash used to when the Kaiser made me wear that crown.

Artemisia is the first one to react. In a few quick strides, she crosses the room to Blaise and slaps him hard across the face, the sound echoing above the rumble, but it has no effect on him.

I've seen Blaise lose control of his powers before, but he has always fought to regain it. It's never been like this. I don't know if he's in his body at all.

The vase on my vanity topples off the edge, shattering against the floor and sending water and limp roses everywhere. I have to grab the wall to steady myself before making my way toward Blaise, my heart pounding against my rib cage. It occurs to me all of a sudden how dangerous this is, not just for Blaise but for all of us. The Sta'Criveran towers are already precariously tall. A full-blown earthquake could topple this one, and the rest would fall like dominoes, crushing the city below. If we don't get through to Blaise, he could destroy the city and kill thousands.

'Blaise,' I say again, reaching for his shoulders. His skin is burning hot even through the material of his shirt, like fire against my skin, but I hold on tight. I try to shake him, but he is rooted to the spot. 'Please, Blaise. I'm fine.'

He shudders and the tremors subside slightly, though they're still pronounced. They're still dangerous.

Without thinking about it, I throw my arms around his neck and hold him as tightly as I can, even as the heat of his body spreads through mine. I comb my fingers through his hair, and before I know what I'm doing, I'm singing him the Astrean lullaby he sang for me when I needed it.

> *'Walk through the fog with me,*
> *My beautiful child.*
> *We're off to dreamland, my dear,*
> *Where the world turns wild.*
> *Today is done, the time has come*
> *For little birds to fly.*
> *Tomorrow is near, the time is here*
> *For old crows to die.*
> *Dream a dream of a world unknown,*
> *Where anything can be.*
> *Tomorrow you'll make your dreams come true,*
> *But tonight, child, dream with me.'*

Gradually, the world around us stills, but Blaise doesn't. He keeps shaking even as his arms come around me and he buries his face in the crook of my neck. It's only when I feel hot, wet tears against my skin that I realize he's crying. None of us speaks for what seems like an eternity, but I know their thoughts as well as I know my own.

Blaise is not in control of his gift and it's getting worse. Another few minutes and he could have killed all of us and thousands of others besides. We have no way to stop it.

Slowly, Blaise extracts himself from my grip and lifts his head.

'I have to leave,' he says, his voice barely louder than a whisper. 'I can't stay here. I can't—' His voice breaks before he can finish the sentence.

Part of me knows that he's right. He's a danger here, to himself and to everyone around him. But I can't bear the idea of sending him away.

'No,' I say, forcing my voice not to shake around the word. 'That . . . You didn't mean it.'

Artemisia stares at me incredulously. 'It doesn't matter what he meant,' she says. 'He nearly . . .' She trails off, shaking her head. 'I didn't realize how bad it was.'

'None of us did,' Heron says. 'But we knew it would come to this eventually. There's no cure for mine madness.'

It's the same thing Søren said to me on the *Wås*. I didn't believe it then, not really. I still don't want to, even with the evidence right in front of me.

'It can't be mine madness,' I say, trying to sound sure even when I'm suddenly not sure of anything. 'He would already be dead if it was.' I close my eyes, searching for some explanation. 'His gift is strong, and because of that it's unstable. You just need to practice controlling it,' I tell Blaise, but I don't quite manage to convince anyone, least of all myself.

Blaise swallows. 'Theo, I don't want to leave either, but—'

'Then don't,' I say. 'Stay and fight it. Stay with me.' I don't mean to say that last part, but the words are out before I can stop them.

Blaise holds my gaze for a quiet moment. I can see the emotions do battle over his expression. 'I've never felt it that strongly before. My body didn't feel like mine, I was just watching helplessly.' He swallows and shakes his head. After what feels like an eternity, he turns to Artemisia, eyes level and resolute. 'Next time it gets that bad, Art, you'll put a dagger through my heart.'

Artemisia's eyes widen, and for a second, I expect her to refuse. 'If I think you're going to hurt people, I'll do it,' she says carefully.

Blaise nods, though he still looks uncertain. 'I don't know what's happening to me,' he says.

'Maybe it's happened before,' Heron offers. 'Maybe there have been Guardians whose powers aren't stable.'

'I never heard any of those stories,' I say.

'We wouldn't have,' Heron says. 'Who would have told that sort of thing to children?'

It's true that all the Guardians I knew as a child were in control of their gifts, but they would have to be, wouldn't they, to be so close to the Queen? The idea of other Guardians – Guardians like Blaise – never occurred to me, but Heron has a point. Where would I have learned of them?

A thought comes to mind and joins with another – a foolish, desperate idea taking shape. 'Erik and I made plans to go back to the refugee camp today to bring more food,' I say. 'That's where I was – visiting Søren with Erik. If there are any Astreans left who may know something about mine madness, maybe they're there.'

'Maybe,' Artemisia says, though she doesn't sound sure.

'How much food have you amassed, Heron?' I ask him. It's a struggle to speak normally with the debris from Blaise's outburst all around us, but I force myself to. If I dwell on it and what it means, I'll go mad myself. It's a problem I have to solve, that's all, and I can do that while helping the refugees at the same time. I focus on that – the solution rather than the problem – and it's the only thing keeping me from falling apart.

'Not enough,' Heron says. 'But then, I don't think it's possible to smuggle enough out to feed them all without it being missed. If I take another couple of passes through the kitchen, though, I should have all that we can carry with us.'

I nod. 'Do it, then,' I say. 'Erik and Hoa are coming as well, we're meeting them in an hour. Art, will you see what you can overhear people saying about the earthquake? I can't imagine anyone would think it was anything other than natural, but I want to be sure.'

They both nod and hurry out, leaving Blaise and me alone.

I wring my hands. Blaise and I go to such lengths to avoid talking about his worsening instability that I'm not sure how to bring it up now.

'I can't stay in the palace, Theo,' he says after a moment passes in silence. 'I can set up a tent outside the capital walls, far enough away that I won't hurt anyone. But I'll be close enough to help if you need me.'

'You would leave me here alone?' I ask.

He winces. 'Don't do that,' he says. 'You wouldn't be alone. You would have Heron and Art.'

'It isn't the same. They don't see me the way you do. They never knew me before all of this. I need you, Blaise.' My voice breaks and I shake my head. 'We'll go to the camp first. We'll find information. If you still want to leave after that, I won't stop you.'

He shakes his head. 'We can't just ask strangers about this. If anyone else finds out—'

'Heron and Artemisia know and they haven't done anything,' I point out. 'They don't treat you any differently.'

'Because they're my friends,' he says. 'But even Art will

if it happens again. Strangers? They'll try to kill me on the spot.'

'Well, we won't tell them it's you. We'll just ask some hypothetical questions, gather general knowledge.'

'There's no way that won't sound suspicious,' he says.

'Then we'll hide one inquiry in another,' I say, an idea coming to me. 'We'll see if anyone knows something about what happened to Cress, why she has Houzzah's gift after drinking the Encatrio. And then we can go from there.'

Blaise gives a labored sigh, but he doesn't disagree, and that's something.

'Chances are it won't lead to anything,' he says after a moment, toying with the Earth Gem bracelet I gave him half a lifetime ago. He keeps it tucked in his pocket usually, but now he's rolling it between his fingers absentmindedly. 'There's no cure for mine madness.'

It isn't mine madness, I want to say, but I'm not sure it isn't anymore. What is mine madness, after all, but a gift given to someone unable to handle it? Maybe it isn't something completely separate from being blessed. Maybe they are two sides of the same coin. I realize with a jolt how little I know about my own country. Though I'm more adult than child now, I understand little more about the gods and the mines than I did at the age of six.

Blaise is holding the Earth Gem bracelet so tightly his knuckles have gone white.

'Maybe you shouldn't have that,' I say, nodding toward it. 'Maybe it's making it worse.'

His grip tightens even more. 'No, it helps,' he says. 'It channels it into something manageable, more often than not.'

I bite my lip and look back up at him. 'I can't lose you, Blaise,' I tell him quietly. 'If there's even the slightest chance that we can help you, we have to take it.'

Blaise doesn't say anything for a moment, his jaw clenched tight. Finally, he nods. 'All right, Theo,' he says. 'We'll try. But if it comes to nothing, I'm leaving.'

A sick feeling spreads through my stomach at the idea, but I nod my head. Tentatively, I step forward and fold him into my arms again. At first, his body is stiff and unyielding, but finally he softens, holding me like I'm as fragile as the vase was before he shattered it.

'I love you,' I tell him, my voice muffled against his shoulder. Maybe it is another manipulation, more words wielded like the only weapon I have at my disposal, but that doesn't make them untrue. It feels good to say them out loud.

Blaise's breath hitches and a part of me feels guilty. As honest as the words might be, I know my motivations for saying them here and now are tangled. I'm telling him what he needs to hear in order to give me what I want.

I push my guilt aside and focus on Blaise, standing in front of me. Blaise who needs to keep fighting, no matter what. Blaise, who I don't know how to survive without. I don't want to learn how to. I just want him, healthy and happy at my side, ready to reclaim our home, save our people, and avenge our parents.

'I love you, too, Theo,' he says, his voice barely louder than a whisper.

Though I already knew that, his words still send a flutter through my chest. I pull back slightly to look at him.

'Then don't you dare leave me. I don't care if Glaidi herself tries to usher you to the After. You say, "Not today." Do you hear me?'

Blaise swallows, the lump in his throat bobbing. 'I hear you,' he says.

The words don't mean much; we both know that people don't have a choice in when death comes for them – we've lost far too many people before their time. But it's nice to pretend for a moment that we do have some control over it.

DISGUISE

———— ✦ ————

ONCE WE'VE EATEN BREAKFAST AND dressed, the four of us go to meet Erik and Hoa by the palace entrance. The sunlight is so bright it's blinding, and I have to shade my eyes as I step out the front door of the palace. Artemisia reported that the damage from the earthquake was, thankfully, minimal – mostly just cosmetic damage to the palace tower. Nothing more than some broken knickknacks and baubles, a few wall sconces that fell, some cracked tile floors. Nothing that King Etristo won't be able to have repaired quickly.

Nothing this time, I think, though I force the thought aside.

'Queen Theodosia,' a voice calls out. When my eyes adjust to the brightness, I realize that it's only Coltania, dressed in a red silk dress that wraps tightly around her figure, highlighting the curve of her waist and the swell of her hips and chest.

Though I'm relieved it's her and not a Sta'Criveran courtier, annoyance still sparks. Why is she out and about when Søren is locked away in a dank dungeon? She should be working on the truth serum so he can prove his innocence. I can't imagine she's doing any work in that dress.

'*Salla* Coltania,' I say, forcing a smile.

She holds her hands out to take mine before leaning in to kiss each of my cheeks twice. She laughs when she sees my surprise.

'An Orianic custom for greeting friends,' she explains. 'An old habit, I'm sorry.'

'Not at all,' I say, though I can feel traces of her sticky red lip varnish left behind on my cheeks. I resist the urge to wipe them away – I know it's not the same, but it reminds me of the Kaiser marking me with an ash handprint at banquets.

'Did you feel that earthquake earlier? Quite frightful. But it's a lovely day out now. Marzen and I were going to have another picnic – you should join us.' She glances at my Shadows, gathered behind me. 'Your . . . companions are welcome to come, too, of course.'

I force a smile. 'It was a frightful earthquake, but I understand they're common in the area,' I say, though I don't know if that's true. Coltania frowns, but before she can question it, I continue. 'That is a very kind invitation, but I'm afraid with Prinz Søren imprisoned, I've decided not to meet with any suitors. He is my diplomatic liaison, after all, and I require his guidance in these matters. Surely you understand – this is a decision that should not be made lightly.'

Coltania's eyebrows lift. 'I didn't realize his guidance was so necessary to you, Your Majesty,' she says.

I laugh. 'Why else would I keep him on my council?' I fake a look of surprise. 'Oh, *Salla* Coltania, you didn't believe those rumors, did you?' I ask.

She looks torn for a moment before her expression softens. 'What rumors?' she asks with a wink.

I change the subject. 'I understand that you're the one helping King Etristo's apothecaries with the truth serum?'

'Yes, it seems the least I can do to get to the bottom of this mess. After what happened to the poor Archduke – and what nearly happened to you!'

'Tragic,' I agree. 'I am glad that you're helping. With all your scientific skills, I'm sure Søren's name will be cleared in no time and we can get back to business.'

She inclines her head. 'Of course, Your Majesty. I will do my best, though it could take as long as a week, depending on the availability of some of the rarer ingredients.'

I reach out to squeeze her arm. 'I believe in your talents. Please enjoy your picnic and tell your brother I say hello. Hopefully, I will be able to spend time with you and Chancellor Marzen again soon.'

When we walk away from Coltania and down the palace steps, Artemisia comes to walk beside me, leaving Heron and Blaise trailing by a few feet.

'I honestly can't tell if you like her or not,' she remarks.

'I don't think I know myself,' I admit. 'I respect her, at least.'

As we come down the steps, I search the bustling crowd for Erik and Hoa. In their Gorakian brocade, they should stand out, but I see no sign of them. When we reach the bottom step, two figures approach, covered from head to toe in ecru robes. With their hoods drawn up over their heads, their faces are cast in shadow. At first, I think they must be two of the Manadolian priests, who always wear dour, conservative clothes, even in the sweltering heat, but when one draws his hood back slightly, giving me a look at his face, I realize it's

Erik. Which means that the smaller figure beside him must be Hoa.

'That is quite a disguise,' I say to him in Kalovaxian. 'Though it seems a bit unnecessary.'

'Easy for you to say,' he mutters. 'The Sta'Criverans don't spit at *your* back and call you *enta crusten*.'

I frown. *'Enta crusten?'* I repeat.

His face reddens. 'From what I gather, it's Sta'Criveran for *"the cursed."* A bit of a blanket term for Gorakians. It seems our presence is being blamed for that earthquake. Apparently, Sta'Crivero has not had an earthquake in centuries.'

I struggle to keep my expression even. 'Is that so?' I ask before I remember something. 'Søren said the Sta'Criverans thought of the refugees as cursed, that they locked them up behind that wall to keep their curse from spreading.'

As if being conquered by the Kaiser and ravaged by his Kalovaxian armies were a disease that can be passed from person to person, country to country. As if it were that simple.

'You should keep your hood up then,' Heron tells Erik, glancing around to see if anyone's noticed him. 'At least until we're out of the city.'

Erik sighs but draws his hood back up, though not before winking at Heron. 'Seems a pity to hide this face from the world, but I suppose you're right.'

As the group of us files through the city streets, I glance over to see that Heron's face is the color of strawberry jam.

Erik, Hoa, and I fall back so that Blaise, Heron, and Artemisia can barter for horses without worrying about us being recognized. The unfortunate side of it is that we can only take three horses. I'm all right with the arrangement, since I can't ride anyway, but Erik seems a bit miffed at the idea of sharing a horse with another rider.

'I haven't ridden as a passenger since I was a child,' he says.

'If you'd rather lead the horse, it doesn't matter to me,' Heron tells him, though he's having trouble looking Erik in the eye as he says it. 'I mean . . . if you *want* to ride with me. You could ride with Blaise, too, or Art, I suppose, though I doubt either of them would let you take the reins.'

Erik is surprised for a moment, looking at Heron like he's not quite sure what to make of him. 'All right,' he says finally. 'Thank you.'

Heron shrugs and looks away again.

'I'll take Theo, then,' Artemisia says in Astrean before Blaise can offer. 'Blaise, you'll take Hoa.'

Hoa looks confused, having understood only her name. I quickly translate for her.

Hoa considers this for a moment, sizing up Blaise before giving a decisive nod. 'He will do,' she tells me.

'As much of a pain as it is, I think we'll have to speak Kalovaxian so that everyone understands each other,' I say. 'Otherwise we'll have to keep translating for Erik and Hoa.'

Artemisia rolls her eyes. 'I hate speaking in this language,' she says in harshly accented Kalovaxian, mispronouncing a few words. 'It feels like yet another violation.'

Hoa looks at her like it's the first time she's seen her. 'I'm sorry,' she says. Her Kalovaxian is more fluid but still uneven.

Artemisia is surprised at the apology and gets a bit flustered – a new look for her but one that I can't help but take some pleasure in.

'It's all right,' she tells Hoa after a moment. 'I just meant . . . It was nothing against you. I was only complaining.'

'She does that a lot,' I tell Hoa. 'You shouldn't take it personally.'

Artemisia glowers at me but doesn't protest, just pinches my arm.

'And for that,' she tells me, 'I'm going to ride *extra* fast.'

My stomach churns in anticipation.

'Then I'll vomit all over you,' I reply.

Hoa laughs, a sound I've never heard before. It's a melodic laugh that reminds me of birdsong at the start of the day. It's beautiful.

OJO

———◆·◆———

M Y THREAT OF VOMIT SEEMS to have worked – the horse practically glides over the flat expanse of the desert with Artemisia at the reins. She leads the pack the whole way there, but I find I don't mind the speed as much as I thought I would.

When we arrive, Heron, Blaise, and Erik unload the packs of food attached to each of our horses while Hoa, Artemisia, and I start for the gate. I can't help but glance over my shoulder at Blaise as we go, looking for signs of his outburst only hours earlier, but he's just as he always is and there is something both comforting and disconcerting about that.

The guards outside are the same as last time, with the stone faces and the curved blades sheathed at their hips. When we approach, they barely spare us a look.

'We're here to . . .' I start, but trail off. How was it phrased last time? 'Look for labor. And we've brought payment for past labors,' I add, gesturing behind me at the boys carrying the food.

The guards exchange skeptical looks, but apparently they don't care enough to call me out on the lie. With an annoyed sigh, one of them opens the single door, ushering us through.

Again it is like hitting a wall of hot, stale air that smells of disease and rot. I'm expecting it this time, so I don't react, but Hoa is not prepared. Next to me, she coughs and gags, covering her nose and mouth with an arm to block out the stench. Her dark eyes dart around the decrepit camp – the small houses that are falling apart, the dirty streets, the people in their torn clothes, some of whom are so skinny that their bones jut out beneath their skin like they aren't fully of this world.

For a moment, there's horror and disgust and sadness in her expression, but just as quickly as it appeared, it seals itself away behind her mask of placid stoicism.

Suddenly, I see it – that other life she lived before I knew her, the emperor's daughter she once was, raised to greet every situation with a level head and diplomacy. Never emotional, never vulnerable. I can't believe I ever saw her as anything else.

'There are refugees from every country the Kalovaxians have conquered here,' I explain. 'Some families have been here for generations. They speak a kind of mishmash language, words and phrases taken from one country or another. And there is a council of Elders who represent each community. That's who we'll be meeting with.'

A group of children – the same ones from our last visit – run up with their hands out, wide smiles stretched over crooked teeth. I can't help but smile back, as much as the sight of them with their protruding ribs and grimy faces breaks my heart. I dig into my pockets and take a handful of jewels I picked off of the dresses left in my closet. One by one, I pass them out to the children who cling to my skirt and tug at my arms.

'*Ojo*,' one of them shouts, and the others quickly join in, chanting the word until their voices blend into one.

Next to me, Hoa stiffens. I don't know what the word means, but she does.

She clears her throat. '*"Prinzessin,"*' she says to me. '*Ojo* was our word for it in Goraki, what we called the daughter of the emperor. It was what they called me then. It's what they're calling you now, though you're more than a prinzessin. They don't know that yet, but you will show them.'

She sounds so sure of me, more sure than I've ever felt. For so many years we suffered side by side. She was a stranger, sealed away behind her silence and the distance she kept to protect us both. But I was not a stranger to her; I was a girl she bathed and dressed and put to bed every night. She saw more of me than she did of her own son.

I reach out and take hold of her hand, squeezing it tightly in mine. Her eyes fill with tears but she blinks them away before they can fall. '*Ojo Hoa*,' she says, so quietly that I nearly don't hear her. But she isn't speaking to me anyway; the words are only meant for her own ears, a name that was taken from her the same way mine was.

'We're looking for the Elders,' I tell the children in Astrean.

They blink in confusion, exchanging a look. They must only understand a word or two.

'Can you ask them in Gorakian where the Elders are?' I ask Hoa in Kalovaxian.

She nods and translates. Understanding dawns on a few of their faces as they put it together, using some Astrean and some Gorakian words.

One of the older girls, maybe nine years old, takes hold of my hand and leads me through the streets. A younger boy of about four takes my other hand, and when I look back at Hoa and Artemisia, I see the children scrambling to hold their hands as well – even Artemisia softens a fraction when a boy grabs her hand and beams up at her with a smile that is missing one front tooth.

They lead us through the grimy streets and I hesitate only long enough to make sure that Blaise, Heron, and Erik got in without issue. They're inside the gate, unloading their packs of food while a group of adult refugees look on with hungry eyes. I'm not sure how we can possibly fairly divide the food we brought – even if we could, it still wouldn't be enough. A bandage on a gaping wound, nothing more.

I look down at the two children grasping my hands like they're terrified I'll slip away. There must be more I can do, but I can't think of what it is. I don't think I've ever felt so helpless in my life, not even when the Theyn was standing over me with the whip in his hand.

The children lead us to the same shack as before. Just as we're stepping up to the front door, it opens to reveal Tallah standing with one hand on her hip, her expression inscrutable.

'You again,' she says to me in heavily accented Astrean. Her eyes dart to Artemisia, then to Hoa. 'And a new friend this time. This is not a park for you to come play in, you know.'

I feel my cheeks grow hot. 'We brought food, as much as we could manage. It still won't be enough, but it's . . . it's all we could carry.'

Her nostrils flare as she stares at me so intently I feel like I'm going to turn to stone on the spot.

'This is Hoa,' I say when Tallah remains quiet, gesturing to where she stands at my right.

Realizing she's being introduced, Hoa stands a little straighter, lifting her chin an inch. 'Ojo Hoa,' she says. '*Ta Goraki.*'

Something flashes in Tallah's eyes. 'There was a time when I never imagined I'd ever meet a princess. Now you seem to be multiplying.'

'I'm a queen, actually,' I say, even though I can hear Dragonsbane's voice echoing in my mind. *Queen of what, exactly?* I push the voice away, but the ghost of it lingers.

Tallah laughs and pushes her door open farther. 'Very well, Queen. Come in, the three of you,' she says before looking down at the children and saying something I don't understand, waving her hands. They giggle and scurry away and we step inside.

The Elders are all here. They must all share the house, small as it is. Sandrin is sitting on a threadbare mattress with a book in his hands that appears to have lost more than half of its pages. When he hears us come in, he looks up, the space between his eyebrows wrinkling.

'Your Majesty,' he says, getting to his feet. 'I thought we'd seen the last of you.'

Guilt swarms through me even though I'm not sure how I could have managed to return any sooner. Maybe I should have never left. No matter how fine the Sta'Criveran palace is, I think I'm more comfortable here, where doing good for my people means giving out food and jewels and thatching a roof instead of selling myself to a strange ruler of a foreign country. But smuggling food and thatching roofs are temporary solutions. The only way I can really help these people is to give them a country to call home.

'I'm sorry,' I tell him. 'It's difficult to get away, but we brought food with us. Blaise and Heron are unpacking it with . . . another friend. Erik.'

He looks confused. 'No Prinz this time? Did we scare him away?' He doesn't sound very sorry about it. In fact, I think I see a smile tugging at the corners of his mouth.

'He's otherwise occupied today,' I say. 'But this is Ojo Hoa of Goraki. Her son, the Emperor, is helping unpack the food near the gate.'

Sandrin turns his attention to Hoa, but before he can say anything, another voice breaks through.

'Ojo,' a man says, his voice all breath. He's Gorakian, with black hair so short it's patchy in places. His face is gaunt and his eyes a rich deep brown. 'Ojo Hoa.'

Hoa stares at him, bewildered, as he falls to the ground at her feet. It's only when he lifts his head to say her name again that I realize he's crying. For a moment, Hoa is at a loss, but after looking around the room she drops to the ground beside him and places a hand on his cheek before speaking softly in Gorakian, the words slipping together as seamlessly as drops of water in a stream. The man nods fervently, his eyes boring into hers. After a moment, Hoa rises, taking the man's hand and bringing him up with her. Her eyes have turned to steel.

'It is not enough,' she tells me in Kalovaxian. I don't understand what she means until she clears her throat and tries again. 'It is not enough to bring food here. We must also bring them hope.'

*   *   *

Hoa insists on seeing the camp in its entirety, and all I can do is trail after her. I don't know how she does it – how she can look at so much ugliness and pain without flinching from it. How she can ask to still see more. I don't want to see more – I want to turn and leave and bring more food in a few days if I can, but I don't want to understand this place the way she does. I can't take it.

I follow her anyway as we go from house to house, walk down every street, and I try to mimic her grace, how she holds herself together in the face of so much misery.

'*We must also bring them hope,*' she said, as if it were a physical thing we could deliver in a basket tied with ribbon. As if it were easy to share with others when it's hard enough to keep my own hope from dying.

When I say as much to Artemisia, she shakes her head. 'Hope is contagious,' she says. 'When you have enough, it spreads naturally.'

MINA

———— ◆ · ◆ ————

Back at the house of the Elders, I find Sandrin with his book again. Though he glances up at me when I approach, he goes back to reading immediately after. I almost think him rude, but I try not to take it personally. If the book's well-worn condition is any indication, it must be an engrossing story. I gingerly sit down next to him on the mattress and wait for him to finish. When he does, he marks his place with a scrap of paper and sets the book aside.

'Can you read?' he asks me.

I blink. 'Of course,' I say before biting my lip. 'I mean, I can read Kalovaxian perfectly well. I can read some Astrean – my teacher told me I was advanced for a six-year-old, but now . . . well, I wouldn't say I'm even average for sixteen. Astrean was forbidden in the palace. I was forbidden to speak, to write, to read.'

His mouth purses. 'We will have to teach you, when there is time.'

I can't imagine when there will ever be time for that, but

I don't say as much. It's a kind offer, and I accept it with a smile.

'Your friend is quite popular,' he tells me. 'Where is she now?'

'Hoa is helping with the food distribution,' I say. 'The Elders were concerned it would cause a mob, but she's keeping the crowd calm and organized.'

He nods. 'She has a gift with people,' he says. 'In Astrea, we would have said that she was a *storaka*.'

'A child of the sun?' I ask, picking apart the roots of the word.

'Who doesn't love the sun, after all? Some people have that same energy about them – they draw others in, make friends out of strangers with a single smile,' he says. 'You are not a *storaka*,' he adds.

I should feel slighted, but I can't deny he's right. I don't have the gift that Hoa has. I am not an easy person to love.

He looks at me with appraising eyes. 'There was a story in Astrea that you might remember hearing as a child, about the rabbit and the fox?'

Bits and pieces of it come back to me – there was a rabbit who wanted to please everyone, so she rolled in mud for a pig, stuck feathers to herself to please a chicken, painted spots onto her fur to impress a cow. Then she came to a fox.

'The fox said it would like the rabbit best in a pot of boiling water,' I say. 'The rabbit hopped right in and the fox cooked her alive and ate her for supper.'

Sandrin smiles grimly. 'There is no pleasing everyone without losing yourself,' he says. 'And you are surrounded by foxes. What will make you happy?'

'It isn't that simple,' I say, frustration leaking into my voice. 'It isn't just about me, it's about them' – I gesture to the door, to all the hungry refugees in the camp – 'and it's about the people in Astrea wearing chains. My happiness is irrelevant if it comes at the cost of theirs.'

He considers this.

'And what does saving them cost you?' he asks.

'The cost is . . .' I start before trailing off. 'The cost is marrying a stranger with strong enough armies to take on the Kaiser.'

I wait for his admonishment, for him to tell me again that queens don't marry, but he doesn't. Instead, he pats my hand. 'That is a difficult decision,' he says.

'It is,' I say, my throat tightening. I blink back tears, focusing on my reason for coming to speak with him. 'Sandrin, do you know anyone who knows about Guardians?'

His hand falls away from mine and he sits up a little straighter. 'What about Guardians?' he asks.

I hesitate, a confession about Blaise's earlier outburst rising to my lips. I push it down and choose my words carefully. 'There was a Kalovaxian girl I became friends with – or, I thought we were friends, I suppose. I'm not sure what we were, really. Before I left, I poisoned her and her father with Encatrio and it killed him, but she survived.'

Sandrin stiffens. 'She survived,' he echoes. 'But she is not the same.'

I shake my head. 'She's scarred by it and she has . . . she has Houzzah's gift.'

He takes this in, his expression unreadable.

'It's impossible,' I say when he remains quiet. 'Houzzah

would never bless a Kalovaxian. He would let the poison have her and be done with it.'

His smile is tight and grim. 'To try to understand the reasoning of the gods is to court madness.'

'No,' I repeat. 'I don't believe it's possible. I don't believe . . .' I trail off because I have no choice but to believe it. I saw it with my own eyes – I felt the heat her touch left behind on the cell bars that separated us, hot enough to burn.

'What is to be done, then?' I ask. 'A Kalovaxian with those kinds of powers . . . and she's the Kaiserin now as well.'

'I have no answer to that,' he admits. 'None you don't already know.'

I swallow. 'You mean I'll have to kill her.'

It isn't the first time I've been told this, but the last time, Cress was innocent. She was just a girl who liked pretty dresses and wanted to marry a prinz. It still feels like a fist closing around my heart, but it's different this time. Sandrin is right – I knew somewhere deep down that killing Cress was the only way to stop her. All those nightmares that have been haunting me, they all ended with her ending my life, and dreams or not, I know there is truth in them.

I push the thought aside before Sandrin can see how much it affects me. 'And . . .' I trail off again, unsure of how to phrase my next question. Blaise was right; if anyone suspects he's unstable, they'll kill him. I'm not naive enough to believe that Sandrin is an exception to that.

'Have you ever heard of someone going mine-mad and surviving it?' I ask him.

Sandrin frowns. 'That, in and of itself, is a contradiction. Mine madness by its very definition results in death. If it doesn't, it isn't mine madness.' He pauses. 'But then again, I suppose death comes for us all in the end, so perhaps that isn't fair. How long has it been?'

'It's not . . .' I tell him. 'It's hypothetical.'

He doesn't believe me, I can tell. For a second, I expect him to press me for details, but eventually, he shakes his head.

'Mine madness is not a disease, no matter how we might treat it like one. It's the magic in the mines – some people can handle it, some people can't,' he says.

'It depends on the gods' blessings,' I say, nodding. This much I know.

He cocks his head to one side thoughtfully. 'That is the most common explanation, yes. It has always been the one I have chosen to believe, but there are others. Less poetic ones. There are some who believe it comes down to other factors – a person's blood, or their constitution. Perhaps it is all true, in a way.'

'If this is philosophy, I don't think I care for it,' I tell him. 'How can they both be true?'

'I've always thought that belief in something lends a kind of truth to it. In this case, we may never have a sure answer, so belief is the only truth we have.'

Frustration bubbles up in me. 'That's not an answer, it's only more questions,' I say. 'Have you ever heard of someone who's gone mine-mad and survived?'

He eyes me warily for a moment before shaking his head. 'No,' he says. 'I've never heard of a case of mine madness lasting more than three months before the sufferer perished,' he says.

Perished. It's a pretty word, prettier than *died*.

'How does it happen?' I ask, though I'm not sure I want to know the answer.

He shakes his head. 'I saw it once, with my own eyes. Not in battle – this was years before the siege. A poor, frightened man ran away from the temple when he realized that he was mine-mad. They used to kill them, even before the siege, though I imagine there was more mercy in it. Still, he panicked and ran to a nearby village for shelter. No one else was hurt when he finally lost all control, but it was a terrible sight all the same. There wasn't much left of him afterward, and the village had been razed to the ground. It's better if you don't know anything more than that, and I hope you never have to see it yourself.'

I want to press him for details, but I hold my tongue. I don't want those images in my mind; I don't want to see it happening to Blaise every time I close my eyes. Awful as my nightmares about Cress are, I know I would prefer them to that.

'What if it does last longer than three months?' I ask him instead. 'What if someone survives the mine, if they have a gift, the way a Guardian would . . . but if they sometimes can't control that gift?'

Again, he's quiet for a moment, his eyes growing faraway as he turns his mind over for an answer. 'Is it dangerous?' he asks.

I pause, though I know the answer well enough. It was only hours ago that Blaise nearly destroyed the entire Sta'Criveran capital. How many people would have died in a disaster like that? I would be surprised if anyone managed to walk away alive.

'They haven't hurt anyone,' I say.

It isn't a full answer, and Sandrin seems to realize this. He heaves himself to his feet with a groan and holds a hand out to me. 'Come,' he says. 'I want to introduce you to someone.'

Sandrin leads me through the maze of crooked streets. They're empty, since everyone is waiting for food at the gates, but there's something disconcerting about the quiet. It looks, more than ever, like a dead place. At the thought, I have to suppress a shudder and I quicken my step to catch up with Sandrin.

He finally leads me to another house with a sagging roof and a door that barely covers the entrance. Instead of walking up to the door, however, he leads me around back to a small patch of dry dirt where a few scraggly plants are growing. There are bright yellow peppers, violet eggplants, and pale green globes of honeydew. It is a welcome shock of color.

Near the garden, a stoop-shouldered woman with short black hair tends to a weak fire. Hanging over it, suspended by a rusted metal frame, is a large cast-iron pot.

'Mina,' Sandrin says as we approach, and the woman turns to look at us over her shoulder. Her expression is severe, but it softens when she sees Sandrin.

'Come to make yourself useful?' she asks him, nodding toward a burlap sack next to her filled with oblong, orange sweet potatoes. 'They need to be peeled.'

'We came to talk about something, actually,' Sandrin says before clearing his throat. 'The mines.'

Something flickers across Mina's expression. 'You can talk

and peel,' she says. 'Give me a second.'

Turning back to the fire, she holds her hands toward it, twisting them in the air around it. At her coaxing, the small fire grows larger, until its flames lick at the bottom of the pot. There are no tools, no matches, nothing but her.

'You're a Guardian,' I blurt out. Another Guardian! And one from before the siege, one who understands her power and the gods more than Heron or Art or Blaise. And a Fire Guardian at that! I think of my own hands growing warm and tingly; I think of waking up with scorch marks on my bedsheets. Perhaps she'll have answers for that as well.

Mina turns back to us, this time looking at me. 'Who are you?' she asks, her voice sharp.

'This is Queen Theodosia,' Sandrin tells her.

Mina scoffs. 'There is no Queen Theodosia,' she says, her eyes locked on me. 'Only a frightened little princess under the Kaiser's thumb.'

'I told you the Queen came, remember?' Sandrin asks.

'Of course I do. The entire camp wouldn't stop talking about it. That doesn't change anything. You aren't a queen,' she says to me. 'You can't be queen of a country that doesn't exist.'

It's the same thing Dragonsbane said to me, more or less, but there's no bite in her voice. Instead, she sounds sad.

'Sandrin said you could help me,' I tell her. 'And he was right. I didn't know there were any Guardians here. I thought the Kalovaxians had killed them all after the siege.'

Mina holds my gaze a moment longer before glancing away and shaking her head. 'I'm not a Guardian, child,' she says.

I frown. 'But I just saw you—'

'You've seen Fire Guardians before, no?' she asks. 'You've seen them create fires with a snap of their fingers, seen them hold a ball of flame in their hands like it's a toy, seen them touch it without ever getting burned.'

I nod. I'd seen Ampelio do all of that and more when I was a child.

She nods toward the fire. 'That is the most I can do. And even that was a struggle,' she says. 'What do you know about Guardian magic?'

I shrug my shoulders. 'There's magic in the caves that ran under the old temples – in the mines now. Some people who spend a prolonged amount of time there are blessed by the gods and attain gifts – like the Fire Gift. But most aren't. The power turns them mine-mad. They have feverish skin, they don't sleep, their gift is unstable, until it kills them.'

Mina purses her lips. 'You are more or less correct, though you have a very juvenile understanding of it – all sharp edges and black-and-white rules. Nothing in the world is as simple as that, and magic certainly isn't.'

'What do you mean?' I ask.

She considers it for a moment, casting her gaze around until an idea lights up her expression. She beckons me closer. When I'm standing just in front of her, she takes a pail and lifts it up so I can see the water sloshing around inside. 'Some of the last of what your friends brought when you came before,' she explains. 'Now, imagine the water is the magic in the mines – this exact amount is what imbues whoever stays there for an extended amount of time. And now imagine that the pot is a such a person.'

She pours the contents of the pail into the pot and it fills it almost three-quarters of the way full.

'We would call this person blessed,' she says. 'The magic fills them up but doesn't overflow. Were the person a smaller container, so to speak, the magic would be too much and they would be, as we call it, mine-mad.'

I frown. 'But that doesn't make sense,' I say. 'I have a friend who's a Guardian and she's close to my size. Surely bigger people than that have gone mine-mad.'

'It isn't physical size she's referring to,' Sandrin says.

'It's something internal, some unknowable thing that determines it, unrelated to genetics or any other factor, as far as we could tell,' Mina adds.

' "We"?' I ask.

'Before the siege, I studied the caves with a group of people who were curious. I wanted to know what had happened to me,' she says.

'And what did?' I ask her.

Mina turns back to the pot. 'Imagine a larger pot,' she says. 'The magic is still there, but it doesn't fill the person up as much. It doesn't come to them so easily. For me, I could feel the magic, but bringing it to the surface was difficult, and it was rarely worth the effort when I did. People like me – we weren't strong enough to serve as Guardians, so we went back to our normal lives. It was shameful, in a way – not to be chosen by a god, nor killed by one, but merely overlooked. No one liked to talk about it. I would imagine it's the case for many in the mines now – why they haven't gone mine-mad but why they also don't present any gifts. The magic is in them, but it's too small a concentration to allow them to do much – if anything at all.'

I struggle to make sense of it. 'So to be blessed by the gods, you must be precisely the right size vessel?' I ask.

'Some believe the gods still choose those capable of carrying the volume of the magic,' Sandrin says. 'That they are still the ones who bless certain individuals above others.'

'And some believe that it is all more unpredictable and random than that,' Mina adds with a shrug.

'You don't think the gods have a hand in it at all?' I ask, surprised.

Mina doesn't say anything for a moment. 'I don't know,' she admits finally. 'But to consider that they choose those who are blessed means that they are also responsible for all of those who don't survive it. I don't believe the gods are capable of that kind of cruelty, and if they are, I certainly don't wish to worship them for it.'

Sacrilegious as it may be, I have to agree with that sentiment.

'So what about someone who has a gift – a strong gift – but they can't always control it, especially when they're angry? And if they don't sleep and their skin always runs hot, but they've been like this for over a year?'

Mina glances at Sandrin, who shakes his head. 'She claims it's hypothetical,' he explains, to which Mina gives a derisive snort before approaching the pot.

'So, when it comes to using magic, imagine this flame is the energy you're exerting to use magic. What would that do to the water?'

'It boils,' I say, an understanding slowly taking shape.

'Yes. For me, the harder I strain to use my magic, the stronger it is. Just as boiling water bubbles to the top of the pot. For your average Guardian, using their power for big things, for long stretches of time, would bring them just to the rim. You say your hypothetical friend is more powerful than most, yes? So when they use their gift too strongly or for too long—'

'It boils over,' I guess.

She inclines her head. 'There were old texts where I read of such people, but I never encountered one myself.'

Sandrin clears his throat. 'From the stories I read, they often appeared in times of trouble. A drought in the West brought about an unusually strong Water Guardian who could produce enough water to satiate an entire village without growing weary. A famine one year was offset by an Earth Guardian who could turn barren soil fertile once more. Scholars remarked that it was as if the gods had answered their prayers.'

'What happened to those Guardians?' I ask.

Sandrin and Mina exchange looks.

'They used their power and saved thousands,' Sandrin says.

'Until they boiled over,' Mina finishes.

It's too much to think about right now and there are still so many questions to ask, so I push Blaise from my mind and look at Sandrin.

'What we spoke of before, the Encatrio?' I ask. 'Is that related to this? I know that it's water from the Fire Mine and people have survived it before, but how?'

'We're getting out of my field,' Mina says, shaking her head. 'But as I understand it, Encatrio is a very concentrated dose of magic. More than the water that was in the pail –

double that, maybe. Very few can handle it.'

'But when they do, they're as gifted as if they'd gone into the mines,' Sandrin says.

'More gifted,' Mina corrects. 'It's difficult to know without performing tests, but I imagine it would be possible that this hypothetical friend and your other hypothetical friend may in fact be in similar situations.'

For a sharp second, I don't think about how this means that Cress is vulnerable, or even more dangerous because of it. I don't think about how much power she must have, how many people she could hurt. I only think of how she must be suffering, just as Blaise is. I wish I could help her, before I remember that I can't.

'One more question,' I say, forcing my mind clear. 'How is it possible that someone who had never set foot in the caves – the mines – or had a drop of Encatrio . . . how could they have a gift?'

Sandrin looks bewildered, but something flashes in Mina's eyes.

'This person,' she says. 'Would they – hypothetically of course – be around your age?'

'Yes,' I say. 'Why? What does that have to do with anything?'

'There was a phenomenon starting, just before the siege. Rumors and reports of children with gifts – small gifts, nothing like a Guardian's power, not even like mine. A mother once told me her son's temper tantrum had caused a glass of water to tip over. Another swore her daughter cried the leaves off of one of their trees. It was all secondhand accounts, things that could have been caused by other things. But there was a pattern forming. Before we could dig too deep into it, the Kalovaxians came.'

There could be others like me. The idea is both blinding and comforting.

'Did you learn anything else before they came?' I ask.

Mina shakes her head. 'But if this hypothetical friend of yours ever wants to find answers, I may be able to help them.'

Part of me wants to ask her for help right here and now, but I hold my tongue. It isn't the most pressing concern. I'm fine and I haven't had any real outbursts since the ship. Though I know better, I can't help but hope that whatever was happening to me has gone away on its own.

'Thank you,' I say instead.

SACRIFICE

———— ◆ • ◆ ————

THE RIDE BACK TO THE capital is harder than the ride out. The sun is high in the sky, beating down so hard I can feel it burning my skin even through my clothes. We have to stop halfway, beneath the meager shade of a group of large boulders. Artemisia uses her gift to produce a stream of water for each of us to drink, but even her powers are faltering in the dry heat and the effort leaves her winded. She sits down, leaning against the side of the boulder.

'I just need a few minutes,' she says, but she barely manages to finish the sentence before dozing off.

We decide to rest in the shade ourselves and wake her in half an hour. With Mina's words still haunting me, I take the opportunity to follow Blaise when he goes to check the horses, even though the idea of leaving the shade is nearly unbearable.

'Do you need help with anything?' I ask him as he gives the horses the last of the water to drink.

'No, I've got it,' he says, not looking at me. 'You should stay in the shade.'

'I found someone in the camp,' I tell him, the words rushing out before I can stop them. 'Someone who studied the mines and the magic in them.'

He glances at me, brow furrowing. 'Did you tell them about me?'

'No,' I lie. 'I just asked about Crescentia, like I told you I would.'

Blaise nods, though his eyes are still troubled. 'And?' he asks.

I tell him about Mina and the theories she and Sandrin shared about the gods and the mines. I tell him about the boiling water and what it meant – that he wasn't quite mine-mad, and that if he kept calm and didn't use his power, he could stay that way. I tell him that he isn't the first, that there have been others, but that they worked themselves to death. Blaise stays quiet while I talk, running his hands over each horse's back to spread the extra water to cool them down.

I lay my hand on top of his and squeeze, smiling so widely my face hurts. 'So all you have to do is refrain from using your gift,' I say. 'You'll be all right. You'll survive it.'

But Blaise doesn't seem to share my relief. Instead, his mouth twists down and he avoids looking at me. My eyes search for the bracelet I gave him – the one I stole from Cress with the hundreds of tiny Earth Gems, but I can't find it.

'Where's the bracelet?' I ask him.

He reaches into the pocket of his trousers and retrieves it. In the bright light of the afternoon sun, the brown gems glow.

'You shouldn't wear it anymore,' I say. 'It adds to your power. Erik said that when they sent the berserkers into battle, they gave them a gem to "push them over the edge." I didn't understand that before, but I think I do now.'

I move to take it from him, but he stops me, his hand wrapping around my wrist.

'Theo,' he says, his voice low. 'I need it.'

'You don't, though,' I say. 'It's only going to make you worse.'

He shakes his head, finally looking at me. 'It's going to make me stronger,' he says, barely louder than a whisper. 'Don't you see? Those Guardians you mentioned – the ones who were like me – they appeared in times of trouble and they were the only ones who could help. You said it yourself.'

'And they *died*,' I remind him.

'They were heroes who served their country,' he corrects. 'That's what all Guardians are meant to do.'

I twist my arm out of his grasp. 'You promised me.' I hear my voice growing higher and higher, but I can't help it. 'You promised me that you would be all right, that we would do whatever we had to, to fix it.'

'To fix me,' he adds quietly. 'That's what you mean. To fix *me*.'

'To cure the thing that's killing you,' I correct him.

He doesn't say anything for a long while, his gaze focused on the sand beneath his feet.

'Who am I without my gift?' he asks finally, his voice so soft I almost don't hear him. 'Because that's what you're talking about.'

'Your gift,' I repeat slowly. 'The gift that almost killed all of us this morning?'

He has the decency to flush at that. 'Ampelio said that I was stronger than any other Earth Guardian he ever knew. He said that if I could control it, I could help change the course of this war. I could help save Astrea.'

'But you can't control it,' I say, harsher than I mean to. He flinches like I slapped him. I soften my voice and try again. 'Your control over it is getting weaker, not stronger, and who is left to help you?'

His jaw hardens and he turns back to the horse, looking away from me. 'The gods have their reasons for doing what they do. They had their reasons for doing this to me. You believed that, too, once, before Søren convinced you there was something wrong with me.'

I take a step away from him. 'That isn't what this is about and you know it. You caused an earthquake today, Blaise. You're dangerous – to yourself, to me, to everyone around you. That isn't a gift.'

'It might not be a gift to you, Theo, but it will be to the Kalovaxians when we finally meet on the battlefield and I unleash every last ounce of whatever kind of power this is – gift or curse, I will use it against them just the same.'

The proclamation knocks the air from my lungs. I imagine a pot boiling over. 'That would be suicide,' I tell him. 'Is that what you want? To die at seventeen by turning yourself into a weapon?'

He's quiet for a moment, taking a shuddering breath. 'I want to save Astrea,' he says finally. 'Whatever it is that happened to me in that mine, it made me stronger. Stronger than other Guardians. Stronger than I ever could be without it. If you take that away from me . . . I have nothing.'

I try to bite back the words, but they slip out anyway.

'You have me,' I tell him. The words are a whisper, almost lost altogether in the harsh desert wind.

He shakes his head. 'I love you, Theo. I said that and I meant it. But I would rather have you safe on your throne without me than be with you for the rest of a long life spent running and cowering and hiding from the Kaiser.'

'It doesn't have to be one or the other,' I tell him, stepping around the horse so that there is nothing between us. 'I want to take that throne with you at my side, like Ampelio was at my mother's.'

His smile is bitter. 'I don't think you learned anything from those stories of the gods we loved as children,' he says. 'Didn't you ever notice what they all had in common?'

I shake my head. 'Monsters and heroes and acts of stupid bravery?' I ask. 'Happily-ever-afters?'

'Sacrifice,' he says. 'The hero never wins if they don't sacrifice what they love to do it. You want everything, and you aren't willing to give anything up to get it – not your freedom or me or the *Prinkiti*. But I think I can sacrifice enough for the both of us, when the time comes.'

Blaise finally turns to look at me, though his thoughts are sealed so well behind his eyes that it feels like I'm looking at a stranger instead of the person I know best in this world.

'If you won't give up your gems, you're a danger to all of us,' I tell him, struggling to keep my voice steady even as I force myself to say the hardest words I've ever said. 'You have to leave.'

His shock and hurt last only an instant before they are sealed away again behind his placid expression. He nods. 'I'll take Hoa back to the capital, but after that, I'll go. It won't be far – I'll make camp a mile outside the wall. If you need me, you can send word through Heron or Art.'

I always need you, I want to say. *I wouldn't have escaped the Kaiser without your plans. I wouldn't be any kind of queen. I would still be just a scared girl, cowering before the Kaiser. I don't know who I am without you.*

The words die in my throat, smothered by my pride and my anger. This is his choice, I remind myself.

He doesn't wait for my response anyway, instead turning and walking back to the others with his empty bucket, leaving me alone in the hot sun with a shattered heart.

MASK

---◆·◆---

I HEARD SOME KALOVAXIAN SOLDIERS WHO lost appendages in battle talk about how they could still feel their limbs even though they were no longer there. For me, it's the same way with Blaise. Even when we return to the palace without him, I still feel his presence. It's a shock every time I look for him, only to find Heron and Artemisia. They seem to feel his absence as well, and when we all retire to my room that night, a blanket of silence drapes over us.

As I lie in bed, I try not to imagine Blaise, alone outside the capital wall with the Sta'Criveran heat bearing down on him even in the dark, amplified by the heat burning through him. But of course I fail and I know sleep will not come anytime soon.

Sleep, however, is not what I was planning on doing tonight.

This time, when I leave Heron and Artemisia asleep to visit Søren, I write them a note so they won't worry. I take my dagger with me. Little good it might do, but it's sharp, and that will count for something if it comes down to it. I hope.

Erik is already waiting when I slip out the door and close it quietly behind me. He leans against the far wall with his arms crossed over his chest. He still doesn't seem comfortable in his Gorakian clothes, but I can't help but think that he looks better in them than he did in his ill-fitting Kalovaxian suit.

'We can't do this during daylight hours?' he asks when he sees me. 'You can't tell me you aren't exhausted – at least I got some sleep last night. You didn't get any.'

It isn't until he says it that I realize he's right. With everything that has happened in the last two days, sleep has been the farthest thing from my mind.

'I'm fine,' I tell him. 'I can sleep late tomorrow. King Etristo gave me leave to visit Søren whenever I like, since he's still my advisor, but I worry that if I do it when the King is awake, he'll find some way to stop me.'

Erik laughs. 'I'd like to see him try,' he says before pausing. 'You aren't like you were in Astrea – you don't let anyone tell you what to do here, not even your friends.'

I shrug and start toward the riser. He quickly falls into step next to me. 'I always take their thoughts into consideration,' I say. 'But when it comes to Søren, their opinions are always biased. They tolerate him and I think maybe they even like him on some level, but at the end of the day, he's a Kalovaxian. They don't trust him.'

'Why do you?' Erik asks.

It's a question I've asked myself countless times without ever being able to find a full answer. This time is no different, but I try.

'Søren loves me. Or he thinks he does, at least. Maybe he's still confusing me with Thora, but that doesn't matter, because his intentions are fueled by that feeling,' I explain.

'Don't misunderstand me – his hatred of his father is real, his guilt over the berserkers is real, his convictions are real.' I think it over for a moment. 'But I also know where he stands. I know what he wants, and I know what he wants from me in particular. Because of that, I trust him more than King Etristo or any of the suitors. I trust him even more than I trust Dragonsbane.'

Erik considers this for a moment. 'More than you trust me?' he asks.

I glance sideways at him. 'Yes,' I admit. 'I trust your intentions, Erik. But I still don't know what you're hoping to accomplish by being here, and until I do you're still an enigma.'

'I rather like being an enigma,' he says with a grin, making me laugh.

We ring the bell for the riser and Erik slumps against another wall to wait, even though it'll only be a moment. He looks like he wants to ask me a question, but doesn't know how. It's a show of uncertainty I'm not used to seeing from Erik, who usually masks his doubts with layers of false bravado.

'What is it?' I ask him.

He shakes his head, looking down at the ground. 'Nothing.'

'Well, now you've piqued my interest even more. Come on, I'm not going to bite you.'

He hesitates a moment longer, and when he looks back up at me, his whole face is pink. 'Do you know . . . does Heron like . . . is he interested in other boys?'

I don't know what I expected him to ask me, but the

question is so entirely out of the blue that all I can do is laugh, though I'm not sure why I am. After all, Heron is interested in boys – at the very least, he was interested in *a* boy, and the way he looked at Erik before makes me think it wasn't a singular case.

Erik's face turns an even deeper shade of pink. 'I was only wondering. Some boys do, you know, just like some girls like other girls.'

'I know that,' I say, managing to get a hold of myself. 'I'm sorry, I wasn't laughing at you about that. You just surprised me is all. Do *you* like other boys?'

He shrugs. 'Mostly I think I just like everyone.'

'I didn't realize,' I say.

'I don't exactly lead with it in conversation,' he says. 'Some people think it makes me . . . unnatural.'

'Some people are fools,' I tell him before hesitating. 'Does Søren . . .' I trail off.

Erik nods. 'I think he's known about as long as I have. I didn't even have to tell him.'

I sigh. 'Since I doubt you want me telling strangers your personal business, I'm not telling you Heron's. If you want to know, you can ask him yourself.'

Erik considers this for a moment. 'Maybe I will,' he says.

I press my lips together, thinking of Heron and his broken heart. After everyone he's loved and lost, I don't know how he would survive another heartbreak.

'Just . . . be careful,' I tell him. 'I like you, Erik, but if I have to choose between you and my Shadows, I will choose them every time.'

He stares at me. 'Huh,' he says.

'What?'

'Nothing.' He pushes off the wall to stand just as the riser whirs into place. 'I think I caught a glimpse of the real Theodosia underneath all those masks. And she's a lot softer around the edges than I'd thought.'

HELPLESS

———— • ————

THE SAME GUARD, TIZOLI, LETS us in the dungeon again, leaving us outside Søren's cell and promising to come back as soon as he's called for. Luckily, this time Søren is already awake, sitting against the back wall of the cell, looking like he's expecting us. Though I know he won't say a word of complaint, his time down here is wearing on him. Even in the dim torchlight, his skin looks sallow and I can make out dark circles under his eyes. He's beginning to smell quite awful as well.

But when he sees us, he manages a smile.

'I was hoping you'd come back,' he says.

'Of course we came back,' I scoff. 'How are they treating you? You're being given enough food and water?'

Just as I expect him to, Søren waves away my concerns. 'They're treating me fine,' he says. 'Food, water, all of that.'

'And you're actually eating the food this time?' I ask him. 'You aren't pulling that stupid stunt again?'

He laughs at that, but it's not as loud and full as I am used to. 'I'm eating plenty, and I think they'd prefer me to drink a little less water, honestly.'

I frown. 'What do you mean?' Wasting food, I understand. Food costs money, food costs resources. But water has no cost.

'They're in the middle of a drought,' Søren says, surprised at the question. 'You didn't know? There's been no rain in years.'

'But the city was built on a spring,' I say, remembering what Dragonsbane told me when we came here. 'That's why the air is cooler here, that's why I've been made to bathe morning and evening.'

'Springs run dry,' Erik says with a shrug. 'But I don't think they like people to know. Sta'Crivero is supposed to be a paradise.'

'How do *you* know, then?' I ask him.

Erik snorts. 'Guest of the King I may be, but I'm still Gorakian. They know I'm not worth anything to them. Do you think they waste more water than necessary on me? They measure out each glass we drink and charge us by the ounce. And baths? None of my people have washed since we arrived, and believe me, some of us are beginning to ripen.'

The revelation is a four-fingered glove, missing something important.

'But the Sta'Criverans use so much water. The garden alone must use hundreds of gallons a day, not to mention what it takes for everyone to drink and bathe.'

'The *courtiers* use so much water,' Søren says. 'But for people who live on the ground, it's strictly rationed. I overheard some guards complaining about it.'

Sta'Crivero seems so lush and wealthy because that is how they want it to appear, but what good will their bejeweled gowns and ornate towers be when they have no more water to drink?

'I hate this place,' I say after a moment. 'I hate the palace and the shallow people who act so superior, even while those around them go thirsty. I hate King Etristo and the way he calls me "my dear" like I'm an ignorant child who can't make her own decisions. And I hate that camp and what they have done to those people. I . . .' I trail off before I can finish the thought.

Søren eyes me uncertainly. 'Theo,' he says quietly. 'Leaving now would be an insult to King Etristo and the entire country. They're the only ally you have.'

'Technically, that's not true,' Erik says. 'She has me and Goraki.'

'And Vecturia,' I add. 'The Chief told me I can call on them next time I need them.'

Søren shakes his head. 'Grains of sand next to a mountain.'

'I *know* that,' I snap. 'I know it's not enough, that it will never be enough. I know that I have to marry someone with a bigger army. I just . . . I like imagining a circumstance where I could walk away and tell King Etristo to eat dirt.'

For a long moment, both boys stare at me, mouths agape. Finally, Erik begins to laugh and a moment later Søren joins in.

'*Eat dirt?*' Erik asks. 'Is that the worst insult you can come up with?'

'I don't think I've told someone to eat dirt since I was six years old,' Søren adds.

'I'm pretty sure you said that to *me* then and I told you it was babyish,' Erik replies, making them both laugh even harder.

My cheeks heat up. 'It was the first thing that came to mind,' I say. 'What would you say?'

Søren stops laughing long enough to think it over. 'I'd tell King Etristo to eat a plate of dung,' he says thoughtfully.

Erik shakes his head and clicks his tongue. 'Still amateur,' he says.

'You go on then,' Søren challenges.

Erik thinks long and hard about it, stroking his chin thoughtfully before a grin spreads over his face. 'I'd say, *"King Etristo, may I extend the humblest invitation for you to eat a fine delicacy of scorpions drenched in piss and a pig's anus stuffed with beetle dung."*' He adds a deep bow for effect.

I double over gagging, but Søren roars with laughter until he's red in the face. After a moment, I have to laugh as well. I wish Erik *could* say that to King Etristo, if only so I could take pleasure in seeing the King's face when he did. When we're all spent from laughter and tears are leaking out of our eyes, I lean forward against the bars separating Søren and me.

'You know that I wouldn't leave anyway, right? Even if I could without consequence?' I say quietly. 'I wouldn't leave without you if King Etristo promised me an army of millions.'

Søren smiles sadly, looking down at his hands. 'You could,' he says.

Even when we move on to our Astrean lesson, his words stay with me and I wonder if he's right. If it came down to it, could I leave Søren behind to rot here? Even if it meant saving Astrea? I'm not sure what the answer is and I'm not sure what I want the answer to be.

When we leave the dungeon hours later, Erik is uncharacteristically quiet. At first, I think it's only because he's tired, and I can't blame him – I feel half-asleep myself – but when I glance sideways at him, I see that he's deep in thought, his brow furrowed.

'What's on your mind?' I ask him as we step out of the riser and onto my floor. Erik offered to walk me to my door, and I'm not proud enough to refuse, with an assassin still lurking around somewhere.

Erik looks like I've just shaken him awake from a deep sleep. 'Nothing,' he says, but the lie is obvious and he realizes it. He sighs. 'I'm just thinking about the camp. I don't think I've stopped thinking about it.'

'I know,' I say. 'I haven't either. I hate feeling helpless.'

Erik nods. 'It's strange, though, because they *aren't* helpless, are they? Many of the adults have been doing physical labor for the Sta'Criverans. They're strong. And they wouldn't have survived if they weren't smart. I don't think they want pity or even charity, really. They just want a chance to fight for a fair life and a place to call home, the same as the rest of us.'

They want to fight. The words echo in my mind over and over again until I stop short, gasping.

'Erik,' I say.

He stops as well, turning back to give me a worried look. 'Everything all right? Tell me there wasn't some kind of poison dart or something. I think your Shadows would actually murder me if something happened to you on my watch—'

I shush him, holding up a hand. A single piece of a plan is joined by another, and another, until it begins to make sense. Until it becomes something solid.

'How many refugees do you think there are in that camp?' I ask him.

Erik shrugs his shoulders. 'Three thousand,' he guesses.

'And if you take out the children and the elderly? And anyone who can't or won't want to fight? How many are there who could be warriors?'

Something in his mind clicks and he smiles, seeing where I'm going. 'One thousand, maybe more,' he says. 'Not enough, Theo. Not even with a Gorakian army and a Vecturian army.'

'No, not enough for a war,' I agree. 'Not enough to take Astrea back. But would it be enough to take control of a mine?'

He frowns, considering it. 'Maybe, for a time. If it's a surprise attack against only the guards of the mine,' he says. 'But even then, we could hold it for just a few weeks until the Kaiser hears the news and sends more troops. Then whatever victory we had would be swiftly canceled out. He has too many men, too many trained warriors. Even with the element of surprise on our side, it wouldn't be enough. It would get us time, that's all.'

'Time,' I agree. 'And the Fire Mine. Another twenty-five hundred Astreans are there, roughly. And we wouldn't stay long. By the time the Kaiser sent more troops, we'd be gone.'

'To another mine,' Erik supplies. 'To free more people, and recruit more warriors at the same time. By the time we take all four mines, you could have a real army.'

'Everyone gets a choice,' I add firmly. 'If they don't want to fight, we'll still give them all the protection we can. But I don't think it will be a difficult choice, after everything. They're angry – let's give them a chance to use that against the people who took everything from them.'

Erik nods slowly, eyes intent. 'But if you leave now, King Etristo will have no reason to keep Søren alive – unless he sells him back to the Kaiser out of spite,' he points out.

Only minutes ago, Søren told me that if I had the chance to save Astrea I should leave him behind to do it, but now I have that chance and I know that I can't do it.

'I can get more people,' Erik says after a moment. 'There are other camps – one in Timmoree, one in Etralia. They might not be as big as this one, but they'll still be sizable. I can go and try to recruit more people and at least make sure they aren't being treated as badly as they are here. And it will take some days to get to each and return to Astrea. That will buy you time to get Søren out of that dungeon, time to get a message to Chief Kapil in Vecturia to take him up on his offer to help. It'll mean playing their game a little longer.'

'I think I can manage that,' I say dryly. 'After the Kaiser, it should be easy.'

'Maybe it would be if there weren't also an assassin to contend with,' he reminds me, which is a fair point.

'I'll be fine,' I say, waving a dismissive hand. 'How soon can you leave?'

'Within hours,' he says. 'The rest of the Gorakians have been ready to go since we got here. They don't like it in Sta'Crivero.'

After what Erik said about the way they were mistreated and spit at, I can't blame them.

'How will we keep in touch?' I ask him. 'Gods forbid anything goes wrong, but it would be nice to have some kind of communication plan in place if it does.'

Erik nods, face drawn tight in thought. 'Let me talk to Master Jurou,' he says after a moment. 'He has some inventions that he's been keeping to himself, but one of them might work for that.'

'What sorts of inventions?' I ask, suspicious. 'You said he was an alchemist, didn't you? Doesn't that involve creating gold?'

At that, he smirks. 'Of a sort,' he says. 'How do you think I've been paying King Etristo for the privilege of fighting for your hand?'

All I can do for a moment is stare at him. 'Master Jurou created gold?' I ask slowly.

'Of a sort,' he repeats. 'It's close enough to fool the King, but the illusion of it might not have held for much longer anyway.'

I shake my head. 'Magic or science?' I ask him.

Erik shrugs. 'As I understand it – which is admittedly very little – it's a bit of both.'

MOLO VARU

———◆·◆———

Though I'd like nothing better than to hole up in my room all day and plan for our eventual escape from Sta'Crivero, I find myself instead preparing for a walk in the garden with Coltania. Her invitation was quite insistent and I'm hoping I can convince her to hurry her truth serum along in order to get Søren out of prison as quickly as possible.

Artemisia sits in one corner of my room, polishing her ever-growing collection of daggers, while Heron tries to mend one of my dresses. Skilled as he might be, it's difficult to hide how many jewels I plucked off to give to the children in the camp.

After what Søren and Erik said about Sta'Crivero's drought, I can't help but worry that Artemisia's Water Gift might make her a target. But she's only one girl – she couldn't do much good for them in the long run – and it would mean King Etristo showing his weakness, which he would be unlikely to do for such a small reward. Still, I'm glad that we'll be leaving this place soon.

'Tell me again what Blaise said when you told him our plan,' I say to Artemisia from my spot at the foot of the bed, pillow clutched tightly in my lap.

Artemisia rolls her eyes. 'I don't know how you expect me to quote him any more directly than I already have. He said, "All right." '

'That was it? Nothing else?' I ask.

'He asked what you needed him to do. I told him to get your letter to someone who could get it to the Vecturian chief. He thanked me and took the letter plus the food and water I brought for him and I came right back,' she said, her voice clipped and impatient. It's a warning not to push her any harder, though it's a warning I ignore.

'But how did he look when he said it? Did he think it was a good idea or was he begrudging about it?'

She slams her dagger down on the ground beside her with a sharp thud that echoes through the room. 'He looked like he was hot. And thirsty.'

To that I don't know what to say. Part of me wants to apologize, but I suspect she would call me a fool if I did. What would I be apologizing for? Letting him leave the palace? He's dangerous and he has no desire to change that. All I can do is try to make sure he doesn't hurt anyone else.

A knock sounds at the door and Heron and Artemisia are on their feet with their weapons drawn before I can so much as blink.

'I doubt an assassin would bother knocking,' I point out, but Artemisia waves for me to be quiet and crosses to the door herself, opening it the same way she always does – with the point of her dagger in the guest's face. This time, it's a very alarmed Erik on the other side of her blade. When she sees him, Artemisia gives a loud sigh – as if he's inconveniencing her by *not* trying to kill me – before reluctantly lowering her dagger.

'Erik,' I say, when she steps aside to let him in. 'Is everything settled for your trip?'

He nods, glancing at Artemisia and Heron. 'Do they know everything?'

Before I can answer, Artemisia jumps in. '*I* think it's a stupid plan, but Heron thinks it's brave,' she says.

I frown at her. 'You told me you thought it was a good plan,' I point out.

'I did *not* say that,' she says with a snort. 'What I said was that it was marginally better than marrying someone with no personal stake in Astrea besides lining his pockets.'

'Well, from you that does actually sound like a ringing endorsement,' Erik says wryly.

To my surprise, Artemisia laughs. She looks surprised by it as well and frowns before sitting back down in the high-backed chair and returning to polishing her collection of daggers.

'If either of you wants to come with me, I wouldn't mind the company,' Erik adds, his gaze lingering on Heron.

Heron meets Erik's gaze, and it might be my imagination, but I think his cheeks turn a bit pink. There's enough of a pause that for a moment I think he might agree, but he eventually shakes his head. 'Our place is with the Queen,' he says finally. Selfish as it might make me, I'm glad he says it. I don't know what I'd do without him and Artemisia.

'Apparently, you aren't the only ones who feel that way,'

Erik says with a sigh before turning to me. 'My mother has also decided that she wants to stay with you, which I'm trying not to take too personally.'

I smile. 'I'm glad to have Hoa with me,' I admit. 'I feel like I'm only just beginning to know her.'

Erik rolls his eyes. 'Yes, yes, she said the same things about you,' he says, sounding somewhat put out. 'She also said that the Sta'Criveran attendants were dressing you too garishly for a queen and she needed to stay to put a stop to that.'

I shake my head. 'She isn't my lady's maid anymore and she has plenty of other worries to tend to now, I'm sure, as the mother of the Emperor.'

Erik shrugs. 'You would think, but she says appearance is important for a female ruler – more important than it is for a male one, since it's what she's judged on first. Apparently, you need her help more. Which is truly saying something, since she was my Gorakian translator.'

I raise my eyebrows. 'How will you manage without her, then?'

He frowns, screwing his face up in concentration. '*En kava dimendanat,*' he says. 'That was either "I'll be all right" or "I have a fat donkey." But I meant the former. All of my donkeys are terribly scrawny.'

I laugh. 'Maybe ask her to write down some phrases before you go?' I suggest.

He nods, then says, 'Oh, I nearly forgot why I came here in the first place.' He digs into his pocket, pulls out two identical nuggets of gold, each the size of my thumb, and passes one to me. 'A gift from Master Jurou. It's called a *molo varu,*' he explains.

'Is this some of that fake gold you mentioned him making?' I ask, lifting it to my eye and looking carefully.

'No, that is the genuine material. Only it's been . . . shall we say, tampered with?'

I shift my gaze from the piece of gold and look at him instead. 'Tampered with how?'

Erik waves a dismissive hand. 'He explained the whole tedious process to me, through my mother of course, but even translated it was quite unintelligible. The gist of it is that gold is a malleable metal. With enough pressure . . .' He trails off and sticks his piece of gold into his mouth, biting down hard on it.

Beneath my fingers, I feel my own piece of gold shift. I nearly drop it altogether. When I hold it up, I see a set of teeth marks shallowly indented in the gold's surface.

'How . . .' I start, but I trail off, looking at it from all angles, expecting it to disappear, but it doesn't.

'In Gorakian, *molo varu* means *"mimic stone."* They're connected. What happens to one, happens to the other.'

'That's . . .' I stare at the stone. '. . . either incredible or frightening,' I finish finally.

'Both, I think,' Erik says, taking the stone from me and tossing it to Heron, who catches it deftly. 'Can you keep an eye on it? You don't have to bite it, of course. A hot enough tool could carve words into it. Keep it in your pocket, and if you feel it get warm, you'll know I have a message for you. And vice versa.'

'It's perfect,' I tell him.

Erik smiles. 'Grumpy as he might be, Master Jurou is something of a genius,' he admits grudgingly.

'Pass along my thanks,' I tell him. 'And safe travels, Erik.'

Erik nods, glancing at Artemisia and Heron before looking back at me. 'Take care of my mother. I'll see you both at the Fire Mine.'

DEAL

———◆·◆———

THE GARDEN IS NEARLY EMPTY when I meet Coltania. Only a few clusters of Sta'Criverans mill about in their jewel-toned, heavily embellished silks that seem designed to compete with the exotic flowers surrounding us. In the midst of so much color, Coltania looks like a particularly lethal bloom, dressed in a high-necked black gown that hugs her figure. Her dark hair is arranged on top of her head and secured with a single jet pin. As usual, her lips are painted deep red, the only hint of color on her.

When she sees me, those lips spread into a smile that reveals two rows of straight white teeth.

'There you are,' she says, coming toward me. 'I was beginning to worry.'

'I'm sorry I got delayed,' I tell her. 'I had a friend stop by unexpectedly.'

She waves a dismissive hand. 'You're here now, and that's what matters,' she says, linking her arm through mine and starting to walk down one of the garden's many paths.

Suddenly, I miss Crescentia so much it feels like a knife twisting in my gut. How many times did we walk together arm in arm like this through the gray garden? We would talk about everything and nothing, all light laughter and jokes no one else understood. It was easy and it was simple and it was a lie, but there is a part of me that would give anything to go back to it.

Coltania is not Crescentia, I remind myself, though I'm sure Coltania is hoping to give the impression that she is a silly socialite with no worries beyond having a new dress ready for the next party. She isn't very good at it. She doesn't know that there is always something beneath the surface with girls like Cress, whether it's a sharply strategic mind or a love of poetry or a kind heart. No, Coltania grew up watching girls like that from a distance, resentful and hungry for a life like theirs, and so she has only managed a cheap imitation of what she believed them to be.

But I can play along with that illusion easily enough.

'You were very kind to invite me for a walk, *Salla* Coltania,' I tell her, squeezing her arm. 'I'm sure you are exhausted after all the effort you are putting in to clear Søren's name. And to think – this was supposed to be a break from your work. I hope we haven't inconvenienced you too terribly.'

That seems to catch her off guard. 'No, not at all, Your Majesty,' she says after a beat. 'I'm happy to help in whatever way I can, truly.'

'That's very good of you,' I tell her with a smile so broad it's actually painful. 'I know I will certainly feel *much* more at ease once Søren is free and I can go back to the matter of selecting a husband. How long will it be before your serum is ready?'

Coltania's smile wavers for just a second. She's very good

at hiding her emotions, but not quite good enough. Not as good as she would be if she'd been groomed to be watched from childhood, the way Cress was. The way I was as well, in a way.

'These kinds of potions can take time, Your Majesty, and we are far from my usual laboratory. I'm making do as well as I can here,' she says.

'I'm sure you are,' I say, giving her arm a reassuring pat. 'Is there any indication of when the potion might be ready?'

Coltania is smart enough to think over her next words very carefully. 'A couple more weeks,' she says finally.

'Didn't you say one week when we last spoke?' I ask her.

She only shrugs her shoulders. 'The timing can be so finicky. These are only guesses. However, I do worry that some of the suitors might become impatient if you refuse to meet with them that long, given the money they must pay King Etristo for each day they stay here.'

She says it easily enough, but I hear the challenge there. She wants to know which of us will blink first. It won't be me.

'I worry about that as well,' I tell her. 'Though I suppose anyone so impatient for me to make such a monumental decision isn't the right choice, don't you agree?'

'Of course, Your Majesty. Patience is of paramount importance,' she says, turning the words back on me.

I grit my teeth. 'It's unfortunate, though,' I tell her with a loud sigh. 'I was just saying to my advisors the other day, before all the nastiness occurred, that I was ready to put an end to all of this. Of course, King Etristo wants to draw it out as long as necessary,' I say, lowering my voice conspiratorially. 'You know how he is.'

Coltania nods. 'In Oriana, we have a saying – "greedy as a Sta'Criveran king."'

I don't have to fake a laugh this time, and Coltania laughs as well.

'That is very true,' I say. 'And to think I was ready to accept the Chancellor's offer of marriage.'

Coltania's back goes ramrod straight.

'Prinz Søren agreed with the decision,' I add. 'In fact, I would argue that he was one of the Chancellor's strongest advocates.'

'Is that so?' she asks dryly. 'I was never under the impression that the Prinz cared for my brother. I would have guessed his favor was with the late Archduke, if he weren't planning on throwing himself into the mêlée, of course.'

Søren did say that the Archduke was the best option if I had to pick one, I remember, but I don't think he ever gave that impression publicly.

'Goodness, I don't know which idea is more ludicrous,' I tell her with a laugh.

Coltania doesn't join in laughing this time. 'There's a rumor going around that I feel I ought to alert you to, as a friend,' she tells me, lowering her voice to a whisper. 'One of the prison guards says you've been visiting Prinz Søren in the middle of the night and that you stay for hours with him. Most people don't think that sounds like a strategic meeting.'

'*Most people* must not realize that with Prinz Søren in prison, meetings have to take place at night, when the prison isn't busy and loud, and that since a large part of those meetings is spent making certain he's being fed and well taken care of, they are of course going to go on longer than they might otherwise,' I snap before catching myself and forcing a smile. 'Another reason I am anxious to get him out of that prison – so that we can waste less time and get this suitor business done with. I'm afraid that two weeks is such a long time, so much can change, don't you think?'

Coltania purses her lips. 'You're saying that if the Prinz's innocence were to be proven in a more timely manner, you'd choose a husband,' she says. 'The *right* husband.'

There it is, a thinly veiled bribe. But if she can play games, so can I. I look her in the eye and nod.

She pauses for a moment. 'I may be able to hurry the potion along so we can settle things officially.'

Before I can respond, we're interrupted by shouts that shatter the fragile peace of the garden. One voice I recognize immediately as King Etristo's.

'It is unacceptable,' he roars, louder than I believed possible for him. 'We had a deal, Reymer.'

The Sta'Criverans wandering the garden recognize his voice as well and immediately scatter from sight, heading back indoors to give him space. Part of me wants to do the same, but if he's talking with Czar Reymer, I fear it has something to do with me.

'Here,' Coltania whispers, tugging me into a copse of trees with wide trunks and thick bushes that hide us completely. The bushes poke and scratch and tear at my dress, but my heart is thudding so loudly in my ears that I barely even feel them. When I glance toward Coltania, she's peering out with alert eyes, her finger raised to her lips to hush me before I can even consider speaking.

I follow her lead and find a space in the bushes where I

can see out to the empty clearing in the garden just seconds before Czar Reymer stalks into view, trailed by King Etristo at a much slower speed, bent over a bejeweled cane.

'It is not *safe*,' Czar Reymer hisses, turning to face him. 'First the Archduke and now this – I will not risk my life and the life of my son on the off chance that a cold fish of a queen deigns to make him her powerless husband. Not even a king! Just a consort. Talin has other prospects. And far better ones, too.'

The hairs on the back of my neck rise and my heartbeat grows faster. What does he mean '*and now this*'?

King Etristo laughs but it's too sharp to be genuine. 'You are missing out on a rare jewel, Reymer,' he says. 'Queen Theodosia isn't much of a prize, to be sure, but the real treasure is Astrea itself and the magic there. You've seen what those stones can do. With the Kalovaxians done away with, you would control their sale. Apart from the Water Gems, as we discussed.'

The Water Gems. The words click into place, the missing piece of the puzzle. What Etristo was getting out of hosting me. What arrangement he and Dragonsbane had. It was never about helping me; it wasn't even about money. It was about water. Before my thoughts can linger too long on that, the fighting continues.

'This is your problem, Etristo,' Czar Reymer scoffs. 'You always want more, more, more, but you want too much. Etralia is wealthy enough.'

King Etristo spits at the ground next to his chair. 'There is never such a thing as *wealthy enough*,' he says.

'There is when the Kalovaxians are involved,' he says. 'The

Kaiser is not someone to be crossed – surely these murders are proof enough of that.'

Murders. Not *murder,* as in only the Archduke. The Czar said *murders.* My heart lurches and my mind spins with thoughts of who else might have been killed in my stead this time. I think of Blaise and Artemisia and Heron, too busy trying to protect me to watch their own backs. *If an assassin thought I was in my room and found them instead . . .* I can't let myself finish that thought.

'The Kaiser is after the girl. He has no interest in hurting you or making an enemy of Etralia,' King Etristo says.

It's Czar Reymer's turn to laugh, though it sounds vaguely hysterical. He covers his face with his hands and shakes his head before letting them fall to his sides again.

'Surely you aren't blind, Etristo – the girl has never been the target of these attacks. If the Kaiser wanted her dead, she would be. The Kaiser is targeting *suitors* and sending a message to anyone who might stand against him. I hear that message loud and clear, and you would do well to listen as well.'

King Etristo throws his arms up. 'Fine, then. Go. Run back to Etralia with your idiot son like the cowards you are, but I will not be reimbursing you for the funds you have already given me.'

At that, Czar Reymer's face turns bright red and he takes a step toward Etristo. 'That is *my* money. We had an arrangement, Etristo, and you guaranteed me that the girl would choose Talin. Since she hasn't, that money was spent in ill faith and it will be refunded before we leave in an hour's time.'

King Etristo only glares in return, and though he is at a height disadvantage, you wouldn't know it from the intensity of his look. 'I don't make deals with cowards,' he says, practically spitting the word out.

Czar Reymer takes a step toward King Etristo, towering over him. 'You've spent your life in your high tower, Etristo, surrounded by your walls and your deserts. You should not be throwing that word around so easily. You don't know what a real war looks like, but I would be happy to enlighten you.'

With that, King Etristo is silenced for the first time since I've met him.

'I want that money refunded in an hour's time and then my son and I are leaving this place before we end up dead as well.'

Without waiting for a response, Czar Reymer turns on his heel and storms away, leaving King Etristo alone with thunder in his expression.

Coltania and I wait until King Etristo leaves the garden before we emerge from our hiding place in the bushes. Though my mind is a panicked flood at the thought of another murder, Coltania remains quite calm. More than that – she simmers with a quiet anger.

'That gilded guttersnipe,' she mutters, eyes stuck to where the King stood seconds ago. 'I can't believe he promised the Czar your hand when he promised Marzen the same thing.'

I stare at her, mouth agape. 'Didn't you hear them? There has been another murder, Coltania, and the Czar made it sound like it was a suitor. It could be your brother.'

She shakes herself out of her thoughts and looks at me. 'No,' she says. 'No, it couldn't be Marzen. We hired food testers and extra guards after the Archduke.'

I go through the other suitors in my mind, but in my gut I already know who's been poisoned. After all, if the assassin is going after suitors I've shown favor to, there is one glaring probability. Before I can follow that train of thought, I'm already running out of the garden, ignoring Coltania's cries for me to slow down.

VICTIM

———◆·◆———

FOR ONCE, I ACTUALLY YEARN for the stairs, long as the trek would be, because at least I wouldn't have to stand still and wait, watching countless floors pass me by in the riser. It feels like every level inches by, giving my mind eons to wonder what I will find when we finally arrive.

Erik, dead. Erik, suffering the same fate as the Archduke. Erik, poisoned. Because of me. Because the Kaiser doesn't want to kill me; he wants to hurt me, to scare me, to toy with me the way a cat toys with a mouse before devouring it.

The doors finally open on the Gorakians' floor and I don't even thank the riser operator before bolting down the already bustling hallway. Sta'Criveran courtiers in their bright clothes are milling about, speculating about what might have happened. As I run past, I hear only snippets.

Such a tragedy.

After all they've been through, they really are cursed.

The boy was too close to Queen Theodosia.

Maybe she's cursed, too.

No, no, no, my mind screams, ignoring those voices as I hurry toward Erik's room. Just when the door is in sight, a hand comes down on my arm.

'Theo,' Dragonsbane says, her voice low in my ear. 'Come, you don't want to make a scene.'

Though the words are sharp, there is an undercurrent of something else in her voice that I can't put a name to, though distantly I think it might be something akin to kindness.

There are a thousand things I want to say to her about our last conversation, but none of that matters now. No words matter now. I yank my arm out of her grip and pick up my pace until I'm running, weaving around Sta'Criveran courtiers and ignoring her calling my name.

I don't stop until I'm at the entrance of Erik's room, where two guards are standing at attention, keeping the gawkers from getting too close. When I finally stop in front of them, they exchange uncertain looks.

'Let me in,' I tell them.

'Queen Theodosia, the King gave specific instructions that you aren't—' one of the guards starts, but I don't wait for him to finish. I take them by surprise and push in between them, forcing my way into the room, only to find no sign of Erik at all.

Instead, it is Hoa, lying on the ground next to a table holding a bowl of grapes. Her body is twisted at an awkward angle, with a cluster of grapes lying discarded next to her open right hand. Her face is twisted the other way, staring at me with glassy eyes that see nothing and a trickle of black blood dripping from the corner of her open mouth.

I stumble back a step, bringing my hand up to my own mouth. I'm going to be sick. I'm going to fall to pieces. I don't know how I'll put myself together again. Not this time.

Suddenly, I'm seven and she holds me while the Kaiser has my mother's garden burned. I'm eight, waking up from another nightmare in which I watch the Theyn kill my mother. I wake up crying, but Hoa is there with a glass of water and a handkerchief – the only comfort she could provide with my Shadows watching. I'm nine, ten, eleven, onward, and she's tenderly applying ointment and bandages to welts from my punishments. For a decade, Hoa lingered in the periphery of my life, but there is no doubt that she kept me alive in the only way she was able to.

And I couldn't do the same for her.

I don't realize I'm on the ground sobbing until strong arms lift me up and I find myself crying into a cotton shirt. I'm carried out of the room, away from Hoa, and I want to scream, to make this person put me down so I can go back to her, so I can stay with her just as she always stayed with me, but the words die in my throat, drowned out by more tears than I knew I had left in me.

Blaise carries me back to my room. Some part of me knows that he shouldn't be here, that it's dangerous, but he is and that is all I care about right now. Nothing exists outside my tears and the image of Hoa burned into my mind's eye. I don't care why he's here, or how hot his skin is, as long as he keeps holding me. I can't make myself stop crying, no matter how I try to force my breathing to slow.

He sets me down onto unsteady legs, but he keeps an arm around my shoulders.

'Someone should slap her,' I hear Artemisia say, not unkindly. 'She's going to pass out if she keeps breathing like that.'

There's a sigh that sounds an awful lot like Heron's, and sure enough, he steps in front of me, filling my entire frame of vision. He looks torn and for a second I worry he's actually going to follow Artemisia's advice.

'No,' Blaise says, looking toward him in alarm. 'Heron, don't you dare—'

'She's going to hurt herself worse if you don't,' Artemisia says. 'Do it now.'

Heron looks between them, eyes wide, before finally looking to me. He steels himself before taking a step toward me. Blaise moves to stand between us, but Artemisia takes him by surprise, tackling him to the ground.

Then Heron gently touches my hand and everything goes black.

I wake up in my bed, swaddled underneath the covers, and for a blissful moment I forget what happened before. For a moment, Hoa is still alive. But then that moment ends and I want to burrow farther under the covers and sink into a deep, forgetting sleep once more.

'Are you all right?' Blaise's voice interrupts my thoughts, quiet and wary. I look around the moonlit room to find him watching me from the sofa. Heron is fast asleep on the floor and Artemisia is on the other side of the bed, her back to me.

I force myself to sit up. It feels like someone knocked me over the head with a boulder, and my whole body is throbbing. My mouth feels like I swallowed cotton.

'You shouldn't be here,' I say, ignoring his question. It's a stupid one anyway – how can I possibly be all right?

He shakes his head, getting up from the sofa and coming to my side of the bed, crouching down beside me and speaking low. 'I gave Art my gems for safekeeping. Just until I leave again tomorrow,' he says. 'I was getting food in town when I heard the news. I thought . . . I don't know what I thought.'

'You thought I'd need you,' I say quietly, my heart aching. 'I'm glad you were here.' The confession takes everything I have. *He left me*, I remind myself, but suddenly that doesn't matter anymore, because when I needed him, he chose me over his power. Right now, that is all that matters.

Blaise takes my hand in his and squeezes it tightly, his skin burning hot against mine. 'Even without the gems, there's still a chance I could lose control. If I start to, even a bit, Artemisia agreed to kill me before I could hurt anyone,' he says.

'That was kind of her,' I say, looking to where our hands are joined, fingers entwined. The pads of his fingers are rough and callused, but they are a comfort all the same. I never want to let him go.

He takes a deep breath and I worry he's going to talk about Hoa. I don't want him to. I can't talk about her yet or I know I'll fall to pieces. As always, though, Blaise seems to know my mind as well as I do.

'Dragonsbane tried to come earlier; she said she wanted to ensure your safety, but I told her you were safe with us,' he says.

I let out a mirthless laugh. 'I'm sure she took that well,' I say. 'She had a deal with Etristo, you know. It's why he's helping us – in exchange for Water Gems.'

He doesn't say anything for a moment, then lets out a long

exhale. 'I wish I could pretend I were more surprised.'

'I thought her capable of an awful lot before,' I say. 'But this is somehow worse. Ampelio was right – her help comes at too high a cost, Blaise. I don't want it anymore.'

I expect him to argue with me, to remind me that we need her and her fleet, that we wouldn't have gotten this far without her help, no matter how many strings were attached. Instead, he surprises me by nodding.

'Then cut ties,' he says. 'You have the Gorakians and the Vecturians and the refugees. Dragonsbane's help isn't enough to tip the scales one way or another. This plan will live or die on its own either way.'

I swallow. 'We'll talk about it with the others tomorrow. We shouldn't make plans without them. It's Art's mother, after all,' I say before taking a deep breath and asking the questions I've been dreading learning the answer to. 'What happened? How did Hoa . . .' But I can't finish. My voice breaks over her name.

Blaise looks away, understanding well enough. 'As far as we've been able to surmise, the grapes were meant for Erik, but after he left, Hoa moved into his rooms and . . .' He trails off, and I'm glad he doesn't finish the sentence.

'The Kaiser is killing suitors,' I say. 'I was never the target.'

'Why, though?' he asks, frowning. 'That doesn't make any sense. The Kalovaxian sailors were very clear – the Kaiser wanted you dead or alive. He has nothing to gain from attacking them instead.'

I shake my head, which screams in protest. 'Because he may want me dead, but he wants me alive more. You remember the discrepancy in the rewards. He wants me suffering. He wants to be the person behind it, even if he isn't holding the whip himself.'

Blaise nods slowly. 'I'm sorry, Theo,' he says after a moment.

The words are a stab to my gut, and again I see Hoa in my mind as I last did, lifeless and empty.

'How am I supposed to tell Erik?' I ask after a moment, my voice cracking. 'He'd just gotten her back and I . . . He told me to take care of her and I couldn't even do it for a few hours.'

'He won't blame you,' Blaise says. 'There was nothing you could have done. It's the Kaiser . . . it's *always* the Kaiser.'

'He's taken all of our mothers, hasn't he?' I ask him quietly. 'Yours, mine, Heron's. Even Søren's. And now Erik's. Artemisia is the only one of us left who has a mother still.'

'I think he took mine, too, in other ways,' Artemisia says suddenly. I wonder how long she's been awake – if she heard us discussing her mother a moment ago – but before I can ask, she rolls over to look at me. I let go of Blaise's hand so I can turn toward her as well, the two of us facing each other like some kind of bewitched mirror. We look nothing alike, but staring into her eyes in the moonlight, I think I see a ghost of a similarity there. We must both have our fathers' eyes; it's not a physical similarity but a reflection of something deeper. A fire that I think we must have inherited from our mothers.

'She was different before the siege. *Softer,* I suppose, though

I don't think she's ever been soft. Happier. Less hungry all the time. Less angry at everyone who couldn't satiate her. But then the Kalovaxians captured my brother and me, and I was the only one who managed to come back. . . . I don't think she ever forgave me for that.'

For a moment I don't know what to say. Blaise is similarly struck by silence. He concentrates on the duvet beside me, picking at the stitching idly to keep from looking at her. I think he's worried doing so will open something between them he'd rather keep closed.

'I don't think she's angry with you for surviving, Art,' I say. Hard and unyielding as Dragonsbane is, that seems cruel in a way I don't think she's capable of.

'No,' she admits. 'But I was the one who got us caught – I was the one who was reckless and foolish and it was my fault we ended up in that mine. The least I could have done was get him out, but I didn't.'

It's such a rare moment of vulnerability from Artemisia that I don't know quite how to reply. Even breathing too loudly feels like it will break the spell that's fallen over us.

'I'm sorry,' I say finally.

She shrugs and rolls over again, turning her back to me.

'I don't need your pity,' she says. 'But the Kaiser ruined my family, too, even those of us who survived him. He ruins everything.'

Venom is not a new thing for Artemisia – it infuses all her words and it has as long as I've known her. It fills up her every glare and makes her every movement potentially lethal. Still, I don't think I've ever heard her so full of hate before.

I inch closer to her and reach out to touch her shoulder

gently. I expect her to shrug me off, but instead, after a moment, she softens and I wrap my arms around her. She turns toward me and buries her face in my shoulder. I don't realize she's crying until I feel her tears against my skin.

BOLENZA

———◆•◆———

I MUST FALL BACK ASLEEP, BECAUSE the next thing I'm aware of is a light knocking at my door. I sit up, blinking the exhaustion from my eyes. Heron and Artemisia are still sleeping and oblivious to the visitor and there's no sign of Blaise at all – he must have left again, I realize with a pang. The knocking starts anew and I climb out of bed, slipping my dressing gown over my nightgown and fitting the dagger beneath it so that it's secure at my hip.

I tiptoe toward the door, careful not to wake the others. Even though I know that an assassin wouldn't knock, I still hesitate before opening the door.

'Who is it?' I whisper.

'Coltania,' a voice whispers back.

I let out a sigh of relief even as irritation prickles at the back of my neck. I think I've had my fill of Coltania and her bribes and bargains. I've had enough of pretending I want anything to do with her smarmy brother.

Still, I might yet need her to get Søren out of prison, so I open the door.

Coltania stands there in the same black, high-necked gown

she wore earlier. In her hands she holds two mugs of tea.

'I hope I didn't wake you,' she says, though her words are crisp and perfunctory.

'You did,' I tell her, stepping out of the room into the hallway and closing the door behind me so as not to wake my Shadows. I'll be back in bed before they can miss me.

'Apologies, then,' she says, though she doesn't sound sorry at all. 'I was just awake and thinking about how upset you must be after yesterday. I understand you and the Ojo were close.'

The Ojo. She means Hoa. I'm glad she doesn't say her actual name – I don't think I could stand hearing it right now, especially from the lips of someone who didn't know her.

And you did? a voice whispers in my mind.

'I've known her most of my life,' I say, and that at least is the truth.

Coltania's sympathetic expression falters at the blunt acknowledgment. 'Well, I thought you might like some tea and a friend to talk to. Shall we take a walk so we don't wake your advisors?'

I have friends to talk to, I think. *Friends who aren't trying to get something else out of me.*

But *I* still need something from *her*. I need Søren out of prison. So I force myself to take one of the mugs.

'That's very kind. Thank you, *Salla* Coltania,' I say, following her down the hall toward the riser. 'How are you and your brother faring? I'm sure you're both quite shaken, all things considered.'

'It's been difficult,' she admits. 'We discussed following the Czar's lead and leaving ourselves, but Marzen decided against it. He's quite brave.'

The last thing I want is to hear her sing her brother's praises again. I'm too exhausted and heartbroken to even pretend to care one whit about the Chancellor. Instead, I take a sip of the tea, wincing because it's too hot and much too bitter. Even after I swallow it, the aftertaste remains. It reminds me of the way wood smells, but mixed with grass after a rainstorm and with an undercurrent I can't put a name to. It might be the foulest thing I've ever tasted.

'I'm sorry,' Coltania says, seeing my expression. 'I wasn't sure which type you liked, so I just made you my favorite. It appears we don't have the same taste.'

'It's fine,' I say, even though it isn't. She opens the door to the riser and I follow her inside, nodding toward the operator. 'I'm used to drinking coffee, I suppose. The way we make it in Astrea is much sweeter. It'll just take some getting used to.'

'Acquired tastes are usually the most delicious, once you actually acquire them,' she says. 'The garden, please,' she adds to the operator. The door closes with a metallic clang and the operator begins to turn the crank. The riser starts its journey up.

I lift the cup to my lips again because it would be rude not to, but I only take a small, tight-lipped sip.

'Better?' she asks me.

'Better,' I lie. 'Have there been any developments with the truth serum?'

'I'm afraid not,' she says, though again she doesn't sound apologetic in the least. 'With all the excitement yesterday, there was no time to work on it.'

Excitement. I resist the urge to hit her, but only barely.

'It's more important to me than ever that Søren is released from prison,' I say, trying to think up a lie that will appeal to her. 'Søren was very close with Ho . . . with the Ojo.' I can't say Hoa's name – it sticks in my throat.

'I'm sure he'll be quite upset,' she agrees.

'Not only that. Do you know why the Kaiser kept her alive for as long as he did? Even after he left Goraki behind?'

'I've heard rumors. They say she was quite beautiful, once,' she says.

Once. The dismissive way she says it rankles me. It's true that Hoa's youth had left her, that she looked older than her years, that the Kaiser had left his mark on her in too many ways to count, but I think of how Hoa looked in the refugee camp and I think she was more beautiful than Coltania with her painted lips and feline grace.

'I don't think the Kaiser is capable of love, but obsession is a whole other thing,' I say, forcing myself to continue. 'When the Kaiser finds out she was killed instead of her son, he'll be furious. It's important that we settle this marriage business as soon as we can and leave before the Kaiser attacks Sta'Crivero. I know I alluded to it earlier, but now let me make myself quite plain: once Søren is free, I will choose your brother as my husband and we – all of us – can get out of this place before the Kaiser arrives. I think that is in all of our best interests.'

Coltania considers this for a moment. 'I couldn't agree more,' she says before nodding at the cup still cradled in my hands. 'You ought to finish your tea before it goes cold.'

I look down at the green liquid. The aftertaste from my first couple of sips still lingers in my mouth, like twigs and rust. This time, when I lift the cup to my lips again, I seal them against the bitter liquid.

'See? It's growing on you, isn't it?' Coltania asks with a smile.

The riser jerks to a stop, causing some of the tea to slosh over the rim of my cup. It falls to the floor of the riser, staining the cream-colored carpet an ill yellow. What I wouldn't give for a cup of strong, sweet, spiced coffee instead.

'Come,' Coltania says, tugging my free arm and leading me out of the riser. 'Some fresh air will do your heart good.'

The garden is deserted this time of night, which makes the hair on the back of my neck stand on end. Danger aside, though, empty and dark, it feels straight out of a fever dream, full of smoky, subdued color and fragrances so overwhelming I feel drunk on them. It's enough to make me dizzy. I grip my teacup tighter. There's still half left and I don't want to drink any more, but Coltania's attention is so focused on me that I'm not sure I can refuse. She still holds Søren's fate in her hands. I meet her gaze and take another tight-lipped pretend sip.

'Delicious,' I lie, but that earns a smile from her.

'The flowers are beautiful in the moonlight, aren't they?' she asks me as we walk down the path. Her fingers trail along the top of a bush full of white buds that almost seem to glow. 'Most flowers are loveliest in sunlight, but a few thrive at night – like these. *Bolenzas* – it translates to "night blooms" in Yoxian. There's a natural compound that coats their petals and makes them glow like this. Isn't it something?'

'It's lovely,' I tell her, even though I don't want to talk about flowers.

'Lovely,' she echoes. 'But that same compound can be stripped from the petals and boiled to a concentrated liquid that can be lethal if ingested.'

She says the words casually enough, but they knock the breath from me. Pieces slide into place. A picture becomes clearer.

'You were never worried about your brother,' I say slowly. 'Even when the Czar said another one of the suitors had been killed. You already knew who the target was.'

Coltania doesn't deny it. She languidly blinks at me like she's already bored of the conversation.

'Why, though?' I ask her. 'Why work for the Kaiser?'

At that, she laughs, taking a step toward me. I take a step back, a bush scratching my legs even through the skirt of my dressing gown.

'In Oriana, there's a story we tell children about a grotesque monster who will snatch them out of their beds and eat them if they misbehave – the Kaiser is your monster. Just the mention of him is enough to frighten you. I needed you frightened because I thought it would push you to make a decision faster. The Kaiser was just a story to nudge you along.'

'But the servant girl said it was the Kaiser,' I say. 'She'd had the truth serum. Or was that fake?'

Coltania lifts a shoulder in a shrug. 'She told the truth as she knew it and she only knew what she had been told – that the Kaiser was behind it and she would be well compensated for assisting him.'

I remember the girl falling to the floor, her body convulsing as she died, and I feel sick.

'Why the Archduke, though?' I ask, my voice rising in a vain hope that there is someone in this garden who will hear. Someone who will help me.

She shrugs. 'I heard you talking to Prinz Søren in this very garden, telling him Archduke Etmond was your first choice of the suitors. King Etristo had promised me that you would choose Marzen, but I feared he didn't have as much control over you as he thought.'

If she heard that, then she must have heard the conversation that followed. The one where Søren told me he loved me. That's why she's been so sure there's something between us.

'And that's why you framed Søren for it,' I say. 'It's why the truth serum is taking so long. You never started brewing it, did you?'

She shakes her head. 'I didn't want you distracted. I didn't want you to actually consider his proposal,' she says. She takes another step toward me but there's nowhere for me to go this time. My vision blurs and suddenly there are two of her before she sharpens back into a single figure with bright, alert eyes. A predator. And I was too blind to see it until now.

I need to keep her talking so I can get a hold of myself.

'We were poured the same wine, though,' I say, forcing myself to focus even though my mind is a blur. 'How did you know I wouldn't be poisoned? Was it the cup?'

'No, not the cup,' she says. 'Too many things could go wrong that way; there are so many servants in this palace. I couldn't control all of them. No, I didn't poison the wine, but I did lace it with a touch of strawberry juice. Not dangerous to you, but the Archduke was allergic.'

I remember Archduke Etmond's face swelling up and

turning red, him grasping his throat. Coltania breathing into his mouth in an attempt to save him – or so it appeared.

'You weren't trying to save him, were you?' I ask.

'I was making sure no one else could. He might have recovered on his own, if I'd let him,' she says.

'The poison was on you,' I guess.

She smiles, red lips stretching over white teeth. With my vision blurring as it is, for an instant I swear she has fangs.

'Clever girl. My lip paint is mixed with distilled bolenza – not the first time I've used it for that purpose. I've built up a tolerance over the years.'

The rumors, I remember – the mysterious deaths of her brother's political rivals. His clear path to the chancellorship.

I open my mouth to ask her another question to buy a little more time, but before I can, blinding pain shoots through my head and I cry out, dropping the teacup. It shatters against the stone-paved path, spilling the rest of the tea over the stones. In the moonlight, the liquid glows.

Coltania watches me for a moment, curious, until the pain passes as quickly as it came on. I gasp for air, struggling for a coherent thought.

'Sorry about that,' she says. Again, she doesn't sound sorry at all. 'A side effect of the poison. Don't worry, though. Once it knocks you unconscious, the pain will cease.'

Another wave of pain hits. It feels like my head is being cleaved in two. I double over, hands on my knees to brace myself. I let myself scream as loudly as I can. Someone must be here, someone must hear me.

'Why poison me?' I ask her when the pain recedes again to a dull throb. 'What could you possibly gain by this?'

'Oh, it won't kill you,' she assures me. 'It'll just . . . make you easier to handle. Now that we know Etristo's deal with Marzen and me wasn't exclusive, I'm not taking any more chances. It won't be easy to smuggle you out of Sta'Crivero if you're kicking and screaming.'

Out of Sta'Crivero. She isn't killing me, but kidnapping me isn't much better. And if no one came after that last scream, no one will come at all.

I still feel the dagger at my hip, but if I have trouble wielding it when I'm in perfect health, I certainly can't do it now, in this state.

Another wave of pain hits, stronger this time. So strong that I would vomit if there were anything in my stomach, but empty as it is, I only retch until the pain ebbs again.

'If you'd had more of your tea like I told you to, it would have done its job by now,' Coltania says with a heavy sigh, as if my pain is inconveniencing her.

I slump down onto the ground, my vision swimming with black spots. Part of me wants to give in to the darkness and let reality slip away to save myself from another wave of pain, but I fight through it. I force myself to hold on to what is happening around me. The sharp edges of the stones beneath me, the scratch of the branches at my back. Coltania's face looming above me, watching me like I'm a most peculiar specimen that she can't quite figure out.

The pain comes again and I dig my fingernails into my palms to anchor me here – a trick I used during the Kaiser's punishments as well to keep from passing out. I scream again, trying to scream even louder.

'No one will hear you,' Coltania tells me, but even as she

says it I hear footsteps coming toward us. My heart leaps but whatever hope there was disappears when Chancellor Marzen appears, looking between his sister and me in shock.

'Coltania,' he says, bewildered. 'You said you were only going to talk to her.'

'We've put too much money into this ploy to risk it failing because of one girl's indecisiveness. Favoring you one day, the Prinz the next, the Emperor another. Who knows who she will favor tomorrow?' she says, never taking her eyes off me. 'I did what I had to do, Marzen, just as I always do. Once we get her away from her advisors and her guards, she will be far more amenable. But you were right about one thing, Theodosia – the Kaiser will come when he does actually learn where you are – and I imagine the Czar will be alerting him soon in a vain attempt to curry favor. We'll be long gone by the time he comes, though. We'll keep you safe, isn't that right, Marzen?'

The Chancellor doesn't look at her, though. His eyes are on me, wide with shock as his mouth hangs open.

'This isn't what we planned,' he says, more to himself than to either of us.

'Plans change, Marzen,' she snaps. 'You never complained about the way I handled things in the past; I don't see why you should start now. The pain will end in a moment and then she'll be out. I'll stay with her; you go make sure everyone in our entourage is ready to leave immediately. If anyone realizes she's missing while we're still here, there will be no escaping.'

For a moment, Marzen doesn't move. He stays rooted in place, his eyes stuck on me. Another wave of pain washes over me, sending spasms through my body. I scream again, less out of hope that someone will hear and more in order to elicit some amount of sympathy from him.

Whatever sympathy he has, though, it isn't enough. Tearing his gaze away from me, he looks at his sister and nods.

'Hurry,' he says. 'If anyone finds out about this, they won't let us leave this city alive.'

And then he squares his shoulders and hurries away without a backward glance.

My mind blurs around the edges. The dark spots grow larger. The pain gets worse. I can't hold on much longer, but I must. I will not be made into someone else's prisoner again, I will not be played like someone else's pawn. The next time the pain hits, I hunch forward and scream again, reaching into my dressing gown for the hilt of my dagger. I find it, but my grip is weak. I can barely hold it, light as it is. I don't know how I'm going to summon the strength to wield it.

I have to, though. There is no other choice. I hold the dagger as tightly as I can before sitting up. I roll my eyes back in my head and let my body go limp, sagging against the bush.

'Finally,' Coltania mutters. I hear her footsteps grow closer and feel her crouch down next to me. I tighten my grip on the dagger, hidden in the fold of my dressing gown. My heart thunders in my chest, all that is keeping me awake and alert now. One chance is all I'll get.

I remember Artemisia's lessons, how to hold the blade, where to aim. I remember her stoking my anger, but I don't need her petty taunts now. Coltania killed Hoa. I see her body in my mind as I last did, the image of her that will never leave me. Coltania killed her, and that knowledge is all the fire I need.

When Coltania reaches under my arms to hoist me up,

I take my chance and thrust the dagger into her stomach.

It is not the best place to strike. It is not the heart or the throat or the thigh, any of which Artemisia told me would cause a quick death. Those places are difficult to reach at this angle, difficult to accurately pierce in my current state. The stomach is easy, even if it will be slower. The blade slides in, slicing through skin and muscle like they're nothing but air.

Coltania gasps in my ear, pulling away from me. Her eyes go wide and panicked as they search my face, struggling to make sense of what I've done. I stare right back at her as she slumps to the ground and I fall beside her.

It takes a long time for the life to leave her eyes, but I don't look away until it has.

SHOCK

———◆·◆———

I DON'T KNOW HOW MUCH TIME passes. I am paralyzed, sitting beside Coltania's body. Her poison lingers in my veins, blurring my sight and making me dizzy, but the pain at least has stopped. I thank the gods that I didn't drink more than a couple of sips. I imagine waking up in Oriana, or en route there, alone. Would my Shadows have figured out where I was? I like to think so, but I can't say for sure. I'm glad I won't have to find out.

A stick crunches behind me and I whirl my head around, making myself dizzy in the process. There's no one there, though, only flowers and trees and – I see it now, a telltale shimmer in the air.

'Heron,' I say, bringing my hand up to my heart to slow its frantic beat.

Heron comes into focus, his eyes wide as he takes me in, my bloodstained dressing gown and Coltania dead at my feet, my knife's hilt still protruding from her belly. I see him piece together what must have happened, though he can't possibly understand why.

'She was the assassin,' I tell him. 'Not working for the

Kaiser, though, only for herself and her brother. To make sure I chose him. They grew tired of waiting, so they were going to kidnap me and make me marry him. I . . .' I trail off. 'I did what I had to.'

Heron's eyes are still wide as the moon overhead, but he nods.

'Come on,' he says, reaching a hand out to me, which I take. His hand envelops mine, an anchor I desperately need right now. 'This changes things.'

It's such an understatement that I nearly laugh out loud. I'd spent days looking over my shoulder, thinking that the Kaiser had found me. That I would never be safe from him. That might still be true, but it isn't right now. It was never the Kaiser – just a brilliant woman with more ambition than sense. Just a *dead* woman. A woman I killed. I'm not sure how I feel about that yet – when I think about what I did, I go numb. So I won't think about it now.

'King Etristo will have to let Søren out, at least,' I say. 'And then we'll leave, just as we planned.'

Heron leads me back inside and to the riser, where the same attendant is waiting. He takes in my bloodstained clothes and what I'm sure must be my half-wild expression without a word, though someone will be alerted any moment. Then they'll find Coltania's body and . . .

'They won't believe me,' I say, more to myself than to Heron.

He replies anyway. 'I think there's plenty of evidence to support your story,' he says.

I shake my head. 'There was plenty of evidence to get Søren out of the dungeon as well, but King Etristo didn't listen to it because it didn't fit the story he needed to tell. He needed Søren imprisoned to use as a bargaining chip,' I say slowly. 'And he'll have an awful lot to gain by arresting me as well now, especially since most of the suitors have fled. He's losing money.'

I'm thinking out loud, but I stop there, glancing at the attendant warily. My heart thunders in my chest even harder now than it did with Coltania standing over me. Heron glances at the attendant as well and the color drains from his face. His eyes meet mine and I know the same thought passes between us.

We need more time than we have and there is only one way to fix that.

Heron acts so swiftly I nearly miss it, aided by his Air Gift, no doubt. Before the attendant can even react, Heron has one arm around his neck, crushing the attendant's windpipe. As the man struggles, he lets go of the crank, which causes the riser to come to a sharp stop that makes my stomach flip. The attendant is bigger than Heron and he fights against him hard, but a measure of peace comes over Heron's face and he holds on tight until, finally, the man's eyes close and he goes slack in Heron's arms.

Heron doesn't make the same mistake Coltania made with me, though – he doesn't assume he's unconscious just because he's still.

'Can you handle the crank?' he asks me, keeping hold of the operator. 'It should be easy, going down instead of up.'

I nod, not trusting myself to speak. Instead, I focus on the crank. Even going down, it takes a lot of strength to turn it. I only make it two floors before Heron tells me to stop.

'We'll get out here and take the stairs,' he says, finally letting go of the attendant's body. He opens the gate and ushers me out.

It's only then that I finally speak the thought that's been nagging at me.

'King Etristo's lost a lot of money on me,' I tell Heron. 'The only way he can make it back is by selling Søren and me to the Kaiser.'

Heron must have reached the same conclusion, because he doesn't look surprised. 'We have to leave now,' he says.

My heart thunders in my chest, but I manage to nod.

'Yes,' I say. 'But not without Søren.'

Artemisia is waiting in my room, sitting in a chair near the fireplace, when Heron and I hurry in. She turns to me, annoyed at first, but then she takes in my bloody clothing and panicked expression.

Before she can say a word, I tell her everything that happened since I left with Coltania only an hour ago. I'm surprised by how calm my voice sounds, even as I feel nothing but panic inside.

'What do we need, then?' Artemisia asks when I finish, her tone brisk. 'Get Søren. Send news to Blaise. The refugees – we'll need to find enough ships to carry them. Food to feed them. Weapons to arm anyone who wants to fight.' She ticks the list off on her fingers and my stomach sinks lower with each task.

'There's no time for all that,' I say, shaking my head. 'We can't do any of it—'

'Not so fast,' she interrupts. A smile spreads over her face, reaching all the way up to her eyes. It's a rare smile from Artemisia, and every bit as frightening as she is. 'Luckily for us, the Sta'Criveran harbor keeps many large trade ships filled with all sorts of things, but primarily food and weapons.'

'So all we have to do is march into the harbor and steal a bunch of ships,' Heron says slowly, looking at her like she's mad. 'There's no way we'll be able to do that. There are only three of us – five if we manage to get Blaise and free Søren, and even that seems like a slim possibility at this point.'

'There will be five of us, with Søren and Blaise,' Artemisia agrees. 'But three of us are Guardians and it's the dead of night.' She pauses, glancing between Heron and me. 'It's a mad plan, but it could work.'

'I can get Søren if you can get Blaise and the ships,' I tell them. 'Three thousand refugees. That was Erik's estimate. How many ships will we need?'

Heron shakes his head. 'We'd need a fleet, Theo,' he says, voice heavy. 'I think even Art would agree that it won't be possible.'

Artemisia does falter, but her lips purse and her brow furrows and I know that she has a ghost of a plan already.

'What if . . .' Heron starts. 'I know we don't want to talk about it, but what if we don't take all of the refugees. We would only be dragging them into a war most of them won't be able to fight in. It would be dangerous—'

'Not as dangerous as staying here after King Etristo realizes I've gone – and stolen a fleet of his ships and the country's cheapest workers in the process,' I point out.

'He'll kill them if we don't take them. I won't leave anyone behind, whether they want to fight or not. Art, what are you thinking?'

She lets out a low sigh, shaking her head. 'There is one option, but it's a risk that might backfire,' she warns. 'We'd need my mother's help and her crew.'

I shake my head. 'She might well turn me over to King Etristo herself,' I say. With everything that's happened, I almost forgot what I overheard him tell the Czar earlier. 'She offered him Water Gems, in some capacity. That's why he agreed to host me. Sta'Crivero is on the verge of a drought.'

For an instant, Artemisia looks like she's going to deny it. But she can't. She knows what her mother is capable of better than anyone. 'We need her, Theo,' she says instead. 'Or Heron is right. Our only chance is to leave two-thirds of the refugees behind.'

Frustration burns through me, blistering hot. Everything is falling apart and I can't see a way out of this that I could happily take. I think of Coltania's body in the garden. In a few hours, Sta'Criverans will be going up there for morning walks or to have breakfast and they will find her. They will find the guard in the elevator first. It won't be long before he wakes up and King Etristo puts together the pieces. It won't be long until I'm in that dungeon next to Søren and the Kaiser is on his way to collect us both.

I was supposed to have more time, but there's nothing to be done about that now.

'Come on, Art,' I say. 'If I'm waking your mother up at this hour, I'm not doing it alone.'

When Dragonsbane answers her door, she looks ready to murder whoever is on the other side. In her white nightgown, with her hair in a frizzy cloud around her pillow-creased face, she doesn't look anything like the Dragonsbane I've come to know and – if we're being honest – fear.

I want to ask her about the Water Gems up front, but I hold my tongue. After all, I need her right now.

'There had better be a good reason for this,' she says, her sharp glare shifting between Artemisia and me.

Artemisia elbows me and I take that as a suggestion that I start.

'Well, I did just murder *Salla* Coltania in the garden after finding out she was the one who assassinated the Archduke and Hoa,' I tell her. Petty as it is, I can't help but enjoy the look of shock that comes over her. 'We're fairly certain that when her body is discovered and a riser operator recovers his wits, King Etristo will have me arrested and then sell Søren and me to the Kaiser to make up whatever loss he's facing over this disaster of a suitor search. Since I'd really rather that not happen, we're leaving now and commandeering a fleet of merchant ships in the harbor so we can take the refugees from the camp with us back to Astrea to liberate the Fire Mine. Oh, and Erik is going to meet us there with refugees from the other camps. Would you like to join us? You are quite good at commandeering ships.'

Dragonsbane stares at me for a few moments, her mouth hanging open. She starts to speak, then cuts herself off, then tries again. It happens a few times before she finally manages to say words.

'Are you mad?' she asks me. There's no accusation in her voice – she sounds genuinely curious.

'I'm desperate,' I say. 'But I suppose the two are close enough.'

Dragonsbane shakes her head, blinking away the sleep still left in her eyes. 'All right,' she says with a beleaguered sigh. 'I'll help you get out and get the ships, but after that you're on your own—'

'Mo – Captain,' Artemisia says before clearing her throat. 'I think . . . I believe that's the wrong choice. We need you not just to take the ships but for the battle as well. We need you to be able to win this.'

The want in Artemisia's voice feels like a punch to my gut, but Dragonsbane is unmoved. She looks at her daughter the same way she would at any other crew member who dared to question her decision.

'King Etristo has crossed me and so I'm leaving and taking compensation with me in the form of ships,' she says.

'*He* crossed *you*?' I ask before I can stop myself. The words rush out and I know they are stupid even as I say them, but I say them all the same. 'That's laughable. Tell me, just how many Water Gems did you offer him for auctioning me off to the highest bidder?'

She holds my gaze, unflinching. 'I offered him the mine,' she says.

Heat gathers at my fingertips but I clench them into fists at my sides. *Not now,* I beg.

'That wasn't yours to offer,' I say. The warmth in my fingertips begins to spread, working its way up my arms, prickling my skin. I try to ignore it, squeezing my fists tighter and digging my nails into my palms, the pain a welcome distraction.

At my side, Artemisia casts me a bewildered glance, looking down at my hands.

Dragonsbane shrugs. 'Someone had to think of Astrea,' she says, drawing Artemisia's attention back. 'I knew you wouldn't do it, so I did. One mine for our country back. One-quarter of our power for the rest. It was an easy decision to make.'

'It wasn't yours,' I repeat through clenched teeth. 'You aren't a queen, no matter what you like to think. I am my mother's heir. You are just a pirate.'

I mean the words as an insult, but they only slide off Dragonsbane's back.

'Etristo doesn't know how to wage battle,' she says, tearing her gaze away from me and looking at Art instead. 'Taking his ships will almost be easy and he won't give chase once we're out. But I won't throw my crew into the crossfire of a war with Kalovaxia – a war we can't win. And you shouldn't either, Artemisia. As Theo put it, we are only pirates, after all.'

Her voice is sharp, but for the first time, Art doesn't flinch away from it. Instead, she stands up a little straighter. 'The Water Mine destroyed me, you know, and it built me up again from nothing. King Etristo doesn't deserve a single stone from its depths. Some things are worth fighting for even when the fight seems hopeless. Even if I'm not worth it to you, I would hope Astrea would be.'

Dragonsbane doesn't answer her. Instead, she looks at me.

'I don't want your crown, Theo. It would bury me,' she

says, her voice quiet. 'I have always done what I believe is best for Astrea, but that does not include storming into a battle we aren't ready for. I'll get you your ships, but then we part ways.'

There is nothing left to say, so I only nod and turn away from Dragonsbane. Artemisia and I leave without another word, hearing the door close firmly behind us. We only get halfway down the hall before Art grabs my wrist and forces my clenched fist open. In the candlelit hallway, we both look at the red skin of my palm.

I want to pull it away, to hide it from view, but that wouldn't do any good. Art knows – she must have suspected even before. I swallow.

'It's been happening for a while,' I tell her quietly. 'Little things at first. Flickering flames would match my heartbeat, Fire Gems would call to me. But it's getting stronger. It seems to happen when I'm angry.' I don't tell her about the worst incident, the one that happened after my nightmare about Cress.

Artemisia doesn't reply at first. She reaches out to touch the skin but immediately pulls back with a hiss. 'It's hot,' she tells me.

'I don't feel it,' I admit. Though I've been dreading this moment, it feels good to tell someone. I'm glad that it's Art, which surprises me.

She touches my palm again, but this time her touch is cool. It feels like dipping my hand into a pool of cold water, and the feeling spreads through the rest of me. The heat in my veins abates. 'Does anyone else know?' she asks.

'No,' I say, the word coming out in a whisper. 'I don't want them to.'

For a moment, I expect her to argue, but instead she simply sighs. 'Can you still get Søren out?' she asks.

I nod. 'I'll be fine.'

'Good,' she says, the word crisp. 'One problem at a time.'

BREAK

———•———

Søren is in his usual position, slouched against the wall. He looks up when he sees me, the dark shadows beneath his eyes a stark contrast against his pale skin. Even in the warmth of the candlelight, his pallor is sallow. He hasn't left this cell in days now, and whatever he's eating isn't nourishing him.

When it comes time for a fight, he won't be in peak form. I'm only glad that Søren on a bad day is still a better warrior than most on their best days. I hope it will be enough.

Tizoli leaves us to return to his post, giving us privacy.

'You look deadly, Theo,' Søren tells me, his voice quiet. 'Is there a reason you're so much later tonight than you usually are?'

'There were some . . . complications,' I say carefully.

Søren must hear something in my voice, because with a labored exhale, he pulls himself to his feet. I shrug off my cloak and pull the sword out from its place strapped to my back. The cragged wrought-iron Kalovaxian blade isn't as ornate as Astrean blades, especially with the Spiritgems pried from the hilt. I remember Søren prying the first one out to give to the Guardians we met in the Astrean prison, but someone on Dragonsbane's crew must have taken out the rest after he was disarmed.

When he sees it, Søren breaks into a grin. 'Sturdax,' he says, reaching through the bars for it. 'I thought it was lost after we left Astrea.'

I pass it to him, unable to hide my amusement though I know this isn't the time or place for it. 'Dragonsbane had it but Artemisia got it back for you,' I explain. 'You . . . named your sword?'

He barely glances at me; all his attention is on his blade, which he swishes through the air a few times experimentally. He looks at the blade so tenderly I half expect him to kiss it.

'He feels different without the stones,' he says thoughtfully before registering my question. 'And of course I named him. We've been through a lot together over the years – I like Sturdax more than most of my friends. I might like Sturdax more than I like *you*.'

'I hope that's not true, since I'm about to ask an awful lot of you,' I say.

Søren tears his gaze away from his sword and looks at me, jaw set.

'Where do we begin?' he asks.

A few moments later, I call out to Tizoli that I'm ready to leave. When he comes down the hallway with his ring of keys already out, I have a moment of doubt. Of everything I've done tonight or will do, this might be the only part I actually regret. Because Tizoli is by far the kindest Sta'Criveran I've met.

I still jump on him as soon as he turns his back to me. I still wrap my arms around his neck the way Heron taught me to, squeezing with all my might. I still kick the keys out of his hand and into Søren's cell.

I just feel a bit bad about it when Tizoli finally sinks to his knees and his eyes finally flutter closed. I hold on to him until Søren unlocks his cell and comes toward us with his sword drawn and ready. Finally, I let go of Tizoli and climb off him, watching as Søren prods him as gently as he can in the shoulder with the point of his sword. Tizoli doesn't move, but his chest rises and falls.

'You didn't kill him,' Søren tells me, and even though I can see that myself, I'm glad to hear the words out loud.

I nod and pull out my dagger from its place at my hip.

'It's nearly sunrise and we need to be on our way to the camp before the palace wakes up,' I tell him.

'I'm feeling a sense of déjà vu, Theo,' Søren tells me. 'It seems like only yesterday *I* was rescuing *you* from a dungeon.'

'The difference is that this time I don't know of any secret tunnels,' I admit.

He looks at me warily. 'What's the plan, then? We walk out the front door? It's the middle of the night but there will be people awake.'

'I know,' I say, my heartbeat thundering louder in my chest. 'The Sta'Criverans love a spectacle, though; I say we give them one.' I nod toward Tizoli's body, clothed in plain trousers and a shirt with a guard's jacket over. 'You two should be close to the same size.'

Søren stares at me incredulously, but I can see the gears in his mind turning. He nods. 'Turn around.'

I roll my eyes, but do as he says. 'Modest all of a sudden?' I ask him.

'Not particularly,' he says. I hear him shuffling out of his clothes, the thud of shoes being removed. 'But you need to keep your wits about you, and I wouldn't want to rob you of any of them.'

I can't help but snort. 'Certainly there's a better time for bad jokes than right now,' I say.

'I'm not sure about that,' he says. 'Running for my life isn't quite as terrifying as it should be when I'm doing it with you. You can turn around now.'

I do and the first thing I realize is that Tizoli and Søren are *not* the same size. The shirt and trousers fit in the sense that they button closed without tearing, but on Søren's broad chest, the shirt gapes between the strained buttons and the sleeves and pants are both an inch too short. Søren seems to have realized this issue as well, though he's far more amused than troubled by it.

'What can be done?' he asks, tugging at the shirt in a vain attempt to make it fit better. 'It'll just have to work. What are we going to do about you, though? You are fairly recognizable.'

I pick my cloak up off the floor and slip it back on, drawing the hood forward so that my face is in shadows. He starts to pick up Tizoli's uniform jacket, but I stop him. 'We still might bring some attention,' I admit. 'We just have to make sure that when we do, we give them a good show.'

We take the stairs instead of the riser, scrambling up the decrepit steps that seem to crumble beneath our feet. They're so out of use now, with the invention of the risers, that they're falling apart. But in the dead of night, we don't run into another guard until we're back on the main level, and by that point we are stumbling and laughing a little too loudly together. I lean most of my weight on Søren as if I can't stand up on my own, and he leans back on me.

Any chance of our proximity bringing up old feelings is quickly quashed because Søren still smells like the dungeon – all mold and darkness and old sweat. I never thought I'd be grateful for such a smell.

The guard yells something at us in Sta'Criveran that I assume must be a question. He's red-faced and blustery, gesturing to the open stairway door behind us, so I assume that question must be something like *'What were you two idiots doing down there?'*

Søren understands, though, and he swaggers up to his full height, nearly losing his balance in the process. He puts an arm around my shoulders to keep upright. He gestures to me and says something in Sta'Criveran, slurring the words together like he's had a few drinks too many. He lifts his eyebrows at the guard suggestively – giving the guard a very lewd excuse for our presence in the dungeon and for the fact that he's covered in dirt and grime, I'm sure.

The guard frowns at me and I pull back further into the safety of my hood. He says something to me that I don't understand, but Søren's quick to interrupt with a raucous laugh.

He says something to the guard that I imagine to be along the lines of *'She's very shy and is very embarrassed to be caught after our dungeon rendezvous, so if you don't mind, we should be on our way.'*

The guard frowns at him and says something else. The only word I catch is *Etralian*. But the way he says it makes me realize that he thinks *Søren* is Etralian. I suppose that isn't surprising, since Kalovaxians and Etralians are similarly pale and fair. It may prove to be a problem, though, since the Etralian delegation left with the Czar yesterday.

Søren remains calm, though, and babbles on in slurred Sta'Criveran with a few words I'm pretty sure are Etralian in order to really sell it. He draws me closer to him and gestures wildly at me. I wish I could tell him to tone it down a touch.

The guard gives a loud harrumph and glowers at Søren, which sends him into another slurred but jovial spiel.

After what seems like an eternity, the guard rolls his eyes and ushers us on with one last shouted warning, which I'm sure is something like *'And don't go having rendezvous in the dungeon again.'* A warning I am only too happy to heed. If I never see another dungeon, it will be too soon.

Søren and I keep up our drunken swagger and giggles all the way through the main hall, drawing the attention of the only people up this early – maids and cooks and deliverymen, all of whom stare at us and laugh at our foolishness, likely enjoying the sight of two of the wealthy elite who employ them making asses out of themselves.

When we finally emerge from the palace, I laugh for real. Søren laughs, too, and even though we don't have to pretend anymore, we both still lean on each other.

'He asked why I was still here when the Etralians left yesterday, so I told him that I'd decided to stay and marry you,' he explains through laughter. 'And he got mad and said foreigners were stealing Sta'Criveran women. I told him he was welcome to go to Etralia and I would introduce him to my cousins. I think he might actually try to find me again and take me up on it.'

Despite everything, I let out a snort of laughter. 'Come on,' I tell him. Without thinking about it, I take his hand and pull him down the empty street.

'You enjoy this, don't you?' he asks, following me.

'Running for our lives?' I ask him over my shoulder. 'Of course not.'

'The danger,' he clarifies. 'The wolf at your heels. The purpose.'

I consider it for a moment before shrugging. 'I think I enjoy acting and not waiting for something to happen,' I say. 'I enjoy having a plan and I enjoy following it through instead of being at the mercy of someone else's decisions.'

'This was not the original plan, though, was it?' he asks, a question I've been dreading since I handed him that sword in the dungeon.

'No,' I admit. As we weave through the streets, I tell him about the plan I hatched with Erik, then about Hoa's death, about Coltania and the poison and her body left in the garden.

'I'm sorry,' he says when I finish.

I glance back at him over my shoulder. 'For what?' I ask.

'I was wrong – you aren't enjoying this,' he tells me. 'You're in shock. I've seen it on the battlefield – soldiers who've watched their friends die next to them or who made their first kill and watched the life leave another man's eyes. They continue to fight anyway, because they have to. The blood pumps hotter in their veins. They're always fiercer and stronger and sharper than they were before. Their minds seem to focus in on just surviving the battle . . . but the battle always ends and the shock ends with it. That's what I'm sorry for.'

I swallow and tear my gaze away from him. 'We should hurry up,' I say softly. 'Let's put some distance between us and the city before King Etristo sends his guards after us.'

FLEE

———— ◆ • ◆ ————

S ØREN USES THE MONEY ARTEMISIA gave me to lease a horse
from the stable, and while the stablehand is saddling it up,
Søren takes the opportunity to clean up a bit with a wet rag.
It can only remove so much of the dungeon grime from his
skin, but it does help measurably. He changes into a fresh set
of clothes he bought off the stablehand, which are too big but
at least more comfortable than Tizoli's.

We have a long ride ahead of us and I'm honestly not
sure which I'd prefer – him smelling like the dungeon or him
smelling like his usual self. Like sea salt and driftwood in a
way that brings me back to times it's better not to think about.

When the stablehand brings the horse around, Søren helps
me up onto its back before swinging on in front of me. He
takes the reins from the man and with a lurch we are off. I
wrap my arms tightly around Søren's waist as the wind whips
against my skin. Once we are outside the city, I finally push
my hood off my face.

We did it, I realize with a thrill. We made it out of the
city before Coltania's body was found and before the riser
attendant could wake up and tell anyone what happened.

Even if either of them is discovered now, the guards will never be able to come after us in time to catch up. When they do put the pieces together, they'll assume we've left the same way we came, through ships in the harbor. They won't think to look at the refugee camp.

I tighten my grip on Søren's waist.

'All right?' he asks me, his voice all but lost in the wind.

I nod against his shoulder. 'I wouldn't have left you, you know,' I tell him.

He doesn't say anything and for a moment I think he didn't hear me at all – understandable since the wind is so loud I can barely hear my own thoughts. Just when I've given up on getting a response, he gives one.

'You never have. Even when it would have made things much easier for you.'

I think about the decision to save him from the dungeon and how much easier it truly would have been to leave him. I would be with my Shadows on a ship now, and we would have been spared an awful lot of trouble and eliminated plenty of risk as well. I remember my deal with Dragonsbane on the *Smoke* and the sacrifice I made to get Søren out of the brig. I remember when I myself was in a dungeon, telling Blaise not to save me because I knew Søren would and I knew we could use that to our advantage.

Having Søren in my life has complicated things – but I realize now that I wouldn't wish it to be any other way.

In the garden, I told him that he couldn't love me because he didn't really know me, and I still believe that. But it doesn't change the fact that I know him. It doesn't change the fact that I'm in love with him.

* * *

By the time the walled camp appears on the horizon, the sun is rising, hanging low in the east with the bottom of it still grazing the sand dunes. It's bright enough to see that we aren't the first to arrive – there is a group already approaching the entrance with weapons drawn. From this distance, the only detail I can make out is the shock of Artemisia's blue hair.

Søren pulls the horse to a halt atop a sand dune that overlooks the camp, and we linger there, watching the fight unfold below us. A mere half-dozen guards rush toward the wall from their barracks nearby. Artemisia makes quick work of one of them, even though he wields two swords to her single blade. First she knocks one from his hand, but when he insists on keeping hold of the other, she responds by cutting off that hand in its entirety.

I tear my gaze away, though the man's screams carry up to our perch.

'It'll be over quickly – the guards are outmatched,' Søren tells me, dismounting and helping me down after him.

I nod. 'They were here to keep the refugees inside the walls,' I say. 'They were charged with keeping thousands of unarmed people in a pen – little more than shepherds, really. They never dreamed anyone would want to attack from the outside.'

Søren glances at me, and he must see my discomfort when another of our warriors runs a blade through a guard's stomach, cutting straight through to the other side.

'You don't have to watch,' he says. 'I can tell you when it's done.'

For a moment, I consider staying to watch. I ordered this, after all – even if I'm not down there in the thick of it, all of this blood is still on my hands. The least I can do is bear witness to it. But as Søren said, the battle will be over quickly and there are still more preparations to be made.

'Thank you,' I tell Søren, walking around to the other side of the horse and shedding my cloak. I smooth my crimson gown, but that does little to help the dirt and wrinkles it's accumulated from the ride. It'll have to do.

Søren glances back at me with raised eyebrows.

'I didn't realize we were going to a ball. It would have been more practical to ride in trousers.'

'Artemisia said I need to be aware of the image I'm presenting,' I tell him. 'I need them to follow me, and they're more likely to follow someone who looks like a queen than they are a dirty street rat.'

Søren snorts. 'Are those her words?'

I shrug. 'She has a point,' I say. 'They already see me as a child with no idea what I'm doing.'

His eyes linger on mine for a moment, even as another scream pierces the air.

'I don't know that it has much to do with the dress,' he tells me. 'Maybe it does make you look more regal, but that won't make them follow you.'

My stomach sinks. 'Then what will?' I ask him.

He shrugs, eyes dropping away from mine as he turns back to the camp. 'You don't need to look like a queen – you already are one. Show them the girl who was brilliant enough to escape from under the Kaiser's nose, who's fierce enough to protect her people with her life, who's strong enough to stand on her own two feet, even with the weight of the world on her shoulders. You are a queen, Theo, and they would be mad not to follow you.'

He doesn't look at me as he says it, and I'm grateful for that. He doesn't see what the words do to me, how they cause heat to rise to my cheeks. After a moment, I walk toward him and straighten up. The guards all lie in the sand, dead or disarmed, and it is time to see if Søren is right.

REFUGE

———◆·◆———

BY THE TIME SØREN AND I make our way to the entrance, the others are waiting. Amid the bodies of the guards, Heron and Artemisia stand together with their bloody swords still drawn. Dragonsbane is there, too, which surprises me. I thought she'd stay on the ship and out of what she thought was a foolish plan, but here she is. She looks my way when we approach, her eyes narrowing slightly. Though fury still burns through me when I think of her offering Etristo the Water Mine, I force myself to nod my thanks. We couldn't have gotten this far without her help.

I walk toward Heron and Artemisia. It's only been a few hours since I saw them last, but part of me wants to embrace both of them. The blood staining their clothes and skin is the only thing that holds me back.

'Well done,' I say instead. 'What happened back in the harbor? Did you get enough ships?'

Artemisia nods. 'Plenty,' she says. 'Food, weapons, all of it. My mother is still a bit begrudging about the whole thing, but her crew is much more enthusiastic – I think more than a few of them might join us at the mine.'

I smile. 'That's wonderful,' I say. 'And Blaise?'

'We sent him ahead of us to meet with the Elders,' Artemisia explains. 'He took them your offer so that everyone could think it over and would be ready to go by the time we got here.'

I nod, swallowing down my nerves. 'Let's get them onto the ships, then. We can sort out who wants to fight and who doesn't once everyone is safe.'

When Heron and one of Dragonsbane's men push open the door, I see that the entire camp has already gathered in the streets, huddling together, clutching loved ones tightly to them, with all their worldly possessions clutched to their chests in meager bundles.

Even when I walk in with my Shadows at my back and Dragonsbane and her warriors behind them, none of the refugees appears terribly reassured. They came here for safety, after all, and now I am bringing war to their door.

But they aren't safe here.

I watch as Elders guide them into a line that files past us and out of the camp that has been their only home for years. Decades, in most cases. I feel their eyes on me as they pass, and I stand up a little straighter, square my shoulders a little more. I try to look like a queen before I remember what Søren said – there is no such thing as looking like a queen.

I've been trying to emulate my mother, I realize, who was always graceful and confident, but I am not her. I would be a fool to be confident and no one needs my grace. They need shelter and food and a path forward, and those are all things I can give them. They will have to be enough.

Sandrin breaks through the crowd and comes toward us, bowing at the waist. Blaise follows him a few paces behind, dark eyes hard and wary. The circles under his eyes are starker than I remember them, and there is an energy about him that startles me. It seems to vibrate in the air around him.

'Your Majesty,' Sandrin says, drawing my attention back to him.

It's the first time he's called me that, and the title feels strange coming from his mouth. It doesn't feel like something I've earned yet.

'Sandrin,' I say, inclining my head. 'Thank you for your help. As soon as we get everyone on the ships, we'll depart. We have little reason to believe the Sta'Criverans will give chase. They aren't much for fighting.'

He nods. 'I've passed your message on to everyone,' he says, glancing at Blaise behind him. 'Many are still considering it.'

'It isn't a choice to be made lightly,' I say. 'There will be time to discuss it more on the ship. You'll stay aboard mine, won't you? And all the Elders as well. I would appreciate all of your guidance going forward.'

He looks surprised by that but nods. 'I would be glad to,' he says. He bows again before joining the other Elders in leading the refugees out of the camp.

Blaise approaches when he's gone, thoughts clearly weighing heavily just behind his eyes.

I'm not sure what to say, so I settle for thanking him.

'I was glad to be of use,' he says. 'Artemisia thought the battle would be too dangerous for me.'

It was a smart decision, but Blaise doesn't sound happy about it.

'I needed you here,' I tell him. 'How do you think it went? I know Sandrin said that many were still considering it, but . . .'

Blaise knows what I'm asking and a grim smile tugs at the corners of his mouth. 'I think that for most of those who can fight, their first impulse was to say yes and I think that impulse will end up outweighing their hesitations.'

I smile, an ember of hope sparking in my belly.

For a moment, he mulls over his words. 'I gave Art my gems,' he says. 'It's too dangerous for me to go on the ship with them.'

He gave them to Art like before, for safekeeping. Not for good. He'll still take them back; he'll still try to do something stupid and noble. But not today. Today he is here and he is safe and he is just Blaise.

He reaches for me, his arms encircling me. The embrace is too hot, especially under the Sta'Criveran sun, but I hold him back just as tightly. 'We're going home, Theo,' he murmurs in my ear. In his voice, the word *home* is spun sugar, sweet but delicate.

It echoes in my mind long after he releases me – a word, a prayer, a promise that I will see fulfilled.

SAIL

———— ◆ · ◆ ————

T WO THOUSAND PEOPLE AGREE TO fight.

It's a tight fit on the fifteen ships Dragonsbane's crew took from the harbor, but we manage to get everyone on board. Cramped as it is, I think they have more room than they did in the camp. Dragonsbane's own fleet takes many of the refugees who can't or don't want to fight, though I'm not sure what she's going to do with them.

I might not trust Dragonsbane with much – I don't always trust her loyalties or her judgment or her opinions of others – but I have to believe that she'll do right by these people after failing many of them so terribly the first time around. We both want what is best for Astrea, even if we might disagree on what that is more often than not.

When we go our separate ways, it's difficult not to feel a twinge of sadness. She failed me, too, in smaller ways. Forgivable ways, if she ever gave me a chance to forgive her. That isn't Dragonsbane, though. She doesn't want forgiveness from anyone. She didn't want it from my mother and she doesn't want it from me. She won't even ask for it from her daughter, though Art knows better than to expect anything else.

We stand together on the aft of the ship, watching her small fleet disappear into the distance. Though I keep hoping they will turn around and come with us after all, Artemisia only looks resigned.

'It's what she does best,' she says after a moment. 'It's why she's survived this long – she knows when to run.'

There's a layer beneath the factual tone of her voice, a layer I might have missed even a few weeks ago when I didn't know her as well as I do now. She never expected her mother to stay, but she wished it all the same.

'I'm sorry,' I tell her.

She shrugs her shoulders, the move sharp and graceless, without any of her usual swagger. Her jaw is clenched so tightly I'm surprised she can get words out.

'Only fools waste time with wishes and apologies,' she says, but the words don't have their usual bite.

We're both fools, then, I think, though I don't say it out loud. This isn't something Art wants to talk about and she doesn't need to. So I don't press her to share her feelings; I don't even try to touch her the way I think I would like someone to touch me if I were in her position. That isn't what she needs. She needs someone to stand at her side and pretend not to notice when her tears begin to fall. So that is what I do.

That night, my cabin feels too quiet. I've taken the captain's quarters on the lead ship, and it's sizable, as far as cabins go – it has room for a desk and a dining table and a cot – but after my grand room in Sta'Crivero, it feels cramped. The styling is simple and minimalistic, without the grand Sta'Criveran flourishes and embellishments, though those, at least, I don't miss. Instead, I find comfort in the weathered wood and worn blanket, the roughly hewn desk and the hard chair with its uneven legs. It is a space that feels homey and comfortable, and I find that is what I crave now more than luxury.

The quiet leaves space for too many thoughts, though, too many nightmares to play out behind my eyes even before I have a chance to fall asleep. I could be leading these people into a slaughter. Thousands of people could end up dead and it would be because of a choice I made. I might as well plunge a dagger between their ribs myself.

Once, I thought that the blood on Søren's hands was so thick that they would never be clean again, but now my own don't feel much cleaner. I killed Ampelio and Coltania myself, but how many others lost their lives because of me? Elpis, Hoa, the Archduke, the Guardians in the Astrean prison, the servant girl Coltania enlisted whose name I don't even know. All those dead guards outside the refugee camp, even.

I know that these deaths were unavoidable, but guilt eats at me all the same. And here I am leading more people – thousands of people – into a battle I don't know if we can win.

It's foolish and irresponsible and – and it's the only way forward. It's the only way home.

A knock sounds at my door, light and questioning.

Grateful for the interruption, I drag myself from my narrow cot and pull my dressing robe over my nightgown, tying the sash around my waist. When I open the door, I'm surprised to find Søren on the other side. I don't know who I expected it to be. Blaise? He's bunking with Artemisia, who's promised to kill him if he starts to lose control. He wouldn't risk leaving her side for even a moment.

I search my feelings. Am I relieved it's Søren? Was there a part of me that wished it was Blaise instead? I don't know. All I'm sure of is that Søren's presence feels like lightning striking in my belly, filling me with a dangerous warmth.

I open the door farther and gesture for him to come in. The door closes behind him with a firm click.

'Are you all right?' he asks me, his voice low. 'With Hoa and Coltania and everything?'

I bite my lip and turn back to him. Images of Hoa's lifeless body and Coltania's eyes locked on mine as she took her final breath fill my thoughts. Coltania is easier to think about, so I bury Hoa in my mind and focus on her.

'Do you remember what you told me after I killed Ampelio?' I ask him, sitting down on the edge of my cot.

Søren stays standing before me, frowning. Whatever he was expecting me to say, it wasn't that. 'I believe I tried to comfort you and I made an ass out of myself in the process,' he says slowly.

I smile tightly. 'You did,' I agree. 'But later, when you mentioned it again, you were right. Killing is never easy, even when it isn't your first time doing it. Even when you have no choice – when it's a matter of self-defense. It leaves its mark on you.'

Søren holds my gaze. 'You did what you had to,' he says.

'I know,' I tell him, looking down at my hands. I debate my next words, whether it's wiser to say them out loud or keep them locked inside. I can't find the answer to that, yet in the end I force myself to give them voice. 'But in that moment, when I forced the dagger into her stomach, I wasn't thinking about defending myself. I wasn't thinking about what would happen to me if I failed. I was thinking about Hoa, about what Coltania had done to her – how she'd taken another person away from me. When I killed her, I wasn't only fueled by self-defense. I was fueled by rage. I was fueled by vengeance.'

It's an ugly confession, made here in a quiet cabin in the middle of the ocean, but Søren doesn't flinch away from it. He holds my gaze, steady and sure like he can see straight through to the deepest parts of me, the parts I'm ashamed of. The parts I try to hide from everyone else, even Blaise. Søren sees the ugliest parts of me, the cowardice and the conniving and the manipulating. He sees it all and he understands it. He looks at me like I'm his favorite book, one he's read every page of too many times. One whose secrets he's uncovered but he keeps coming back for more anyway.

I'm still not sure if I'm Thora in his eyes, or Theo, or some bleeding watercolor of both together, but in this moment, we are the only two people in the world and we are not Thora and the Prinz. We are Theo and Søren and it feels like he knows me as well as I know myself.

I stand and close the few steps of distance between us until we are only inches apart. He doesn't step back, but he doesn't move closer either, though his breath hitches. He makes no move to touch me, his hands hanging limp at his sides. He won't, I realize, because I asked him to keep his feelings to himself.

It's easier that way, smarter to leave things as they are. He is my advisor and my friend, and that is all he can ever be. But standing this close to him, it's difficult to remember why that is. It's difficult to remember Blaise, only a few cabins away, telling me he loved me. It's difficult to remember the Kaiser, sitting on my mother's throne with my once closest friend at his side. It's difficult to remember the thousands of people who have agreed to follow me into battle, people who see Søren as their enemy.

'Søren,' I say, his name little more than a breath.

His eyes find mine – they're the same shade of blue as the Kaiser's, but even that reminder is dim now, a ghost in the back of my mind.

Tentatively, I reach up to touch his cheek. He's in need of a shave and his stubble is rough against the palm of my hand.

Søren looks like he wants to say something, but whatever it is falls away when I roll onto the tips of my toes and brush my lips against his. With that touch, all Søren's restraint falls away and in an instant he is kissing me back. One hand reaches up to cradle my face while the other settles at my waist, anchoring me to him. It is a gentle kiss, like the ones we shared back in Astrea, sneaking through palace tunnels and taking midnight sails when we were still strangers to each other, but we aren't strangers anymore. I know him and he knows me and the darkest parts of our souls match.

The kiss deepens. Søren tastes like the fresh bread and spiced wine we had at dinner. The kiss turns hungry, devouring, consuming until I'm not sure which breaths are his and which are mine. Our edges blur together, hands and skin and lips and teeth. When his mouth leaves mine, I want to pull him back, but all too quickly he's kissing my jaw instead, my cheek, the shell of my ear, sending a shiver through me that feels like fire.

'Theodosia.' He whispers my name like a hymn. It doesn't

sound too big anymore; it fits me as perfectly as his hand fits the curve of my waist, as perfectly as his mouth melds to mine when he kisses me again.

I don't have to ask Søren to stay the night with me. The invitation hangs in the air without words, and he accepts it, shucking off his boots and crawling into my bed. We curl up together under my threadbare blanket, my head on his chest, his arms around me.

'If they find me here in the morning, there will be talk,' he says through a yawn.

'I know,' I say. I listen to the beating of his heart, steady and sure and in time with mine.

His fingers trace patterns on my back through the thin material of my nightgown. 'In the garden, you told me not to mention my feelings for you because you believed them not to be true,' he says slowly.

'Søren—' I start, but he interrupts.

'Just let me say this, please,' he says before pausing. 'In Astrea, who you were – Thora – I wanted her. I wanted to protect her from my father, the way I never could protect my mother. I wanted to run away with her and save both of us. You were right about that. But what I felt then, it's a shadow of what I feel for you, Theo.'

I open my mouth to tell him to stop again, but the words die in my throat. Dangerous as they are, I want to hear them so much it almost breaks me.

'I don't want to protect you. I don't *need* to protect you. You have others for that and you've done it yourself enough times by now. I don't want to run away with you; I want to stand at your side and fight – fight for something I never even thought that I wanted, but I do. I'm stronger with you, and braver, and I never want to go back to living like I was before. I love you, and it isn't anything to do with who you pretended to be. I love *you*.'

'I love you, too,' I tell him softly.

When his breathing turns slow and even, I can't help but think about Blaise saying those same three words to me only days ago. When Blaise said them, they were a balm for a wound he hadn't delivered yet. Søren says them like he's breaking the chains that bind us together and hoping I will stay anyway.

STRATEGY

———◆———

THE SHIP WE'RE ON TRAILS behind the rest of the fleet. Though we made it from Astrea to Sta'Crivero in a week, it takes us twice that to wind around to the southeast coast of Astrea, where the Fire Mine is, and we make no effort to hurry. The two weeks pass in a flurry of training and strategizing, trying to turn our two thousand refugees into two thousand soldiers. The weapons and armor that were looted from one of the Sta'Criveran ships we stole are barely enough, but it will have to do, because the coast appeared on the horizon this morning, the silhouette of Astrea's cliffs jagged against the rising sun. There isn't much more time to wait and train and plan.

Though I know I'd do more harm than good if I tried to physically lead an army, it's difficult not to feel like a cosseted infant in a cushioned cradle. Søren must feel it worse than I do, though he's never complained to me in the nights he's spent in my room, the two of us huddling beneath the covers together, blocking out the rest of the world. Him fighting would be too risky and potentially confusing – Kalovaxian as he is, it would be too easy for a friendly sword to find its way to his heart. Still, I feel his disappointment permeating the air around him.

He tries to make up for it by throwing himself into strategizing. Because he's seen the mines from the point of view of a Kalovaxian commander, his input is invaluable. Even my Shadows, who spent years in the mines themselves, are surprised by the detail in the illustration Søren sketches out on the parchment we've laid out on my desk. We surround it, Søren, Blaise, Heron, Artemisia, and I, our shoulders touching.

'I've circled everywhere guards will be,' Søren says.

I glance from his somber face to the map. There are more circles than clear space.

'It's a lot,' he allows when none of us speaks.

'*A lot* is an understatement,' Artemisia says, pursing her lips.

'The mine won't be as easy to take as the camp was,' Søren admits. 'But we'll still outnumber them and they won't be expecting it, which gives us an advantage.'

'Enough to counteract *their* advantage of fighting on land they know, plentiful with their own resources, with more experience, strength, and gems to aid them?' Blaise asks.

Søren hesitates. 'Maybe,' he says.

Maybe isn't good enough, but it's the best we can hope for. I rub my temples and stare down at the map, pointing to the shore. 'So we'll approach from this direction?'

Søren nods. 'But it would be more effective if we also send a couple of the faster ships around here to come from this direction,' he says, pointing to the shore on the far side of the Fire Mine. 'That way, we'll be attacking on two fronts and it's one less channel they'll have to send a warning to my father.'

I nod. 'Do we have enough men for it?' I ask. 'Or will splitting our resources make it easier for them to pick us off one side at a time?'

Søren stares at the map, brow furrowed in concentration. 'We should have enough,' he says after a moment.

Should. There was a reason Dragonsbane didn't want to join this fight with us – it's a risk, and a big one at that.

'They won't have any ships watching the southwest coast,' Søren adds. 'But they will have some ships patrolling farther north. We have enough ships to take them out, but we'll likely lose a few of our own in the process.'

'Ships we can't afford to lose,' I say, frowning. An idea takes hold of me and I look up at Heron. 'How far can your invisibility spread?' I ask.

He considers the question. 'I can't say I've ever tried cloaking more than a couple of others.'

'Could you cloak the entire fleet?' I ask, though even as I voice the request, it seems like a hopeless question.

Heron's brow creases. 'No,' he says slowly. 'But maybe I could fade us enough that we would be difficult to see, especially if I play with the water's reflection. Not for long, though. Not long enough to get us past them.'

Artemisia tilts her head to one side, dark eyes becoming thoughtful. 'If Heron can fade the fleet, I can manipulate the tides, push us past the Kalovaxian patrol faster. We might not be able to slip by unnoticed before he loses the invisibility, but at the very least, we could surprise them enough to minimize our losses.' She pauses, her eyes flicking to Blaise. 'Or,' she says, her voice wary, 'we could rip their ships apart without giving them a chance to fire a single cannon.'

Blaise meets Artemisia's gaze, eyes widening when he understands what she isn't saying. After a moment, he nods. 'I can do that,' he says, testing out the words. 'Wood is of the earth.'

My time on the *Smoke* with Blaise comes back, how the wood that made up the ship started thrumming as erratically as his heartbeat, how I worried it might splinter apart. Artemisia is right – if we can use that against the Kalovaxian ships, we could deal a great blow before even setting foot on the shore. But at a steep cost.

'It's too dangerous,' I say. 'We don't know what it'll do to you, never mind our own ships.'

Blaise shakes his head. 'My gift is the strongest we have, Theo,' he says.

I remember Mina's words and imagine a pot boiling over. 'It could kill you. If we can get close to them using Art's and Heron's gifts, we can sink their ships in the non-magical way – with cannons – and not take that risk.'

Artemisia makes a noise in the back of her throat. 'We could,' she says slowly. 'It would even be easy, but it would come at a cost still. No matter how much of an advantage we gain by sneaking up on them, we'll still take losses – warriors, a ship even. Losses we can't afford.'

'We can't afford this either,' I say.

For a moment, no one speaks. 'Yes, we can,' Blaise says before reluctantly turning his gaze to Søren. 'Since Art will be otherwise occupied, the duty falls to you, *Prinkiti*. If I seem to be losing control of it and becoming a danger to our ships, you'll kill me before I can. Are we understood?'

Søren glances at me and then back to Blaise. 'We're understood,' he says.

'No,' I say, louder this time. 'It's too dangerous. You could *die*, Blaise.'

Blaise's jaw tenses and he shrugs. 'I can give us an advantage we desperately need.'

I look around at the others, hoping that someone else will speak out against this mad plan, but there is only silence, only friends who won't look me in the eye. An order dances on the tip of my tongue and I know I could use my crown – metaphorical as it might be – as a weapon again. I could order him to stay out of this, to stay safe, but I swallow down the urge. Some choices are not mine to make.

'We'll send a rowboat to pass along the plan to the other ships,' I say instead. 'What happens when we get to shore?'

'You were a Kalovaxian commander,' Heron says, looking at Søren. 'When we attack the mine, how will they respond?'

Søren looks a bit flustered at that. 'I was never posted at the mines, but as I understand it, they're trained differently than most warriors, though getting assigned there was always seen as something of an insult. They won't be the best of men, so there is some comfort there.'

'There would be,' Artemisia says, 'if our army weren't made up of refugees with two weeks of training.'

Søren doesn't have an argument for that. Instead he looks at me. 'We could wait,' he says. 'If we wait for Erik and the Vecturians, we'll have more warriors and the odds will swing more in our favor.'

'But waiting also means the risk of losing the element of surprise,' I say. 'If the Kalovaxian patrol notices our fleet lingering not far from the coast, *they'll* attack *us*.'

Søren nods before turning toward Heron. 'You've been keeping in touch with Erik with that gold,' he says. 'Has there been any more news from him?'

Heron shakes his head. 'Not since the last update I gave. They're on their way from Timmoree and they'll hopefully be here tomorrow, but it could be another couple of days, depending on the weather.'

There are so many variables, so many choices with unforeseeable consequences, so many things that could go wrong. I stare at Søren's map, as if there might be secrets there that I can somehow find, but it's just a map, and one that doesn't put things in our favor.

'What would be the best time to attack?' I ask Søren.

He frowns. 'They'll have a skeleton guard on the night shift,' he says. 'So it would be fewer men awake and ready to fight, but the dark would affect our warriors more than it will affect theirs. The Kalovaxians have trained in the dark, they know how to use it against their enemies. Dawn is our best chance. It'll be light enough to see, but the guards wouldn't have changed shifts yet. They'll be tired, not ready for a fight. Of course, it will only buy us a bit of time before their replacements join them, fully refreshed.'

'And the slaves?' I ask. 'Where would they be?'

'Some would be in the mines,' Heron says. 'The night shift is smaller, but still present. The rest would be in the slave quarters, here.' He points to a place on Søren's map, just next to the mine.

I nod. 'I trust your opinion on this,' I tell Søren. 'We'll attack at dawn.'

I look around at everyone. 'It must be dinnertime, go eat,' I say. 'There will be more time to plan when you're done.'

Everyone stands up from the table, chairs scraping against the wooden floors, but I stay seated. I'm too stressed to be able to stomach food, and I don't want the rest of the ship to see me like this, uncertain and afraid.

'Blaise,' I say when they begin to file out. 'Stay a minute, will you?'

He freezes in the doorway, looking at me before stepping back inside. Artemisia pauses as well and nods, leaving the cabin and closing the door, though I'm sure she will be waiting right outside, just in case. The thought makes me sick and I feel sicker still when I realize I'm grateful for her presence.

Neither of us speaks at first and the air is heavy between us. We haven't spoken much since we left Sta'Crivero, though I'm not sure who is avoiding whom or if it's even been intentional. There has been so much to do to prepare for this battle. But even as I think that, I remember that there has been time for Søren to come into my room every night, time for me to fall asleep in his arms. I wonder if Blaise knows about that; I'm sure he must have his suspicions.

I clear my throat. 'I don't like this plan,' I say.

He's quiet for a moment. 'Do you think I do?' he asks finally. 'Do you think I relish the idea of risking my life like this?'

'I think you relish the idea of being a hero.' The words force themselves out of me before I can stop them.

Blaise reels back like I slapped him. 'It wasn't my idea, Theo. You heard Artemisia and Heron and Søren – they all think it's our best chance. You know it is, too.'

'That doesn't mean I want you to do it,' I say quietly.

For a painful moment, he only stands there. 'Do you believe that Glaidi gave me this gift?' he asks.

'Mina said—'

'I'm not asking what Mina said, or Sandrin, or Heron, or Art. I'm asking what *you* believe.'

I bite my lip. 'Yes,' I say after a moment. 'I believe Glaidi blessed you.'

'Then it would be an insult to her to not use her gift,' he says with a grim smile. 'This is what I'm meant for. Let me do it.'

I shake my head. 'You don't need my permission, Blaise,' I tell him. 'The others agreed with you. I was far outnumbered.'

'That doesn't matter,' he says. He seems to be fighting himself for a moment before he takes my hands in his, squeezing them tightly. His skin is as feverish as ever, but I squeeze them back. 'If you ask me not to do it, I won't.'

It's a cruel offer, and part of me hates him for voicing it, because there is no right answer for me to give. I can't give him my blessing in this any more than I can stop him.

'You know yourself,' I say instead, forcing a smile. 'If you believe that you can do this, I do, too.'

GHOST

———— ◆•◆ ————

THE MOON PROVIDES ALL THE light we need as our ship pulls farther ahead of the fleet. They will wait for our signal that it's safe. On the bow, Heron, Artemisia, and Blaise stand shoulder to shoulder, staring out at the horizon where three Kalovaxian ships patrol the coast. Søren and I hang back, watching and waiting for what can only be called a miracle.

Søren's hand is on the hilt of his sword, his eyes on Blaise. I don't have to ask him if he would actually follow Blaise's direction to kill him if he loses control – I know he will without hesitation as surely as I know that if he does, I will stop him however I can.

Even if it puts everyone else in danger? a voice in my mind whispers, but I push it aside. It won't come to that. It can't come to that.

Everyone on the ship who isn't on duty crowds behind Søren and me to watch the three of them, and it seems that we are holding one collective breath, waiting for the moment we can finally exhale.

Heron begins first, though the only sign of it is his

shoulders tensing with effort. The effect, though, begins immediately, spreading through the ship and all of us. Like it does whenever he's used his gift on me, my skin begins to tingle as if my whole body has fallen asleep. A quick glance behind me confirms that the others are feeling it, too – some look down at their bodies in surprise and bewilderment only to see them begin to fade before their eyes.

But the sensation is not as strong as it was when Heron made only me invisible. He isn't strong enough alone to make the entire ship disappear. However, between his gift and the natural cover night provides, we should be impossible to see.

Artemisia is next, and she has a flair for drama that Heron lacks. The crowd gathered behind me gasps as she lifts her arms and the tides pick up straight away. The fine mist of magic flies from her fingers as she directs our ship toward the Kalovaxian ships on the horizon, faster than I would have thought possible. In the moonlight, her every movement seems liquid, every jerk of her arms and flick of her wrist executed like the ocean itself gave birth to her.

It's a bit like watching her sword fight.

The crowd gathered behind her gives whispers of awe – our ship flies across the sea, propelled by a perfect tide. The plan is working – as long as Artemisia can get us close enough before Heron becomes too weak to hold our invisibility. That is the question, the theory we couldn't test out before putting it into action. That is what this all comes down to. We need to get close enough that Blaise can deploy his own gift.

Some small, stupid part of me hopes that we fail on that account – that Heron will fail to hold our invisibility and the Kalovaxians will see us and that we will fall into a less magical sort of battle, but at least Blaise wouldn't use his gift. He wouldn't risk his life like that.

The prayer goes unanswered. Artemisia's tides propel us toward the Kalovaxian ships swiftly, Heron's gift holding until the moment Blaise steps forward, his body shaking. He takes the gem-studded bracelet from his pocket and clutches it tightly in his fist.

For all his bravado earlier, he is actually afraid, I realize. Without meaning to, I take a step toward him, but Søren grabs hold of my arm with his free hand.

'It's a brave thing he's doing,' Søren says to me, his voice low and his eyes still locked on Blaise. 'Don't rob him of that now.'

A protest lodges in my throat. Søren is right – even though I would rather have Blaise cowardly and alive instead of brave and dead, that is not my choice to make. And so I do the only thing I can do: I watch.

Heron stumbles backward, drained of energy, and Artemisia drops her arms to catch him, keeping him upright. Both of their magic fades, but it isn't needed anymore. The Kalovaxian ships are close enough now that I can make out the shapes of the sailors running across the decks of their ships, close enough that I can hear their panicked shouts. It's too late, though they don't realize that. They will soon enough.

Blaise braces himself against the ship's railing, his body straining like he's being torn apart. Our ship is so quiet I can hear each breath from the crowd behind me, each wave crashing against our hull, each Kalovaxian curse and order being shouted in the distance.

He lifts one hand, extending it forward toward the center

ship, directly ahead of us. Beneath the thin material of his shirt, the muscles of his back strain like something is trying to force its way out of his skin. A crack splits the air like thunder, followed by another and another, each one louder than the last. Seconds later, I see it – the Kalovaxian ship's hull splintering apart, planks of wood breaking off and splashing into the water. The crew begins to call out as the fragmented ship sinks, and a bell rings out. An alarm, I realize, to alert the other ships of trouble.

The ship on the left hears it first and they try to come to the first ship's rescue, but Blaise is ready for that. He lifts his other hand toward them. The power that racks its way through him is so strong that he has to lean the full weight of his body forward against the bow's railing to stay standing. Even above the chorus of destruction, I can hear him gasping and grunting with pain.

'It's too much,' I tell Søren. 'He can't do any more.'

But even as I say it, the second ship begins to break apart, just like the first, plunging wreckage into the ink-black sea.

Two ships wrecked without a single life lost on our side – that's enough. But it won't be for Blaise. I know this even before he turns his attention to the third ship. Unlike their nobler brothers, the third ship isn't making an attempt to rescue the other two. Instead, they are fleeing.

'We can let them go,' I say to Søren, but he shakes his head, keeping his eyes on Blaise.

'They may get help and come back,' he says. 'We can't afford to take that risk.'

Blaise must know this, too. He turns away from the wrecked ships and focuses the brunt of his attention on the one fleeing.

His shoulders shake as he takes a deep, trembling breath and lifts up his hands once more. He lets out an animalistic cry so loud it could break open the sky itself. The power that floods from his hands is not a beam of light shooting from us to them. Instead, it is a tornado, whipping through the air without a target – as aimless as it is brutal.

The fleeing Kalovaxian ship takes the worst of it, dissolving to nothing but splinters as quickly as I can blink, but our own ship is not spared. The crowd behind me screams and drops to the ground, covering their heads as pieces of the ship begin to break.

'Blaise!' I scream, but my voice is lost in the madness. A piece of the mast above my head snaps off and plummets toward me. I am frozen in place, unable to move until an arm snakes around my waist and yanks me out of the way.

'Get everyone to the aft of the ship, to the rowboats,' Søren tells me, drawing his sword from its sheath.

I grab his sword arm. 'No,' I say, the word wrenching itself from my gut. 'He doesn't know what he's doing, you can't—'

'Theo, look around. He's going to kill us all,' Søren says, gesturing around the ship with his free hand. 'He asked this of me and I'm going to honor that.'

I swallow, tears biting at my eyes. 'Let me do it, then,' I say, my voice shaking. 'I owe it to him, Søren.'

Søren's eyes flicker to Blaise and back to me. After a second, he nods and passes the sword into my hands. 'Remember – strike hard and true, end it fast.'

I nod. It's only when he turns away from me and begins escorting the frightened passengers to the aft of the ship that I realize it's the same thing, more or less, that he said to me when I held a dagger to his back.

Steeling myself, I step toward Blaise's figure, still leaning against the ship's railing as tremors rack through his body, making his muscles spasm and twitch. Heron and Artemisia stand on either side of him, too exhausted from their own efforts to do much more than stare and call out his name, though their voices are lost in the overwhelming din of ruin.

The sword is longer than the ones I've practiced wielding with Artemisia, and the tip of it drags along the deck beside me. The ship careens one way and I stumble, leaning on the sword like a cane to stay upright, only to have the ship rock the other way. Each step I take toward Blaise feels like my body is moving through quicksand, but I keep my eyes on him and put one foot in front of the other.

Distantly, I hear Artemisia scream my name, but she feels a thousand miles away. Everything does. It is as if the world consists only of Blaise and me and the sword in my hand.

The air between us crackles with lightning. I reach out and touch his shoulder, hoping against hope that it will be like the last time and my touch will be enough to pull him free from the magic or Glaidi or whatever it is that has a hold on him. But when his head turns toward me and his eyes find mine, there is nothing of Blaise left behind them. They remind me more of Hoa's, staring glassy and lifeless after the soul left her body. He looks at me, but he does not see me.

'Blaise,' I say, his name a whisper.

The deck begins to crack beneath my feet, shards of wood peeling up like fruit skin.

This is not like what happened in Sta'Crivero. Then, there

was enough of him left that I could pull him out again, but now he is more magic than man, unreachable, unsalvageable. I swallow down the tears threatening to spill and lift the sword with shaking hands.

It feels like I am standing over Ampelio all over again, with the tip of a sword pressed against his back. I killed him then to save him from more pain, to save myself, to keep the rebellion alive. How is this so different from that?

My eyes clench closed tightly so that no tears escape. I know what I have to do – drive the blade through his chest, hard and true, just as Søren said.

I take a steadying breath.

I grip the hilt of the sword harder.

I lunge toward him.

The sword twists out of my grasp, the force knocking me to the ground. It takes me a moment to process what is happening, but when I do it's like time itself slows down.

Artemisia with Søren's sword, gripping the blade instead of the hilt. Her fingers digging into the sharp edge, streaking the wrought iron with rivulets of red. She charges Blaise with a guttural yell that I barely hear and my heart tightens in my chest, but instead of stabbing him, she brings the heavy hilt of the sword overhead in an arc, hitting him over the head with every last ounce of her power.

They both fall to the ground and the ship goes still.

With Blaise unconscious and the threat contained, we assess the damage done to the ship. Luckily, it was largely limited to the areas nearest Blaise – the upper deck, the masts, the railings. There are holes belowdecks spouting water, but they are easy to patch up.

'We can't go far without sails,' Artemisia tells me when she reports the progress made. I haven't been to see it myself. When Heron and Søren brought Blaise's unconscious body back to his cabin, I came with them and I haven't left in the three hours since.

'We don't need to go far,' I remind her without looking away from Blaise's still face. 'We're only a mile from the shore. We could coast there. And we have the rowboats.'

Artemisia nods, her eyes drifting to Blaise and then back to me. 'We've sent word to the other ships and they'll meet us there. We should make landfall in an hour.'

When I don't reply, she continues.

'You should try to get some rest, Theo. It's going to be a long day,' she says, her voice surprisingly gentle. Still, the words rankle me.

'You think I could sleep while Blaise is like this?' I snap. 'He might never wake up, Art, and—' My voice breaks and I take a deep breath before forcing myself to continue. 'And if it weren't for you, there wouldn't even be that possibility.'

The confession comes out in a whisper, but it hangs heavily in the air between us. The mattress gives as she sits down beside me.

'I think you're greatly overestimating your aim,' she says.

I know that she's trying to lighten the moment, but I barely register the joke.

'How did you know that knocking him unconscious would stop him?' I ask her.

Artemisia sighs. 'I didn't,' she says. 'It was a guess — a random, dangerous guess. If it didn't work, I would have done what he'd asked and killed him. It just . . . it was worth trying. I didn't want . . .' She trails off, pausing for a moment. 'I didn't want to lose another person.'

'Neither did I,' I say, shaking my head. 'That didn't stop me from trying to kill him when it came down to it.'

Artemisia surprises me by touching my shoulder.

'There were lives at risk, Theo,' she says, her voice uncharacteristically soft. 'You put your country over your heart and that is not something to be ashamed of. Blaise would have understood.'

I nod, even though her words lodge under my skin like a splinter.

Because yes, Blaise would have understood. But he never would have made the same choice if our positions were reversed.

Blaise's eyes open moments later, and in that instant, all the tension wrapped around my heart unspools.

He blinks twice, dark brown eyes focusing on me.

'Theo,' he says, my name a prayer on his lips. I can see the memories flowing back to him. He must remember everything. He said as much when he lost control in Sta'Crivero – that he could see everything even though it felt like he wasn't in his body.

'Is everyone all right?' he asks finally.

'There were no casualties,' I tell him, and his shoulders sag with relief. 'The damage to the ship was easily repaired. We'll be loading up the rowboats to head to shore any moment now.'

He nods, struggling to sit up. I wait for him to ask what happened, how he's still alive. If he does remember everything before he lost consciousness, he must remember me, with the sword in my hand. I can see the knowledge reflected in his eyes, in the uncertain way he looks at me. I can see the question forming on his lips before he decides that he doesn't want to know the answer.

Instead, he shakes his head as if trying to clear it. 'Is there any update from the other ships we're waiting on? The Vecturians and Gorakians?' he asks, changing the subject to easier, more practical things.

'No,' I say. 'But they'll be here. Even if they're late, we have enough warriors to hold our own until they are.'

He's quiet for a second, then asks, 'Why do you trust him?' The question takes me by surprise but it's clear that it's been on Blaise's mind for some time. 'Chief Kapil I understand. You did him a favor and he's repaying it. But Erik? What does he want? You don't even really know him, do you?'

'He wants the same thing we do,' I say. 'The same thing we counted on the refugees wanting. To rebuild our countries. To make a home and protect the people we love. And revenge, of course.' My chest tightens at the thought of Hoa. Erik doesn't know yet. Heron offered to write the news to him through the gold piece, but I told him not to. Some things need to be said in person.

Blaise laughs, but there isn't much humor to the sound. He winces like it hurts his head. 'Revenge,' he echoes, leaning back against the headboard of his narrow bed. 'Not exactly the purest of motivations, is it?'

The words prickle at me. 'The purity of motivations doesn't matter – the strength of them does, and there is no stronger motivation than revenge,' I say.

He looks at me for a long moment. 'That sounds like a very Kalovaxian way of looking at things,' he says finally. And there it is, the barb of an accusation.

Blaise was ready to die, he was ready for Artemisia or Søren to drive that sword through him and end his life because that is who they are and what they do. But not me, it was never supposed to be me.

I shrug and glance away. 'Maybe it is,' I say quietly. 'Maybe that's why Erik and Søren and I understand each other as well as we do – we were all raised by the Kaiser in different ways. It's not an upbringing I would wish on anyone, but I don't think you could call any of us weak.'

It's not an apology, but after what Artemisia said, I can't bring myself to give one.

'I asked you not to risk it, Blaise,' I continue, unable to meet his gaze. 'You insisted – you and Artemisia and Heron and Søren. You thought it was worth it, maybe you still think that. But you almost killed us all and I would have done what I had to do to save us.'

'I asked Søren to do it for a reason,' he says, his voice low and hard. 'His soul is already black; he's killed before—'

'So have I,' I interrupt, startling him.

'That's not the same thing. Ampelio—'

'It's exactly the same thing,' I say, my voice strengthening. 'I killed Ampelio to save myself and to save the rebellion. The same thing was at stake this time, only more so. Hundreds of lives would have been lost if I'd waited a few more minutes. I tried to bring you back like before, but you were gone and I couldn't wait any longer. So I did what I had to do, and if you keep insisting on putting yourself and all of us at risk, I will do it again.'

He's quiet for a moment, looking down at his hands. 'Are you afraid of me, Theo?' he asks, his voice so quiet I can barely hear him even in the silent cabin.

I open my mouth to deny it but quickly shut it again. 'Yes,' I tell him honestly. 'I'm afraid of you.'

He's hurt, but unsurprised. 'I'm sorry. That's the last thing I want.'

'I know,' I tell him. Part of me wants to reach out and take his hand, but a larger part holds back. I try to spin myself an excuse for why that is, but the truth is that I don't want to touch him. I don't want to feel his hot skin and look into his eyes and see him as he was earlier, nothing but an empty face and frightening power. A stranger with the power to kill. I am afraid of him and I don't know how not to be.

'I'm asking you to stay out of the battle tomorrow,' I tell him.

His entire body stiffens but he doesn't look at me.

'You saw my power, Theo. Imagine what I could do on that battlefield. The gods crafted me into a weapon and you have to wield me as one.'

I shake my head. 'You'll hurt too many innocent people in the process.'

When Blaise speaks, it's through gritted teeth. 'The gods wouldn't allow that.'

'I might have believed that before today,' I say. 'After we

reclaim the Fire Mine, we'll take the Earth Mine and we will pray to all of the gods that there is someone there who will know what to do, how to help you, how to train you so that you can use this gift without hurting yourself or us.'

'You're my Queen, Theo,' he says quietly. 'You could order me not to go.'

'I know,' I tell him. 'I'm not going to do that. But I am asking you and I believe that you'll do the right thing.'

He stares at me a moment longer, his expression unreadable, before he gives a sharp nod.

When I leave him alone in the cabin and close the door behind me, I let out a sigh of relief.

READY

━━━◆━━◆━━◆━━

ROWBOATS BRING US TO THE shores of Astrea – they bring us home. Though it has been ruled by my enemies for most of my life, it still lifts my heart to see it. Those rocky shores, the rolling green hills behind them, the quickly fading night sky overhead – all of it is a part of me, deeper than bones or muscle or blood. Astrea is mine and I am hers.

It takes a dozen trips back and forth to unload all the warriors, if they can truly be called that. Though Søren and Artemisia say they've trained well in the last two weeks, they are still civilians – bakers and teachers and potters and such. Some of them are old enough to be grandparents; others are as young as fourteen – children. At least they would be in a different world, a fairer world. All of them asked to fight, they trained hard, and they are all going into this battle knowing that they very well may not survive it.

There will be more blood on my hands after this is done, no matter how it ends. I will have killed them by sending them into this battle.

'How did you do it?' I ask Søren from where we sit on a cluster of boulders, watching the warriors line up. He glances at me, brow furrowed, and I clarify. 'When you led battalions. You knew that not everyone would survive, even when you led them into a battle you were sure you'd win. You knew there would still be casualties. How did you send them into battle anyway?'

He considers it for a moment, his gaze unwavering as he looks out at the assembling troops. His expression is unreadable, carved from stone. There was a time I thought that was all he was – a hard, emotionless shell – but I know better now. I know that expression is its own kind of armor, donned whenever he feels vulnerable.

'I suppose I never really thought of myself as their leader, even when I was giving orders. My men and I were a team and I respected them enough to believe that they knew the risks and were making a choice. I respected that choice.'

'You fought beside them, though. What you asked of them was nothing you weren't willing to give yourself. But I'm ordering them to fight while watching from a safe distance.' It's difficult not to keep the bitterness out of my voice.

My eyes find Artemisia in the crowd, her shock of blue hair making her stand out. She shouts commands, arranging everyone into lines and groups. In a different life, could I have been as fierce as she is? Could I have charged into battle and cut my way through a sea of enemies with ease and grace?

That path must have existed for me at some point, but it's long gone now.

'They're following you, Theo,' Søren says. 'You can't fight alongside them, but you can still be the leader they need, and in order to do that, you have to respect the choice they're making. You have to send them into battle and do everything you can to make sure as many of them make it back as possible. And then you have to honor the fallen as best you can by continuing to fight for a world they would be proud to live in.'

We're both quiet for a moment and I think he's done. Just when I'm about to thank him, though, he speaks again.

'I never really did that,' he admits. 'I sent them into battle and I respected them, that much is true, but I don't think I ever honored them the way I would have liked to. At the end of the day, we were never fighting for anything we really believed in. We were fighting for my father, because he ordered it. They died for his greed and his bloodlust and I let them. That guilt is mine and I'll carry it with me forever, but it won't be yours.'

My throat tightens. Though I appreciate his words, I'm not sure if they're true. Even if we do win, even if we do manage to take back Astrea and destroy the Kalovaxians, I don't think there will ever be a day I don't feel guilty for every life I lost – Ampelio, Elpis, Hylla, Santino, Olaric, Archduke Etmond, Hoa. They were the beginning, but after today I won't be able to recite all of their names.

It's for the greater good, I remind myself. The deaths of a few in order to save the many. There are so many people enslaved in Astrea, so many people we can save, but not without this sacrifice.

The thought makes me feel better for only a moment before I realize '*the greater good*' was what the Kaiser used to say his warriors died for as well.

I turn to Søren. 'Do you still worry that you're the same as your father?'

He tears his gaze away from the warriors and looks at me thoughtfully.

'Not as much as I used to but still often enough,' he admits. 'Why?'

I shake my head, pressing my lips together as if I can keep the words inside, but they slip out anyway. 'Sometimes I worry I'm like him, too. He's left his mark on me, not just my body or my mind but my soul as well. Sometimes I worry he shaped me.'

His eyebrows arch so high they nearly disappear into his hairline. 'Theo,' he says, lowering his voice. 'I have never met anyone so unlike my father as you. The fact that you're worried about that, that you feel guilt over sending your people into a necessary battle, only proves that more.'

'But—'

He stops me by taking hold of my hand, his grip tight and urgent. 'You aren't who you are because of my father. You're who you are in spite of everything he did, in spite of everything he tried to twist you into. Don't give him that kind of credit.'

His words do little to ease the black pit growing deeper in my stomach, but I'm still glad to hear them. I squeeze his hand.

'He can't take credit for you either, Søren,' I tell him.

Søren gives me a small smile that doesn't meet his eyes.

I suppose neither of us really believes the other.

When the sun is a mere sliver over the horizon, I stand before the assembled troops on the shore, feeling small. I can't let that show, though, so I draw myself up to my full height and survey my warriors like I am actually worthy of commanding them. I strengthen my voice so that I sound confident and regal. Like someone who deserves their loyalty.

'I want to go home,' I begin. 'I know that all of you want the same, no matter where that home might be. And I know many of you have no home to go back to – it has already been destroyed in the Kalovaxians' wake, razed to the ground so that life there is unsustainable. Goraki gives me hope that life after a siege is possible, that your countries can rebuild themselves. And if that is not the case, I would offer a new home in Astrea.'

I pause before continuing.

'Today, we begin our triumph over the Kalovaxians,' I say. 'Today we tell them that they have trampled us for too long, they have taken too much, they have destroyed too many. Today we tell them *enough* and we begin to take our revenge.'

Cheers go up throughout the crowd and I stand a little straighter.

'Today, we show them what we are made of. For Astrea,' I shout. 'And for Goraki and Yoxi and Manadol and Tiava and Rajinka and Kota. We will rise, together, and we will show the Kalovaxians how wrong they were to ever think us weak.'

This time, the cheers are so loud they are deafening.

BERSERKERS

————— ◆ ◆ —————

THE BATTLE BEGINS AS THE sun bleeds over the horizon. Surprised shouts, alarm bells, metal clanging against metal, pained screams – all echo between the mountains that surround the camp, amplified tenfold at the cliff I watch from, flanked on either side by Søren and Blaise.

We can't get too close, but the battle can change in an instant and we need to be near enough that we can adjust our strategy and get messages to Artemisia and Heron. We need to be near enough that we can order a retreat if we must.

We don't go too high – none of us is dressed for mountain climbing. I wear my red gown again – the most queenlike outfit I have – while Blaise and Søren are dressed in heavy armor in case they're needed in battle. I can't imagine they will be, but neither enjoys sitting still.

Even I have to admit that it's difficult to keep watch and do nothing. We have more warriors than they do, more than they're prepared for, and in the hazy dawn light, the Kalovaxians are taken by surprise. For a moment, we are winning, our ramshackle army cutting down trained warriors, pushing toward the mine and the camp next to it – but that moment is over before the sun lifts away from the horizon.

Søren was right: the Kalovaxians are skilled enough to make up for the discrepancy in numbers. They fight with precision and strength that our warriors aren't able to match. What I don't think Søren prepared for, though, is the energy of our warriors – the rage and desperation that drives every one of their movements, making them stronger and fiercer than they should be.

'They fight like they know they won't survive it,' Søren says from my right side, a sense of awe in his voice.

'They fight like they *don't care* if they survive it,' Blaise corrects from my other side.

Every time one of our warriors falls, something inside me twists. The first few times it happens, I say a prayer to the gods, but soon there are too many of them, too much blood, too many bodies. Soon it becomes difficult to tell who is fighting for whom.

We are advancing, though, the fight inching closer and closer to the mine and the slave quarters next to it, both ringed by wrought-iron gates, with guard barracks set up around the perimeter. Not much of the slave quarters is visible from our vantage point, just flat tin roofs and thin spirals of smoke.

'Their objective will be to protect their assets – the mine and the slaves,' Søren said when we were plotting our attack. 'They'll know we're there to free them. They'll know that when we do, the battle is lost.'

He's right. The Kalovaxians surround the perimeter of the mine and the slave quarters, holding their line fiercely even when that means they lose their barracks. As our army closes in on them, a few Kalovaxian warriors disappear into a building I didn't notice at first. Small and squat, it sits separate from the slave quarters, almost obscured behind the mine. The fence surrounding it is spiked at the top, and the metal gleams strangely in the sunlight, a brilliant red-orange.

Søren's gaze follows mine and he swallows. 'Iron mixed with crushed Fire Gems,' he says. 'It's a newer discovery; I've never seen it implemented in such a large quantity. It's incredibly expensive to make. Whatever they're keeping in there must be valuable.'

'*Who*ever,' Blaise corrects, nodding toward the building's gated entrance, where the guards have reappeared, but they aren't alone. Ten Astreans stumble in their wake, chains around their ankles binding them together and making their steps slow and sluggish. They shrink from the sunlight when it hits them, raising their arms to block the rays.

Valuable Astreans, ones the Kalovaxians would spend a lot of money to protect. No, not protect, not really.

'Berserkers,' I say, the word barely coming out a whisper. Blaise takes hold of my hand, and this time I barely feel how hot his hand is against mine. I can't take my eyes from those people.

'We knew this was a possibility, Theo,' he says to me. 'We prepared for it.'

I nod because I don't trust myself to speak. It's true that we knew the Kalovaxians would likely use the berserkers they had at the mine, and it's true that we have a plan for how to counter it. It will limit the danger they do to our army, but it will not save them. Though I know there is no saving them, my stomach still ties itself into knots.

'I can't watch this,' I say quietly.

'You don't have to,' Blaise says. Out of the corner of my eye, I can see that he's gone a little green himself.

'You should, though,' Søren says. He swallows, forcing himself to keep his own gaze on the scene. He's the only one of us who knows what we're looking at, I realize. The only one who has seen berserkers in action before.

'She doesn't need to see it,' Blaise snaps at him. 'I think she can imagine it perfectly well after hearing about what you did in Vecturia.'

Søren has the grace to look ashamed. 'It's important to understand it,' he says, his voice clear. 'To *see* it.'

'That won't accomplish anything,' Blaise says, but there's an edge of fear in his voice. His hand shakes in mine; the air around him simmers. I squeeze his hand and the air stills, but his eyes remain wide and afraid.

He doesn't want me to see it, I realize. He doesn't want me to see how he will die if the same fate ever befalls him. I don't think he wants to see it either – it's easy to be noble about dying when it's abstract, but I'm sure it's much harder when the process unfolds before your eyes.

'She's stronger than you think she is,' Søren says. There is no bite to his voice, but Blaise hears one. He turns to Søren with hateful eyes.

'I know how strong she is,' he says, his voice low and dangerous. 'I knew it when you believed her to be a weak flower in need of protecting.'

Søren doesn't say anything to that, though a muscle in his jaw twitches. His hand wanders to the sword at his hip. I know he's taken on Artemisia's usual duty, that he has instructions on what to do if Blaise becomes a danger to us. The thought sickens me. Søren must realize that Blaise is only angry, not dangerous, because his hand stills.

'Right now I believe her to be someone who can make her own decisions,' he says, his voice level.

I swallow, though I force my eyes back to the battlefield, back to the ten Astreans being unchained. They're delirious, stumbling every few steps they take, wobbling on their feet. One man's knees buckle and he falls to the ground only to be forcefully yanked back up by a guard.

'They're drugged,' Søren explains quietly. 'It keeps them manageable, makes them more inclined to follow directions.'

The Kalovaxian commanders press gems into their hands, which they accept eagerly, the way a parched man would accept water.

'To *push them over the edge*,' I remember Erik saying when he told me about berserkers. But he didn't tell me how it affects them. As soon as they touch the gems, it's like something deep in them sparks to life. Something feral and inhuman. The air around them sharpens.

Gems in hand, the berserkers take a few hesitant steps toward my army. Their movements are still slow and drugged, but there is an energy to their movements now that is unnatural. They jerk like puppets on strings being urged forward by some force I can't see.

My army hesitates. It doesn't matter that we knew this would likely come, that everyone had been instructed on what to do when it did. It doesn't matter that a few dozen warriors have arrows nocked and ready for just this moment.

They hesitate in the face of it, and I can't even blame them for that. The figures approaching are not berserkers, after all. That is a Kalovaxian word for a Kalovaxian idea. They are not weapons; they are people. Sick people who need help we can't give them. We can only offer the mercy of an arrow to the heart.

'Shoot,' Blaise murmurs under his breath, his gaze intent. 'Shoot now.'

Søren, however, remains silent, his eyes heavy on the scene.

Finally, one arrow fires, striking a berserker man square in the chest. He looks down at it, the drugs in his system making his reaction slow. He falls to the ground as if he's sinking through water instead of air.

That shot breaks the spell and other arrows follow, some missing, others finding their target. Berserkers drop, one after another, gems tumbling from their slackened grips and rolling away harmlessly. I count them as they die, my heart lurching with each one. They all die mercifully, until only one is left, a young girl who can't be more than eight. Her steps drag like she's forgotten how to walk, and though I'm too far away to say for sure, I think she's crying.

The arrows stop but she doesn't. She takes another step, then another, crossing the field between armies, a figure so tiny that she nearly disappears altogether.

Even Blaise is silent now, though I know all of us are waiting for it, waiting for the arrow to fly and find its target, waiting for someone to end this, to put her out of her misery.

No one does. No one can.

The girl reaches our front lines before stopping short. Standing in front of thousands of armed warriors, she looks even smaller. Too small, surely, to hurt anyone. My armies retreat as quickly as they can, but for many it isn't quick enough.

Something sparks. *She* sparks. One moment she is there, a crying, frightened girl, and the next she is a ball of flame, engulfing everything around her for yards. They scream as they burn, but she screams the loudest.

I stumble back a step and it takes everything I have not to look away, not to turn from the gruesome sight until it's over, but I somehow don't. I keep watching, even when it feels like it will kill me.

The fire dies as quickly as it started, and all that is left is a fifty-foot circle of charred grass and close to thirty burned corpses, including one that is far too small.

I'm going to be sick. I lift my hand to my mouth and breathe through my nose until my churning stomach stills.

'It could have been worse,' Søren says quietly. 'It could have been much worse.'

I know he's right, but I still have to fight the urge to slap him.

Erik told me about berserkers, he told me what happened, what they became, but no words could have prepared me for the reality of it, for the feral humanity of the people, how they cried as they walked to their deaths.

My army is as shocked as I am, and they are slow to respond. The Kalovaxians are not. They use our hesitation to push forward, gaining the few yards that we fought so hard for before my army gets a hold of themselves.

But when they do push back, they are angrier than ever.

BATTLE

THE BATTLE RAGES ON FOR hours, but there are no more berserkers and for that I am grateful. I know it will be a long while before I close my eyes to sleep without seeing that crying girl in my nightmares. I'm not the only one shaken – Blaise hasn't said a word since it happened, though against all odds we actually appear to be winning now. It's a slow progress, fighting for every inch we gain, but it's progress.

By the time the sun is directly overhead, we reach the slave quarters and a few dozen warriors slip in to free the slaves there. There are still Kalovaxians remaining – maybe a couple hundred fighting with everything they have – but I can't imagine they won't surrender any minute, especially once the slaves who want to fight join the fray. Stubborn as Kalovaxian warriors are, they know a lost cause when they see one.

'Should we start making our way down?' I ask, but Søren holds up a hand, his brow furrowing deeply.

'Something isn't right,' he says, staring at the battle still raging as if it's a puzzle he can't solve. 'They should have surrendered by now. It doesn't make sense.' He pauses and the color leaves his face. 'Unless they know help is coming.'

I shake my head. 'That's impossible, Søren,' I say. 'The closest soldiers are days away. They couldn't possibly arrive quickly enough.'

His frown deepens as his eyes scan the horizon, but it's Blaise who finally lifts a finger to point east.

'There,' he says, voice a hoarse whisper.

My eyes follow to where he points and my stomach plummets. There, snaking through the mountain ranges, is another army all dressed in Kalovaxian red.

'It doesn't make sense,' I say, more to myself than to them.

Søren's jaw clenches.

'King Etristo got word to my father,' he says. 'It's the only explanation I can think of. He put the pieces together and figured out where we were going and sent word ahead. We took our time getting here – a single, fast ship could have made it to the capital in half the time.'

My gut sinks lower as I stare at the incoming troops. A seemingly endless red ribbon of soldiers weaving its way through the mountains.

'How many, do you think?' I ask Søren.

He looks at me, his gaze unflinching. 'Too many.'

I nod. I expected as much, but hearing it makes me feel sick all over again.

'We have to retreat,' I say. 'We freed the slaves, that's enough. It's still a victory and there's no other option. If we stay, we'll be slaughtered.'

Søren nods, but Blaise is faster, hurrying around to the opposite side of the cliff, overlooking the sea. He shades his eyes against the sun.

'Wait a minute,' he says. 'There are ships coming from this direction, too.'

My stomach sinks lower. 'Kalovaxian ships?' I ask, struggling to stay calm. If they're surrounding us on all sides, we are done for. We haven't just lost a battle, we will have lost everything.

'No,' Blaise says after a moment that seems to last forever. His voice lifts. 'No, those are Gorakian flags.'

Erik. I send thanks to all of my gods and I make a mental note to ask Erik about his gods so I can thank them as well.

'And . . .' Blaise says, peering in another direction. 'And there are more. A few of the ships have Vecturian flags and, Theo, I . . . I think I see Dragonsbane as well.'

My knees give out beneath me and I would fall to the ground entirely if Søren didn't steady me with his hand on my shoulder. It takes me a moment to realize I'm laughing. Delirious, hysterical laughter, but laughter all the same.

'Will it be enough?' I ask Søren.

'Two camps will give us another four thousand or thereabouts, plus the warriors we still have, plus the slaves we just freed, plus a couple hundred Vecturians, plus Dragonsbane's crew,' he says, tallying up the numbers in his head. After a moment, he nods. 'It just might be.'

'We can still run,' Blaise says. 'All of us can, then regroup and attack another mine.'

I shake my head. 'That's what the Kaiser will expect us to do,' I say. 'He'll expect us to run from him – he's used to people running from him. He'll make sure we don't get another chance to embarrass him like this. It's now or never.'

Blaise nods, eyes somber. 'I'll get word to our army, update them on what's happening, tell them to get the freed slaves armed or to safety as soon as we can.'

I open my mouth to protest, but I know it's the best choice. I can't very well go myself, and if Søren shows up looking like a Kalovaxian, he'll likely wind up dead before my army realizes he's not an enemy.

'Come back quickly,' I say instead.

Blaise stares long and hard at the battle below.

'No,' he says, the word quiet and clear, though he won't look at me. It feels like it echoes in the distance between us, but I think that's only in my head.

No. No. No. It occurs to me suddenly that Blaise has never said that to me. He's disagreed with me often enough and argued his point until I came around to his way of thinking, but he's never outright refused me.

'Blaise,' I say, taking a step toward him. 'After what we just saw—'

'After what we just saw, I know more than ever where I need to be.' He says it quietly, but there's steel in his voice. 'I'll stay close to Artemisia. If it looks like I'm losing control, I trust her to make the judgment call – kill me or let me kill as many of them as I can.'

I take a step closer to him, placing a hand on either side of his face and forcing him to look at me. 'Blaise, you can't. You won't. I'll order you – I'm ordering you to stay here. As your Queen, I'm ordering you.'

I don't sound like anyone's queen, I realize that as I say the words, but in this moment I'm not. I'm just a frightened girl begging a boy she loves not to leave her. I hate it, but I can't stop.

Blaise swallows, his eyes heavy on mine. 'No.' It seems to kill him to say the word.

Tears sting at my eyes and I blink them away furiously. He won't see me cry over him.

'I'll never forgive you if you do this,' I say, biting the words out.

He glances away from me.

'I know,' he says softly, looking at Søren over my shoulder. 'You know what to do if it looks like we're going to lose – even if there's the slightest chance.'

Søren's voice is strained. 'I'll get her back to the ship,' he promises.

Blaise nods before gently extracting himself from my grip. He looks at me for a moment that seems to go on forever. 'I love you, Theo,' he says.

'If you did, you wouldn't do this,' I say, sharpening each word to a dagger's point.

He recoils like my words physically hurt him, then turns away from me.

As he makes his way down the mountain, he doesn't look back once, even though I'm sure he can hear me crying his name until he reaches the bottom.

Erik and Dragonsbane arrive mere moments before the Kalovaxian reinforcements do, and when the troops clash it is a cacophony straight out of a nightmare. Metal clangs against metal, screams pierce the air, battle cries mix and mingle until I'm not sure whose are whose. All of it bounces and echoes off the mountains so that it surrounds me. The scene before my eyes is a blur of bodies and blood that seems to go on forever, but I only watch one figure in particular.

It should be hard to find Blaise at this distance, with nothing to differentiate him the way Artemisia's hair distinguishes her, but it isn't. Even in the madness, I find him easily, sword in hand and a wildness to his every move that is terrifying.

Søren doesn't say anything when I can't stop crying. He seems a bit frightened of me, keeping a careful distance and pretending he doesn't notice. I realize distantly that he hasn't been around many crying women. When my sobs finally do quiet, he allows himself to speak.

'Blaise is reckless, but he isn't stupid,' he says. Though the words are clipped, he seems to be trying to sound compassionate. 'He will be all right.'

'He's not in control of what happens,' I say, wiping my eyes. I remember the earthquake in Sta'Crivero, how close he came to losing all control before I pulled him back from that edge. Who will pull him back if it happens now? Artemisia will put a sword in his back if she thinks he's more of a danger to our army than the Kalovaxians. She will even think it's a mercy.

Søren shrugs. 'He seems to have more control than any berserker I've seen. A few slips don't mean that using his power will kill him.'

I know he's right, but it doesn't bring me much comfort.

Blaise left me, after everything. After everyone I've loved and lost, I can't lose him, too.

'Theo,' Søren says.

'I'm fine,' I tell him, wiping my eyes again.

'It isn't that,' he says, his words tentative. 'I think . . .

I think my father is here.'

That shocks me out of my thoughts. 'What?' I ask, blinking away unshed tears. 'The Kaiser never goes to battle.'

'He isn't fighting,' he says, squinting into the distance. 'He's watching, like we are. And I think Crescentia is with him.'

Cress. My heart lurches in my chest and I hurry to Søren's side, peering in the same direction he is.

'There,' he says, pointing. 'That mountain range, the cliff. Do you see?'

I do. They are difficult to miss in their ornate chairs that must have taken a good portion of the Kalovaxian army to bring all this way. There is even a red silk canopy above their heads, to shield them from the sun. As if it's some kind of festivity they're witnessing instead of a battle. I can't see their faces, but that's just as well.

'Why would he come all this way?' I ask him.

Søren thinks about it for a moment. 'Because you embarrassed him by escaping,' he says. 'Because he wants to see you destroyed.'

My stomach sours. 'Well, he won't,' I say. 'It's a shame you aren't a more skilled archer, Søren. We could end this here and now.'

Søren shakes his head. 'Even if I could make the shot, my father isn't stupid. I'm sure he's as armored as he can be. We can't let them see us, though,' he says, taking a step back into the shade of the mountain and pulling me with him. 'He'll send men here to take us.'

I nod, heart thundering in my chest.

'Søren, can you promise me something?'

He looks at me, perplexed, but nods. 'What is it?'

I swallow. 'If they do come for us, if it looks like they're going to take us – I want you to kill me.'

His eyes widen. 'Theo, no,' he says.

'I won't be his prisoner again, Søren. You can do it or I'll throw myself over these cliffs, though I'd imagine that would be far more painful than if you did it, so I'm asking you.'

Søren holds my gaze for a long moment before nodding once. 'If it comes to it,' he says, though I'm not sure I believe him.

Søren and I huddle together, pressed against the mountain for hours, until the battlefield falls silent.

'Is it over?' I ask.

Søren looks confused. 'I can't imagine so,' he says. 'Wait a moment.'

He slides onto his stomach and crawls to the edge of the cliff, peering over to the battlefield below before glancing back at me.

'They're flying a flag, the fighting's stopped,' he says, his eyebrows tightly knit.

'Surrender?' I ask, surprised. Even in my sweetest dreams, I'd never imagined a surrender this easy.

Søren shakes his head. 'It's a yellow one, for a parlay. The Kaiser wants to speak to the head of our army. He wants to speak with you.'

PARLAY

———◆·◆———

Søren will come with me to meet with the Kaiser, though neither of us says as much out loud. It is simply understood. Søren says the meeting will take place in closed quarters – the mine commandant's barracks, more than likely – with a single guard from each of our armies posted outside. While we are meeting, there will be no blood shed by either party.

Even knowing what to expect, though, I can't shake the bone-deep fear of what it will mean to be in the same room as the Kaiser again – to be in his presence, to hear his voice, to have him look at me.

I don't know if I can do it.

I have to do it.

Artemisia will be our guard. It's possible the Kalovaxian guard will underestimate her – I hope he does.

'Do you have your dagger?' Søren asks me, his voice low. We walk together across the bloodied battlefield, surrounded by a cluster of guards in case any Kalovaxians attack us en route. The soldiers are separated on either side of us. They aren't fighting anymore because of the cease-fire, but they are far from peaceful. Taut as bowstrings, they watch us pass, eyes hateful or hopeful or empty.

I nod, feeling the place where the knife is sheathed at my hip, beneath my dress.

'They won't let me take it in,' I realize, the thought of being defenseless in the presence of the Kaiser making it difficult to breathe.

'Not technically,' Søren says. 'But they won't expect you to be armed – they'll only check me. Hold on to it, but don't use it unless you need to. If you attack him unprovoked, your life is forfeit.'

I nod, swallowing down my fear.

Artemisia looks at me with a level gaze. 'It's time,' she says. 'Are you ready?'

'No,' I say honestly. 'But let's go.'

As soon as we walk into the commandant's barracks, the Kaiser's presence suffocates me. His cold blue eyes settle on me, making my skin crawl beneath his gaze. It's so disconcerting that it takes me a moment to realize that he isn't alone. Sitting at his side with her hand swallowed by his is Crescentia, just as I saw her last, with her ashen skin and brittle white hair. A Fire Gem choker rings her charred neck, but it doesn't hide her disfigurement, it only accentuates it. A black gold crown of ruby flames rests on top of her head.

My mother's crown, I realize with a jolt. The sight of it is enough to make the tips of my fingers burn, and I clench them into fists at my sides to smother them.

I stop short when Cress's eyes find mine, but Søren's hand

at my back gently urges me to keep moving, to not let them see me falter.

I sit down gingerly in the chair across from them, and Søren takes the seat next to me.

A silence stretches between all of us for a few moments. The first to speak, it seems, will be the first to lose something.

Finally, Søren clears his throat and addresses the Kaiser. 'I hear congratulations are in order, Father, on your nuptials,' he says with a grim smile before turning his attention to Cress. 'And you, Lady Crescentia, have my deepest condolences.'

The Kaiser's face reddens, but it's Cress who answers first, her roughened voice cutting through the air like a knife with teeth.

'It's *Kaiserin* Crescentia,' she says coolly. 'I don't suppose similar congratulations are in order for you two?'

Søren might have been the first to speak, but Crescentia is the first to lose, because in that moment, her weakness shows. Even in the middle of a battle, with casualties crossing into the thousands, she is still a jilted girl angry that she lost the boy she wanted to marry.

I can use that.

'Not yet,' I tell her with a saccharine smile. 'When we marry, it will be in the Astrean palace after I retake it.'

Cress's jaw clenches, but I turn my gaze away from her and to the Kaiser, shoving down the fear and nausea that his presence triggers.

'I believe we're here to discuss the terms of your surrender,' I tell him, careful to keep my voice level and strong. I won't let him cow me.

He snorts. '*My* surrender,' he echoes, shaking his head.

'You *did* request a parlay; I assumed it was to discuss terms,' I say. 'We do outnumber you, after all.'

'Battles aren't won with numbers alone, surely you know that, Søren,' he says, addressing only his son despite the fact that I'm the one speaking.

'I'm surprised *you* do,' Søren replies evenly. 'It's been decades since you were last in battle, Father. A lot has changed since then.'

The Kaiser smiles tightly. 'I'm willing to let your armies leave Astrea peacefully,' he says, leaning back in his chair and surveying us. 'All I want in return is the two of you. It seems more than a fair trade – two lives for the thousands more that will perish if you refuse.'

He's trying to play to our honor, a smart move I know him well enough to have seen coming.

'No,' I say flatly. 'We will let *you* and *your* armies go peacefully if you and all of your people abandon Astrea now.'

It's as much a bluff as his offer was – the Kaiser would never let my armies leave alive even if I do surrender, and I certainly will not accept a surrender that doesn't include the Kaiser's death. We both know this, but we pretend anyway.

The Kaiser laughs. 'We are at an impasse, then,' he says before looking at Crescentia. 'You see, dear? I told you meeting with them would accomplish nothing.'

Cress requested this meeting?

I glance at Søren, but he looks just as baffled. What would Cress have to gain by meeting with us? It's possible it was mere curiosity, but knowing Cress as well as I do, I can't imagine that's the case. Her father didn't raise her to be someone ruled by something as trifling as her curiosity. No, there's something else at play here, but it feels like I am looking into a fogged-up window, unable to see more than vague shapes.

My spine stiffens when Cress gets to her feet.

'I suppose I wanted to see them one last time,' Cress says with a mournful sigh, taking a step toward us.

Next to me, Søren tenses as well, as if expecting an attack. She sees this and smiles, like a cat circling a mouse.

'Are you afraid of me, Prinz Søren?' she asks, tilting her head to one side thoughtfully. 'I am quite a frightful creature now, thanks to her.' She nods toward me. 'I offered her friendship and in exchange she poisoned me. Did she tell you that?' she asks him.

'You offered me a collar,' I tell her, struggling to keep my voice even. 'I wasn't your friend, Cress. I was your pet.'

She rolls her eyes. 'So *dramatic,*' she chides, walking around the room with languid steps, trailing her fingers over the desk, leaving a path of burnt wood where she touches. I can feel my heartbeat speed up, and the urge to flee the room is difficult to ignore. When she sees my reaction, she smiles, pleased with herself.

It's the way she used to smile at me from across a crowded room, as though we shared a secret just between the two of us. The memory feels like a kick in the gut, but I push it aside and focus on the present.

'I suppose I should thank you,' she says to me quietly. 'It's really something, isn't it?' She examines her fingers thoughtfully. 'I could burn you both with just a touch, you know. By the time your little guard came in, you would be nothing but ash.' She laughs, her eyes sparking with a malicious kind of joy. 'An appropriate enough end for you,

Ash Princess, don't you think?'

I touch the dagger hidden beneath my skirt, though I know it wouldn't do any good if it came to it. By the time I drew it, it would be too late. My own fingers are still itching and I wonder what would happen if I didn't hold back my fury, if I let it burn through me until there was nothing left of me but flame and smoke and ash. It would anger the gods, I remind myself; it would risk bringing their wrath down on Astrea. It would mean never seeing my mother again.

But when I watch Cress control the fire at her fingertips with a frigid distance, I know she wouldn't hesitate to use it against me. I know that if she tried, I would do whatever it took to stop her. I know that it wouldn't be enough in the end – after all, she knows her power, she understands how to control it. I've been too afraid of mine to do the same.

The Kaiser beams at Cress like she's the most beautiful thing he's ever seen, like he wants to possess her. Cress smiles back at him, but there is something sickening in that smile, something dark and sticky. She paces the room and comes to stand behind him, placing her hands on his shoulders.

'You're awfully quiet now, aren't you?' she asks me. 'No smart retorts to that? Because you know I could do it, don't you?'

I find my voice and hold her gaze even though I want nothing more than to flinch from her. 'You could. But I know you, Cress,' I say, hoping against hope that it's the truth. 'You aren't a killer.'

Her eyes narrow and a shudder racks through her. Without breaking our gaze, she moves her hands along the Kaiser's shoulders until they're around his neck, her elegant, bone-white fingers closing tight over the Kaiser's ruddy throat. She gently tilts his head back, forcing him to look at her before bringing her lips down to his in what can barely be called a kiss.

The Kaiser realizes what's happening an instant too late – by the time he struggles, her touch is already fire, burning his mouth and throat before he can even utter a scream. The smell of burning flesh permeates the room, pungent enough to make me dizzy. I watch in horror as his body turns to ash beneath her embrace, his expression frozen in silent agony.

A scream dies in my throat. I can't bring myself to look away from him as the life leaves his eyes. I have waited years for this. I have dreamt of watching the Kaiser die before my eyes. I never thought it would happen like this. I never thought that when it did, I would be more afraid than ever.

The smell of burning flesh gets stronger, making bile rise in my throat. Søren covers his nose with the sleeve of his shirt, his face pale enough to match it, but Cress doesn't seem bothered. Not by the smell or by what she just did. It can't be the first life she's taken, I realize distantly, and I wonder just how monstrous she has grown since I saw her last.

'There,' she says to me when she finally drops her hands away from the Kaiser's corpse. 'Now, why don't we revisit those terms.'

She crosses behind the commandant's desk, digging through its drawers until she produces a half-full bottle of wine. She sets it on the desk, reaching into the pockets of her dress and drawing out from one a small goblet covered in Fire Stones and from the other a vial of opalescent liquid.

My stomach lurches at the sight of it. Encatrio, the same

poison I used on her and her father.

'Where did you get that?' I ask, my voice barely louder than a whisper.

She shrugs. 'After what it did to me, it wasn't difficult to figure out that it must have come from the Fire Mine. From there, it was a matter of asking the right questions and making people more *inclined* to talk.'

'You tortured them,' I say, my voice cracking. Monstrous indeed, but I started her down that path, didn't I? I shaped her into this.

Cress rolls her eyes. 'I wouldn't have had to if they'd just told me what I needed to know.' Uncorking the poison, she pours a few drops into the goblet. 'That should do,' she says, though I think she's mostly speaking to herself. She pours the wine next, filling the goblet up halfway and swirling the drink around. Picking the goblet up, she comes toward me and I have to force myself to hold my ground.

Søren steps in front of me. 'What are you doing with that?' he asks, alarmed.

Cress only smiles at him. 'I promise I won't pour it down her throat. I'm only offering it to her – she'll drink it herself, every drop.'

'And why would I do that?' I ask, my voice shaking.

'Because if you do, I'll order my armies to retreat. You can keep the mine, you can keep the slaves you liberated – well, *you* can't, because you'll be dead, but your people will live.'

'We're already living,' Søren says. 'The battle isn't over.'

'Not yet,' Cress says, eyes darting to him only briefly. 'But it will be soon enough. It doesn't matter that you have more men. They're untrained, they're weak. They don't have

Spiritgems. Even if you do somehow manage to win this one battle, your army would be decimated and you would only hold the mine long enough for me to fetch more troops. We would return in a week and crush what was left of your army like a bug beneath a shoe.' She pauses, smiling at me. Unlike in my nightmares, her teeth aren't pointed, but her expression is every bit as feral anyway. 'It's a simple exchange, Thora. Your death, or your people's.'

I stare at her, paralyzed. It feels like a sick joke, but there is nothing funny about it. She's serious. She's offering me death and calling it a mercy, and she isn't even wrong in that. If the Kaiser hadn't shown up with reinforcements, we would have kept enough of our army to travel to another mine and wage another battle there, but Cress is right – even if we win this battle, the number of casualties would be too high. It would be our first and last stand.

But if I drink the poison, there would be hope. I'm not foolish enough to believe that Cress would let my army keep the Fire Mine for long, but it would be long enough to make another plan, to find another way to fight. I trust that in my absence, Artemisia, Heron, Erik, and Blaise would keep fighting. They don't need me – Artemisia said so herself back at the Astrean palace. If I fall, the rebellion will keep going.

I have to believe that.

I hold Cress's gaze and step around Søren, taking the goblet from her. For an instant, our fingers touch. I expect hers to be hot, but they feel like mine.

'Theo, no,' Søren says, pleading. 'There are other ways.'

'No,' I say, not taking my eyes off Cress. 'There aren't.'

It may not kill me, I think, a feverishly desperate thought.

It didn't kill Cress, after all. Houzzah's blood burns through my veins, I've seen the proof of that. But it seems even more likely that what fire I do already have will be amplified by the Encatrio, that, as Mina put it, my pot will overflow.

I should trust my gods, I should believe that they wouldn't let that happen, that they would protect me. But they didn't protect Blaise. They didn't protect my mother or Ampelio or Elpis or Astrea as a whole. I can't bring myself to believe they will protect me now.

I lift the goblet to my lips, but I pause before drinking. 'Cress,' I say. Just one word. Just her name.

Something flickers in her expression, and for a brief, fleeting moment I think I've reached through to some part of her I thought was lost. She smiles at me the same way she did once, when we were just two silly girls sharing gossip. But that smile turns hungry.

'Drink,' she says.

I take Søren's hand in mine because I don't want to die alone, and then I tilt the goblet back and drink.

The first gulp is hot, but bearably so. The ones that follow scald. I drink so quickly that wine trickles down from the corners of my mouth, singeing the skin there, but I don't stop. I drink until it is all gone.

The burning starts in my throat, a pain so sharp that it brings me to my knees, banishing all other thoughts from my mind. I don't care where I am anymore, or whose hand I'm holding, or anything that exists outside of my own body. The pain spreads, racking through me until I am shaking, the ground like ice beneath me. Arms come around me, holding me tight, but all too quickly those arms are gone and the only comfort I have left is yanked away.

A scream pierces the air, but it isn't mine. It can't be mine because I can't even open my mouth.

A door opens, figures rush in, too blurry to recognize.

More yelling. Panic. The comfort is dragged away, kicking and shouting the whole time. Even after I can't see him, I still hear him. Calling my name. Calling for Theodosia.

Blue hair. She crouches down beside me, her touch cold. Two hands on my skin like water, but it hurts so much more than the fire ever could. If the poison turned me to fire, this dissolves me into nothing but steam.

Everything goes black.

AFTERMATH

———— ◆•——————

I WAKE UP IN A TENT, the bright sunlight filtering through the stitches that hold the roof together. My skin feels like it's been rubbed raw, every nerve on fire, but the pain doesn't overwhelm me anymore. I can think through it. I remember drinking the poison and Cress screaming for her guard. I remember the guard dragging Søren away and Artemisia coming to help me instead of saving him.

Rolling over on the threadbare mattress chafes my skin and I let out a groan, closing my eyes tight.

'Theo?' a voice says, small and afraid.

I force my eyes open again to find Artemisia sitting on the ground next to my cot, looking at me with solemn, worried eyes. Judging by the dark circles under them, I don't think she's slept in a while. I try to sit up, but it sends another wave of pain through me and I lie back down, bringing my hands to cover my face.

Beneath my fingertips, the skin is smooth but slick with sweat. Not like Cress's charred, dry skin. I check my hair, too, expecting to find singed ends, but it is the same as it's ever been, except for a single piece. When I bring it in front of my eyes, I see that it's stark white. I shudder.

I'm alive, though, I realize, and that thought both stuns and buoys me. I'm alive even though I shouldn't be. I'm alive, but I am not the same. The potion may not have marred me like it did Cress, but it changed me. Where before, heat gathered in my fingertips and spread slowly, now I feel it everywhere, a constant dull heat coursing through my veins. It doesn't scare me anymore, though. After drinking Encatrio, I can't imagine anything will truly frighten me again.

'How long have I been asleep?' I ask, though it comes out rough, my throat aching around every word.

'Two days,' Art says. 'The Kalovaxians retreated. Their Kaiserin gave us a piece of paper saying we own the mine now, though I don't think it's worth much.'

'No,' I agree, though I'm surprised that Cress kept her word at all. She must think I'm dead, I realize. 'And Søren?'

I hear her swallow. 'They took him when they left, said he was a Kalovaxian traitor and he belonged to them. Erik tried to stop them – Heron and Blaise, too – but Søren agreed to go with them to keep anyone else from getting hurt. You're both noble idiots,' she says, but there's no mistaking the fondness in her voice.

'Blaise?' I ask. 'He went into battle. Is he—?' I break off, unable to finish.

'He's alive,' Artemisia says. 'He's been lingering nearby, but he said you wouldn't want to see him.'

I'm not sure how wrong he is. Our argument still echoes in my mind and I see him leaving, no matter how I begged him to stay. But I'm alive and he's alive and both of those facts feel like miracles, so how can I be angry?

'You saved me,' I tell her, remembering how she used her Water Gift on me. The poison would have killed me otherwise, or disfigured me like Cress, if nothing else.

'You saved everyone else,' she says with a shrug. 'It was the least I could do. How do you feel?'

She asks the question like she isn't sure she wants to know the answer. Because she isn't asking about my pain – she's seen that clearly in my winces, heard it in my groans. She's asking about something deeper.

'The same, mostly,' I tell her, unsure how to explain how different I feel.

Artemisia touches my cheek. 'Your skin is still warm,' she says. 'We thought it was a fever at first, but Heron couldn't heal you. He said it was something else.'

I swallow and stare harder at my palm. I saw what Cress was capable of. If I'm going to stand against her, I can't be afraid anymore. I summon fire, imagine it leaping to life there, but something feels wrong. I can feel the fire in me, but it's buried deep. I have to dig for it, fight for it, but at last, with some effort, a small flame appears in my hand.

Artemisia doesn't even jump, she only stares at the fire with a vague sort of curiosity.

'It's different than it was before,' she says. 'You can control it.'

'Yes,' I agree, frowning. 'But it's not like I imagined. It's weaker.'

She nods. 'Well, you won't have to hide it anymore. A queen who sacrificed her life for her people only to rise even stronger like some sort of . . .' She trails off, unable to think of the right term.

It comes to me right away. 'Like some sort of *Phiren,*' I say. She looks confused and I elaborate. 'A bird in Gorakian mythology. Hoa told me about it – it turns from ash to smoke to flame and back again.'

The thought of Hoa hits me with fresh agony. 'How's Erik?' I ask her.

Before Artemisia can answer, the tent opens and Dragonsbane slips inside. When she sees me, she actually smiles, though there is still something feral about it that looks nothing like how I remember my mother's. It looks like Art's smile.

'You're up,' she says with a curt nod. 'How are you?'

Instead of answering, I light up my hand again. Seeing her eyes go wide with fear and awe makes me happier than it should. 'I know that you don't believe in the gods, Aunt,' I say. 'But it seems they still believe in us.'

She doesn't say anything for a long moment. 'Does it hurt?' she asks finally.

I close my hand and the fire is extinguished. 'Everything hurts,' I tell her. 'I owe you my thanks. Without you, we would have lost many more lives.'

'It was a good battle,' she says. 'What you did was admirable. Foolish, but admirable.'

I nod, knowing that from Dragonsbane, that is the highest praise I can expect.

Artemisia clears her throat. 'I'm glad you came as well,' she says, her voice surprisingly small.

The sharpness in Dragonsbane's expression softens slightly, but she can't seem to form words. The energy in the room is fraught, delicate as a spider's web, but when Dragonsbane and Artemisia lock eyes, a thousand silent words pass between them and I feel like an interloper.

Dragonsbane told me that I was lucky my mother hadn't lived to disappoint me, but with a lump growing in my throat, I realize that also means I'll never have a moment like this, to look my mother in the eyes and forgive her for her flawed humanity.

Erik comes to visit me after Artemisia and Dragonsbane leave. In his undershirt and trousers, with his hair down loose around his shoulders, he looks younger than he is. Someone told him about Hoa already, and I hope whoever it was did it kindly.

'I'm sorry,' I tell him, though the words are pitifully lacking.

He sits down beside my cot and takes my hand in his. If he's surprised at how hot my skin is, he doesn't show it. I wonder if word is already spreading.

'The Kaiser will never do what he did to her to another woman.' His voice is cold steel. 'He'll never hurt anyone else. I wish she could have lived in this Kaiser-less world for just a day.'

'Me too,' I tell him before taking a deep breath. 'I killed the woman who killed her. I can tell you it was self-defense and that I had no choice and those things are true, but it's also true that I killed her for what she did to Hoa and I will never regret that.'

He considers this for a moment before nodding. 'One day, I would hear about it in detail,' he says. 'But I've seen too much death lately. Even that one won't bring me any joy.'

I bite my lip. 'Do you think Søren's dead?'

Erik's eyes find mine again. 'No,' he says after a moment. 'He's a traitor, and the Kalovaxians don't show mercy to traitors, but in this case, I would imagine Crescentia is keeping him alive. Her position as Kaiserin is precarious – they've never had a female ruler, and they won't be keen on the idea. She needs to marry him to keep the throne.'

The thought sickens me, but at least it will mean that they won't kill him. Not yet. As glad as that makes me, I can't help but think that death would be merciful compared to whatever hell he's being put through now.

'We'll get him back before that happens,' I tell Erik, as if it's that simple.

Erik must know it isn't, but he nods. 'We'll get him back,' he echoes, squeezing my hand.

The Kaiser's body is already burnt, but we erect a pyre for him anyway. I stand beside it now, close enough to touch his charred skin. I'm barely strong enough to stand for more than a few moments, but I force myself to manage. I remember what I told Blaise what feels like a lifetime ago.

'*When the Kaiser is dead, whenever that may be, I want to burn his body. I want to put the torch to him myself and I want to stay and watch until there is nothing left of him but ash.*'

I believed that when the Kaiser was dead, it would bring me peace, but even as I stare at his dead body and his empty eyes, peace still feels miles away.

My mother was the Queen of Peace, I think as the men building the pyre finish and leave me alone with the body.

But I am not that sort of Queen.

I turn away from the Kaiser to look at the crowd of refugees and freed Astreans who have gathered to watch him burn. It's a good moment for another speech, perhaps, but they didn't come here for speeches. Blaise approaches, torch in hand, eyes downcast. He hasn't looked at me since I woke up, and I'm still not sure if I want him to or not.

I don't take the torch. Instead, I turn toward the Kaiser and hold out my hand. Again, it takes some coaxing. For a moment, there is a hushed, anticipating silence before the small flame appears, licking at the palm of my hand. Feeble as it is, it's enough to elicit gasps and murmurs from the crowd.

I touch the flame to the bed of straw beneath his body and watch the fire catch.

Behind me, the crowd's gasps turn to cheers. Artemisia was right, they don't hold this power against me – they believe it's a new gift, given by Houzzah for my sacrifice.

Maybe it is, but it isn't enough. I saw how Cress wielded her power. She didn't have to dig for it; it was always there, as much a part of her as her skin and sinew and bones.

I barely hear the cheers. I keep my eyes on the Kaiser's corpse and I don't even let myself blink as the flame catches and licks at his already blackened body. It's only then that I notice the faint glimmer of the red gem at his throat, covered by ash and soot but unmistakable. Ampelio's Fire Gem pendant. I reach into the flames, take hold of the gem, and pull it free.

Blaise's hand comes to rest on my shoulder, trying to lead me away from the growing fire, but I don't let myself be moved.

I want to see it all, the moment the Kaiser disappears into nothing but ash. I hold Ampelio's pendant tight in my grip, feeling its power tug at my own.

I would wear a crown of that ash, I think.

Finally, when the flames grow so thick I can no longer see him, I turn and walk away without a backward glance.

I find Mina in one of the Kalovaxian barracks, with a boy and girl a little younger than me. The bunks have been pushed to the edges of the room, leaving a large open space in the middle of the stone floor where the three of them stand. Lingering in the shadows of the doorway, I watch them for a moment, unseen.

'Show me, Laius,' Mina says, placing a bowl on the floor between them. When she sets it down, some water sloshes over the sides.

The boy swallows, fidgeting with his hands behind his back. At first, I think he must have been one of the slaves we freed from the mine, but then I notice the marks on his arms, places blood must have been drawn from.

He's a Guardian. The Kalovaxians must have been studying him before the battle. The thought sickens me, and a quick glance at the girl confirms she has the same marks. How many are there?

The boy – Laius – finally lifts his hands, holding his palms toward the bowl. Instantly, the water streams upward, hovering in the air at eye level in a perfect crystalline sphere.

Mina nods. 'Can you turn it to ice?' she asks.

Laius's brow furrows as he focuses on the sphere. It shifts, the candlelight making it glow, before the surface turns frosted and hard, spreading until it is entirely ice.

'Good,' Mina says. 'Release it.'

Laius drops his hands and the sphere drops, shattering on the stone floor.

'Sorry,' he mutters.

'Quite all right,' Mina says. 'How do you feel?'

She steps toward him to feel his forehead, and when she does, she catches sight of me. 'Your Majesty,' she says, inclining her head in my direction.

Laius and the girl fall into a clumsy bow and curtsy as I step entirely into the room.

'Mina,' I reply before smiling at the other two. 'You found Guardians.'

Her mouth purses. 'I did. There were ten altogether. Nine fire, including Griselda here. Laius was brought from the water mine so they could be studied side by side. Laius, Griselda, would you allow Queen Theodosia to touch you?'

'Why?' I ask. I frown, but they seem to understand what she's asking and nod. Mina beckons me forward.

'Feel their foreheads,' she instructs.

Warily, I reach a hand out to each of them: when I touch their skin, it's hot, like Blaise's. And now that I'm close enough, I can see the dark circles under their eyes, like neither has slept in a long time.

Mina sees the understanding dawn on me. 'Why don't you two go get lunch?' she suggests to Laius and Griselda. 'We'll continue lessons afterward.'

The children hurry off, and I wait until they're out of earshot before speaking again.

'There are more,' I say, not sure what to call them. Berserkers isn't inaccurate, but the word feels like a death sentence.

Mina nods. 'The other eight are Guardians in the traditional sense, but Laius's and Griselda's abilities are unlike any I've seen before. Like the hypothetical friend you described. Is he still hypothetical?'

I hesitate. 'It's Blaise. He's an Earth Guardian.'

'I figured as much. I saw what he did to those ships – more than any Earth Guardian should be capable of.'

'It almost killed him,' I say.

'But it didn't,' she says. 'Not this time.'

I don't have an answer for that. 'You said you were giving them lessons. Is that true, or are you studying them?' I ask instead.

'A bit of both, I suppose,' she says with a heavy sigh. 'The stories I heard said that Guardians like them were rare – there were records of one a century perhaps. Now, there are three altogether and we haven't even seen the other mines. Who knows how many there are in total?'

'What does it mean?' I ask her.

She shrugs, glancing at the door the boy and girl just left through. 'If you were to ask Sandrin, he would tell you that it's part of the gods' plan, and maybe he's right. But maybe there's a higher percentage of people going into those caves, so there are more people who have just enough room for the exact amount of power they are given. Maybe the gods have a hand in that as well.' She turns her gaze back to me. 'You didn't come here about them, though, did you?'

I hesitate before shaking my head. I hold out my hand,

palm up, and after a moment of concentration, a small flame appears, nestled in my palm. Mina watches, her eyes thoughtful.

'It's not much,' she says after a moment. 'It's more than mine, I'll give you that, but if this were before the siege, it wouldn't have been enough to make you a Guardian.'

I close my hand and smother the flame. 'Crescentia – the Kaiserin – the one I told you about who drank the Encantrio . . . she oozes power. It comes to her as easily as breath. She doesn't even have to reach for it, it's just *there*.'

'You want to know if you're a match for her, but you already know the answer to that,' she says. 'You are a pot half full, and she is close to brimming.'

I swallow down my disappointment. It's nothing I didn't already suspect, but it hurts to hear all the same.

'All those people, they're treating me like a *Phiren* who rose from the ashes,' I say, my voice trembling. 'Like I'm the hero they've been waiting for. And I'm not. I can't protect them from her, from any of the Kalovaxians.'

Mina's jaw hardens. 'You survived a stand against the Kalovaxians – few can say the same. You've protected us this far; who's to say you need a gift to keep doing it?'

I smile and thank her, but deep inside, I think we both know she's wrong.

We survived this fight because of luck and little more. Next time, we might not.

BATTLEFIELD

———— ◆ • ◆ ————

THE KALOVAXIANS ALWAYS SPOKE OF battlefields with more reverence than they spoke of their temples. There was even a popular court ballad about one, with its 'grass streaked red with the blood of enemies,' that made a battlefield sound beautiful in its own, violent way.

Walking around the Fire Mine and the ruins of the temple that once stood here when I was a child, I know there is nothing beautiful about a battlefield. Erik and my Shadows are quiet as well, though I'm grateful for their presence. The last thing I want is to be alone right now. My strength is returning, slowly but surely, and I relish every moment I get to spend out of bed.

Like that Kalovaxian ballad, the grass is more red than green now, but the ballad didn't mention that most of it would be covered by bodies, or parts of them, and that it would be impossible to tell which parts belonged to which side. The ballad didn't mention the smell of decaying flesh that would hang in the air, making it putrid and nauseating. The ballad didn't mention that enemy or friend, they would all be mourned by real people.

'A pyre,' Erik says from beside me, breaking the silence.

'It's the typical burial for Kalovaxian warriors.'

'For Astreans, too,' I say, surprised that two cultures as different as ours could have anything in common. 'And the others?'

He hesitates before shaking his head. 'Gorakians are buried, but the rest—'

From my other side, Artemisia speaks. 'Yoxians are buried,' she says. 'Brakkans as well. Vecturian custom says that their warriors should be put to sea in flaming boats.'

'We can't do that,' I say, my stomach clenching. 'We need all the boats we have.'

Artemisia nods in agreement. 'I don't know the customs of the others, but there are enough living that we can figure it out.'

'There are so many,' Heron says, looking around. Apart from the small section where our camp is set up, bodies stretch around us as far as I can see. Hundreds, or maybe thousands. I don't know how we'll be able to sort out which body belonged to which country.

I swallow. 'They'll come back, and when they do . . .' I trail off, unable to put it into words.

'We'll be ready,' Erik says. 'This *was* a victory for us and that means more than just that we survived it. We stood against the Kalovaxians. We are no longer a poor investment. We can ask for help from other countries, and this time we might actually get enough.'

'*Might,*' I repeat.

'The gods blessed you, Theo,' Heron says, a smile tugging at the corners of his mouth. 'And in doing so, they blessed all of us. They're on our side.'

I tear my gaze away from him. Even Heron doesn't know how long I've had this gift, how long I've kept it secret from him, how weak it is now that it's been dragged to the surface. Like most, he believes it was a reward for my sacrifice. It's a pretty story, but it's not who I am. I glance between Heron and Artemisia. 'How does it feel for you? Being blessed?'

They exchange a look, but it's Art who speaks first. 'It feels like a cold drink of water in suffocating heat,' she says.

'It feels . . . full,' Heron adds. 'Like I'm at peace with everything around me.'

My stomach sours. 'It doesn't feel like that for me,' I tell them, my voice quiet. 'I don't feel relieved or at peace. Ever since it happened, I just feel . . . empty.'

My thoughts turn to Cress with her charcoal eyes and flaming touch. *'Our hearts are sisters,'* she said to me in my nightmare. *'Shall we see if they match?'*

Maybe they do, underneath everything. Maybe we are both abominations, but I don't want that to be the case. I would rather be powerless than be this, and that is the difference between us.

'I was born with this in my blood,' I say, my voice shaking. 'I had it forced on me. But I never chose it, not like both of you did.' I look at Blaise. 'You didn't choose it either,' I say. 'It forced its way into you, like a different sort of poison.'

Blaise holds my gaze, and though he doesn't agree, he doesn't protest either.

'The power owns me, but I don't own it,' I say, and my voice doesn't shake anymore. Suddenly, it is sure, because I am sure.

We walk a bit more until we come to the entrance of the

Fire Mine, which has been evacuated and roped off — as if anyone would choose to go in there on their own.

Of course, that's exactly what I'm doing.

When I pause in front of the entrance, the others stop as well. They say nothing until I reach out to move the rope.

Blaise's hand comes down on my arm, pulling it back. His skin is less hot since he surrendered his gems — temporarily again — but it's still warmer than mine.

'No,' he says, the word a whisper.

'It's the only way,' I tell him. 'You know it as well as I do. You feel it, that disconnect between who you are and the power you possess. Because we don't control it. Because it controls us.'

'Walking into that mine isn't going to heal you,' he says. 'After all that poison in your system, it could push you over the edge. It could kill you.'

'It could,' I agree, looking at Heron over his shoulder. 'But it won't. It's the only way to choose this power. It's the only way to exert some control over it, to understand it. The only way I can be the Queen they need.'

'I'm sorry I left, Theo,' Blaise says, his voice breaking. 'I'm sorry I broke my promise, and I swear to you, I'll never leave your side again. Just don't do this. Don't leave me.'

For an instant, I waver. 'You went to battle because it's who you are,' I tell him. 'And it was stupid, but you knew it was the right thing for you to do. This is the right thing for me to do.'

Blaise doesn't answer, but I see the tears welling up in his eyes. I place my hands on his shoulders and roll up onto the tips of my toes to brush my lips against his. For an instant, he's frozen in shock before I feel him melt against me, his arms tight around my waist like he can anchor me to him and make me stay. But he can't and I force myself to pull away and look at my other Shadows.

'I don't know how long I will be in there. If the Kalovaxians return, you'll leave me and run. All right?'

Heron starts to shake his head but Artemisia nods. 'I'll do what must be done,' she says, every word curt.

I look at Erik. 'And when I'm out, we're going to find a way to rescue Søren. And I'm going to finish what I started with Cress.'

Erik looks more serious than I've ever seen him. 'Good luck, Theo,' he says softly.

With a thundering heart, I turn away from them and step into the mine.

EPILOGUE

S ANITY SLIPS INTO AN EPHEMERAL thing, coming and going until I'm not sure which thoughts are sane and which aren't. I don't know where I am or what I'm doing here. I hear Cress's laughter, feel her breath like smoke on the back of my neck, but she is always just out of reach.

It's my mother who finally finds me, cowering against a cave wall with bloodied hands, my head throbbing with thirst. She looks just as she did a decade ago, down to the violent slash across her throat. I don't run to her like I always imagined I would. She doesn't seem to expect me to.

I swallow. My throat is raw, like I've been screaming for hours.

'Is this the After?' I ask her.

My mother shakes her head. 'Not yet, my love,' she says, holding a hand out to me. 'Come, there is much to do.'

I should be relieved to not be dead, but I don't feel much of anything. I stare at her hand but I don't take it. 'You could have stopped the Kalovaxians,' I say to her.

She doesn't flinch from the accusation or try to deny it.

'I died the Queen of Peace, and peace died with me,'

she says after a moment. 'But you are the Queen of Flame and Fury, Theodosia, and you will set their world on fire.'

I take her hand and she leads me deeper into the mine.

Acknowledgments

Writing a book has a reputation for being a solitary endeavor, but if that were the case, I would only have to thank my laptop, and these acknowledgments would be mercifully short. Alas, much like how it takes a village to raise a child, it takes a squad to publish a book. I have been lucky enough to have the best publishing squad out there.

Thank you to Krista Marino, my brilliant editor, for being my sounding board and cheerleader and for not just making this a better book, but making me a better writer. And to Beverly Horowitz, Barbara Marcus, Monica Jean, and everyone at Delacorte Press for giving me and my books an amazing place to call home.

Thank you to my incredible agents – Laura Biagi, Jennifer Weltz, and John Cusick – for building and nurturing my career and helping to shape it into a dream come true.

Thank you to my publicist, Jillian Vandall Miao, for her tireless support and contagious positive attitude. And to Elizabeth Ward, Kate Keating, Cayla Rasi, Mallory Matney, Janine Perez, Kelly McGauley, Alison Impey, Colleen Fellingham, Tamar Schwartz, Stephanie Moss, and Isaac Stewart for your enthusiasm, dedication, and kindness. And, of course, to everyone else at Random House for bringing this book and this series to life in a way that constantly surpasses my wildest imaginings.

Thank you to my NYC writing squad for all the productivity-amping sprint dates: Patrice Caldwell, Lexi Wangler, Arvin Ahmadi, Zoraida Cordova, Sara Holland, Sarah Smetana, Kamilla Benko, Lauryn Chamberlain, Mark Oshiro, Jeffrey West, Jeremy West, Kheryn Callender, Emily X.R. Pan, Dhonielle Clayton, Blaize Odu, Christina Arreola, MJ Franklin, and Adam Silvera.

Thank you to Kiersten White, E.K. Johnston, Karen McManus, Melissa Albert, Jessica Cluess, Amanda Quain, Julie Daly, Tara Sonin, Samira Ahmed, Shveta Thakrar, Claribel Ortega, Kat Cho, Farrah Penn, and Lauren Spieller for all your friendship and support.

Thank you to my dad for keeping me grounded and focused and always encouraging me to step outside my comfort zone, and to Denise for her sage advice and guidance. Thank you to my baby brother, Jerry, for always inspiring me and making me a better person.

Thank you to Cara Schaeffer and Emily Hecht for being my lifelines in times of crisis and of jubilation. You make the highs higher and the lows a little less low.

Thank you to Jefrey Pollock, Deborah Brown, and Jesse and Eden Pollock for being my NYC family.

And last but not least, thank YOU, for embarking on Theo's journey with me. I could not have done any of this without you.

About the Author

LAURA SEBASTIAN grew up in South Florida and attended Savannah College of Art and Design. She now lives and writes in New York City. Laura is the author of *Ash Princess* and *Lady Smoke*. To learn more about Laura and her books, follow @sebastian_lk on Twitter and @lauraksebastian on Instagram.

THE QUEEN YOU WERE MEANT TO BE
THE LAND YOU WERE MEANT TO SAVE
THE THRONE YOU WERE MEANT TO CLAIM

IN A LAND WITHOUT A QUEEN,
THE PRINCESS MUST RISE

ASH PRINCESS

LAURA SEBASTIAN

FREEDOM COMES
AT A PRICE

LADY SMOKE

LAURA SEBASTIAN

The *New York Times* bestseller

THE FINAL BLISTERING INSTALMENT – OUT SPRING 2020

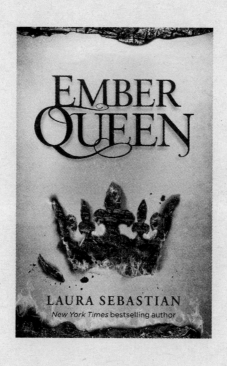